＃ ALEXANDRIANA

ALEXANDRIANA

By LeGette Blythe

CHARLOTTE PUBLISHING
Charlotte, N. C.
1975

Copyright, 1940
by LeGette Blythe
ALL RIGHTS RESERVED
Mecklenburg County Bicentennial Edition/1975

Printed in the U.S.A.
Observer/Craftsman Company
CHARLOTTE, NORTH CAROLINA

For
ESTHER

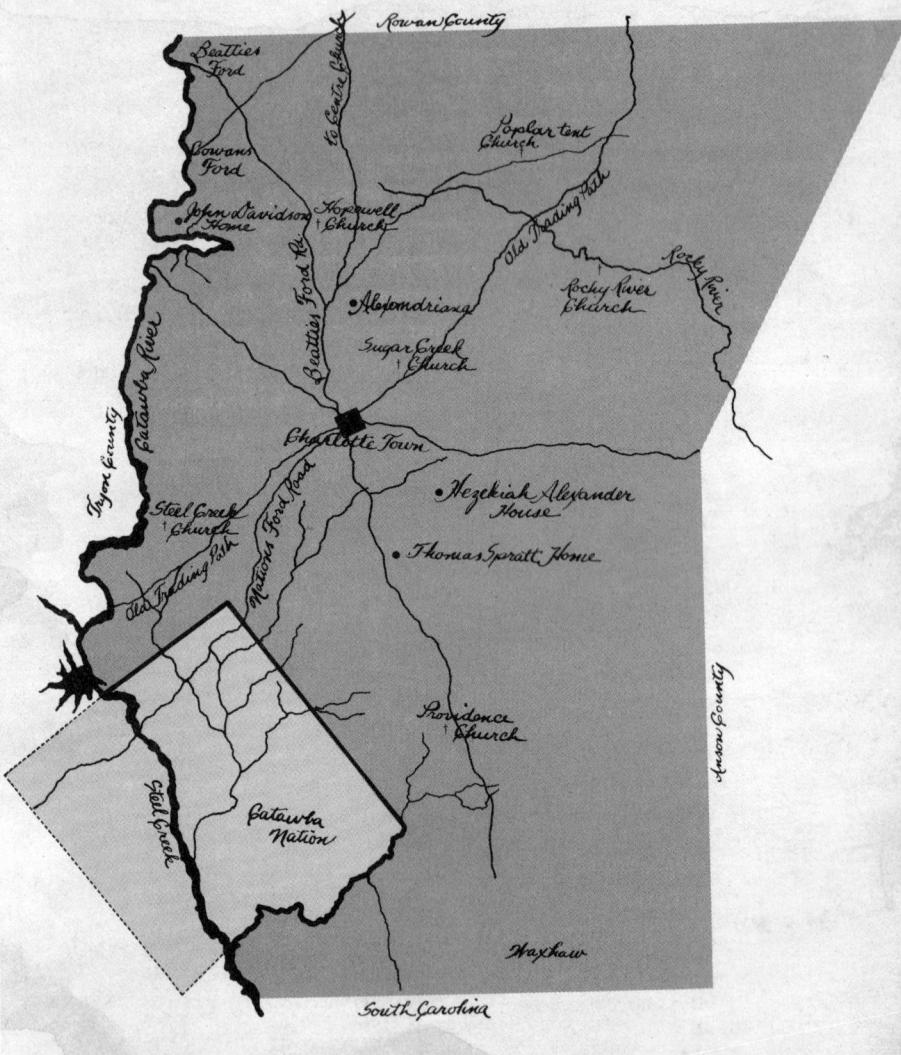

ALEXANDRIANA

I

He SLOUCHED over to the shade of a tree at the edge of the muster-ground, dropped his musket with a clatter and slumped down beside it.

Untying the rawhide laces, he removed his shoes, jerked off the sweaty wool socks that imprisoned his tired feet, and ran a lean brown forefinger between each successive pair of toes.

"Feet hurtin', Jethro?"

"By damn," he whisked the forefinger in front of his nose, "I aint never walked so fur and got nowheres since I was borned. If they'd a-straighten out all this walkin' I done this mornin' it would reach smack over to the Cherokee country. They aint no sense in walkin' hell outer fokes and them got on shoes."

He pulled a twist of tobacco from the pocket of his homespun hunting shirt, stuck the end into his mouth and sawed until he broke off a chew, clamped down on it until he could get his jaws together, and placing his forefinger and second finger on his lips, spit through them fifteen feet into the dust. "What the hell's the use of all this here walkin' jest in order to git ready to th'ow some hot lead at them Regerlators? I can knock a squirrel outer any tree in these here settlements and I aint had to do no drillin' to learn how neither. If'n it warn't fer that there drum o' yourn, Davy, my feet wouldn't be so hot and my new shoes wouldn't be dang nigh wore out."

"Davy's been drillin' too and he's got on shoes."

"Well, he's more used to 'em. And he aint been walkin' all the time. Part of the time he was jest standin' over there by the Guv'ner.

ALEXANDRIANA

He wanted to git a good look at that there pink coat and them milk-colored britches." He let fly another stream of amber juice, glanced slyly at the young drummer-boy. "Thinks mebbe he'll wear clothes like that when he's growed up."

"Not me, Jethro. I won't ever be Guv'ner, and if I do I'll wear reg'lar clothes like Uncle Mac."

"I hope so, Davy. You couldn't go fur wrong doin' 'bout ever'thing like yore Uncle Mac. By damn, that there's a man what could be Guv'ner and he wouldn't have to wear them sissy lookin' clothes and come around drillin' hell outer honest fokes. Look at 'im now. What the hell you reckin he's a-doin' now? He pointed over his shoulder.

"You better not talk so damn loud, Jethro."

Jethro turned to glare at his neighbor. "Look after yore own business, Bedent Spraggins, and I'll thank ye. I aint a-scairt o' that man if'n he is the Big Wolf o' the Cherokees. He can be the Big Tager and cattymount to if'n he wants to be. I'm gonna slip over and git a better look at 'im." He eased into his shoes, picked up his musket, and edged toward the group to which he had pointed.

His Excellency William Tryon, Governor of the Province of North Carolina, had just completed his frequently repeated formality of having two fastidious pinches of snuff, and was now in the midst of the enjoyment of a half dozen discreet sneezes, each a bit more discreet than its predecessor, three from the right nostril, three from the left.

"What the hell did he do?" Jethro, now within some twenty paces of His Excellency, turned to the militiaman beside him.

"Had a couple of sniffs of snuff."

"You mean he put hit up his nose—didn't dip hit like the wimminfokes does?"

"Stuck it up his nose, sniffed it; that's the way the quality do down in the coast country."

Jethro tugged at his mustache, felt of the eel-skin that held his hair in a plait behind his neck and watched intently as His Excellency returned the silver snuff box to the inner recesses of the plum-colored coat, and having probed with white forefinger and

ALEXANDRIANA

fat thumb, brought forth from the lace at his left wrist a dainty handkerchief with which he dabbed decorously at the few particles of snuff that had persisted, despite the sneezings, in clinging to his upper lip. This duty completed, His Excellency brushed lightly his thumb and forefinger and returned the handkerchief into the lace at his wrist.

"Well, I'm damned if'n that don't beat all. Sniffin' snuff up his nose. Pink coat. Silk stockin's. More lace on his shirt 'n on a woman's hoop-petticoat. I'll bet, by damn, he's got lace around the legs of his drawers."

"You better not talk so loud, Jethro. He may hear you. Have you tied up to a tree and have hell whupped outer you. He don't give a damn fer nobody. Had a feller over east gived five hundred lashes."

"This here aint no damned east country. This here's Mecklenburg."

"Yeh, and yore back's got skin on hit now too."

Jethro eased his way through the sprawling militiamen to a position nearer the place where His Excellency was talking with Colonel Moses Alexander and some of the other officers. He wanted a better view of the Governor and perhaps to hear what he was saying, but he did not want to appear to be eavesdropping. He sat down, his musket between his knees, facing toward Sugaw Creek, with the Governor and Colonel Alexander on his right toward Charlottetown. He slumped over in the grass, his right elbow supporting his head, but he was listening intently. The Governor was talking.

". . . and for men of a backwoods settlement unused to the profession of arms, they show good training. I must confess I didn't expect to find them so well trained."

"We are indebted to you, sir, for your compliment." It was Colonel Alexander speaking. "We had hoped to be able to drill a little more before you should have had occasion to review us. But those Regulators over in Anson and Orange seem to be spoiling for a fight, don't they?"

"I'm afraid so, Colonel. They have no respect for the royal

ALEXANDRIANA

authority. Every day they grow more brazen. They are persistent troublemakers. They are continually making charges. They claim the agents of the provincial government are denying them justice." He pulled the handkerchief from his wrist, held it before his mouth to conceal a slight yawn. "If they had justice, Colonel, they would be served a healthy helping of powder and balls, and it's my notion that nothing short of that will instill into their insubordinate hides a proper respect for the King and His Majesty's representatives in this colony."

Jethro ejected along a soaring arc the amber juice that had been accumulating during the Governor's discourse. He had developed a distinct aversion to His Excellency. He could not have given any definite reason for his feeling. Perhaps it was the plum-colored coat. Perhaps the lace at the wrists, the silk stockings and silver shoe buckles, the elegant three-cornered hat. Gentlemen did wear such clothes, he knew. Even McKnitt Alexander and Captain Tom Polk had fine coats and knee-britches and shoes with big square silver buckles that they wore when they went away to Charles Town or Philadelphia. But they didn't flaunt them among their neighbors in Mecklenburg. And when McKnitt Alexander put on a fine coat, Jethro would bet his last shilling, the coat wouldn't swallow McKnitt. No, he'd be damned if you wouldn't see McKnitt instead of the coat. But looking at this dandy fellow all you saw was lace. He spat again.

The Guv'ner and the Colonel were talking. The Guv'ner was giving them Regerlators hell, yes, siree, and there was no mistake about it. Colonel Alexander was mostly agreeing. Sometimes, though, the Colonel was sort of speaking up for the men over in Anson and Orange. Jethro wasn't missing much of the talk. "We've been hearing there's some excuse for unrest in those parts, Your Excellency. There's a right smart of traveling back and forth through these settlements. Of course, Mecklenburg doesn't abide disrespect for the King's laws and there's probably no excuse for many of the excesses being committed. Here in these settlements we haven't had much trouble with the officers of the law. Most of them are our own people. There's been a little overcharging for

ALEXANDRIANA

recording deeds and for marriage licenses and such like, but not much of that." . . . Damned if Mose Alexander warn't tellin' that Big Wolf. Jethro turned his head to face the colonel and at that instant Colonel Alexander beckoned to him. He clambered to his feet, walked across to the group.

"Your Excellency, this is Jethro O'Flannagan. Jethro, His Excellency, Governor Tryon."

"Pleased to be makin' yore 'quaintance."

Governor Tryon nodded curtly. "Well, Colonel?"

"Jethro is one of our citizens, sir. Jethro, I was telling the Governor that there is little complaining in these parts against the officers of the law, except occasionally for overcharging for such things as deeds and marriage licenses. Isn't that about the way you find it?"

"Yes, sir, Colonel. O' course, there's been a right smart o' complainin' on that score agin McCulloh and Frohock, as I can vouch for my ownself."

"How's that?" The Governor was scowling. "Speak up, man!"

"Well, sir, Frohock he tried to charge me too much fer a set o' marriage licenses. They was supposed to cost eighteen shillin' and he wanted three pound."

"Did you pay him three pounds?"

"No, sir."

"Well, how much did you pay him?"

"Nothin'. I didn't git no papers."

"So you didn't get married rather than pay three pounds for the marriage license?"

"Well, sir, I guess it's accordin' to the way you looks at it. Molly and me figgers we's married, I guess."

"How could the minister marry you without a license?"

"Well, sir, didn't any. 'Twon't no preacher handy if we'd got them licenses. And if'n it had been, he'd wanted another pound."

"Well, so you just began living together without benefit of clergy?" The Governor flicked at a sweat-bee buzzing about his ear.

"We started to livin' together, all right. Molly was right smart anxious and I wasn't what you'd say holdin' back. So we started keepin' house and we sorter took fer granted we was married. 'T any rate, I got nine chaps by her. And I don't run 'round none with other wimmin-fokes."

The Governor straightened a bit of lace at his wrist. "I shouldn't think," he observed in casual tone, "that you'd have time."

Colonel Alexander dismissed Jethro and he returned to the place he had been sitting, but he faced toward Charlottetown so he could keep an eye upon David. That was a boy, that Davy. Yes, siree, over there right now talkin' with those two pretty little girls that came with the Guv'ner from somewhere down in the eastern settlements. They had come out in the Guv'ner's carriage to watch the paradin' and now they was talkin' with Davy. Pretty little things, all dressed up in their finery like growed wimmin-fokes with their little lace han'kerchers flutterin' 'round. And them smilin' and talkin' with their pretty airs.

They looked to be 'leven or twelve, but they acted right smart growed up like. And Davy was jest about the right age to start makin' eyes at the girls. 'Bout fourteen. But already strong and muscled out. Yes, siree, danged if Davy hadn't mighty nigh marched him down. And him totin' that danged drum too."

Jethro faced about languidly, busied himself with the rawhide laces of his shoes. He wanted to hear more of what the Governor was saying and he could hear better with his right ear turned that way.

". . . no general disaffection then, Colonel? That seems to be the general impression of the citizens of Mecklenburg. Your man of the large unlicensed family is the first of his kind, I'll confess, with whom I have had the privilege of conversing on this visit into your county." . . . Damn the stuck-up jackass. He thinks he's better'n us fokes in the back-country. Well, jest wait . . . "I talked with several of the Rocky River men at Major Phifer's who were kind enough to assemble there to greet me on my arrival Friday from Salisbury. I talked with others Saturday, and when I accompanied Major Phifer to Coldwater Church Sunday I was happy to listen to a discourse by the minister, a Mr. Luther—"

14

ALEXANDRIANA

"Yes, I know him, Your Excellency."

"He preached upon the necessity of the obedience of all loyal citizens to His Majesty's government. And I trust I can rely upon the loyalty of the King's subjects here in Mecklenburg."

"You can, sir. These are spirited men here in Mecklenburg and the women are the same. We are pioneers, you know, and there's not overly much polish amongst us. O'Flannagan that you just talked with, for example. But he's got sense and he isn't afraid of the devil." Jethro let go of his shoe laces and straightening up, set at a jauntier angle the cap he had fashioned of a piece of buffalo hide with a squirrel tail behind for trimming. "Damn if'n the Colonel aint a-tellin' 'im."

"We aren't inclined to be run over, Your Excellency, but we believe in law and order and we don't allow that folks should be setting themselves up in defiance of the courts and the officers of the law. You can count on us at Hillsboro."

"I am grateful, Colonel. I'm glad to hear what you're saying. Mecklenburg has already shown me much consideration. You have named the principal street of your village for me, and I shall recommend to the Assembly that it be granted papers of incorporation. I confess—" His Excellency smiled broadly, "that Charlottetown is a small place and that Tryon Street in rainy weather must be a damnably muddy road that my carriage would be hard put to travel over."

"You are right, sir, but we hope some day to grow larger, and even to challenge Salisbury."

"You'll never be as large as Salisbury, Colonel. But I appreciate your action anyway. And I want spirited troops. I can see that your men are strong-willed. I trust, sir, that they shall not be insubordinate. Soldiers are meant to obey and fight, not to think—" Jethro shot a stream of tobacco juice that threatened to engulf a bumble-bee on a sprig of goldenrod six paces away. "—and I fear some of your militia are inclined to consider themselves on an equality with their officers, who in turn may lack a proper respect for those in command of them.

"These are bad days, Colonel. Sometimes I wonder what this

province of Carolina is coming to, what with all this spirit of rebellion and insubordination abroad in these settlements." The Governor was gesticulating. Jethro watched the lace at his wrists as he waved his hands. "Nobody in Carolina seems to venerate his betters. And it is worse in the coast country, perhaps, than it is here. I had hardly succeeded to the Governorship upon the death of Governor Dobbs three years ago when a gang of ruffians at Wilmington, angry at the arrival of an English sloop with stamp paper aboard, threatened to burn down my house over my head. The next spring, Colonel, I had a whole ox barbecued and beer and liquor by the barrels carried to the muster-ground. After the drill I invited the people to partake of the refreshments. And damn me, Colonel, if they didn't pour out the beer and the liquor and throw my whole damned ox into the river!"

His Excellency paused, retrieved his handkerchief from his cuff, wiped his lips. "And when we ran out of money in building the Palace at New Bern—the Assembly, you see, had appropriated only five thousand pounds at the start—I asked for ten thousand more. And they argued and debated the need for the Palace, and vilified me no end. And that was just the beginning, Colonel." He returned the handkerchief to its place. "Yes, sir, conditions have become impossible. I have determined that I shall no longer abide them." He raised his voice, so that Jethro and all the militiamen near him could hear plainly. "I shall utterly destroy this Regulation movement and restore respect for the laws and those who represent His Majesty in this colony!"

"Five thousand pounds! And ten thousand pounds more! Fifteen thousand pounds fer a house fer him to live in! Damme if'n I aint a Cherokee if'n they didn't must 'a' made it outer gold!" Jethro turned his back upon His Excellency. "I plumb don't like to hear no sech braggin'."

"I noticed you aint been actin' like you don't, Jethro."

"And I aint seeked yore opinion neither, Elam." Jethro turned around again. The Governor, he saw, was looking directly toward the carriage. He raised a fastidious finger to point. "Look over at the carriage for example, Colonel," Jethro heard him say. "See

ALEXANDRIANA

that little drummer-boy? He does not know his place. A young backwoodsman in hunting shirt and rough breeches talking with those young ladies of my party. Those girls, Colonel, are daughters of two of the finest gentlemen of my acquaintance in Carolina. And look you, even they themselves do not resent the young rascal's impertinence. Who is the young whelp anyway?"

"His name's Barksdale, Your Excellency. Lives at Alexandriana with John McKnitt Alexander, the crown surveyor in these parts. He was bound out to him to learn surveying—"

"What, sir? You mean to say that the brat has the effrontery to stand there almost under my nose and bandy words with the daughters of Cross Creek gentlemen, and he a bound-boy!" He turned to his orderly, spoke sharply. "Bring that drummer-boy to me!"

"The boy meant no harm, Your Excellency. He's but a child. And his father was—"

"That's all very well, sir," the Governor interrupted. I will have discipline in my army. If it must include bound persons, all the more reason that they should know their places. I have had enough of this so-called democracy, this easy mingling of backwoodsmen with their betters. I'll teach these upstart pioneers to recognize authority when they become a part of my army!"

David had come with the orderly. "Boy, what do you mean by leaving the ranks to talk with those young ladies?"

"Our company was at rest, sir. I didn't fall out until the captain gave the command."

"But did I not see you standing there passing pleasantries with those young ladies?"

"Yes, sir. One of them asked me to show them my drum. We jest got to talkin'. I liked to hear them talk, sorter funny like. They don't talk jest like us."

"I suppose not. They are the daughters of gentlemen. Their fathers are loyal subjects of His Majesty." A scowl was furrowing His Excellency's forehead. "That's the way with you yeomen of the back country. Always seeking to worm your way into the confidences of your betters." He spoke sharply. "Understand, boy, I'll have no

17

ALEXANDRIANA

more of this associating with the ladies in my party. Now get back to your place in your company and stay there!"

Jethro's face was flaming, his lips drawn tightly across tobacco-stained teeth, but the Governor was regarding only the drummer-boy. "Wait a minute! For two shillings, boy, I'd have you lashed for your impertinence. The idea of a bound-boy presuming to enter into conversation with young ladies of the Governor's party!" Jethro gripped the stock of the empty musket between his feet. "The damned coward! The damned dirty bastard of a coward! Jest let him offer to have a cut put on Davy!"

But David was not flinching. He stood looking the Governor in the face, and slowly down from his forehead into his bronzed cheeks a flame spread. His lips began to quiver. Colonel Alexander saw it. "Go back to your company, David," he said, quietly.

"Yes, sir." The boy saluted the colonel, turned squarely on his heels, walked toward the carriage, picked up his drum.

"I heard him," one of the girls said, from the carriage window. "It was rotten what he said to you."

"But he must be a bound-boy, Lovelace," said the other.

David, his drum in his hand, stared straight into the girl's eyes, turned, and walked away.

"I must say the brat has spirit." The Governor had been watching.

"We have spirit here in Mecklenburg, Your Excellency. Sometimes, I fear, Your Excellency does not understand us."

"You may be right, in part, at least, Colonel. But I care not a fig. I'm an army man, trained in the ways of the army. I'm a believer in discipline. I believe the citizen must have a reverence for his government and support and obey its officials. I have lost patience with this continual harping about the peoples' rights. What rights have the people except those given them by the government? And the government that protects them in turn demands their obedience and loyalty."

Colonel Alexander's remark had served to launch him upon another oratorical flight. "These people in Carolina, Colonel—" He was gesticulating again—"these people have been away from

ALEXANDRIANA

England only long enough to lose their sense of order and discipline and royal authority, and acquire an independence of mind that brooks no restraint. It bodes no good for the colony. I have a mind His Majesty will soon be losing patience with them." He paused abruptly. "But I didn't come here to make a speech, Colonel. I came here to review your troops. How many have you, sir, and when can you be ready to begin the march to Hillsboro?"

"Our rolls show more than fourteen hundred men from all the settlements roundabout, sir. There are some nine hundred here today. But we are not yet supplied with provisions for the march, and it will be a week or longer before we can start."

"Very well, Colonel. Of the nine hundred select about one-third of the best men you have, equip them as best you can with powder and balls, and provisions. I shall be obliged to leave Captain Polk's tomorrow and make my way back to Major Phifer's on my return to Salisbury, where the Rowan militia is assembling. But I'll be back next week, and at that time I shall be pleased to receive your report on the progress you have made in preparation for the march to Hillsboro." The Governor removed his hat, pulled the handkerchief from his cuff, dabbed at his perspiring forehead. "It's damnably hot today, Colonel."

"It is, Your Excellency."

"The court sits at Hillsboro late in September, Colonel. Today, I believe, is the twenty-third. You have less than a month in which to equip your troops and have them in Hillsboro."

"We shall be ready, Your Excellency. And now, sir, if I may, I'll communicate your orders to the officers."

"Indeed, Colonel. And I must be returning to Captain Polk's. I plan to ride up to see John McKnitt Alexander this afternoon, and it's quite a way, I understand. I've been told he's one of the leaders in Mecklenburg and a man who supports His Majesty's government."

"You've been rightly informed, sir. McKnitt Alexander is one of the leading men in all these western settlements. He supports everything that's right and proper."

II

THE HOUSE at Alexandriana, a large two-story square structure of logs weatherboarded with planks sawed at Colonel Moses Alexander's mill, faced toward Charlottetown nine miles southward on the Great Road. It sat just at the place where the slope up from the big spring a hundred yards in the rear flattened into a level space that dropped gently off on all sides.

A grove of oaks and cedars surrounded the house, some of the trees but recently planted, and rows of small boxwood bordered the walk from the door out to the Great Road. Eastward and across the road were the stables and the granary, and the kitchen, a small log house with a large chimney, sat a few paces from the right rear corner of the big house. Down nearer the branch that ran out from the spring were the quarters of the Negroes.

John McKnitt Alexander's house had been built near the center of his wide rolling acres. Three miles westward, if he could have ridden in a straight line over streams and through thick patches of forest, across flat lands of long waving grass, and into small valleys and up gentle slopes, he would have come out upon Hopewell Church. Had he ridden eastward the same distance he would have neared the western edges of the Poplar Tent and Rocky River settlements. Northward toward Centre Church, where lived the Brevards and the Osbornes and others of his friends, and southward toward Charlottetown he could have ridden other miles. And in all this riding he would never have set his horse's feet upon land other than his own.

ALEXANDRIANA

Some said Alexandriana comprised a hundred square miles. Perhaps that was an exaggeration. A surveyor should have been able to tell within a few acres the amount of his holdings. McKnitt Alexander had surveyed the boundaries; perhaps he knew how many acres they embraced. But land was cheap and easily to be had, and when fourteen years ago as a young man just turned twenty-one he had come southward through the Valley of Virginia from New Munster on the Pennsylvania and Maryland line to claim a share of the grant given his father, James Alexander, he had chosen this section north of Charlottetown while his brother Hezekiah was settling below Sugaw Creek Church.

The Alexander brothers were Scotch. Three-quarters of a century ago their grandfather Joseph Alexander, refusing to endure the religious persecutions in his native Scotland, had moved into Ireland and later had come with his family to America. Joseph years ago had died and now James Alexander was past seventy.

McKnitt on trips north had visited his father. He had also journeyed to Philadelphia on business, for quickly he had become a man of means in the Catawba River settlements now set off as a part of the new county of Mecklenburg. On one of these trips to his old home he had gone on business more urgent than usual and after some weeks he had returned with the new mistress of Alexandriana. She was a pretty girl, the daughter of the Bains, Scotch neighbors of the Alexanders, and her name was Jane, but McKnitt called her Jeanie.

Six years ago Jeanie had come to Mecklenburg. Two years later the first heir arrived, and Jeanie named him William Bain for her father; in another two years she bore a daughter, and McKnitt named her Margaret McKnitt for his mother, but she quickly became Peggy; and seven weeks ago the new baby had arrived, and McKnitt had promptly called her for her mother, but already she was Polly to everybody at Alexandriana.

The babies had been born two years apart almost to the month, and Jeanie, McKnitt reflected, was now but twenty-nine. Perhaps Mecklenburg would not always be a sparsely settled country of buffalo and deer . . .

ALEXANDRIANA

But just now there was little time for reflection. His Excellency Governor Tryon was expected at any moment at Alexandriana from Charlottetown. When the militia had been dismissed after the morning review at the muster-ground, Moses Alexander had sent David racing home to notify McKnitt that the Governor and his party were planning to visit Alexandriana during the afternoon.

Jeanie was in the kitchen superintending Venus and the Negro girls in the preparation of supper. Cato had been called in from the field, and bathed and dressed in an old suit of McKnitt's designed to serve as a butler's livery, was now shooing the flies from the dining room. Upstairs in his room David had stripped off his homespun shirt and hunting breeches and the rough heavy shoes in which he had drilled that morning, and refreshed with a bath from a pail of cold water from the spring, had put on the new suit bought that spring in Charles Town.

David had told McKnitt of the scolding the Governor had given him. McKnitt, packing tobacco in his pipe, had been slow to reply. Having lighted the pipe and puffed until the interior of the bowl was glowing, he removed it from his mouth. "Don't worry about that, David. The Governor doesn't understand us. His idea of what makes a gentleman may be different from ours. Remember, Son, always act a gentleman yourself and folks who are gentlemen themselves will know you are one." He had puffed again, several times. Then he had knocked the ashes and the unburnt tobacco from the pipe, put it into his waistcoat pocket. "Don't worry about it, Son. There are too many heavier things nowadays to think about. You are growing up, David, getting to be a man mighty fast. In a few more years you'll have the weight of a man's work on your shoulders. And I've a notion there'll be a-plenty for you to do. Some time we'll talk about it. But right now we'd best be getting ready for the Governor. When you see him just act like nothing had happened between you. Now go along and dress up."

And now David was ready. His hair brushed neatly away from his temples and knotted behind with a blue ribbon begged from Jeanie, his bronzed face and big rough hands scrubbed clean and smelling of the store boughten soap from Mr. McCafferty's in

ALEXANDRIANA

Charlottetown, and his overgrown feet encased in the freshly tallowed slippers made only last winter by old Shadrach Piggot when the cobbler came to Alexandriana on his yearly visit, he mounted the uppin'-block and searched the Great Road to the point where it disappeared in the woods a half-mile off to the right toward the Catawba. But though there had been no rain in weeks and the corn over beyond the stables was twisting with the heat, there was no dust along the Great Road.

David jumped from the uppin'-block and ran around to the kitchen. "They aint comin' yet, Aunt Jeanie. There warn't any dust showin'."

"You mustn't say 'aint,' Davy. It moughtn's set well with the Governor. You must look to your talk, lad." Jeanie turned from the ham she was basting on the spit before the fire. Her cheeks were flaming and little beads of perspiration had popped out on her forehead. "My, but you look good, Davy. Were I not an old woman and were I but your age, I've a strong notion I'd take a quick liking to you and set out to capture you straightaway, Davy. 'Tis a great pity the Governor isn't bringing some young ladies with him."

"But he may be, Aunt Jeanie. Leastways, there were two girls with him watchin' us drill this mornin'."

"So 'tis that, Master Barksdale, that is responsible for this so sudden transformation—" She sniffed, wrinkling her little nose, now shiny from the heat and the grease of the steaming ham— "and the unasked use of my lavender-scented soap."

"But I didn't use much, Aunt Jeanie. That lye soap Venus made does smell so strong. And I put it back in your room."

" 'Tis all right, Davy, you know. I'm right glad to see you taking interest in your looks. But about those young ladies with the Governor—"

"They're from over Cross Creek way, I think. One of them's father came with the Governor from Hillsboro and they came along too, they said."

"You talked with them, Davy? Well, I do say I'm right glad and I hope they'll come along with the Governor."

ALEXANDRIANA

"I was close to the carriage they rode in out to the muster-ground and when we got through drillin' they called me over there and said they wanted to see my drum."

"And were they nice-behavin' and did you set much by talking with them?"

" 'Twas one of them right smart polite and nice-actin'. But I don't set much store by the other'n."

"And why didn't you set much store by the other one, Davy? What did she say that wasn't to your liking?"

"Somethin' about me, Aunt Jeanie, about my ownself."

Jeanie saw that the boy was reluctant to talk about his meeting with the two girls that morning. She was puzzled. "But . . . But how could she say anything of evil concerning you, Davy? They are strangers in this settlement their ownselves. They had never heard any reports of you, I'll vouch. And did they hear any, they could not be evil."

"I liked not what one of them said. It mought be that she meant no harm, but I like not what she said, Aunt Jeanie."

"What did she say, Davy? You know you can vouch I'll do no talkin' about what you tell me."

"Well . . . the Governor catched me talkin' with 'em, leastways, I reckin he figured in his own mind he had catched me, but I had no notion I was hidin'—and he called me over there to where he was talkin' with Colonel Alexander and he said somethin' about back-country fokes gettin' outer their places talkin' with friends of the Governor, 'specially anybody that was a bound-boy, and he said he ought to have me lashed and told me to get back to my company. And when I went back by the carriage to get my drum one of the girls said he had talked rotten-like, but the other said when she was talkin' with me she didn't know that I was a bound-boy."

The jab of Jeanie's fork into the sizzling ham was vicious. She dropped the fork on the table, turned squarely to confront the boy. "Did she say that, Davy?" Quickly she changed her tone. "Well, now that was not well-actin'. How old were the girls, d'you suppose?" "They was well growed, Aunt Jeanie. Must 'a' been ten or 'leven anyway."

24

ALEXANDRIANA

"Old enough to have better manners, Davy. And what did you say to her?"

"Nothin'. Jest looked straight at her."

"That was well-actin'. Had I been you, I reckon I'd have pulled her hair. But gentlemen don't pull ladies' hair, do they?"

"No'm, I don't reckon they do. But, Aunt Jeanie,—" He hesitated, his bewilderment shown plainly in the serious expression on his tanned face. "Aunt Jeanie, what . . . what is a gentleman anyway?"

"Why . . . why, I'm of a certainty you know your ownself, Davy. Why do you ask? Why are you worried about it?"

"Well, they do say Governor Tryon is a fine gentleman. He wears fine clothes and has silver buckles on his shoes and has a shirt with lace cuffs stickin' out from his coat sleeves, and his hair is all powdered and—Aunt Jeanie, he sniffs snuff up his nose. And he talks proper and is well-actin' to the ladies. But Uncle Mac and Colonel Alexander and Cap'n Polk don't act like him and they don't wear no lace cuffs—leastways, I haven't catched 'em doin' it—and they smoke their 'bacco or chew it. But they are well-actin' to the ladies and to the men, too. And I always set right much store by them bein' gentlemen. But they aint what you'd say like Governor Tryon, Aunt Jeanie."

"Clothes don't make gentlemen, Davy, and you can be sure of it. The Governor lives over in the coast country and they are older settlements. We live in a new settlement and our men wear homespun, most of them all the time. They wear their fine clothes over there, but that doesn't make them gentlemen. A gentleman is from the skin in, Davy, not from the skin out. A lot goes into making a gentleman, Davy. Good blood behind you is a great help and some do say it's altogether necessary. Good stock, just like horses and cows and sheep. But then it takes more'n that, too. I set great store by right-actin' to your neighbors and strangers as showing up a gentleman."

"Then Uncle McKnitt and Mr. Davidson and Cap'n Polk and the Brevard boys and men-fokes in this settlement are gentlemen, too, aint they, Aunt Jeanie?"

ALEXANDRIANA

"Of a certainty they are, Davy. McKnitt Alexander is the finest gentleman in the world, leastways to my way of thinking, and he's just as fine a gentleman when he puts on his huntin' shirt and rough breeches and starts off on a surveying trip as he is when he packs up his blue greatcoat and his fancy waistcoat and goes traipsin' north to Philadelphia or down Charles Town or Camden way."

"That's the way I figured it, too, Aunt Jeanie. I think Uncle Mac's a heapways finer than Governor Tryon." The boy's face was serious again. "Aunt Jeanie, can a bound-boy be a gentleman?"

"Why, what's come over you, Davy boy? O' course, a bound-boy can be a gentleman. If it's your ownself you're referring to, Davy, you are already a gentleman, Son. And if you be a good boy till you're more growed, you'll be a leading man in these settlements like McKnitt and Cap'n Polk and Colonel Alexander and John Davidson and the others. You have let that girl with the Governor give you cause for worriment when she wasn't well-actin' her ownself. Being bound out to somebody doesn't mean you are a slave, Davy. Don't you have all the privileges at Alexandriana that any of us have? And aren't you learning surveying and how to make fine clothes and follow the trade of a tailor so you can earn money and some day have a great place of your own?"

"Yes'm, but I was jest a-thinkin'—"

Gently she pinched the boy's ear. "You should have no time for such thinking, Davy. You are not enough growed. Besides, looks to me like you should be recollecting about that nice-actin' girl and—" she winked, "if I were a-wearing your shoes, Master David Barksdale, I'd set out with a right fair determination to make that other girl take a powerful strong liking for me. That would be my idea of how to get vengeance on her. O' course, that's like a woman. But, mercy o' me, Davy, here we've been talking away and I'm not dressed and the Governor is likely to be here any minute!"

She called to the Negro woman working at a table across the room. "Here, Venus, you watch the ham. It's almost done, I'll vouch. I've a right strong notion I'll not be ready 'gainst their

ALEXANDRIANA

coming if I don't hurry. Davy, you go out to the front with your Uncle McKnitt and watch for them, whilst I run upstairs and put on my dress."

A few minutes later David called from the uppin'-block. "I think they're comin', Uncle Mac! There's dust a-risin' from over the woods down beyond the south field. I can tell in a minute when whoever they are comes out from behind the woods." He watched steadily, keeping his eyes centered upon a point in the Great Road where it emerged from the woods and turned to come in a gentle curve to McKnitt Alexander's house. "Yes, sir, 'tis for a certainty them! It's the Governor's carriage, I'm bound. And there's a man horseback behind. I can't rightly make him out jest now. But it looks like—" He stood on tiptoe. "It looks like Cap't Polk. Yes, sir, 'tis him for a certainty."

"You'd best run tell your Aunt Jeanie they're coming, so she'll be all prettied and composed to receive them, and tell Cato to stir up the stableboys to see after the horses, whilst I wait to welcome them 'gainst their driving up." McKnitt Alexander knocked the ashes from his pipe, returned it to the pocket of his waistcoat. He ran a forefinger around the inside of the top of his impeccably starched stock, flicked a bit of lint from his coat sleeve. He was standing at the gate as the visitors drove up.

" 'Light, Tammas, and rest your saddle."

"Fine day, McKnitt. How're you?" Captain Thomas Polk swung lightly from his saddle, gave the horse's reins to the Negro boy waiting to lead it to the stable, and came over and shook hands with Mr. Alexander. "I've brought you the Governor and some of his friends."

"I'm right glad and honored, Tammas. Did you have much trouble with the carriage on the road from Charlottetown?"

"Not overly much, McKnitt, though in places it was right rough for wheels. Had the weather been rainy 'twould have been troubleful."

The two stepped to the door of the carriage and Captain Polk opened it. Governor Tryon, wearing his plum-colored greatcoat and holding his cocked hat across his chest, was the first to alight.

ALEXANDRIANA

His hair, freshly powdered when he left Charlottetown, was streaked with the dust of the road and the perspiration of His Excellency, and his stock would have been completely wilted had he not taken the precaution of placing around his neck the silk handkerchief he now removed and placed in his pocket.

After the Governor came the two little girls, their faces pink and warm beneath their bonnets. They jumped lightly to the ground and shook out the folds of their silk skirts.

The last to leave the carriage was a florid gentleman of dignified expression who though neatly and correctly dressed was not so lavishly attired as His Excellency.

"Your Excellency," Thomas Polk addressed Governor Tryon, "I have the honor to make you acquainted with Mr. Alexander." He turned to face the master of Alexandriana. "McKnitt, His Excellency, Governor Tryon."

"I am most honored, sir." Mr. Alexander bowed, advanced a step toward the Governor, and they shook hands.

Captain Polk turned to the other man. "Mr. McNeill, I have the honor, sir, to make you acquainted with Mr. Alexander. Mr. Alexander," he faced McKnitt, "this, sir, is Mr. McNeill of Cross Creek." The two bowed and shook hands, as Mr. Alexander welcomed him.

"And now, my friend McKnitt, I come to the most pleasant task of all. I have the honor to present Miss Lovelace McNeill—" He paused, as the little girl curtseyed, "and Miss Belinda Winthrop." The other child curtseyed, and both smiled from beneath their bonnets.

"I am most honored, young ladies, and all of you are most welcome to Alexandriana. And now we'd best go into the house where 'tis cooler. The boys, Tammas, will look after the horses."

Jeanie met them at the door. Captain Polk spoke, and she returned his greeting. "Your Excellency," McKnitt stood beside Jeanie, "I have the honor to make you acquainted, sir, with Mistress Alexander." Jeanie dropped a curtsey. Her husband next presented Mr. McNeill, and then he introduced the little girls, who curtseyed to Jeanie.

ALEXANDRIANA

"We make you all welcome to Alexandriana," said Jeanie, when all the introductions were finished. "We are right powerfully honored to have you. And though we live in this back settlement and sort of 'way from civilization, we hope we can make you comfortable. And now, McKnitt, perhaps the gentlemen would like a little refreshment whilst I take the young ladies upstairs and let them freshen up a bit after the long ride from Charlottetown. I know you must all be tired."

" 'Tis a capital idea, Jeanie," agreed Captain Polk. He turned to the Governor. " 'Tis passing strange, Your Excellency, how McKnitt Alexander succeeded in snaring a woman in whom is combined such cleverness with such beauty."

"Go 'long with you, Tom Polk." Jeanie blushed becomingly, turned to the girls. "Come, young ladies. Let's go upstairs." Half way to the first landing she paused. "You'll find on the sideboard, McKnitt, a pitcher of water freshly fetched from the spring, and glasses. And you know about the rest."

"You gentlemen must be tired and hot from your ride. 'Tis a powerful hot day, leastways, has been to me." He led them into the dining room and toward the sideboard. "Would you have some water first, Your Excellency, before trying something more cooling on a hot day?" He poured a glass, handed it to the Governor, who proffered it to the others before downing it. Then he poured one for Mr. McNeill. "And how about you, Tammas?"

"I have a rule that's seldom broke, gentlemen." Captain Polk smiled broadly. "But I shall break it today. The rule? 'Tis never to drink water when there's brandy handy." He downed his glass at a gulp.

"And now, Your Excellency and gentlemen—" McKnitt opened the door of the big corner cupboard, "Here's something apter to drive off the heat, leastways, to make you unmindful of it."

"You're right, McKnitt." Captain Polk agreed. "His Excellency and Mr. McNeill will vouch there's nothing more calculated to open the pores of the skin and let the heat out than a stiff swig of apple brandy or even plain Mecklenburg corn whiskey."

"Well, gentlemen, there's both here—and there's some Scotch,

ALEXANDRIANA

too, and some pretty tastable stuff I brought down from Williamsburg last fall. 'Tisn't much of this last remaining, but you're welcome to it as long as it lasts."

"I've never tasted this Mecklenburg whiskey you make from corn, Mr. Alexander," said the Governor as he stepped nearer the sideboard, "but I've heard of it." McKnitt was setting out the drinks. "I believe I shall choose to try it."

"I have heard of Mecklenburg corn whiskey, too, even down at Cross Creek," observed Mr. McNeill. "I think I'll have about three fingers of that."

When McKnitt had finished pouring the drinks, he turned to Captain Polk. "And you, Tammas?"

"My usual, McKnitt. I shall not break my rule, gentlemen. And that's never to drink Mecklenburg corn liquor when there's anything else handy except spring water."

They all laughed. McKnitt poured himself a drink from the brandy bottle that had half filled Captain Polk's tall glass. The four lifted their glasses. "Let us each propose a toast, gentlemen," said McKnitt Alexander. "Your Excellency will propose the first one."

"To His Majesty the King!"

McKnitt nodded to Mr. McNeill. "To the utter damnation of the Regulators and all enemies of the King and His Excellency!"

Tom Polk raised his glass a bit higher. "To a wise and happy reign of His Excellency over Carolina!"

The three waited for McKnitt. "To our guests at Alexandriana," said he, "and to the happiness and prosperity of the people of these provinces."

They clinked their glasses lightly, downed their drinks. His Excellency's face grew livid, he reached quickly for the pitcher, poured his glass half full of water, downed it with a gulp. McNeill reached for the glass, poured water into it, drank it down.

Captain Polk, hardly able to restrain himself from laughing heartily, set down his glass. "This Mecklenburg liquor that McKnitt makes is right powerful stuff, Your Excellency, as you'll vouch."

"You're right, Captain Polk. It's potent indeed. No wonder

the Cherokees call it firewater. Everything I've discovered in Mecklenburg, in fact, seems to be strong stuff. I only hope that your allegiance to His Majesty's government in this province is half as strong as that whiskey." He poured himself another drink of water.

"Perhaps Your Excellency would have some other sort?"

"No, indeed, Mr. Alexander. That was quite enough, quite enough, indeed."

"Mr. McNeill?"

"No, no, sir. I am still on fire inside."

"Tammas?"

"Not just now, McKnitt. We shall return, perhaps, before the afternoon is spent?"

"As you say, Tammas."

"That is good, McKnitt. My rule is never to allow one drink of good apple brandy to stand alone and unsupported."

They stepped into the hall. David was coming down the stairs. McKnitt observed with satisfaction that the boy's hair was still neatly combed and parted and his clothes unwilted. "Come here, David," he called. "I want you to meet these gentlemen."

Captain Polk nodded. "Hello, David."

"Hello, Cap'n Polk. How're you?"

"Your Excellency, this is Master David Barksdale. David, His Excellency, Governor Tryon."

The boy bowed low. The Governor nodded. "I believe I have met him before." He spoke directly to David. "This morning at the muster-grounds. Perhaps I was a bit rude. My apologies. But soldiers understand one another, eh?"

"David told me about it, Your Excellency. I'm sure he'll think nothing more about it. And—" He turned to his visitor from Cross Creek. "This, Mr. McNeill, is Master David Barksdale. David, Mr. McNeill." They bowed low to each other.

David walked behind the four men into the sitting room, and had turned to slip out when he encountered Jeanie and the two girls at the foot of the stairway. He stopped. They drew back, startled. "Wait, David, I want you to meet our guests."

ALEXANDRIANA

"But we know him. He's—" The other little girl's disapproving frown cut her short.

"Yes, you talked with David this morning. But I don't know whether you were introduced. Miss McNeill, and Miss Winthrop, this is Master David Barksdale." The boy bowed low, and the girls curtseyed. The McNeill girl spoke to Jeanie. "We talked with him at the muster-ground. He was nice enough to show us his drum and tell us about the way the drummer-boys do in the parading."

"But he looks so different now!" Belinda was looking at David, frankly admiringly. "He was not dressed so nicely this morning. Had on frontier clothes and brogues. I thought he was just another woodsman, and—"

"I am." David looked her squarely in the eye.

"We all are," Jeanie added, with a merry little laugh. "And now I must be seeing to the supper. Would you girls like to go into the sitting room or sit out under the big oak in the yard?"

"I'd much rather go out in the yard with Master Barksdale." Belinda was not hesitant about answering. "I'm sick and tired of hearing about taxes and old Regulators. And I know that's what they're talking about in there. Wouldn't you, Lovelace?" She smiled brightly upon David. "And you, Master Barksdale?"

"Whatever you all want to do will suit me."

"Well, you all run out into the yard then, and I'll go see to supper." Jeanie started toward the kitchen, turned. "And David, maybe the young ladies would like to see your new colt."

"I'd love to," said Lovelace.

"I'd like to ride him," added Belinda.

"But you aren't dressed for riding, Belinda." Lovelace's expression was a reproof.

III

IN THE COOL shadows of the sitting room at the eastern end of the house Governor Tryon was animatedly defending his course of action. Through the window at the right of the fireplace, a window with glass panes brought down from Philadelphia, His Excellency could see out across a rolling plateau cut by two roads that crossed a quarter of a mile to the northeast. They were the Great Road that led up from Charlottetown past McKnitt Alexander's to the Centre Church settlement on the Rowan boundary and the road past Tuckaseegee Ford to Ramseur's Mill and the western settlements.

Some forty miles to the northeast, as McKnitt Alexander traveled the route that carried him over the Tuckaseegee Road to Rocky River and then along the road from Camden to the north, was Salisbury. Another hundred miles north and eastward was Hillsboro, where the Mecklenburg militia was being sent, and it was of this proposed expedition that His Excellency was talking.

"The situation, gentlemen, has become intolerable. The dignity and authority of His Majesty's government are being assailed. These insurrectionists who have the effrontery to call themselves Regulators must be taught a lesson. I trust that a show of power will be all that will be necessary when the court sits next month at Hillsboro. The smell of a little gunpowder, I'll promise you, will set the whole pack of them running." His Excellency turned to his host. "What is your opinion, Mr. Alexander?"

"I'm not so certain that Your Excellency is correct on that last score."

ALEXANDRIANA

"Then you feel that we may encounter trouble?"

"If they are pushed too far, sir. I counsel moderation and fair dealing with them rather than gunpowder. I believe—"

"But I have shown them every consideration," His Excellency interrupted. "At Brunswick I offered them beer and barbecued ox, and they threw my ox into the river; I did nothing to interfere with efforts to repeal the stamp act; I issued proclamation after proclamation, heard delegation after delegation. I instructed the sheriffs to collect nothing above the just taxes. And they? Mr. Alexander, they spurned the entertainment I had prepared at Brunswick, they threatened to burn down my house on my head, they have seized and severely beaten officers of the law engaged in carrying out their lawful duties. Only this past April they fired upon Colonel Fanning's house in Hillsboro, and a few weeks later when the sheriff of Orange arrested Herman Husbands and William Butler, those notorious insurrectionists, and lodged them in jail, they raised a mob and marched toward Hillsboro to set the prisoners free. And when they reached the Eno and learned that the prisoners had already been freed, damn me if they didn't refuse, Mr. Alexander, to send a horse across the river to bring Colonel Fanning across to them to treat them with wine and rum. Instead, they made him wade the river and then refused to touch his refreshments or listen to his pleas." His Excellency was gesturing with both hands to accompany his soaring oratory. "Nor was it until my messenger arrived and read my address to them promising redress of their grievances and protection from what they contended was extortion would they disperse. You see, Mr. Alexander, I cannot permit this sort of conduct to continue longer in this province."

"They are misguided, no doubt, Your Excellency, but I'll vouch they feel themselves aggrieved, and I've a mind if they are led to see that they will obtain justice from Your Excellency and the courts they will be law abiding subjects of His Majesty from now on."

"I think that's right, McKnitt." Captain Polk interposed his view. " 'Tis true they haven't been altogether well-actin' but they

ALEXANDRIANA

may have some rash leaders and there be likely among them some who are bent only upon mischief."

"Well, gentlemen, they'll get a fair trial at Hillsboro, both Husbands and Butler on the one side, and Colonel Fanning, whom they have caused to be indicted, on the other. And I trust I can depend upon the loyalty of the Mecklenburg militia."

"Mecklenburg's militia are on the side of law and order, Your Excellency, and I'll vouch for 'em. But they aren't calculated to stand by indifferently and see injustice rule, and if the court at Hillsboro isn't prepared to give fair trials, then the Mecklenburg militia hadn't best be sent."

"But, Mr. Alexander," Mr. McNeill interposed, "do you mean to indicate that the Mecklenburg militia might constitute themselves a judge and jury to tell themselves whether justice was being done the defendants at Hillsboro?"

"I'm not saying what they would do, Mr. McNeill. I'm only trying to explain the nature of our people of this settlement. They came down here to get away from oppression and injustice. They are strong-willed. Scotch, you know, and a sprinkling of Germans in Rocky River, and some English and French. But mostly Scotch. They fled from oppression in the old country."

"So did I," rejoined McNeill. "After Culloden. I was a young man then." He pushed up the coat sleeve on his left arm, opened the cuff, turned it back. "Look, Mr. Alexander. See that little scar there?" He pointed to a tiny mark on the inside of the wrist. "I opened my own wrist there, drew out my own blood and with it attested a most binding oath. The Blood Oath, we call it. I swore after Culloden an oath to be loyal to His Majesty. Mr. Alexander, I shall never be false to it." He fastened the cuff, pulled down his coat sleeve.

At that moment Cato appeared in the doorway. Mr. Alexander saw him, nodded.

"Beggin' pardon, Marse McKnitt, Mist'ess says supper ready. I done told Marse Davy an' de young ladies."

Mr. Alexander arose. "But, Mr. Alexander—" His Excellency and the others stood up. "We had not planned to stay to dine, sir:

ALEXANDRIANA

I am afraid we have caused Mistress Alexander much trouble. In our discussion of the present agitated condition of affairs we have overstayed our time."

"We had planned to have you all for supper, Your Excellency. We are greatly honored and we would be right smart put out did you not break bread with us."

"Mistress Polk, no doubt, Captain, was expecting us?"

"Yes, she was, Your Excellency, but Susan's a powerful understandin' woman. She usually calculates that when I leave of an afternoon I'll eat before I'm home again. And besides, I'm right averse to leaving without another visit to McKnitt's cupboard."

"I heard your remark, Tom Polk." Jeanie came into the room. "There's just time enough before supper to step over to it. Everything's set out there right handy for you."

The Governor and Mr. McNeill chose brandy, along with Captain Polk and McKnitt, and then they joined the others at the table. McKnitt took his place at the head, with the Governor on his right and Mr. McNeill at his left. Tom Polk sat beside His Excellency. Jeanie was at the opposite end from McKnitt and at her right sat Lovelace McNeill and to her left, beside Captain Polk, sat Belinda. David was between Mr. McNeill and Lovelace.

McKnitt bowed his head. The others bowed theirs and closed their eyes, except His Excellency, who from the corner of his eyes furtively regarded his host.

"Our Father, grant us a blessing on this portion of food to our nourishment and bless us to Thy service. Bless this day the strangers within our gates. May their lives be lives of great joy in Thy service, and at the end, Oh Lord, reward us all with crowns of righteousness. And this we ask in the name of our blessed Redeemer. Amen."

The two little Negro boys who had been keeping the flies from the table with long green peach branches withdrew unobtrusively and McKnitt began working with his foot the treadle that caused the contrivance above the table to move back and forth. Instantly the guests were intrigued.

From a rectangular frame perhaps half as long as the table

ALEXANDRIANA

streamers of gaily colored paper trailed. Suspended from the ceiling by wooden strips hinged at each corner of the frame and at the ceiling, it was free to move back and forth along the length of the table, with the streamers trailing just above the heads of the diners. To the center of the strip joining the suspended arms at McKnitt's end a cord was tied and this ran through a staple in the ceiling to the treadle just under the edge of the table. When McKnitt pumped the treadle, the frame swept back and forth.

"Mr. Alexander, this is most unusual, indeed." The Governor opened his doily, spread it upon his lap. "Is it your invention? I'm sure I have never seen anything like it before."

"I would hardly say that, Your Excellency. I made it, however, and adapted some of my own ideas."

"I believe the idea could be utilized in the dining room of the Governor's Palace at New Bern. The cord by which it is operated could be worked by a servant in an adjoining room, could it not?"

"Yes, that would be easy to arrange."

"Do you like to fashion things with your hands, Mr. Alexander?"

"Yes, Your Excellency. I dabble in a right smart of different things. A sort of Jack-of-all-trades."

"And good at all of them, Your Excellency." Tom Polk interposed the comment. "You should see the work he does at his forge. He has a pair of adjustable pot-hooks he made himself, and they couldn't be beat in Philadelphia. And he's the best tailor in these parts. On top of that, he's the Crown surveyor, and during his spare time he raises about the biggest crops in the western settlements. And every year he goes off trafficking to Camden or Charles Town or Hillsboro or Cross Creek or Philadelphia. And when all that doesn't keep him busy he reads all the books and papers he can get his hands on."

"Tammas Polk, Your Excellency, has very nearly described his ownself. He's the big man of Mecklenburg and these western settlements. We young men set much store by his example."

"Now look a-here, McKnitt, I'm not such a mighty bit older'n your ownself."

ALEXANDRIANA

Jeanie's supper was both varied and bountiful. Besides the ham, still warm from baking on the spit, there was crisply fried chicken and a saddle of cold buffalo from last winter's curing, water cress with boiled eggs, sweet potatoes, whole-grained hominy, the husks of the grains removed with the lye from the ash-pit behind the smokehouse, stewed sweet corn from the late roastin'-ear patch, and field peas. There were little sweet cakes, brandied peaches, blackberry acid, preserved pears, and a great deep brown-crusted family peach pie. And clear, golden elderberry wine, muscadine wine of a deep purplish-scarlet, and Port.

"We like the elderberry best, Your Excellency. But here's Port I fetched up from Charles Town for Jeanie in exchange for corn whisky I carried down there last fall, and this muscadine's right smart sweet and may strike the fancy of the young ladies."

The meal finished, the ladies left. Outside the shadows were heavy under the trees and Cato had lighted the candles. The four men sat about the table smoking. His Excellency and Mr. McNeill were smoking seegars, but McKnitt and Thomas Polk had declined them and were puffing solemnly upon their pipes. The Governor had returned to his theme, the denouncement of the Regulators and the accompanying emphasis upon the duty of the good citizen to support the King and his duly constituted representatives in the Provinces.

But now he stood up. "Mr. Alexander, we have greatly enjoyed our visit, sir, and the warm hospitality of your home. But we must be going. It will be late before we reach Charlottetown and the road is not the best. And I must leave early for Major Phifer's on my return to Salisbury."

"But, Your Excellency, you are now as near Phifer's Mill as you'll be when you get to Charlottetown. We had hoped, sir, that you all would be spending the night at Alexandriana. There's room a-plenty, and we would be most honored."

"But the others of my party in Charlottetown would not know how to proceed and might be anxious at our failure to return."

"That can right easily be arranged, sir. I can send a man on horseback to Charlottetown to notify them that you are staying for

ALEXANDRIANA

the night. And early tomorrow morning you can set out along the Tuckaseegee Road which takes you into the Rocky River settlement and puts you out on the road from Salisbury to Charlottetown right near the Major's."

"That wouldn't be necessary, McKnitt," spoke up Captain Polk. "I must be going home and I can notify them myself. But I am reluctant to forego the honor of entertaining His Excellency and his friends another night."

"Now gentlemen, you are most kind, and I wish it were possible that I could stay with both of you. But I must think first of my own convenience, as you can well understand, and select a course that will be best calculated to get me along earliest to Major Phifer's, for I fear that while I have dallied here in Mecklenburg things may have been getting a bit out of hand over Hillsboro way."

"It would save you the trip back to Charlottetown, Your Excellency, did you stay here at Alexandriana, though I would like right smart to have you return with me, sir. But I could notify your party—"

"Now, Tammas, we did expect you to stay likewise. I can send Cato over to fetch Jethro O'Flannagan and have him ride to Charlottetown to bear the message."

"No, McKnitt, I must be going home. And, Your Excellency, I shall be delighted to have the pleasure of your company and Mr. McNeill's and the young ladies'. But do you think it best to stay, I shall right gladly bear any message you might wish to send the others."

"Perhaps, then, Mr. McNeill, it would be best for us to remain here with Mr. Alexander and get an early start tomorrow. And perhaps we had best notify Miss Lovelace and Miss Belinda. It may be that they may have some message to send to Charlottetown. And you can notify my orderly to make certain that all my baggage is sent along from Charlottetown."

At the front Captain Polk took leave of them. McKnitt had sent Cato to have the captain's horse brought. When he had gone, the three men walked into the sitting room.

ALEXANDRIANA

McNeill turned to his host. "The ladies are outside, are they not?"

"Yes, sir, I believe so, Mr. McNeill. With David, and Mistress Alexander is with them, I'm right certain."

"It is getting a little late now and the air is cooler. Don't you believe they had best come in? The night air, you know."

"Perhaps so. But there aren't many swamps in this section, and the country is not low, as it is down in the Governor's country of the Neuse and the Trent, or even down in your own Cross Creek settlement, nor do we boast the mosquitoes that His Excellency has down in the coast country." He sent Cato to call Jeanie and the others inside.

When they came in, they sat at one end of the large room, while the men, engaged in animated discussion of public affairs, at the other end remained engrossed in their own talk.

"I must slip out and run upstairs and see about the children," Jeanie said, apologetically. "David, you entertain the girls until I get back." She retreated noiselessly from the room.

When she returned a half hour later David was telling them of the trip he had made to Charles Town with McKnitt last fall. "And after I get back with the militia from Hillsboro Uncle McKnitt might take me with him to Philadelphia," she heard him say.

"Oh, that would be lovely." Lovelace's blue eyes were beaming. "Think of all the fine things you would see—ladies and gentlemen and beautiful clothes and fine carriages and houses. And think of all the gorgeous shops with fine things from London. Couldn't you have a wonderful time just looking?"

"And think of the trip up there. That's what I'd like best about it." Belinda, too, was excited. "Riding all day and stopping at night at the taverns. I've always wanted to stop at the Raleigh Tavern in Williamsburg. They say that is the swellest place anywhere. Have you ever been to Williamsburg, Master David?"

"Not yet, I haven't. But I've heard Uncle Mac speak about the place. He's been there right smart. We'll go through there when we go to Philadelphia, or else we could go up through the Moravian Settlements and the Valley past where Uncle Mac's pappy still

ALEXANDRIANA

lives. That's at New Munster and most of the fokes in this settlement comed from up that a-way. It aint such a far piece from there to Philadelphia, they do say."

"But it's not as civilized up that way as it is by the eastern route through Williamsburg and Richmond, is it? I should think it would be best for you to come over to Cross Creek and then go north through Halifax."

"I reckon it would be more civilized goin' that a-way, but it would be right smart out the way to go by Cross Creek. If we went by Richmond we would take across the Tuckaseegee Road and go up to Salisbury and on to Hillsboro and Halifax. That would be a right smart nearer. O' course, there'd be Indians if we went up the western way, but we'd take our muskets. Uncle Mac's been that a-way a right smart and he aint had any trouble."

"That's the way I'd go," Belinda declared. "I wouldn't mind taking a crack at an Indian my ownself. But it would be nice if you came by Cross Creek, Master David, like Lovelace said."

"I hate to break in," interposed Jeanie, "but you young ladies have a long trip tomorrow and it mought be a right smart tiresome. So maybe you'd best be getting ready to go to bed. And you too, David. You are likely to have to do some riding for McKnitt your ownself. As for the menfolks, it looks like they can never get enough of talking about taxes and such like."

They quickly said their good-nights and withdrew. In the hall three candles sputtered in their stands on the walnut drop-leaf table. "I'll lead the way." Jeanie picked up one of the candles. "You take yours and come behind us, David."

Lovelace followed behind Jeanie. Belinda was just a step ahead of David. As they neared the top of the stairs, she reached back, found his free hand, and in the shadows squeezed his fingers. Just as quickly she let them go.

"Good-night, David." Jeanie, holding the candle high, turned toward the front room at the right.

"Good-night, Master David," said Lovelace.

Belinda was a step behind. "Good-night, Master David." She turned quickly, followed the other two.

ALEXANDRIANA

The boy for a moment was dumb. "Goo-o-d-night," he stammered. Quickly he walked down the hall toward his room door. But he was in strange surroundings. Was this the same hallway he had walked a thousand times, this the door to his room? The floor was a long way off, the candle-holder in his hand without weight. His whole body was tingling with a strange feeling, a strangely delicious, unworldly feeling, that same feeling that had overwhelmed him when the girl had touched his hand there on the stairs.

He set the candle down on the dresser. In the room on the other side of the partition he could hear the chatter of the girls' voices, and Jeanie was saying something about getting them some things to sleep in. Now she was crossing the hall to her room. He stood rigid, tense, until Jeanie had returned from her room with the nightgowns. Then he heard her say good-night.

He blew out his candle, flung off his coat, removed his shoes, stood tense again. The girls were still chattering, but he could understand only an occasional phrase. With sudden resolution he stripped off his remaining clothes and walked across the floor to the closet to get his nightshirt. As he opened the door, through a tiny crack in the partition above his head he saw a faint ray from the girls' candle. Instantly, as he stood there naked in the darkness of the closet, the strange feeling engulfed him, set him tingling all over his body.

The tiny ray was swallowed in blackness. They had blown out the candle. Listening, his ear to the partition, he heard them climb into bed. Without feeling for the night-shirt on its peg near the closet door, he tipped back into the room, climbed into bed, pushed his naked body between the cool sheets.

He closed his eyes, although he was already enveloped in darkness, and concentrated upon the re-enactment in its every detail of the incident on the stairway. A strange thrill swept over him. He raised to his nose the fingers she had squeezed. There still hung about them, he was sure, the faint perfume of her little hand.

And now he was tense again, listening, all his faculties eager and alert, as a tiger crouches in wait for its expected prey. Stealthily

ALEXANDRIANA

he slipped from the bed, moved noiselessly over to the closet, listened intently. But all he could hear was a low mumble that soon ran out to silence.

In his bed he lay stretched out, now excited, tense, now cool, relaxed. He clamped his eyes shut, and the girls materialized before him. Lovelace—sweet, gentle, dependent, the sort of girl a boy, yes, a man, would want to protect, would fight Indians for, would trap and hunt and survey and work in the fields to get rich in order to buy her pretty little ribbons and dresses and things, would go tramping off to Charles Town and Philadelphia for, and fight Regulators or Governor Tryon's soldiers for . . . And Belinda. He clamped his eyes tightly shut . . . The thrill of that moment on the stairway overwhelmed him. She was different from Lovelace. The boy didn't know how, why . . . Fire, that was Belinda, fire smouldering under ashes, fire that would break forth at a slight fanning . . . Not to be protected, but to be conquered. Yes, she had called him a bound-boy, that very morning she had called him a bound-boy, and laughed. She had felt contempt for him and his back-settlement ways . . . Yes, but that squeezing of his fingers . . .

He was vaguely, vastly troubled, exhilarated. Strange currents ran along his spine and down into his toes and out his fingertips, juices heretofore unknown to the boy coursed his frame, charged his strong, sinewy body . . .

And after a while, still not knowing what had come upon him, he drifted off into a strange deep sleep in which his dreams followed one upon the other along the paths of an inexplicable maze . . .

IV

" 'TIS NOT so fine a coat, Davy, as your Uncle McKnitt made last year for Mr. Andrew Bowman, but neither has it cost so much, and I'll vouch it'll serve you in just as good stead."

" 'Tis a good coat, Aunt Jeanie, and a likely looking one to boot. I'll vouch there'll be no better one on the back of any drummer-boy in the Mecklenburg militia, and likewise in the Rowan militia, too."

"I wouldn't say as to the Rowan militia, Davy. Salisbury's a right smart city and there's more things to be had in the stores there than in our little village of Charlottetown. I do think it was in Salisbury that was boughten the buttons for Mr. Bowman's greatcoat, and likewise the thread, if I do remember rightly."

"That was a fine coat, warn't it, Aunt Jeanie?"

"One of the best McKnitt ever made, and if I do say so there's not a better tailor in all these settlements than your Uncle McKnitt. If'n he had the time to put to it, he'd be making fine clothes for folks from Sugaw Creek to Centre Church and Rocky River to Hopewell."

"Mr. Bowman's coat had a lot of little buttons and big buttons, too, as I remember, and they cost right smart, didn't they?"

"Yes, there were nine big buttons, as I remember, Davy, and three or four little buttons, and the buttons and the thread were both right costly. And the button holes were worked in mohair thread. Your Uncle McKnitt used more'n three yards of broadcloth and that cost two pounds and fifteen shillings. And the buttons and thread, I think I'm right, cost two shillings. And your Uncle McKnitt charged him seven shillings for making it. But it was worth more. It was a fine coat, I'll vouch, wasn't it, Davy?"

"Yes'm, but this here coat will serve me just as well as that one serves Mr. Bowman, and maybe a right smart better. It'll be good in cold weather over my huntin' shirt. Do you reckon we'll be at Hillsboro overly long, Aunt Jeanie?"

"I trust and pray you won't, Davy. It's not to my likin' that you're going, as you right well know, I'll vouch."

"But Uncle McKnitt doesn't think there'll be any trouble, Aunt Jeanie. And if there's any fightin' the drummer-boys won't be calculated to get in it, likely. The militia's bein' took mostly to keep down trouble while the court's goin' on."

"Still, Davy, where there's folks with grievances or fancy themselves with grievances there's likely to be trouble. And they do say there's hotheads among those Regulators and some would enjoy nothing better than to get up a right sharp fight. And I fancy my ownself there's right smart reason for those Regulators to be feeling like what they do."

Cato rode with David to Major Phifer's early Monday morning, and returned long after nightfall with David's horse. "Hit was a powerful lot of mens at the Major's, Marse McKnitt," he reported. "'Bout three hundred, they 'lowed. An' Marse Davy he was the best lookin' drummer-boy in the whole passel."

"How many drummer-boys were there, Cato?"

"Somebody said dere was seven all told. They was keepin' up a powerful racket."

"Were they about ready to start for Hillsboro?"

"Yas, suh, 'bout. Was goin' to try to make Salisbury 'fore night. But they'd have to do some powerful steppin' did they git dere 'ginst black dark."

Ten days after the Mecklenburg militiamen left Major Phifer's in the Rocky River settlement the court convened at Hillsboro. Never before in his life had David seen so many soldiers. All the grog shops and the taprooms in the taverns were overrun. The fat landlords and bartenders in their greasy aprons, sweating and

ALEXANDRIANA

bowing and rubbing pudgy hands over fat paunches, had all but given up hope of assuaging the thirsts of the soldiers. Soldiers from the coast country, from the central counties and the western settlements jostled each other, drank beer and rum and Scotch whiskey and laughed uproariously at their own jokes that under the mellowing of alcohol and the stress of excitement had gone pointless but had lost none of their bawdiness.

Some of the militiamen had brought tents to Hillsboro, some had improvised sleeping quarters in barns and smaller outbuildings, others were quartered in the homes of residents of the town and nearby community. David shared a room with Jethro O'Flannagan and Elam Dawkins in the home of a young carpenter named James Few. McKnitt Alexander had given Jethro strict instructions to keep an alert eye upon David. A detachment of soldiers had been quartered in the house and on the grounds of Colonel Fanning, for word had been whispered about that this time the Regulators were going to complete the job they had begun in the spring when they fired into the roof of the Colonel's fine mansion.

Colonel Fanning was under indictment along with Herman Husbands and William Butler. The colonel was charged with extortion. "And he's as guilty as a dog, too," James Few told Jethro. "That man would do anything for money. He wears fine clothes and has fine manners and he lives in a big house, but he's as sorry and rotten as they come. He charges the people double and more what they owe in the court costs and fees, and how can they protect themselves? A lot of 'em don't know what the fees are due to be according to the book and if they did they couldn't fight against Fanning and his crowd."

"And to my way of thinkin', and I aint got no book larnin' and I live in the back settlements," observed Jethro, "there's a sight o' justice behind these Regerlators' demands."

"You're right. It's that kind of doings that has brought on the Regulators. They are set against being unjustly dealt with. And it's a sight the crookedness that goes on by the officers of the Province, and I'm not exceptin' the Governor, neither." He paused. "And I'm telling you, and you can mark my words, if they clear

ALEXANDRIANA

Fanning, Mister O'Flannagan, there's goin' to be trouble and a-plenty."

"I been hearin' today that these here Regerlators is a-gatherin' fast. They do say there's three-four thousand down on the river a-waitin' to see what the court's goin' to do with Fanning and these other fellows."

"I been hearin' those same words my ownself. But they aint come for trouble. They're only wantin' justice. They can't go on payin' out everything they make in taxes and not havin' anything to live on after they've settled with the sheriffs. The Governor better do like was done about that tax on tea." The young man's eyes were burning bright; there flamed on his face the bright intense earnestness of the zealot. "They listened to the people then and they better do it now if'n they don't want trouble."

"That's right, young man. 'Fact, this here's more important, to my way o' thinkin'. I never did git het up over that there tea business. I bought a batch o' tea over to Salisbury onct jest to see what it was like on account o' so much talk about it, but it warn't no good to my way o' thinkin'. My wife she cooked the stuff two-three hours but still it was so tough and bitter couldn't nobody eat it and she th'owed it out and the danged chickens wouldn't even touch it. Far as I was concerned, they could 'a' put the tax a hundred shillin's a pound on tea and it wouldn't 'a' made no difference to me. But I stick with the crowd and if they don't like no tax on it, then I don't neither."

Herman Husbands came to trial before the Honorable Martin Edwards, Esquire, the chief justice, and the Honorable Maurice Moore and the Honorable Richard Henderson, Esquires, His Majesty's associate justices. He was indicted on four bills of having conspired with a mob to riot. Three of the bills were found ignoramus. The fourth was found a true bill. But in the trial that followed he was acquitted.

Colonel Fanning, tried before the same justices on charges of having extorted wrongful fees, was found guilty on seven counts and fined one penny in each case.

"The Jedges," observed Jethro, when news of the verdict

ALEXANDRIANA

reached the militiamen stationed outside the courtroom, "was mighty danged rough on him."

William Butler and two others were tried and found guilty of rioting. They were given long prison sentences and ordered to pay heavy fines. But in the confusion of the recessing of the court, two of the prisoners broke away from their guards and found safety among sympathizers swarming the grounds. The other prisoner refused to run, and the court discharged him.

The militiamen were becoming restive. Conviction of Fanning, even though his fine had been ridiculously small, had served in the minds of the Governor's troops to justify the arguments of the Regulators. And when the soldiers began to grow ill of the flux, His Excellency, glad of an ostensible reason for such action, ordered the militia to return to their homes, and proceeded himself to return to the enjoyment of his great palace at New Bern.

The next morning they told James Few and his parents goodbye. "Look a-here, young man," said Jethro to the young carpenter, "why don't you come over into Mecklenburg with yo' saws and hammers and things? Charlottetown's building up; hit'll be a big town some day. And say," he thumped Few on the chest, "why don't you git busy with that fine lady I seen you keepin' company with? Man, she's as purty as a speckled pup."

"Maybe I'm doin' better'n you think. The next time you're over in these parts we'll likely be married." And for a fleeting moment Jethro saw on his face that same intense burning brightness.

And now David, home again at Alexandriana, was seeking, even though without conscious intent, to construct to his own satisfaction a pattern out of the things he had seen and heard and thought during the expedition to Hillsboro.

Sometimes he saw Jethro, and occasionally Elam, and they reviewed the trip, and often he talked with McKnitt before the big fireplace on winter nights. And sometimes he thought of Governor Tryon, austere and contemptuous, and the carpenter James Few and his beautiful lady to whom he was paying court, and sometimes on cold nights as he crawled between icy sheets that soon warmed to the touch of his tough and hot young body, he

ALEXANDRIANA

lay still and consciously recalled with a certain secret delight the vision of the girl Lovelace.

And as the image of Lovelace slowly faded and merged into the teasing vision of Belinda, he would feel again the squeeze of her hot little fingers upon his own, and instantly he would come alive, his body taut and tense under the racings of sensations, vaguely painful, infinitely pleasurable, impelled by the flame in his brain . . .

V

David pointed with his riding switch. "Uncle Hezekiah's over at the mill, Jethro. That's his bay mare tied up over there at the hitchin'-rack. But whose is that other horse?"

"I don't know that horse. It's a strange one on me. But I tell you, Davy. That mebbe aint yo' Uncle Hezekiah. It may be that young lawyer feller that lives at yo' Uncle Hezekiah's house. Likely as not he's come out here to git old man Abraham to sign some court paper, and brought somebody 'long with him."

"Maybe so, Jethro. That would be Mr. Avery then. Do you know him?"

"I couldn't say I do, even if I have made his 'quaintance. Me and yo' Uncle McKnitt was down at old man Pat Jack's when he comed in the taproom with Duncan Ochiltree, and he bought the toddies for the crowd."

"I'll bet old man Ochiltree didn't offer to do no settin' up."

"You're right there, boy. Not the way that Scotchman likes money. W'y, he'd th'ow his old grandma in the Catawba fer a couple o' half-Joes—and push her under, by damn."

"What did you think of Mr. Avery?"

"I didn't have no chanct to find out much about him. I guess he's all right. He's one o' them college fellers and was all dressed up. But he bought my toddy and 'taint no reason I should be a-runnin' him down."

"I made his 'quaintance one day we were down at Uncle Hezekiah's house. I like him right smart, Jethro. He's a pretty clever

ALEXANDRIANA

fellow if'n he does wear fine clothes and talk proper. He went to Princeton College and that's where I reckon they learned him his fine ways. But he's got spunk and I'm a notion he wouldn't be feather-legged if'n somebody was to stir him up. Uncle McKnitt says he's goin' to make a fine lawyer. We been to his office down at Charlottetown. It's on Tryon Street up above the courthouse a little piece. And he's sure got a lot o' books and papers and suchlike."

"He's all right, I reckin, Davy, as far as lawyers goes. But I aint got overly much use fer no lawyer. See that there big hunk o' mistletoe up there in that big hickory—" He pointed with his switch. "Well, that there mistletoe don't have to do nothin' but jest live off'n that there hickory. Hit don't push no roots down in the ground. Hit jest sets up there and looks purty and sucks the sap out'n the hickory. And to my notion that's the way with a lawyer. He jest dresses up in fine clothes and talks big words out o' big books and lives off'n fokes what works. Yes, sir, Davy, that's Mr. Avery, all right." Three men had come out on the porch of the mill. "That's him and 'Squire Alexander, all right, but who is that there tall young feller with 'em?' "

David didn't know the stranger. "Maybe it's a traveler from down in the coast country. Maybe it's somebody from the Cross Creek settlement."

"Now you wouldn't be thinkin' 'bout Cross Creek, Davy." Jethro grinned. "Some day purty soon I'll vouch you'll be goin' down that way with yo' Uncle McKnitt." He spat an accumulated stream of tobacco juice toward a fleeing rabbit that had jumped from its bed beside the trail. "And I might say, Davy, that I wouldn't blame you nary bit. Them was mighty purty young ladies and I noticed they sorter had eyes for you, too. I been a-wonderin' though if'n you had sorter picked betwixt 'em. I thinks to myself it's sorter accordin' to what a man likes in gals. One of 'em is nice and sweet and womanish-like and t'other 'pears to be full o' fire and snap. It's sorter like a good ripe pear off'n one o' yo' Uncle Mac's trees the middle o' October set up beside a juicy Winesap apple that makes you screw up yo' face when you bite int' it but tastes so good too, or yet mebbe like Kate here which is a good gentle beast and carries a pack all day without complainin' with her eyes lookin' at you, and Lady, which has got a good gait and is a handsome beast but which would like nothin' better'n to th'ow hell outer me right now, and which makes me danged certain I'm gonna ride her or git my neck broke tryin' to. And that's sorter the way I got those young ladies figgered out, Davy."

David's face was reddening. Jethro saw it. "I hope 'Squire aint got no grindin' ahead o' us. I'd like to git th'ough and git home afore night, wouldn't you?"

"Yeh, and I 'spect Uncle McKnitt'll want to start makin' this run tomorrow."

They tied their four horses at the hitching-rack, pulled the sacks of corn from the pack horses.

"Leave your corn be, boys." 'Squire Alexander called to them from the porch. "I'll send the boys out to get it and set it up here. Come on over. I want you to meet two of my new friends."

"Howdy, 'Squire Alexander, how's all?"

"Moderate, Jethro. And how're you, Davy?"

"Moderate, 'Squire. How's all?"

The magistrate turned to one of the men standing beside him. "Waightstill, this is Jethro O'Flannagan, one of our Mecklenburg citizens. Jethro, make the acquaintance of Mr. Waightstill Avery, the new lawyer over at Charlottetown."

Jethro took off his hat, bowed. "Done made his 'quaintance, 'Squire. Mr. Avery bought me a toddy over at old man Jack's t'other day."

"That's right. Glad to see you again, O'Flannagan. And I know this young man, too, 'Squire Alexander. This is Master David Barksdale, and he lives at your cousin McKnitt Alexander's. And a strapping fine lad he is, too."

"Thank you, sir." David's face flushed.

"Waightstill," said 'Squire Alexander, "you'll make a politician, sir. I can see it all over you."

He pointed to the other man. "And now, boys, this is Reverend Mr. Balch, and you boys—Jethro, I'm talking to you now—had

ALEXANDRIANA

best mind your language, because he's the new pastor of Rocky River and Poplar Tent Churches." He was a tall, sandy-haired young man. He wore a plain black cutaway coat, dark knee breeches and cream colored wool stockings, and black shoes with large square silver buckles, drab habiliments beside the blue cutaway, fawn breeches and pale blue silk stockings and black shoes of the lawyer.

The young minister bowed. "I am very glad to meet you both. I hope to see you again—at church, perhaps?" He smiled, and David saw with delight that there was a lively sparkle in his blue eyes.

"Hezekiah—the parson here—and I were classmates at Princeton College," Lawyer Avery explained. "He's a very young man, as you can see. He's a year younger than I am and a much better student. I guess that's why the Synod of New York and Philadelphia sent him down here as a missionary to us."

"Well, we no doubt need all the missionaries we can get," observed Abraham Alexander. "And all the more now since we've lost our pastor at Sugaw Creek."

"Mr. Craighead?"

"Yes, sir, Mr. Balch. Alexander Craighead."

"He was a great man. I have already heard much of him, and all of the highest praise."

"Never a finer man walked the soil of these western settlements."

"You spoke the truth there, 'Squire." Jethro nodded his head. "Mr. Craighead was the finest man I ever seen. I could sit and listen to him preach by the hour. He preached the truth. I bet when Mr. Craighead started for his pullpit the Devil he flinched."

Young Balch laughed. "That's good, Mr. O'Flannagan. An unusual expression, but it conveys a distinct meaning."

"Yes, sir, he was a preacher. And he was one of the commonest men you ever seen, too. Didn't put on no style and no fancy clothes—" He stopped, looked sheepishly toward Lawyer Avery. The lawyer was beaming, and the minister laughed heartily again. "Beggin' yo' pardon, Mr. Avery; 'twarn't no offense meant."

ALEXANDRIANA

"Go ahead. I like to hear you talk, and I like to see my preacher friend losing his ministerial dignity. Go right ahead."

"Well, 'twarn't no more to be said, I reckin. But Preacher Craighead were a man o' God and he didn't mind speakin' out fer the right whether he was upbraidin' sinners like me or great fokes like —like King George or Guv'ner Tryon, by damn!" Jethro stopped abruptly, his face reddening. "Beggin' pardon, Mr. Balch. I don't so common use sech words, but when I thinks o' King George and Guv'ner Tryon—"

"When you think of King George and Governor Tryon," the preacher finished Jethro's sentence, "you are no doubt justified in slight slips of the tongue." Jethro saw in his clear blue eyes a lively sparkle.

"I understand Preacher Craighead didn't have any high respect for the King or the Governor."

"You're right there, Waightstill," 'Squire Alexander assured him. "Mr. Craighead didn't live but a year after Governor Tryon took over after Governor Dobbs died. But he learned a lot about him in that time, I'll vouch. Mr. Craighead came down to these settlements from Pennsylvania to find a free land. He had to have freedom. I've many a time heard him say he couldn't seem to get his breath in a country that wasn't free. He came over from Ireland as a young man and I reckon the Irish stayed in him. He couldn't abide these taxes and restrictions the English were putting on us. He preached against it and he talked against it. I reckon Mr. Craighead had a lot to do with the way we feel about such things in Mecklenburg. He was a good man, a great man, was Mr. Craighead." He paused, turned to face the young minister. " 'Twill take a great man, a pious, God-fearing man that is willing to work hard and ride much to step into his shoes in these settlements."

"You are right, Mr. Alexander. I only hope and pray to the Lord that I may in my weak way emulate him."

"And I hope and pray to the Almighty, Son, that you can, too. These are grave times that have come upon us. Nobody knows what's ahead in these troubled days. It's a job you young men—you and Waightstill and Jethro here and Davy and the rest o' you young folks—must soon be taking on your shoulders. There's things stirring in the air. There's wrongs to be righted, there's maybe battles to be fought, though God forbid it will come to that."

"That's the God'lmighty's truth, 'Squire." From the mill porch Jethro cut loose a stream of pent-up amber. "This here Tryon and Fanning and the likes o' them has got to be teached a lesson and I'm 'bout ready to start larnin' 'em any time somebody ups and says the word, dam'me, if I aint! And beggin' yo' pardon agin, Preacher. Sometimes I let an onpolite word slip out when I gits sort o' excited like." He spit again. "But me and Davy didn't come over here to talk politics and git started on no Regerlators' business nohow. We got an oncommon big turn o' corn here, 'Squire, and Mr. McKnitt's wantin' to start a run o' liquor tomorrow. And if'n you gent'mens will excuse us, me and Davy'll be gittin' it ready fer grindin.' "

"Just leave that corn be, Jethro. The Niggers'll look after it. The run the White boys brought in this mornin' from Rocky River won't be through for a while."

"Those White boys 'round?"

"No, they rode off a while. Said they'd be back by the time the corn was done."

"Them's spunky boys. Any of 'em been in a fight lately?"

"Didn't see any signs of it and hadn't heard tell of any."

"They'd fight a bob-cat."

"Yes, that's right. Those Rocky River boys are pretty independent fellows." He laughed. "We're talking about some of the preacher's congregation, Jethro. Maybe he can sort o' tame 'em."

"I like 'em with spirit," said the preacher.

Jethro started toward the porch steps. "I could be puttin' some o' that there corn—"

'Squire Alexander stopped him. "Just leave that corn be, Jethro. Waightstill and the preacher here said a little bit ago they had to be gettin' on and you and Davy will have to stay here and entertain me 'gainst the return of the White boys. McKnitt don't have to have his liquor for a few weeks yet. Where's he figuring on taking this run, down to Charles Town or over Cross Creek or Hillsboro way."

"I don't b'lieve I've heard him say. Have you, Davy?"

"Unhh-uh. I don't know whether he's decided yet."

"You and Davy most'n generally go 'long, don't you, Jethro?"

"Most'n generally Mr. McKnitt takes us, yes, sir."

"Well, where'd you rather go this time?"

"Don't make much diff'ence. But mebbe down Cross Creek way. Them Charles Town fokes is so all-fired high-falutin'. And I jest cain't understand what they's sayin' half the time. Strangest-talkin' fokes I ever runned up aginst. But I wouldn't mind goin' over to Hillsboro. They's tellin' 'round that the Regerlators is warmin' up over in Orange and I wouldn't mind goin' back over that way and gittin' a earful o' the news my ownself."

"You know, Jethro, I've half a notion you'd like to get in a fight."

"I believe you're right, 'Squire. It looks like Jethro is hankering for a crack at Governor Tryon. But I tell you, Jethro—" Waightstill Avery carefully folded the paper he had been holding in his hand and placed it in his inside coat pocket—"that man Tryon, I'm afraid, would make monkeys out of our militiamen. Whatever else you can say about him, you've got to admit he's a soldier."

"He mought, and then agin he moughtn't." Jethro shot a long stream of tobacco juice through his fingers that rolled up in the dust of the mill yard. "I've a notion we'uns in Mecklenburg could give him more'n he wanted."

"And I have the same notion, Jethro," agreed the young minister. "But heaven forbid that there'll be any fighting. I hope the troubles are settled satisfactorily. But look here, Waightstill, we must be getting along. I've got to get over to Charlottetown and then out to Poplar Tent. And that's a lot of riding."

"You're right, Hezekiah. We've got to be going. 'Squire. Thank you for looking after this matter for me. And come in to see me. You know where my office is—a little way up the street from the courthouse." He looked at Jethro and grinned. "A little way up Tryon Street."

ALEXANDRIANA

"And a hell of a name to put on it, I do say. Beggin' yo' pardon agin, sir. But it jest comed out."

"Your language is a bit direct—" The young minister laughed heartily. "But Waightstill pushed you to it, and I don't know, my friend, but that I agree with you again."

"I tell you what, 'Squire," observed Jethro, when the lawyer and the preacher had mounted their horses and ridden off, "that there lawyer feller is a purty good feller, fer a lawyer, and that there other boy, too, has got all the sense you're lookin' fer. If'n he don't watch out, 'Squire, he's goin' to make a hell of a fine preacher."

VI

"I WANT TO GET started for Philadelphia in another two weeks, Mr. Alexander, I've got a pretty good sized batch of hides collected up and I don't want to have to take too big a pack train. And my stock here in the store is getting a little low besides."

"Well, Mr. Wilcox, you ought to run into some interesting news up Philadelphia way. It's been quite a spell since I was there and a lot has happened in the meantime."

"You'd better go 'long. You can send David and Jethro and Elam on back with the horses and go with me. I'd be powerful set up to have your company. It's not so far from Cross Creek back to Mecklenburg, is it, David? You wouldn't be afraid, would you? Aint likely to be any Indians bothering you 'tween here and there."

"But how about the Regulators, Mr. Wilcox?" David's grin betrayed his purpose in asking the question.

"They won't hurt you. O' course, you are just trying to feel me out. Well, I don't mind telling you and your Uncle McKnitt what I think. I wouldn't talk like this to everybody—" Although no one else was in the store, he lowered his voice—"but I feel like I sorter know the folks from Mecklenburg. I think that in most ways the Regulators are in the right. That's what I think. There's some of 'em, I'll admit, may take things too far, but they've been pushed to it. The way these sheriffs and clerks of courts been robbing honest folks is a sight. And I don't mind telling you I think so." He paused, turned to Mr. Alexander, as if for the Mecklenburger's approval.

ALEXANDRIANA

"I agree with you, Mr. Wilcox. O' course, in Mecklenburg we don't get the straight news maybe about what's going on, like you people over here in Cross Creek or up around Hillsboro. But what I do hear leads me to agree with you."

"It's a fact, Mr. Alexander. But, as I said, I'm in business and I can't afford to talk too much. You know a man that's running a store has to hear a lot o' things without taking sides too much. Now I wouldn't tell a lot of folks down in this section what I'm telling you all, folks like Mr. McNeill, for instance. Now he's a fine man, but—"

"We're going to spend the night with him tonight."

"Well, now, Mr. Alexander, I'd rather you wouldn't repeat to him any of this as coming from me."

"No, no, o' course not. In fact, I hope we can avoid the subject of Regulators."

"That would be better if you could. Mr. McNeill, as I was saying, is a fine man, a fine upstandin' Christian man, but he just don't see things like we do. He was at Culloden, you see, and he took that oath."

"Yes, so he told me when he was at my house."

"And he's a friend of the Governor."

"That's right. The Governor was with him when he came to Alexandriana."

The storekeeper laughed. "You do beat all, Mr. Alexander. A man would think, hearing you talk and all, that you and Governor Tryon were close friends your ownselves."

"He was my guest. I don't believe in his policies, all of them, at any rate, but of course, I had to treat him with courtesy."

"That's right, Mr. Alexander, that's exactly right." He paused. "While David's looking out to see if Jethro and Elam haven't strayed off, maybe you would run back to the office with me. We could be figuring on what your liquor and hides will come to."

"Yes, David, you run out there and see if you can find those boys. I'm afraid they're overstaying theirselves in some tavern or other."

When they reached the little inner office and the storekeeper

ALEXANDRIANA

had closed the door, he opened his safe and pulled forth a sheaf of papers.

"This is really what I wanted to get you back here in private for, Mr. Alexander," he explained. "I didn't want any prying ears to hear us. You see, Herman Husbands—you know who he is if you don't know him your ownself—"

"Yes, I've heard a lot spoken of him."

"Well, he's a relative some ways off—some kind of a cousin, I reckon—of Dr. Franklin up in Philadelphia, and I sorter act as messenger between them. I don't most'n generally carry any letters, but just bring messages by word of mouth. That's safer, you know, in these times, and 'specially when a man's in a public business like me." He selected a printed pamphlet, handed it to Mr. Alexander. "Well, sir, on my last trip I fetched down this pamphlet from Dr. Franklin wrote by him and printed in Philadelphia, which he called 'State Affairs.' But Herman Husbands had some copies struck off and he had the name changed to 'Sermons to Asses,' as you'll see there. He left me some to hand out among my friends, ones I was willing to trust. You might like to look it over, but I'd thank you not to say you got it from me did anybody ask about it."

"I'll be glad to read it, Mr. Wilcox. I'm an admirer of Dr. Franklin. I had the honor of making his acquaintance some time ago in Philadelphia but I don't reckon he'd remember me. I didn't get a chance to talk with him."

"Well, I'm right glad to know that, Mr. Alexander. Dr. Franklin is a great man, a very great man, sir. And that being the case—" He went to the office door, opened it and called to his clerk on the other side of the store. "If anybody comes in and calls for me, Hector, just tell him I'll be out in a minute, and to wait." He closed the door carefully, lowered his voice. "Mr. Alexander, did you know that Dr. Franklin has some pretty pronounced notions about the way things are going and what ought to be done, some pretty radical notions, I'd reckon you'd call 'em?" He did not pause, however, for an answer. "Well, sir, he does, and I'm going to tell you about it, but don't breathe it to anybody that I told you,

ALEXANDRIANA

and it might be best not to talk to anybody except your most trusted friends at all." He paused, lowered his voice until he was talking in almost a whisper. "Dr. Franklin and Herman Husbands have been passing messages to each other agreeing that the colonies ought to separate from Great Britain."

"You mean—"

"Not so loud, Mr. Alexander."

The Mecklenburg man lowered his voice. "You mean that Dr. Franklin thinks we should be independent of England, and should set up our own government and be a free country our ownselves?"

"That's what he believes, Mr. Alexander. But he's not talking it out yet. And be careful how you talk it, Mr. Alexander. And I'll thank you not to mention, should you say anything about it to anybody, that I told you."

VII

"I'VE GOT A surprise for you, Master David." David thought he could detect just a suggestion of challenge in her announcement. He thought too that there was a faint trace of a blush on Lovelace's cheeks. He wasn't sure. "Don't you want to know what it is?" He had been watching her, had been more interested in watching her than in the surprise she was promising. "I'll give you three guesses."

"I was just thinkin' how much you've growed."

"Well, you have growed your ownself. You're most a man a'ready." She wrinkled her forehead. "But still you haven't asked me what the surprise is."

"You got some news about Governor Tryon and the Regulators?"

"Go 'long with you, Master David. You menfolks always thinking of those old Regulators. Don't you ever think of anything else?" He thought now that he saw another expression, maybe in her eyes, maybe in the way she looked a little to the side, a little beyond him.

"Well, lots o' times I think about you."

"Go 'long, Master David. You had no eyes for me." She looked straight into his eyes, challenging. "Now don't you know what the surprise is?"

"No'm, I truly don't."

"It ought to be a thrill for you, Master David. Mama's letting me have a dance tonight and Belinda's coming!"

David was certain now that Lovelace was blushing. It wasn't

ALEXANDRIANA

just the color reflected from her little wine-colored silk dress. There was something, too, about the way she looked past him, a little over his shoulder, and the way her eyelashes drooped a bit. He felt a strange stirring, a tingling that ran up the inside of his arms, that met across his chest . . .

"Well, aren't you thrilled? You haven't said one thing. You're just standing there."

"I'm not much of a dancer. And I don't have any dancing clothes, neither. These here shoes would shake down the house."

"Oh, Master David." The girl laughed. "You say the most amusing things." Suddenly she was serious again. "But I didn't mean about the dance. I meant about Belinda's coming. Master David, you well know what I meant."

A quick little sqeeze of hot fingers upon his fingers on the stairway at Alexandriana. A gleam of candlelight through the crack in the closet. The feel of cool sheets as he pushed his warm, naked body down between them . . . "That's the girl," he said, "that was with you when the Governor and you all came to see Uncle McKnitt, aint it?"

"You right well know she is, Master David, and I'll thank you not to try to appear to be so clever. I'm no child, Master David Barksdale. I'm fourteen, I'll have you to know, and I ought to understand what I see with my own eyes. And I saw how you looked at her when we were at Mr. Alexander's." She looked him straight in the face. "But I'm warning you, sir, that she has a beau and he's bringing her tonight and they do say they're engaged and might be getting married soon. Belinda's most fifteen and she's well growed." She looked away again, over his shoulder, and her lashes dropped. "But I can tell you she was right smart took by you then and maybe—maybe when she sees you again Angus MacDougald might have to be looking well to his knittin'."

"Who is he?"

"Well, he's the son of a rich man at Cross Creek here. And he's right good looking, though he's not nearly so big and strong as you, Master David, but he's eighteen, and they do say he's got marrying on his mind."

ALEXANDRIANA

"How does he stand on politics? Is he 'gainst the Regulators?"

A frown clouded the girl's face. "Why must you always be talking about politics and Regulators and such, Master David? Folks down here aren't always talking it. And Angus—well, he thinks about other things that—that I reckon you aren't interested in." David saw a pout on her lips.

"You mean about girls and such." Now the pout was deepening. "Well, why should I be thinkin' 'bout her when she already has a beau and—and—"

"And what?"

"Well, why aint you talkin' about who's goin to be fetchin' you?"

"Master David, I'm giving it. You see, the hostess doesn't have to have a beau."

"But she could, I reckon, if she wanted to, couldn't she?"

Now her eyelashes were drooping low and she wasn't even looking over his shoulder. She seemed preoccupied with the inspection of her polished little pink fingernails. "Yes, I reckon she could if—if anybody was to ask—"

"And it looks to me like when you are somebody's company and they're havin' a dance and you don't know anybody looks like she ought to see after gettin' you a partner."

She looked up, brightly, her eyes challenging again. "There will be several cute girls coming and I'll get an extra one for you."

" 'Taint worthwhile goin' to all that trouble. Howcome you couldn't sorter pair up with me if you don't have a beau comin'?"

"That would be fine, Master David. But I thought you'd want to dance mostly with Belinda. But Lawsy me, I've got to be getting things ready. Mama's going to play the harpsichord and you should just hear her. There's nobody in Cross Creek can hold a candle with her. And we'll have a fiddle and a banjo and a guitar, too. Won't that be fine for a dance? And now, Master David, you can run out and talk politics and Regulators in Papa's study with him and Mr. Alexander whilst I start getting ready."

But David did not go into Mr. McNeill's study. Instead, he went to his room, opened the worn old bag in which Aunt Jeanie had

ALEXANDRIANA

packed his clothes, and laid out his suit across the bed. He had protested when Aunt Jeanie had suggested bringing the new suit, made only last winter by Uncle McKnitt of materials fetched up from Charles Town to Duncan Ochiltree's store in Charlottetown. But Aunt Jeanie was a wise little woman. She had known what she was doing. She had visioned the possible need of the suit. Perhaps she had said something about it to Uncle McKnitt.

She had put in the black shoes with the silver buckles, too. And stockings, and a freshly starched white shirt. And a ribbon for his hair.

He was downstairs when Lovelace came down.

"I thought you said you didn't have any party clothes with you. You look grand, Master David."

"Aunt Jeanie put my Sunday suit and shoes in the bag. But they aint fine like you all wear down here at Cross Creek."

"Indeed they are. I've a notion you'll be the handsomest young gentleman at the dance."

"And I'll vouch there'll be none here pretty as you." He had said it before he had thought. He could feel a flush upon his cheeks. But he didn't care. He would say it again. In the instant since he had said it he was feeling light, sort of floating, and there was that funny feeling along the inside of his arms, across his chest.

"Go 'long with you, Master David," he heard her saying. "I've a notion you're as quick with your flattery as these young men around Cross Creek and Campbelltown, even if you do talk much of your pioneer ways." As she looked up and directly into his eyes from under her long lashes, David saw that her cheeks were flushed too. But she looked down quickly, shook out the folds of her hoop-petticoat. "It's only that you haven't seen my new dress. But most of the others have, I'll vouch. 'Twas got when Father went to Philadelphia and they do say it was made in England."

It was a pretty dress. Silk, David supposed. Must have been yards of cream-colored silk in the quilted hoop-petticoat. The gown over it, open in front and drawn to the sides in billowing folds over the tight-fitting bodice, was light blue silk. The bodice was cut low, too, David was quick to see, and revealed much of the V between firm little breasts emphasized by the upward push of the corset. And her waist was squeezed in so tightly that David wondered fleetingly how she managed to breathe at all. Sometimes he had helped Aunt Jeanie wind herself into her stays. But that had been years ago, before he had been well growed. And he hadn't noticed such things as bodices and low-cut gowns then.

Lovelace was smiling at him. "Do you like it? And the bouquet?"

"The bouquet?"

"Yes, you were looking at it. Would it be prettier to take off the flowers and just have the breast-knot?"

Just below the V where the breast-knot, of a blue to match the gown, was fastened to the bodice, she had pinned a small bouquet. "I think the flowers are mighty pretty," he said, "but I'd like it either way." And he felt his cheeks warming again.

"You are of a truth a flatterer, Master David." A carriage had driven up; from the driveway came the shrill high laughter of a girl. "Somebody's coming. And if you think my dress is pretty, then just wait until you see Belinda's."

They had pulled back the sliding doors between the parlor and the dining room and danced several sets before Belinda and her escort arrived. When they came in Lovelace ran over to them. "Darling, I've got the best surprise for you!" She was helping Belinda remove her cardinal with the attached hood so that she wouldn't spoil her hair. "I just know you can never guess what it is."

"A new dress. But no, that's not it, for you'd be wearing it. Your father's going to Hillsboro and you're going with him? Or to Charles Town? Or maybe Williamsburg?"

"No, nothing like that. Guess again. Something that might interest Angus. Might make him jealous."

"A man! Whoever could it be? Not Duncan McNeill home from William and Mary College?"

"No, silly. Brother couldn't get off this time of year. You know that. Guess again."

"I haven't any idea. Could it be—" She hesitated.

"Who?"

ALEXANDRIANA

"I won't say. It couldn't be, though."

"Maybe it could. Who?"

"I'm not going to say. No. I'm not." She stamped her little black satin shoe that peeked from underneath her ruffled petticoat. "Who is he, Lovelace? And where is he? Bring him out if he's here!"

Lovelace stepped back into the recess formed by the landing from which the stairway went up on both sides of the entrance hall. Presently she emerged, leading David by the hand.

"David Barksdale!"

David bowed. "You wasn't lookin' for me down this way, I'll vouch." He knew his cheeks were burning, for Belinda was looking directly into his eyes.

"Where in the world did you come from? And, my, but you have got big and tall. I'm right glad to see you, Master David."

"I'm glad to see you, too. And you are right smart growed your ownself."

"Tell, me, Belinda," said Lovelace, "was Master David who you were thinking the surprise might be?"

The other girl's cheeks colored. "I'm not going to say, Lovelace. I told you I wasn't going to tell you."

A tall, sallow young man appeared on the stair landing.

"Did you find where to put your things, Angus?" Lovelace asked him, and he nodded. "Come on down; I want you to meet a friend of ours from the western settlements."

He came down and Lovelace introduced them. "Glad to make yo' 'quaintance." David bowed, offered his hand.

"Pleased to meet you," said the other young man, diffidently. But he did not offer his hand, and David, embarrassed, quickly withdrew his own. The girls, if they noticed it, appeared not to have observed what could have been a deliberate slight. But there was an awkward pause.

"David stopped to see us with his uncle, Mr. Alexander. Wasn't it lucky I was having the dance tonight, because they say they are determined to leave in the morning."

"Yes, wasn't it?" Belinda's delight was evident.

Angus yawned ever so slightly against the back of his hand.

"You are here on business, I take it. Came down from the back country with a pack train of things to trade?"

The girls were conscious of the deprecating tone. "Why, Angus—"

Lovelace interposed. "Mr. Alexander and my father are good friends, and we are always happy to entertain him and Master David here."

"Of a certainty I came down with Uncle McKnitt on business, and we fetched a pack train, too. Else how do you think we'd been able to fetch all those buffalo hides and mink hides and stuff and all that good liquor? And I've a notion, sir, 'twouldn't do you no harm were you to down a right smart slug o' that liquor, neither. Might cheer up that sad face o' your'n."

Lovelace paled a trace. Angus MacDougald swallowed, flushed, but said nothing. And Belinda, David saw out of the corner of his eyes, was looking upon him now with plainly revealed admiration.

"But here we stand talking," spoke up Lovelace, a quick smile lighting her face, "and all this fine music going to waste. Don't you think the music simply wonderful, Belinda? Mama's playing the harpsichord. She'll think you perfectly stunning. Don't you want to go over and speak to her now?" They walked around the ring of dancers toward the musicians at the end of the parlor.

Presently the set ended and the four formed a square, Lovelace with David and Belinda with Angus.

"We're goin' to dance 'Lady 'Round the Lady,' " explained the caller, as he signaled for the music to start again. "Lady 'round the lady and the gent don't go;" he shouted. "Swing yo' pardners and promenade!"

Belinda and Angus moved around the circle, Lovelace and David stayed at home.

"You said you couldn't dance," Lovelace whispered to him, when for a moment they came together.

"I can't much. Sometimes I go over to Rural Retreat when the Davidsons are having a dance. But I don't like to much." He realized he had said the wrong thing. "Unless'n it's with you."

"You can dance well, Master David, but you're better at flattery."

ALEXANDRIANA

When the half set was finished, they exchanged places and Lovelace and David moved around the ring while Belinda and Angus stayed at home.

After a while, for there were only five squares and a half set was quickly danced, Lovelace and David came back to their starting point. "I'm so glad to see you again." Belinda whispered it in his ear as the movements of the figure brought her to him. "I've thought about you so much since—since—" She looked up into his face. "I wonder if you remember anything that happened that night at your house—on the stairs as we were going up to bed? And she squeezed his fingers.

David felt himself go tense. And just as quickly he was relaxed, floating. The music was a long way off and he was skimming above the heads of the other dancers. He was going through the steps mechanically. His feet were away down there . . . And now icicles and hot coals were chasing themselves along his spine . . .

He crushed her little hand in his hard palm, pulled her almost roughly to him. He could feel her firm little bosom within her corset stays swelling against his chest, burning into it. The fragrance of her hair in which he was burying his face was engulfing him . . . "Don't, David. Don't . . . You mustn't." She was whispering in his ear, her lips close to it, her hot breath upon him . . . "You mustn't. Not—not now."

The caller had stopped yelling; the dancers were changing partners. David vaguely felt it. And here was Angus waiting. And Lovelace waiting for him. Angus' sallow face was flushed, scowling. Perhaps it was flushed from the exercise of the dance. Perhaps he had seen. David was certain he didn't care.

He could feel, as he relinquished Belinda to Angus, the ends of his fingers digging into his right palm, his hand tingling along the line of the knuckles . . . And a few whirling steps with Lovelace and the music stopped. The set was ended.

VIII

"YES MR. ALEXANDER, I'm afraid there's going to be trouble, serious trouble. That's why I came out to see you. I hesitated about coming. I haven't been in Mecklenburg long and I'm a young man—"

"All the more reason for your being interested, Waightstill. But look here, I'm not so old myself. I won't turn thirty-eight till next month. And I'd rather you wouldn't remind me of my approaching senility by calling me 'Mister.' Save that for Hezekiah. He's forty-three—old enough to deserve it and has the dignity to wear it properly."

"Well, sir, you're not so old, I'll agree. But I'm new around here and you're a leader in these settlements—"

"And so are you your ownself."

"Well, it's good of you to say so. Perhaps after a while I'll be able to call you by your first name. But anyway, I wanted to talk with you, and your brother suggested I should ride up here."

"I'm glad you did, Waightstill. In fact, you're not the first one who's been here today. Ephraim Brevard was in Charlottetown—maybe you saw him—"

"Yes, I did."

"Well, he stopped here on his way home. He lives up in the Centre Church settlement, you know, and he always stops over for a while with me if he's not in too big a hurry. And he was telling me pretty much the same thing you are. He was right smart worried his ownself."

"I'm glad to know it strikes others as it does me."

ALEXANDRIANA

"And the other day I was talking with John Davidson and he was worried, too. So's Tammas Polk. Last week I was down to his mill and we talked about the prospect. 'Tisn't the best, Waightstill, and it's getting worse instead o' better. I saw that when I was down in the Cross Creek settlement. It's bounden to come to a head, Waightstill. But I'd rather it wouldn't do it in Mecklenburg. Did they offer to do any damage to the Governor's powder?"

"No. I couldn't say they did. When the wagons got to Charlottetown with the stuff—there were three wagons, if I remember aright, and they were loaded with powder and flints and blankets and such stuff—when they got there nobody was willing to provide wagons or teams to take it on over to Salisbury. You see, the teams that brought it up from Charles Town couldn't go any farther; that's where they were to turn back."

"Was there much talk when Moses Alexander impressed the wagons?"

"That's just it. There was a lot of muttering. O' course, they don't talk so freely around me. Some of them have the same notion about me that those Regulators had over there at the ferry on the Yadkin."

McKnitt chuckled. "They really gave you a pretty fair tanning, eh, Waightstill?"

"Of a certainty they did. I thought they were going to beat me to death."

"How'd you get away from them?"

"I reckon I outtalked them. A fellow can do some powerful pleading before that kind of a court."

"Well, Waightstill, maybe it sharpened your knowledge of human nature, and that's a right handy thing for a lawyer to have, I'm bound."

"Maybe so, but it's a damnably hard way to get. But that makes it all the stranger to you, I'm bound, and to my ownself, I reckon, too. Here those Regulators catch me and give me a first-rate licking, and threaten to kill me, and still I've got a strong feeling that I'm supporting them in their fight with Tryon. That's hard to understand, eh?"

ALEXANDRIANA

"No, it's not, Waightstill. You see, you aren't defending those fellows who beat you up so much as you are defending a principle. You realize that they jumped on you mainly because you wore fine clothes and were a lawyer. They associate fine clothes and lawyers with Tryon and his type, with the cause of the King in general. They have been oppressed by lawyers and clerks and judges and sheriffs and lawmakers and officials of one sort and another until they just bunch them all together—and you were just in the wrong bunch, that's all."

"That's exactly what they said. Old man Hamilton was making them a speech when they brought me up to the main crowd. 'What business has Maurice Moore got being a judge? He aint a judge; he aint been appointed by the King. And neither has Henderson.' That's the sort of talk he was making to them. 'The Assembly don't make good laws. They make laws against the common fokes and it's the damned lawyers that makes 'em!' Then they all looked over there at me. 'The best thing that could be done for the country,' old man Hamilton went on, waving his arms and shouting, 'would be to kill all the clerks and all the lawyers. We ought to kill every blasted one of 'em! Them and their fine clothes paradin' around while the common fokes has everything took from them by the sheriffs for taxes!' And there I was in my new broadcloth clothes and my brand new shoes and hat. Old man Hamilton's speech of a certainty wasn't helping my feeling of safety. And for a while I thought they were going to take him at his words, too. And, still and all, sir, I'm bound they have justification."

"Maybe it would pay you when you take trips, Waightstill, to wear a huntin' shirt and rough back-country breeches. But we're getting off the subject. What do you think's likely to happen to those powder wagons?"

"I've a notion they may never get to Hillsboro. They got started before daylight. But the word got out ahead of them. Some of the Rocky River boys were in Charlottetown last night—a bunch of them at Jack's Tavern. I heard there was a good deal of talk. And old Pat Jack, you know, is pretty free about expressing his views on Tryon, King George and the English in general. He's got his

ALEXANDRIANA

Irish blood up. There was some talk that the wagons might get held up over around Rocky River. I—I—well, to be frank, I sort of hope the wagons won't get to Hillsboro, but I realize that if anything happens to that powder it will infuriate Governor Tryon, and it may of a certainty set off some big fireworks."

"I just this morning started David and Jethro O'Flannagan—he's an Irish fellow who lives on the place—"

"I know him. Met him at Jack's Tavern last fall and again one day when he was out at 'Squire Abraham Alexander's mill with David. He's quite a character."

"Yes, Jethro's a little wild maybe, but you can depend upon him. And as I was saying, I've just started him and Jethro to Hillsboro on some business for me. They were figuring on stopping for the night over about Phifer's Mill. I hope they don't run into any trouble, but if it's any fightin' anywhere near Jethro you can trust him to get in it, I'm bound."

"Well, I wouldn't be surprised if—"

He stopped, as Jeanie appeared in the doorway, rose from his chair, bowed. McKnitt had risen beside him. "Come in, Jeanie. Waightstill was just telling me—"

"It's high time you were coming to see us, Mr. Avery," she interrupted.

"But, Mistress Alexander—"

"You needn't offer any excuses. You haven't even been out to see my baby. And she's worth riding many a mile to see, sir, I'll have you know. But do sit down, sir, and don't begin making excuses. I shan't hear them anyway. All you men talk about these days is taxes and Regulators and Governor Tryon—the conceited prig—and such like." But the young lawyer, as the three sat down, saw that her eyes were beaming.

"I have meant for a long time to come to see the young lady," he began. "And I've often asked about her of Mr. Hezekiah and Mistress Alexander and the girls. And how is she now? I do want to see her. I hear she's mighty pretty."

"W'y, she's most growed now. She was born way last November and here it's May and you haven't seen her. And we do think she's pretty. She's picked up so much lately and we do hope she will keep on improving so she'll have a good start for the hot weather."

"Mistress Alexander was saying some time ago that you had had a hard time getting a wet nurse."

"Yes, we did. One of the Negroes had a young baby just a week older than Abigail, but she took to havin' weed-chills and we had to take Abigail off her. She didn't have enough milk for the two of them anyway. But the baby of one of the other women died and with her milk Abigail's been improving right along."

"You were fortunate. I'm mighty glad she's doing so well and I want to see her before I leave if I won't disturb her sleeping."

"O' course you can. But you all can start back on politics now, because I must be running out to the kitchen." She arose, and the men stood up. "Do sit down. We are expecting you to stay for supper, Mr. Avery, and to spend the night if you will."

"That is mighty good of you, Mistress Alexander, but I've got to be getting back to Charlottetown. I've still got some work to do before I head back out Sugaw Creek way."

But Jeanie had already turned to go. "Supper will be ready shortly," she called back from the doorway, "and you aren't so busy that you can't stay for a bite."

"Sit down, Waightstill. Of course, you're going to stay for supper."

"Thank you. But I ought to be going. And I might add, sir, that you are a very lucky man."

"I am, for a fact. Jeanie is a powerful fine little woman."

"She is of a certainty. Seeing you all here at Alexandriana makes a bachelor begin to have ideas."

" 'Tis about time you were thinkin' of a family, Waightstill."

"Well, I'm twenty-four. I reckon I am old enough. But, to get back to what we were talking about, I'm afraid that regardless of whether anything happens to the Governor's powder and flints or not, there's trouble ahead for us, and not far off, at that."

"Waightstill, the party that's got the upper hand in England doesn't seem to understand that we in America are men with the same rights they have. We are no slaves. They can't seem to see that. And if they don't change their policies, I'm afraid you're right."

"You're right. We've got the same blood, the same traditions, the same rights they have on the other side. Look here," the young lawyer leaned forward, an intense expression on his serious face, "they've got no right to lay taxes on us for the support of the British government, especially when we've got not a word to say about it. That's not right, sir. And on top of all that, they're not providing a fair and honest government in this colony. Had they done so, there'd have been none of this Regulator business. And you well know it, sir." He sat back in his chair.

"Yes, of a certainty that's the truth, Waightstill. I've a notion that if the liberals—Pitt and his crowd—don't restrain Lord North and his Tories, there's going to be trouble, and right serious trouble, at that. And you know—" He removed his pipe from his mouth, knocked the ashes from the bowl into his cupped hand and threw them toward the fireplace, cheerless now that early May had brought warm afternoons. Then he stuck the pipe into his waistcoat pocket. "You know, Waightstill," and he was deliberately weighing his words, "it wouldn't be an oncommon silly notion, either, to think that it just mought start right here in Mecklenburg with those powder wagons of the Governor's."

IX

"Get along Nellie! Get along." 'Squire White nudged the horse he was riding, tugged jerkily upon the rein of the pack horse he was leading. "Step up, Kit! We got to be gettin' home afore it's black dark." The two beasts, plodding along lazily this warm spring evening, raised their heads, stepped a bit livelier. "If it hadn't a-been for that there Jethro O'Flannagan, the dad-blasted rascal," the Rocky River 'squire reproved himself, "I'd 'a' been home a long time afore now. He can tell the funniest stories I ever heared, I'll vouch, and the way that fellow can stow away grog's a sight in this world."

The mention of grog, even to himself, reminded him again and painfully that he was getting home late to supper. "The old woman's likely to be raisin' holy Ned." He kicked his horse, jerked again on the rein of the pack animal. "Get up, Nellie! Step along! That little nip I had won't help her disposition none either."

Nellie stopped, precipitately, almost throwing the Rocky River yeoman from the saddle and almost upsetting the grain that had been balanced across the horse in front of the pommel. The pack horse, coming alongside Nellie, stiffened her forelegs too, stopped in her tracks.

'Squire White, regaining his equilibrium and righting the bag of grain, dug his heels viciously into the horse's sides. "Get on with you! Goin' plum' to sleep here in the middle o' the road. Get up, Nellie! Get up! Get along—"

A man stepped from the bushes that fringed the roadside. He grabbed the horse's bridle.

ALEXANDRIANA

"What d'want?" 'Squire White's bold tone betrayed a trace of nervousness. "Take your hand off that bridle." He peered into the face of the fellow. "You black devil. Whose place you runnin' off from? Take your hand off, I tell you, and stand back. If'n I had my pistol!"

Two other figures slipped from the bushes. "Get down!" commanded the first one, who continued to hold the horse's rein. One of the others grabbed the bridle of the pack horse. "We want to borrow your horses."

"You black devils. You'll not get 'em. I'll have the sheriff on you!"

One of the men pulled the sack of grain from the pack horse, deposited it by the roadside. When the second sack had been deposited beside the first, two of the men hauled 'Squire White, protesting and kicking, from the saddle and stood him beside the bags of grain.

Now he changed his demeanor. "But I'm two miles from home. Let me take my stuff home and then you can have the horses."

"And let your boys shoot us for our trouble."

"Shut up." One of the men whirled upon the one who had just spoken. "You talk too much. You all get on Nel—" He stopped. "Get on that horse." He pointed to Nellie. "I'll ride this one."

In an instant they were galloping away.

"You're not Niggers!" 'Squire White, standing beside his two bags of grain, shook his fist at the departing highwaymen. "No, sir, you're no Niggers, you and your black faces. I'll have the law on ye, too!" 'Squire White stood in the road shaking his fist until he could think of no further inprecations to call down upon them. And then he turned his painful gaze upon the bags. "Two miles from home and all this stuff to tote!" He sat down upon one of the bags, pulled out his handkerchief and mopped his perspiring forehead, shook his head slowly. All at once he stopped. "I wonder,"— He sat up straight. "—how that fellow happened to know Nellie's name. I wonder—" But he said no more. Instead, he clambered to his feet, started the long walk home.

"Well, you were powerful smart, I do say. Holler at me to shut up. Say I'm talkin' too much. And then up and tell us to get on Nellie."

"I didn't quite get the name said."

"You got enough of it said, I'm bound."

They had slowed the horses to a walk to let them catch their wind.

"It was a shame to make the old man walk and carry those bags home."

"He won't carry 'em. He'll borrow a horse and fetch it back to get 'em. Besides, there wasn't no time to be lost."

In a few minutes they came up with a larger group of riders. "Well, I see you boys got the horses. Come over here, all you fellows. We want to get our plans fixed up." The man who appeared to be the leader motioned to the others.

"The wagons are at Phifer's Mill, boys," he revealed, when the riders had crowded about him. "I don't think they are guarding them very good. Aint expectin' trouble. That makes it all the better for us. We want to get everything done and get away without causin' too much fuss. And then we'll scatter. It's likely to make Moses Alexander powerful mad, and Tryon still madder, and we'll have to lie low. You fellows aint forgettin' what you swore, remember. Now let's get goin'."

Fifteen minutes later a sleepy wagoner, tired after the long drive from Charlottetown and dozing on the straw-filled sack he had pulled from the wagon seat and placed at the foot of an oak he was now slumping against, observed through half-closed eyes a man standing in front of him.

"Get up!" The man was waving a pistol. The wagoner scrambled to his feet. "Where are the rest of your crowd?"

"Ezra's right over there on the far side of that there wagon. I 'spect he's sleep."

"Ezra's bein' took care of, pardner. Where's the others at?"

"Over there in the tavern—right smart drunk by now, more'n likely."

"Well, you step over here 'longside o' Ezra so's one fellow can look after the two o' you. The rest of us's got work to do and we aint got much time." He raised his voice. "All right, boys, let's get at it."

There were three wagons. Quickly they lifted out the kegs of powder, stove in the heads, and dumped the powder into a big pile. Then they tore the blankets into strips, threw them on the pile, and the flints and the other things from the wagons with them. "We've got to work fast," cautioned the leader. "We don't want to have no trouble when they come pilin' out from the tavern. We want to be ready to ride."

Jethro was standing at the bar, his foot on the rail, his glass hoisted in the middle of a story. A half dozen men grouped about him had almost forgot to sip their grog. "—and I says to him, I says, 'Tom, the only way to handle a woman—"

A man came running in from the tavern porch. "There's some men down there at them wagons fixin' to blow up that there powder!"

The crowd downed their drinks; there was a general surge toward the door. Jethro finished his drink, moved toward the front. "By damn, it won't make me cry none if they blow hit to hell."

"Shut up, Jethro." David, sitting at a table near the door with a young Rocky River man, was almost within reach of Jethro when he made his observation. He arose, followed him out the door. "There's folks around here we don't know, Jethro. You got to be more careful."

"Ye're right, Davy. I got too much mouth. But I've a notion these here wagoners wouldn't mind gittin' shed o' that stuff they're haulin' nohow." He pointed. "Look a-yonder. They's already piled up the stuff and that there feller—That there one, over there. See 'im—He's makin' a powder train."

There was still enough light to see men moving about down at the camping place. Now David pointed. "Look at 'em, Jethro. They're Niggers!"

"No, they aint. 'Twouldn't no Niggers do that. They's white men blacked up. But watch out, and don't git too close. That stuff will make a hell of a 'splosion and it might blow some of them wagons—"

ALEXANDRIANA

"Stand back!" A fellow was waving a gun. "We aint wantin' no trouble but this here powder's got to go. We aint goin' to have it shootin' hell out o' none o' our fokes." He turned to face the group down at the wagons. "Go ahead!" He waved his free hand. "Let her shoot!"

A man fired his pistol into the powder train. There was a small explosion, and David saw a stream of fire racing along the ground toward the pile of powder. A deafening roar, and a blast of air solid as a plank slapped him to the ground. Instantly Jethro was over him. "You hurt, Davy? Anything hit you?" He pulled the boy to his feet. "No, aint nothin' wrong. You just wasn't lookin' fer it. There was a lot o' powder. I sorter got braced, but it danged nigh knocked me down too."

The man who fired the pistol, they saw, was on the ground. As he arose a bit unsteadily Jethro saw blood streaming from his face. As Jethro and David pushed forward, a man from his crowd ran over to him. "I'm all right," said the bleeding man. "Damned stave from one o' those kegs hit me, I reckin." He mopped blood from his eyes. "But damned if we didn't get shed of Tryon's powder in a hurry."

A tall man was waving furiously. "We got to be gittin' away from here, boys!" The light from the burning wagons danced full upon them as they ran to the place where their horses had been left, mounted them, and in a moment were galloping off. "To hell with Tryon!" one of them shouted, as he turned in his saddle for a last look.

"Davy, don't say nothin', boy, but you and me knows some of that crowd and I'll vouch did I have a horse I could beat that feller home that got his head cut. But we aint talkin'. Y'understand? We don't know nothin' 'bout them—them strangers. See?"

"Sure, we don't even know they live in Rocky River settlement."

Jethro laughed. "You got plenty sense, Davy. And as you was sayin' a little bit ago, the best way o' showin' sense, I reckin, is keepin' yo' mouth shut. There's a lot o' fokes gits in trouble beca'se they was talkin' when they ought to 'a' been listenin'." He kicked the hub of a ruined wagon wheel. "But look a-here, this here's been nerve-upsettin' doin's. Hit calls fer another drink. We better be moseyin' back before this crowd gits there and drinks hit plum' dry."

Next morning 'Squire White called his boys to breakfast early. "We got to be gettin' some seeds in the ground, boys," he announced, when the boys had sat down at the table, "and you all will have to put off some of that dancin' and playin' long-balls 'til crops's laid by." He poured his coffee into the saucer to cool.

"But what I was wantin' to ask you was if you ran into any strange goin's-on over at Phifer's Hill yesterday. The funniest thing you ever seen happened to me last night. I was comin' home from the mill when three men—three Niggers, I took 'em to be—held me up, pulled me and the stuff off the horses and rode 'em off. There I sat in the road with two big bags and nothin' to ride and two miles from home. Well, I walked home and borrowed a horse from Neighbor Newell and went back and got the stuff. But here's the funny thing: when I went to the stables this morning to get his horse and take it home I found my horses in the stable all right except they'd been rode hard. And Mr. Newell, when I took his horse home, said he'd just got word they'd blowed up a passel o' powder last night over at Phifer's Mill."

He looked straight toward one of his sons. "Look a-here, Jim." His forkful of big hominy was poised in midair. "I've been tellin' you all about this long-balls. That's a rough game. It's worse'n a gander-pullin'. Look at that there cut in your forehead. Might 'ave knocked your head off."

"It's just a scratch, Pa."

"Well, you're gettin' too old to be playin' it anyhow. But as I was sayin', they blowed up the wagons with the Governor's powder and there's bound to be trouble. If I had been in it I'd sure lie low and keep my mouth shut. Not that I would 'a' been 'gainst bein' in such a trick my ownself had I 'a' been a few years younger. But 'twould pay anybody that was in it to keep quiet and mind his own business." He lifted the saucer expertly to his lips, took a long swallow. "But I can't understand about them horses. Been wonderin' if there was any connection 'tween them fellows takin' the horses and the powder blowin'-up. They was Niggers that held me up—black as coal. Still, Niggers wouldn't 'a' had nerve enough to blow up the Governor's powder, I'm bound."

He chewed his hominy silently, poured more coffee into his saucer, blew on it, took another swallow. "Jim, if I was you, I'd clean out that there scratch. Look's sorter like there's dirt in it, black looking. You better clean it out good and put some turpentine in it. And, John, you and Bill better wash a little behind your ears. Folks prying around's likely to figure you don't wash much."

And in their father's eyes the White boys were certain they saw a sharper glint.

"Didn't any of those hold-up fellows offer to harm you, did they, Pa?" There was the trace of a grin on Jim's tanned face.

"Me! They didn't have the nerve. I could a-licked the whole passel of 'em." And he poured himself another cooling of coffee.

X

"Look a-yonder, Davy. Aint that Bedent Spraggins? Yeh, it's him; it's him shore'n hell. I wonder what he's doin' way over here in Rowan."

He hailed the man approaching. "Hi, there, Bedent! You must be lost, man. This here's a hell of a ways from Sugaw Creek. And jedgin' by the way yo' mule's all lathered up, you must 'a' been makin' time from somewheres."

"Hi, Jethro. Hi, Davy." Bedent pulled on his mule's rein; the beast seemed willing enough to stop. "What's you'ns doin' over this a-way yo' ownselves?"

"We're headed to Hillsboro, Bedent. Where you been?"

"You better be headin' back to Mecklenburg 'longside o' me if'n you aint lookin' fer trouble."

"Looks like somethin's been scarin' hell out o' you yo' ownself, Bedent."

"Well, hit's plenty o' trouble makin' up 'tween here and Hillsboro. That's why I'm goin' home."

"Where you been, old man?"

"I been with old man Hugh Waddell. But I'm pullin' out on 'im."

"You mean you aint got no discharge papers, eh?"

"I reckin that's how you'd put it, Jethro. But they's a damn sight more'n me done left 'im."

"What's the trouble, Bedent? You don't like the smell o' gunpowder, old man?"

" 'Taint that, Jethro, as you damn well know. But I aint a-goin' to

ALEXANDRIANA

be a-killin' fokes what's in the right jest to uphold this here damned Tryon. And there's plenty o' the likes o' me, too. I aint the only one what pulled out o'camp."

"Where is the General anyhow?"

"He was over 'tween Tradin' Ford and Salisbury when I left. I wouldn't doubt but what he was still farther this a-way by now. We crossed the Yadkin and started to join Tryon at Hillsboro but we hadn't went far when we come on a big batch o' Regerlators. They was 'tween us and Tryon and they 'lowed to us we wasn't goin' no farther. A lot of our crowd didn't want to nohow. We didn't have much powder neither. Old man Waddell and Grif Rutherford and some of the rest of the officers helt a council and decided to come back acrost the Yadkin, which we done. There was some talk that the Regerlators was comin' acrost after us. But 'twon't be no use 'cause dang nigh all o' Waddell's crowd has about runned out on him anyhow."

"How was the General a-figurin' on getting more powder? You say he didn't have much."

"He was waitin' on a batch comin' up from Charles Town. It ought to be due 'bout now. Thought I'd 'a' met the wagons but they might 'a' gone t'other way."

"Bedent—" Jethro, sensing the importance of the dramatic announcement he was about to make, shifted the cud of tobacco from one side of his mouth to the other, and spit a voluminous stream of amber toward an unoffending small rock beside the road, "the General needn't be lookin' fer that powder no longer."

"How come, Jethro?"

"Beca'se it's gone. Blowed up."

"What you talkin' 'bout?"

"Well, me and Davy here seen it did. We stopped at Major Phifer's and along after night some Niggers come along, busted up the kags, set a-fire to it and blowed it up. Everything—wagons, flints, blankets, the whole endurin' batch o' stuff."

"Well, I'm damned if that aint somethin'. Niggers, you say? Don't sound like Niggers."

"Maybe it won't Niggers, Bedent. But you needn't be goin'

'round sayin' so. They blacked their faces to look like Niggers but they didn't fool nobody, leastways not me and Davy. Hit was a bunch o' them Rocky River boys, I'll vouch. But don't you be a-tellin' it. Hit mought cause 'em trouble if things keep a-goin' like they seems to be headin'. But how 'bout them Regerlators? Is they many o' them?"

"They say the whole danged woods 'tween Tradin' Ford and Hillsboro's full of 'em. Hit looks like there's goin' to be fightin'. But Waddell aint goin' to git much done, I'll vouch. Tryon is a-raisin' hell and he's got some o' them eastern settlements soldiers at Hillsboro and they do say he is comin' this way to join up with Waddell. If'n he does, he's likely to git in a fight somewheres over 'bout Alamance. And it'll be a damned shame fightin' them Regerlators. They aint done no harm. They's only tryin' peaceable like to git their rights and they aint wantin' no trouble."

"You're right there, Bedent; aint he, Davy?"

"That's the way it looks to me. I aint never had much use for Governor Tryon since that time he did me that way in Charlottetown."

"I 'member that." Bedent pulled up the reins that had slipped down along his mule's neck. "I seen it. I was right close by when he was talkin' to you. And I aint got no use for him neither, damn him. But look-a-here, I got to be gittin' on down Sugaw Creek way. You fellows be careful and don't git in no trouble. Hit mought be sort o' dangerous like over t'other side o' the Yadkin." He jerked on the reins. "And if'n you sees Tryon, tell him fer me to go to hell."

Farther along the road to Salisbury they met other men heading westward, some riding, some plodding along on foot. "They may call it desertin' if they like," declared one man who stopped to talk with them a moment, "but I'm not goin' to turn no gun on men that aint wantin' nothin' but justice and fair dealin'. And that's the way most of us feel, I'll vouch, mister."

At Salisbury they turned in at the Mansion House. When they had helped the hostler water and feed their horses, they went inside. The taproom was crowded. "Soldiers," explained the maid who came to wait on them. "General Waddell's soldiers. Going

ALEXANDRIANA

over Hillsboro way to join the Governor. Leastways, that's what I hear. And some of them are just Salisbury folks come to hear the news. They do say there might be a battle."

She brought them their food, and from time to time as they ate she came back to their table. "Anything else I can do for you gentlemen?" They were almost finished.

"You might bring me another hunk o' yo' butter and some bread," Jethro replied. "And some more coffee. Hit's oncommon good or I'm mighty blasted hongry one or t'other."

"And you, sir?"

"I'd like some more coffee, please ma'am."

She brought it. "You gentlemen staying for the night?"

"We 'lowed to."

"You'll want rooms then. And maybe—" She stared at the palm of her hand, slowly lifted a meaning eye to meet Jethro's.

"One'll do us, eh, Davy?"

" 'Twill unless'n it's mighty powerful little."

The girl laughed. "There's plenty room in 'em. But sometimes gentlemen like to be private."

"Me and Davy got nothin' private to keep from one another."

She laughed again. "Well, 'twouldn't make no difference about that. We wouldn't mind, o' course."

"What you mean, we, sister?"

"Myrtle and me. I thought maybe you'd be wantin' some company after 'while. Myrtle's red-headed and pretty lively, and good-looking—"

"You aint to say ugly your ownself, girlie."

"But you ought to see Myrtle, mister. Now if you'd want me to get you Myrtle and did the young gentleman here want me—"

"Listen, sister, you needn't bother 'bout Myrtle nor your ownself neither. We done got our room and hit aint got but one bed in hit, and hit's jest wide 'nough fer me and Davy. You run 'long and play with the General's soldier-boys." He gave her a playful spank on her broad bottom.

"Salisbury's a big town, aint it, Davy? Got everything you're lookin' fer. Reckin' Charlottetown'll ever be this big?"

ALEXANDRIANA

"I don't reckon so. Maybe though, in a hundred years."

That night David slept soundly. But from the depths of exhausted slumber there arose confused images, kaleidoscopic, now focused sharply and distinct, now blurred and merging, revolving, expanding and contracting, coming forward, receding . . . Soldiers in coonskin caps, Regulators chasing General Waddell's soldiers . . . Belinda, dressed in apron and cap, standing before his table, a coquettish smile in her challenging eyes . . . Lovelace . . . lovely, lovely . . . soldiers and horses, horses and Regulators . . . Belinda again . . . "Anything else you want, David?" . . . Governor Tryon in mouse colored breeches and a purple coat, and a lace handkerchief . . . A red-headed girl squeezing his hand on a stairway . . . No, Governor Tryon, squeezing him tightly in the shoulder . . . "I should have you lashed, you young backwoodsman!" . . . Shaking him, shaking him . . .

Up from the depths of deep sleep he was being lifted . . . Up, up . . . Slowly he opened his eyes. "Time to get up, Davy." Jethro released his grip upon the boy's shoulder. "The horses's been fed. 'G'inst we git a bite it'll be time to be hittin' out fer the Yadkin and Tradin' Ford."

Hard riding over the road that turned northward beyond Trading Ford brought them by nightfall to a tavern at the crossroads where one route led northwestward into Salem and the Moravian Settlements and the other turned sharply eastward toward Hillsboro.

In the taproom they met two men who had come from the Alamance section. "It looks right smart like there's goin' to be fightin'," one of them reported. "The Regulators are gatherin' from all sides. There are hundreds of 'em. They are expectin' to get satisfaction out of Tryon by a show of their strength, but I doubt if they'll scare Tryon. He's a mean devil, all right, but there's one thing you got to admit: he's not scared and he's a soldier. They said he was headin' this way with a big bunch of men. When he comes on the Regulators there's bound to be fightin'. Tryon's mad. He don't like the way the Regulators did his crony Fanning over at Hillsboro when they tore up the court over there."

ALEXANDRIANA

"How was that?"

"Well, you know there's been trouble a long time. You know how the King's officers have been robbin' the people with their big fees? I guess there's been some of it done in Mecklenburg?"

"Yes, some. But what I meant was what's happened lately to make the Guv'ner extry mad?"

"Well, at the court last September there was a bunch of the Regulators—some of the hot-heads in the crowd—broke in and took out some of the lawyers and give 'em a good lickin' and tried to force old Judge Henderson to try their crowd that had been indicted before. They tried to make the judge pick the jury from their crowd. Rednap Howell—you know, that poet fellow—and Herman Husbands and Jim Hunter was 'mongst them, and they generally raised the devil. But the judge was too slick for 'em; he adjourned court 'til the next day and that night he slipped away from Hillsboro."

"We got wind o' those doin's, but what's happened lately?"

"Well, it was the same thing, only worse, at the March term this year—two months ago. The same crowd come to court and raised so much devilment that they adjourned court 'til next September. But the Regulators weren't to be outdone. They catched Lawyer Williams on the street and give him a powerful beatin' and they dragged Fanning out the courthouse by his heels and whupped him something terrible, and that night they kept him in their camp. And the next mornin' when they found out court had been adjourned, they beat him some more and plum' tore down his fine house. Yes, siree, tore it plum' down. They even found a bell Fanning was keepin' for the Episcopal Church and they thought it was his spice mortar and they broke it up too. They raised hell, friend. But it wasn't the general run of the Regulators; it was the hot-heads. And you can't much blame them, at that."

"You can't, pardner. You're right about that." Jethro took another swallow from his mug, licked his lips. "But I can see how that'd make the Guv'ner madder'n hell. And when he meets up with them Regerlators, it's bound to be fightin', as you 'lowed."

They stayed at the tavern the next day, for their horses were

ALEXANDRIANA

exhausted. But the following morning they started eastward and by early afternoon they had reached the fork where one road turned off to the right down the country toward Cross Creek and the other continued toward Alamance and Hillsboro.

"Three days steady ridin' down that road, Davy—" Jethro pointed with his switch—" and we'd come out at Cross Creek. Would you rather take that road and sorter go 'round them Regerlators and Tryon's soldiers?"

"But that would take too long, Jethro."

"Mebbe in the long run 'twouldn't take as long as 'twould goin' this a-way. But that wasn't jest what I was thinkin' 'bout. I was thinkin' you might like to call by Mr. McNeill's house. Or mebbe by that other young lady's house." He was watching David. The boy was conscious of it.

"Well, I wouldn't mind seein' them. But you know Uncle McKnitt's business can't wait too long. And I'm not afraid of the Regulators or Tryon neither."

But he looked down the road that led to the southeast. And there came to him the picture of a little girl in a cream-colored hoop-petticoat, a light blue gown over it, a tight-fitting little bodice, a breast-knot at the bottom of the V formed by firm little breasts . . . And he remembered fiddles, and a banjo and a guitar and a harpsichord . . . And he remembered a girl close to him, her little bosom pushing hard against his chest, her fingers squeezing his fingers, the fragrance of her hair in his eyes, in his mouth . . .

He jerked the reins. "Jethro, we got to be makin' time if'n we get far today."

Jethro kicked his animal in the ribs.

"Giddap," he said.

XI

"Hold up, there, strangers!"

A man on a mangy gray horse came threshing out of the undergrowth at the side of the trail. He was a cadaverous looking fellow and his head sat at the end of a red thin neck that arched forward from shoulders and back in the exact symmetry of his horse's rump.

"Where you'ns a-goin'?"

David saw that most of the front teeth were missing from his shrunken blue gums, and the ashy stubble of beard that pushed up almost to eyes that flamed out from sunken sockets heightened the intense, hungry look of the fellow.

Jethro with unhurried deliberation turned in his saddle and discharged a stream of tobacco juice that clipped the front hoof of the man's horse. "We aint on no secret business, brother," he observed with an emphasized casualness, "but that bein' agreed on, me and my friend here aint figurin' where it's any o' yore business."

"Well, that could be a matter of argyment, mister, and I might add that we aint fancyin' no smart lip neither."

"We? What you mean by we? If you're talkin' 'bout that there spavined nag, you can crawl off'n it and git down where I can give you a taste o' my fist."

" 'Twon't be necessary, mister. I aint got time to be cloutin' no thick skulls nohow." He turned around in his saddle. "Hey, you fellers ride over this a-way. Here's a couple o' fellers we got to look into."

David spoke in low tones to Jethro. "Don't talk too much, 'member. Aint no use makin' 'em mad."

ALEXANDRIANA

The stranger confronted David. "That's right, young feller. You talkin' sense. We aint after botherin' you'ns." Several other men on raw-boned horses and two on mules had ridden out of the bushes. The man who had stopped Jethro and David turned to one of the others. "You talk to 'em."

"You fellers be soldiers?" The man, evidently the leader of the detachment, spoke directly to Jethro.

But David answered. "No, sir. We were just on a trip over Hillsboro way."

"You aint Waddell's men?"

"No, sir."

"Where you come from?"

"Over in the western settlements—Mecklenburg."

"Mecklenburg? You're a hell of a ways from home, son."

"Yes, sir, right smart."

"Did you know there was trouble 'tween here and Hillsboro?"

"No, sir, not for certain. But at Salisbury they did say Governor Tryon and the Regulators was 'bout to get at it."

"Well, that's likely to be so." He looked toward Jethro. "You fellows friends o' the Governor's?"

"Who, us?" Jethro's tone betrayed his indignation. But he stopped. "How'n hell does I know if you aint his friends yore ownselves?"

"Well, now that's a fair question, stranger. But don't we carry the answer our ownselves? Do friends of Tryon look hongry and ragged like us? We don't look like no Frohockeses and Fannings, do we?"

"That's a fact, you don't. And how about me here? Do I look like the bastard's done fed me?"

"You aint what you'd say no 'ristocrat looking feller." The man who had been questioning Jethro laughed, and so did the others. But the one who had stopped them spoke up.

"It's a lot o' Waddell's soldiers don't look like no 'ristocrats," he observed. "How do we know this here feller aint a slick spy tryin' to find out what we're up to?"

"Well, now that jest could be so, though it's onlikely, Bud. But

ALEXANDRIANA

I tell you what. You fellers says you're headed over Hillsboro way. We're headed in that direction our ownselves. You all might jest ride 'long with us and we'll sort o' pervide protection for you in case we should run into any o' Tryon's soldiers." He turned to the man he had addressed as Bud. "Rednap'll know if'n they're all right."

"Look a-here, we aint no spies or no soldiers neither. And I don't fancy bein'—"

David interrupted Jethro. "But if you all are goin' towards Hillsboro where we got business, mister, we'd be glad o' havin' your company."

"Son, you got sense."

After a few minutes they turned off into a thick underbrush through which they pushed their way until they came out upon a little clearing down by a creek. Horses were hobbled about the open place or tied to trees, and men lounged around, some of them talking in little knots, some sprawled separately under bushes, their hats across their faces.

"We got two strangers here, Rednap," said the leader to a man who came across to meet them, "and they says they's headed over Hillsboro way. They come along with us and we thought maybe you'd like to talk to 'em." He turned to Jethro. "This here's Mr. Howell, and I didn't git yore name."

"Jethro O'Flannagan. And this here's Master Barksdale. And I'm glad to make yore 'quaintance, Mr. Howell. Be you the one they calls Rednap?"

The man nodded.

"I've heared tell o' you. And from what I've heared you aint to say much of a friend o' Guv'ner Tryon."

Rednap Howell laughed. "Not exactly. You've been hearing aright. But look here, Mr. O'Flannagan, you can't get to Hillsboro now without running squarely into Tryon's bunch. Yesterday he raised his camp and crossed Haw River and last night he was on the Alamance. He's not more than six or seven miles from us now."

The fellow who had first halted Jethro and David put in a word. "We thought maybe these two was Waddell's soldiers tryin' to

ALEXANDRIANA

git back to Tryon with some sort of a message or else spyin' on us."

Jethro glowered at the man. "Hit's a lie, Mr. Howell. We aint no spies or no Waddell's soldiers neither. We was goin' to Hillsboro on business fer Mr. McKnitt Alexander—"

"I've heard of him," interrupted Rednap Howell. "Lives over in the western side of Anson."

"Mecklenburg now."

"Yes, I remember it was cut off a few years ago. I tell you, Mr. O'Flannagan, you and your young friend had better stay along with us until this trouble blows over. We think we can get it straightened out tomorrow. We're sending a propositoin to the Governor and we believe we'll be able to avoid fighting. We are not in much shape to fight, but we have a lot of men and more are coming all the time. We think we can impress him with our numbers and get a fair compromise out of it."

"I tell you, Mr. Howell, I wouldn't mind gettin' a crack at Tryon my ownself. If I thought 'twas a right smart good chanct of it, I'd right gladly put off gittin' to Hillsboro, eh, Davy?"

" 'Twould suit me."

"Well, it just mought be that there'll be a fight. But I hope we can get it settled."

When night came the campfires blazed from the woods and around the campfires men were singing and telling bawdy stories, and some were drinking brandy, while others, more impressed with the seriousness of their situation, sat together quietly and talked.

There was no effort to be secretive about their strength; the Regulators, in fact, were hoping Governor Tryon would think them stronger than they really were.

"I aint no soldier, leastways, much o' one, Davy, but this here aint no way to be doin', I can tell you that." Jethro lay sprawled on the ground, his head supported on the heel of his hand, his elbow braced at a strained angle against the ground. He was staring into the dying coals of the fire on which their supper had been cooked. "No, siree, this aint no way to be gittin' ready to do any fightin'."

ALEXANDRIANA

"But they won't be any fightin', will there, Jethro?"

"I wouldn't be s'prised. Tryon's a hell of a dominatin' feller and he'll likely try to show off how smart he is. And these fellers aint ready. Why look over there at them guns stacked there; bet aint more'n two out o' three here's got a gun. They figure this here's a picnic. A lot of 'em's comed out to see what's goin' to happen. Yeh, and they'll likely see more'n they want to. Look over yonder. Them fellers' pretty well lit up. 'Twon't be long 'til they'll be singin'." When a feller gits lit the first thing he thinks 'bout is singin'."

"Look a-here, Rednap, what was that there 'bout old man Fanning and Frohocks? That was a plum' good piece. Git up there and say it off. You ought 'o be able to; you writ it." The fellow chuckled.

"Go ahead, Rednap, go ahead," another man urged, loudly. "Give us that piece 'bout them fat bastards. I heared you say it off t'other day."

"See there, Davy. What'd I tell you? Now they's hollerin' fer poetry. Tryon'll be givin' 'em more damn poetry than they want, I'll vouch."

But let's slip over that a-way and see what he's goin' to say. It mought be a pretty good piece. I've heared a lot about this Rednap my ownself."

Rednap Howell was standing near the center of the group. The flickering light played upon his face, chased little shadows across his coarse hunting shirt opened at the neck. "I tell you, men. Maybe I oughtn't to be saying pieces about two such fine gentlemen as Colonel Fanning and Mr. Frohock." Several of the men guffawed. "Maybe you wouldn't 'preciate having your good friends made fun of. But I'll say you a piece that I heard the first time at a wedding over in Chatham some five or six years ago. You see, Colonel Fanning—this one's about him—has been popular a long time in these parts."

"Go ahead and say it," someone interrupted.

"Well, it was something like this." He leaned his head back slightly and the firelight played full across his amused features. "If I can remember aright:

ALEXANDRIANA

When Fanning first to Orange came
He looked both pale and wan,
An old patched coat upon his back
An old poor mare he rode upon;
Both man and mare wa'nt worth five pounds
As I've been often told
But by his civil robberies
He's laced his coat with gold."

There followed an outburst of cheering and coarse laughing and one fellow lifted his bottle. "Here's to that old mare. I hope he'll ride her smack damn to hell and back." He recovered himself after he had fortified himself with a healthy swig from the bottle. " 'Scuse me; I didn't mean back. 'Twas a slip of the tongue." He wiped his mouth with his shirt sleeve.

"Now, how about that piece you wrote your ownself, Rednap?"

"I aint said that piece in a long time. I've maybe forgot it. It goes something like this, though:

"Says Frohock to Fanning, to tell the plain truth,
When I came to this country I was but a youth,
My father sent for me: I wa'nt worth a cross,
And then my first study was to steal for a horse.
I quickly got credit and then ran away,
And haven't paid for him to this very day.
"Says Fanning to Frohock, 'tis a folly to lie,
I rode an old mare that was blind of an eye;
Five shillings in money I had in my purse,
My coat it was patched, but not much the worse;
But now we've got rich, and it's very well known,
That we'll do very well if they let us alone."

Another guffawing greeted the end of his poetic effort. His slightly inebriated critic raised his bottle again. "This here one's to—to—" He faltered. "No, I didn't mean back. 'Twas a bad mistake, bad mistake." He downed another big swallow, belched loudly, and wiped his lips with his shirt sleeve. "T'hell with Tryon," he concluded feebly, and set down his bottle.

ALEXANDRIANA

Through the night and during the next morning more men came into camp. Some carried their muskets, many had come without weapons to see what was happening. Toward noon when the messengers returned from a visit to Governor Tryon, Rednap Howell told Jethro that there were perhaps more than a thousand men with the Regulators.

"We sent some men over to the Governor to ask him for a proposition," Rednap explained. "We asked him to let us know within four hours. But he put them off and promised to have his answer ready by noon tomorrow. I believe we have him frightened, got him playing for time."

"Mebbe." Jethro bit a large chew from his twist of tobacco. "And then, mebbe not. Tryon's tricky."

"Preacher Caldwell went to see him today, with Alexander Martin. He's trying to get him to compromise with us. That's all we want. Preacher Caldwell's got a lot o' his members in this bunch and he's pretty much concerned. And he ought to stand pretty well with Tryon. He's working on him."

That night the fellow who had stopped Jethro and David the day before came over to them as they lay stretched on the ground beyond the heat of the fire. "Look a-here," he said to Jethro, "you fellows come 'long with us. They's goin' to be some fun over acrost the t'other side the woods. Some o' the boys catched a couple of Tryon's soldiers prowling 'round and they're goin' to marry 'em off tonight. We jest 'bout got time to see the show."

"Marry 'em off? What you mean?" David didn't understand.

"You'll see, Son, when we git there. You all come 'long with us."

A few minutes later they walked into the circle of light made by another campfire. The thing that first caught their attention was a man tied to a small tree. He was stripped to the waist. And as they walked into the circle of Regulators they noticed a few feet away another man tied in the same way to a small oak. He, too, was stripped to the waist; his shirt hung down around his knees.

"Come up, gents," one of the men greeted them. "We're fixin' to have a big weddin'. This here's—" he pointed to one of the men

ALEXANDRIANA

"Captain Ashe, so he says, and this other gent is Captain Walker. They're good friends o' Governor Tryon. They come slipping up to see what we was a-doin' and we catched 'em. And now we fixin' to marry 'em off to these two saplings here. Step up, gents, so's you can see 'em hug their brides." The group moved in closer. "All right, boys, go ahead." Two men stepped forward. Each had a whip made of a stick about two feet long with a leather thong attached.

David stood aghast as they raised their whips, almost in concert, and swung them downward. He saw the thongs strike full across the bare backs of the men, saw livid pink marks dart across the white flesh behind the sickening dull thuds and rise quickly into pale red welts, saw them press bare chests into the bark of the trees as tortured flesh recoiled from the lashes. In the pit of his stomach he discovered a nauseous emptiness . . .

"Look at 'em!" shouted the fellow who had been doing the talking. "Look at 'em hug their brides, boys!" The men were hoisting their whips again. "Mebbe this time they'll do some singin' fer 'em."

The whips descended with a hissing, and new welts sprang up across the first ones. The men with the whips hesitated. "What you slowing up fer, boys? Tryon, they says, most'n generally gives five hundred, and we don't want to slight these two gents. It'll take a right smart time and you better be gittin' on with yore work."

The whips swung downward again. One of the prisoners, when the lash struck, grunted. It was more the mechanical expulsion of tortured breath than a weakening of the man's spirit. He twisted his head around from the tree, looked the man who had been giving the commands full in the eye. "Damn you bastards," said he. "In the name of King George you'll pay for this!"

"Lay it on 'im!" shouted the fellow, now enraged. "He can't call us no names like that and git away with it. And damn King George besides!"

The whip cut a new welt that lay crazily across the heaving marks of the others, and David saw a thin trickle of blood.

Jethro stepped forward, stood between the prisoner and the

man with upraised whip. "Hold on, here, men! This aint no way to be doin'. I aint no lover o' Governor Tryon nor King George neither, but this aint no way fer folks o' this here colony to be doin' feller citizens. This here's Tryon's way. I don't know what these men's done but they's had enough anyhow. I says untie these here men."

"He's right!" A man on the outer rim of the circle came pushing his way into the center of the group. "This aint no way to bring peace to this province. I say this man's right, and I says untie 'em, too."

Jethro took out his knife, with one swift downward sawing stroke cut the thong that bound the man's wrists. Then he stepped across to the other tree, cut the thongs that held his companion. "Pull up yore shirts and set down." He turned to face the crowd. "Be there anybody here who don't like my doin's, he can step out and say so." He stood quietly surveying the circle of faces. The fellow who had been supervising the whipping, he saw, had pushed back into the crowd.

But another figure was emerging from the circle. He was coming straight toward him. "Well, I'm damned if—" Jethro's tanned face broke into a smile that turned up the corners of his tobacco-stained mouth—"Davy, boy, you hadn't ought'o be gittin' into this."

David stood beside Jethro. The sickness in the middle of his stomach had vanished. He was conscious of a tightening in the calves of his legs as he stood back upon his heels. And a tingle ran along the knuckles of his clinched right hand.

"The same thing goes for me," he said, and his voice was entirely calm.

XII

HIS EXCELLENCY, the Governor of the Province of North Carolina, laid down his quill, replaced the stopper of his ink bottle and blew gently upon the document in front of him. "It will be dry in a moment." He extended his silver snuff box to the Reverend David Caldwell, who declined with a polite shake of the head and murmured apologies.

From the box His Excellency drew a pinch of snuff which he forthwith inserted into his right nostril. When the expected succession of polite sneezings had been duly completed, he inserted a pinch into the left nostril, and promptly initiated a new succession. Having finished this formality, he replaced the snuff box in a pocket of the velvet waistcoat revealed beneath a campaign coat less resplendent but more serviceable than the plum-colored coat now reposing in a scented drawer of a great chest in the Governor's Palace a hundred and fifty miles southeastward.

"Dr. Caldwell, I promised you I should do everything within reason toward effecting a compromise with these damned rebels. And I promised them yesterday they should have my answer today. Here it is; I'll read it to you." He picked up the paper before him, cleared his throat:

"Great Alamance Camp, May 16th, 1771," he began, and cleared his throat again: "In reply to your petition, I am to acquaint you that I have been attentive to the interest of this country, and to that of every individual residing in it. I lament the fatal necessity to which you have now reduced me by withdrawing yourselves from the mercy of the Crown and the laws of your country, to require you who are assembled as Regulators to lay down your arms, surrender up the outlawed ringleaders, and submit yourselves to the laws of your country, and then rest on the lenity and mercy of the government." He paused, saw with evident satisfaction that the minister was listening intently. "By accepting these terms in one hour from the delivery of this dispatch you will prevent an effusion of blood, as you are at this time in a state of war and rebellion against your King, your country and your laws. William Tryon."

He paused, added: "To the people now assembled in arms, who style themselves Regulators."

The Governor laid the paper down again. "Well, Dr. Caldwell, there it is. Do you wish to bear it back to them?"

"But, your Excellency—"

"That is the best I can do for you, sir."

"An hour, Your Excellency, is a very short time, considering the number of men, and they are scattered over a long front, you know."

His Excellency smiled, and for an instant a sharp glint flared in his eyes. "Yes, I know they are scattered. But I shall scatter them all the more." He picked up the paper. "You may carry it back to them, sir."

"Very well, Your Excellency. I shall get Thompson and Mateer and go over and report right now."

"I am very sorry, Dr. Caldwell, but you must allow Thompson and Mateer to remain with me." He smiled, and again the fierce glint in his eyes betrayed his feelings. "As hostages, let us say, sir," he added.

He summoned an orderly. "See that those two rebels, Thompson and Mateer, are kept under close scrutiny."

"Yes, sir." The man saluted, walked away. Dr. Caldwell picked up the paper. "These are hard terms, sir. I shall do my best, however, to get them to accept them as perhaps the better of two hard choices."

"Well, sir, I can offer no more lenient terms. But just a moment, Dr. Caldwell." The minister halted. "There are two of my men in

ALEXANDRIANA

the camp of the Regulators, and I understand they have been severely dealt with by those unprincipled ruffians. You may tell them that if they will release Captain Ashe and Captain Walker, I shall release to them the seven Regulators I hold as prisoners. That is fair enough, I'd think."

"I'll report that offer to them, Your Excellency."

But the Regulators, strung out along a ragged line roughly fronting the troops of Governor Tryon, quickly demonstrated they were uninterested in His Excellency's terms.

"That's a hell of a compromise." Jethro nudged the man beside him, spoke out of the corner of his mouth, for Dr. Caldwell was not far away. "That's like the cat compromisin' with the bird after he's catched it."

"Ye're right, friend. That won't do. If that's the best old Billy Tryon can do, then we'd better feed him some powder and balls."

The minister heard him. "But, my friend, you aren't prepared to resist the Governor. You aren't organized; he is. You haven't six rounds around, and half of you don't have guns. You don't have any cannon, and he does. And where are your leaders? He'll drive you like chaff before the wind. Courage won't be enough. To fight a battle, you must have organization. You must submit now, and work and pray for another day."

Another Regulator spoke up. "I'm agin submittin'. It'll mean the rope for us, Parson. "I'm for fightin' as long as we can. And we might whup him, at that. I don't b'lieve his crowd will fight us anyhow—"

"Let me read the message once more." Reverend Mr. Caldwell held up the paper. "Listen men, let us hear the message just once more and then calmly consider it." He cleared his throat. " 'Great Alamance Camp, May 16th, 1771. In reply to your petition, I—' "

"We don't want to hear it no more, Parson," shouted a man near him. " 'Taint nothin' good in it. 'Taint worthwhile readin' it no more. We jest as well be gettin' at our business, which is to give old Tryon hell, and this very day."

The preacher's reading was drowned out in a chorus of protests, some flavored with oaths that gave emphasis to the belief

ALEXANDRIANA

that there was no longer any efficacy in treating with His Excellency. "Look at 'em!" shouted one man, pointing across toward the Governor's troops. "They're movin' up on us. He's tryin' to scare us. But he won't do it. Them boys over there aint goin' to fight us noway."

"But how about exchanging prisoners? You haven't decided about that."

"We aint got no time for that now, Preacher Caldwell." The Regulators were beginning to surge forward toward the line of the Governor's troops. A man shook a clinched fist toward His Excellency across the narrowing space between the two lines. "Damn you, Billy Tryon. We're a-fixin' to git you, you dressed up bastard." He spied a man near the Governor, and his face reddened. "And you too, Fanning, you dirty, stinkin', robbin' devil in them fancy clothes. We'll soon be a stripping' 'em off'n you, you low down bastardly coward. Jest come across if'n ye dare." He snatched open his shirt front, baring his hairy chest. "Jest take a crack at me if'n ye're got the guts!"

Along the straggling line others were joining him in challenging Tryon to start the battle. They waved bedraggled three-cornered hats and coonskin caps and shook knotty fists at the quiet soldiers across in front of them. "Come on! Step on over this a-way if'n you aint scairt. We're yore own fokes. Shoot at us if you think more o' that fat fine-dressed bastard than you do o' us!"

Preacher Caldwell mounted his horse, raced up and down the line. "Listen, men, I am your friend, I am the pastor of many of you. Listen to me! You must not have a battle today. All of you who are not too far involved in this should go quietly home. You are not ready to fight, you are not—"

"But what about the rest of us, Parson? You want us to stay and git hung?"

"You must submit. I promise to try to prevail upon the Governor to be lenient, to be merciful. I promise I'll do my best—"

An old man who had come running along the line interrupted. "It's too late now, Pastor. You'd best be riding off, sir." He ran over to two young men wrestling on the ground, kicked the man

ALEXANDRIANA

on top a healthy whack on his backside with the flat of his foot. "Get up, boys! Get up! This is no time for that stuff. The Governor's gittin' ready to charge you." He ran along the line. "Get your guns ready, men! You what's got guns get 'em ready—"

"Damn if'n it aint old Pat Mullen. We goin' to have some fun, Pat?"

"More'n you want, likely. Get lined up over there boys. Here, you, get up off'n your hind-end and get in line. And you over there, get your gun ready. You'll be needin' it afore long, I've a notion."

The Governor's troops by now were hardly fifty yards away. Calmly they regarded the disorganized, undisciplined thin ranks of the Regulators across the clearing. And the Regulators from the edge of the woods watched them approach, many of them still unconvinced that there would be fighting, that they faced any imminent danger.

And now the troops stopped, and from their side walked a man bearing in his hand a piece of paper. In front of the scowling Regulators he stopped and began reading from the paper.

It was a renewed demand that the Regulators lay down their arms, and surrender their leaders to the mercy of the Governor. As the messenger read, an angry growl along the ranks grew quickly into a roar.

"Get back over there and tell Billy Tryon we says to go to hell!" shouted a Regulator in the ranks near the messenger. "Tell him we aint goin' to surrender nobody to be hung by him. Tell him if he wants to fight to come on, damn him, the low-down, good-for-nothin', lyin' bastard!" All along the line they were shouting at the fellow, and he quickly turned heels and moved back toward the troops.

Jethro faced David. "This aint no place for you, Davy. It looks like there's goin' to be fightin' as shore as the devil. You better be pushin' on back and seein' after the horses. They mought 'a got loose with all this racket goin' on."

"How about your ownself?"

"I'll be back there in a little bit. I want to stay around a while though and see what happens."

ALEXANDRIANA

"I'm stayin' too." David squeezed the stock of his musket. "I'm not scared and I'm not leavin' till you do. Besides, somebody's got to take care o' you." He grinned. But the twinkle in his eyes, Jethro knew, concealed something else. He clapped a rough hand on the boy's shoulder. "Davy, boy, you're a good 'un. And all at onct, boy, you've growed up. Since last night you've been well growed."

The man standing beside Jethro nudged him in the ribs with his elbow. "Look over yonder. That Tryon's arguin' with somebody. Look." He pointed a bony finger. "Damned if'n 'taint Bob Thompson what went over there with Preacher Caldwell and that feller Mateer. What's he fixin' to do?"

"It looks like he's fixin' to leave the Governor and come back to us. He's walkin' off and leavin' the Governor talkin' to his back. And damn if'n Tryon aint mad. Look at him. Well, I'm damned—the dirty, low-down devil—"

Robert Thompson was walking straight toward the Regulators' line at the edge of the trees. He had turned his back squarely upon Governor Tryon. And now the Governor, his face livid with rage, had grabbed a musket from a soldier near him, was leveling it . . . The musket rang out. Robert Thompson threw up his right arm, and his extended fingers cut a swift arc as his arm dropped. He stumbled forward, his knees bulged, he fell upon his face. The Governor handed the gun back to the soldier, pulled forth his handkerchief, wiped his hands. From under the left shoulder of Robert Thompson a red trickle pushed out into the dust . . .

Two Regulators ran over to the man on the ground, carried him quickly into their lines, and along the front an angry muttering grew swiftly into a bedlam of imprecations.

But Tryon displayed no nervousness. Having returned his handkerchief to his pocket, he mounted his horse, which an attendant had been holding, and rode along the front of his line. At the flank he paused, called an orderly. A moment later the orderly moved across the open ground toward the Regulators, and in his hand he carried a white flag.

Shots rang out. Tryon, watching from his horse, saw the orderly drop the flag, pause, and come stumbling back. The Governor

ALEXANDRIANA

wheeled in front of his men. "When I give the command, fire," he shouted, and galloped his horse back to the flank of the line. "Ready, aim, fire!" The command rang out. But there was no volley.

Tryon rose in his stirrups, shouted: "Fire on them, or fire on me!"

A spatter of firing followed the command. A Regulator slapped his hand upon his hip, darted behind a tree. Another Regulator grabbed up the musket the first one had dropped, fired point blank across the opening.

From both sides the firing increased. Jethro, peering from behind an oak, saw a detachment hovering about one of the Governor's six-pounders. Presently there was a roar and a ball plowed up red dirt twenty yards out to his left and went crashing into the woods. In the lull that followed for a moment Jethro heard one of the soldiers at the cannon shout to the gunner, "Get it up this time; I told you that was aimed too low." The cannon roared again, and a six-pound ball clipped off limbs just above the heads of the Regulators.

And now from behind the trees and rocks the Regulators poured hot lead upon the troops of Governor Tryon. But the soldiers held their ground, despite the disadvantage of their position, for the steady fire of the Regulators kept them in the open in front of the trees.

The troops were firing by platoons, the Regulators were fighting Indian fashion, each man for himself. Jethro handed his musket to a man behind a tree near him. "Here, take this here gun, and let me have yore'n, pardner. If I'd a-knowed we was goin' to have this sort of a fracas I'd a brought some more powder and balls. You'd better tie up that hand whilst I'm shooting fer you. It's bleedin' pretty bad." A bullet chipped off bark a foot above Jethro's head. He whirled around. "Always a-talkin' at the wrong time." He crouched behind the tree, poured in powder, dropped his ball into the muzzle, rammed in the wadding. Then he straightened up, peered across the opening, through a hole in the smoke took careful aim. The musket roared. "A little hot tea, Yore Excellency, from Mecklenburg."

ALEXANDRIANA

When the smoke had cleared a bit, he peered again around the tree. "Hell, I missed the damned bastard. His horse must 'a jumped jest as I pulled the trigger."

Slowly the troops began to fall back. In a short while a man came walking toward the trees with a white flag held high on a stick. But as he neared the Regulators a shot rang out from behind a rock over on a flank. "Hold on, there!" yelled old Pat Mullen. "That's a flag of truce. Hold on, boys." But two or three other shots followed, and the soldier with the flag turned and fled.

From the Governor's troops now came a volley, and from the woods the Regulators poured another offering of hot lead. The troops gave way, fell back until they were a hundred yards from their original position. And as they abandoned their cannon, several young Regulators rushed out and seized the field pieces. David was in the group.

But there was no ammunition. Nor did the youngsters know how to fire them. By the time they had wheeled the cannon about, the smoke was clearing, and the Governor's troops, seeing only a few Regulators remaining on the field, came charging back.

The powder and balls of the Regulators had been exhausted. The few still on the field turned and took to their heels through the woods.

Beside one of the cannon a wild-eyed young man, hatless, his hair streaming down his powder-blackened face, was working feverishly to wheel it round. "Help me here!" he yelled to the two or three with David. "I've got to shoot this cannon at Fanning! See him over there. Look!" He pointed toward the Governor's troops. "See him? I've got to kill him. He's my enemy. He got my sweetheart with a baby. I've got to kill him!" David saw the man's eyes. They were flaming. "I've got to shoot him down like a dog. I have been sent by Heaven to relieve this world from oppression and the Lord told me to start here in Carolina with Fanning!" The man was mad. Brooding had made him irresponsible. That was it. He was beating upon the cannon with his blackened fists. "I've got to kill him. He ruined my beautiful sweetheart. The Lord has sent me to rid this world of evil!" His eyes were losing their flame now. He was muttering, blubbering, his arms flung about the cannon, his hair streaming.

Suddenly David remembered him. Hillsboro. Yes, he and Jethro had stayed at his house. He was quiet then, quiet and unassuming. And he had been planning to marry a beautiful girl. Yes, that was the fellow. James Few, the Hillsboro carpenter.

David was conscious now of another commotion. He looked up. A squad of the Governor's soldiers had surrounded them. He glanced quickly toward the woods. The Regulators had fled. There was no sight of them anywhere. Or of Jethro.

XIII

DAVID WALKED across to the table behind which sat Governor William Tryon. The leather thongs that bound his arms behind his back cut into his wrists and his legs still ached from the shackles that a moment ago had been removed from his ankles.

His Excellency looked up, and David met his eyes calmly.

"Indeed. A young rebel, and a likely looking one. Where'd you get him?"

"He was captured trying to turn one of our cannon upon us, sir."

"Well, that's bad for him. Too bad, too bad. A likely looking young fellow to have to be hung. Might have made us a good soldier. What's your name?"

"Barksdale, sir. David Barksdale."

The Governor's eyes narrowed. Searchingly he looked into the boy's face.

"Seems that I have seen you before. I wonder— Where're you from?"

"Mecklenburg, sir."

A smile spread over His Excellency's face. "Indeed. I thought so. McKnitt Alexander's bound-boy. Well, well, well." He toyed with the quill before him. "And now you're my bound-boy." His laugh was high and thin and mirthless, and behind his back David's aching hands doubled into fists that itched along the knuckles. But quickly the laugh turned into a scowl. "Was McKnitt Alexander with you? Speak up, boy!"

"No, sir."

"Where was he?"

"At home, I reckon, sir."

"Who was with you? How'd you happen to be mixed up in this business?"

"Uncle McKnitt had sent me and Jethro O'Flannagan over Hillsboro way on business for him and this is the far'est we got."

"Jethro. Ah—" the crafty smile spread over his features again. "He's that funny back country fellow that had so many children?"

"Yes, sir."

"Where's he?"

"I don't know, sir. I haven't seen him since before the fight was over."

The Governor turned to the officer. "Have you got him among the prisoners?"

"No, sir, there's nobody by that name."

"That's most unfortunate. He would have made pretty sport hanging him. And he well deserves it on general principles besides." He hesitated a moment as he looked David in the face. "You got anything you want to say for yourself, young man?"

"I don't know anything to say, sir, I reckon, as would do any good."

The Governor laughed again. "You're very likely right there, young fellow." He turned to the officer. "Take him back. Hold on a minute. There's one of the prisoners Colonel Fanning wants me to have a look at." He turned in his chair to confront a lavishly dressed man some steps away at his right. "Who was it you wanted me to see, Colonel?"

"A fellow named James Few, Your Excellency. A particularly obnoxious and dangerous outlaw from over Hillsboro way."

The officer conducted David back to the prisoners, readjusted the shackles about his ankles. Having finished securing him, he walked over to a young man lying on his side, his arms pinioned behind him, his feet bound tightly together. He was bending over him, trying to untie the thongs, when the Governor called out: "Don't bother with untying his feet. I don't mind. Bring him on over."

ALEXANDRIANA

"Get up, Few."

James Few twisted to a sitting position, tried to raise himself. "I'm sorter stiff," he explained, with a wan smile. The officer helped pull him to his feet, supported him as he shuffled slowly across to the Governor's table.

"Well, here he is, Colonel. Go ahead. What do you want to say about him?"

Colonel Fanning walked across to confront the prisoner. "This man, Your Excellency, is a very dangerous man, a distinct menace to our Hillsboro community. He is a fomenter of trouble, a veritable hothouse of sedition—"

"He's a liar!" James Few's face was crimson. He tried to lunge forward, but the thongs and the hand of the officer on his pinioned arm restrained him.

"Hold your peace!" The Governor's command was an angry shout. "Another word out of you until it's asked and I'll have you lashed unmercifully!"

Fanning smiled benignly, spoke calmly. "You can see, Your Excellency, that this man has an inordinate temper. He has demonstrated here before you the violence of his nature. He is a dangerous man, I tell you, sir, and the community could well be rid of the danger his presence in it imposes. He is—"

"He lies! He lies!" The carpenter screamed his denunciation, his eyes flaming with an intense wild burning, and he struggled madly with his captor. "He is telling lies. He wronged me! He has wronged everybody! He wronged my sweetheart! The Lord has sent me to rid the world of evil, to begin with him!" The mad words rushed one upon the other in a torrent of released pain and anger. "The Lord has sent me, the Lord—"

Governor Tryon picked up a small riding whip lying on the table, walked calmly across to the charging wild youth. "—has sent me to avenge the world of oppression, to rid Carolina of this evil—" The whip slashed across the face of James Few, and a red welt sprang up along a line that crossed his cheek and ran above an eyebrow.

Few staggered, but the officer held him on his feet, and as his head slumped forward a bit he began to blubber and yellowish foam flecked his lips . . .

"I told you to hold your peace," said Governor Tryon, as he pulled his lace handkerchief from his wrist and wiped his hands.

He sat down again. "Colonel Fanning, he did say one thing, one thing that intrigued me, and I would go into it a bit." He smiled and a cunning light blazed in his narrowed eyes. "He spoke of your having ruined his sweetheart. I didn't know, Colonel, that you were capable of such conquest, though I can well believe you'd be willing."

"She was a damned tempting bit of womanflesh, that wench he speaks of, Your Excellency." The trace of a sneer shadowed his fleshy face. "Too damned juicy a morsel for the likes of him." The sneer gave way to a sardonic smile. "I don't think I ruined the wench, Your Excellency, though they do say the baby looks like me. I wouldn't say she was ruined, not for good anyway, just temporarily not in prime condition, I'd say."

The Governor slapped his open hand upon the table, threw back his head, laughed uproariously. "You're a good one, Fanning, a damned cunning rogue." He leaned forward, slapped the table again. "A damned clever villain. You didn't ruin her. You just taught her some fancy new tricks, eh?" And his laughing shook the rough table as he leaned against it.

David could see the face of James Few as he stood before the two men. The carpenter's madness had subsided; he had ceased even his muttering and blubbering. Upon his face David saw the cold hopeless look of utter despair, and suddenly he realized he himself had gone sick at the pit of his stomach. But as he continued to watch the lean face of James Few, David saw a flame spreading over the thin cheeks, saw brightening from deep-set eyes new furious fires . . . Suddenly, before the Governor was aware of any change in his prisoner's demeanor, James Few jerked away from the officer who had been holding loosely to his arm, lunged forward, lost his balance, and fell sprawling upon his face in front of the table. "He's a liar!" he screamed. "Fanning's a dirty contemptible liar! And you're no better, Bill Tryon! You're

ALEXANDRIANA

both dirty low-down knaving bastards! You're both bound to hell, damn you. And King George with you!" He was pawing the dirt with his hobbled feet, and the foam from his bleeding lips was smearing his face with the dampened dirt.

Governor Tryon rose from his chair, walked with deliberate tread over to the helpless man raving at his feet. David turned his head. But Tryon did nothing. "Pull him back over there with the other prisoners," he commanded, and walked back to his chair.

"Colonel Fanning and you other officers of my staff, I shall constitute myself a court-martial and try one James Few." He turned to Fanning. "I believe that is his name, as you gave it to me?"

"That's his name, Your Excellency."

"I shall constitute myself an extraordinary court-martial and hear the case of James Few," he reiterated. "I suppose the charge against him is rebellion against the government of the Province of North Carolina and against His Majesty the King, is it not, Colonel?"

"That should serve, Your Excellency, though inciting to riot and other high crimes might be added to the bill of indictment."

"I shall now hear evidence against the prisoner. Colonel Fanning, you may take the stand."

Fanning's evidence was delivered at some length with a benignity betrayed only by the venom in his eyes and the half-sneer upon his puffy lips. He was followed by a subordinate officer who told of capturing Few as he fled into the edge of the woods from a cannon of the Governor's troops he had been trying to fire. The Governor called upon Few to speak in his own defense if he wished, but the carpenter, slumped upon the ground, said nothing.

"We pray the verdict of the court." Fanning spoke calmly.

"I shall give it. I am ready. I reach it without difficulty. The verdict is guilty as charged."

"And the sentence, Your Excellency?"

"Death by hanging."

"Shall the prisoner be brought before the court?"

"Yes." He nodded to an orderly. "Fetch Few back."

ALEXANDRIANA

"Do you have anything to say before sentence is passed upon you, James Few?"

Few was entirely calm. The rage that had burst within him had burned out. He straightened himself upon his tortured feet.

"I have nothing to say. There is no need. I would not be heard. But I am not guilty. I have done nothing except fight for the rights of a free man." He looked Tryon full in the face. "And now listen to me, William Tryon. You won yesterday. You will hang me and maybe these others. But your day will come. These people of Carolina will be free. They will rid themselves of tyrants like you and this bastard friend of yours who has been a leech sucking the life blood out of our people. You'll hang me, but there'll come a day—"

"I've heard enough. You have been found guilty, and the sentence is death. You shall be hanged, and as soon as the necessary arrangements can be made."

"But you'll be in hell, Bill Tryon, afore me!"

"Take him away. And now, Colonel, shall you make the arrangements for the execution?"

" 'Twould be a waste of lumber and precious time, Your Excellency, to build a scaffold. Yonder limb, I fancy, would serve nicely."

"Always ready and anxious to get out of work, Fanning. But what's a man's head for if it's not to save his feet? The limb will do nicely. But we must have some troops and draw them up in a hollow square, and a little drum rat-tat-tatting. Who would deny the right of any poor devil to be drummed to his own hanging, eh, my good Fanning?" The Governor laughed gaily at his own cleverness.

"I shall get the troops, Your Excellency, and a cart for him to stand in before making his grand leap into the arms of Saint Peter."

"Very well, Fanning. But don't forget the drums. And say," he called to an orderly. "Go cut the cords about his feet so he can shake them around and get the blood to moving so he'll be able to keep step to the music."

"There is one other thing, Your Excellency." Fanning spoke

ALEXANDRIANA

pleasantly, without any trace of rancor. "The family of this man, his father and mother, have been aiding and abetting him in fomenting unrest and rebellion. They have a house in Hillsboro. Perhaps Your Excellency would like to take action—"

"Indeed, Colonel. I shall order any removable goods confiscated, and the house I shall have burned to the ground. We must destroy every trace of this damnable rebellion against our authority."

"Thank you, sir. We admire Your Excellency's courage and sagacity in the face of this insolent uprising."

An hour later the troops had been drawn up in a square about the tree. His Excellency with evident relish supervised the plans, and when the necessary arrangements had been completed he and members of his staff took their stations near the center of the hollow square. Under the limb a cart had been placed.

"Captain, you may fetch the prisoner. In fact, bring all the prisoners. I wish them to have first choice of seats at this event, sir."

The captain stepped forward two paces, saluted, turned to face his detachment.

"Just a moment, Captain. The prisoner should be granted the ministrations of a chaplain before he is launched into eternity. Do we not have a chaplain?" He turned to the little group of officers standing with him near the trunk of the tree. There was a hurried consultation. "We do not have a chaplain, Your Excellency. He was unable to leave New Bern."

"Very well. Perhaps a chaplain wouldn't do him much good anyway. I could never see any especial need for them. They look too damned pious and they're no help with a gun when you get in close quarters. Bring them along, Captain."

The prisoners, with two drummer boys beating a slow march, walked between files of the soldiers through the opening in the hollow square. James Few came first, and then Captain Messer. Behind him walked David, and James Pugh and Captain Merrill and the others followed in single file. David held his head high, but the nausea in his stomach was pushing up into his throat. Desperately he wanted to sink down, to embrace the cool earth, to lie upon his stomach. But he fought off this weakness, and when

ALEXANDRIANA

he saw Tryon standing with his aides beside the tree, cool and arrogant and apparently relishing with sadistic delight the pitiable plight of these captured Regulators, he lifted his chin a bit higher . . . A few days ago he was back in Alexandriana. He wondered what they were doing. Aunt Jeanie, Uncle McKnitt, the children, Venus, Cato . . . Lovelace, Belinda . . . the bound-boy. Well, he was a bound-boy now. A few days ago he was at the tavern in Salisbury with Jethro . . . Old Jethro, only yesterday Jethro was standing beside him pumping hot lead at the Governor's troops. He was going to protect Jethro. He wondered where Jethro was . . .

"Halt!" The command was sharp. It ended his reverie. Twenty paces away was the tree. The cart stood directly underneath a big limb. The horse hitched to the cart was methodically switching with his tail at a fly that buzzed about his flanks.

"Let the prisoners form a line facing the gallows, Captain."

The line was quickly formed. "Proceed with the execution."

James Few was led forward, helped into the cart. His feet were bound together; his arms were already pinioned behind him. A noose had been tied in the rope extending downward over the limb. It was placed about his neck, adjusted with the knot under the left ear, and the rope was pulled over the limb until the slack had been taken up, and tied around the trunk. The hangman stepped back.

"James Few, do you have anything to say for yourself?"

"I would like to say a few words, Governor."

"Then go ahead."

James Few, the rope around his neck, faced the little group of prisoners and the troops behind them. "This is what I want to say. I am innocent of any rebellion against the government of Carolina, any rightful government. I have been wronged, and you have been wronged, and we fought for our rights as free citizens of a free country. For years we have been robbed by crooked public officers—clerks of the courts and sheriffs and deputies. Such men—" he turned to confront the little group around the Governor, "as Edmund Fanning over there, and Frohock over in the western settlements, and dozens of others. The Governor has refused to protect us from these crooks and instead has helped them to rob us. He has refused us justice—" he turned back toward the prisoners, "and he'll hang you all too, no doubt, as he's hanging me. But his day is coming, men. The good Lord won't let him and his kind rule forever. The good Lord has sent us—" David, watching the man on the cart, saw his lips begin to quiver and his eyes were flaming up— "the good Lord has sent us to end the oppression of our people. He has sent us to avenge Carolina, to drive out such men as Bill Tryon and Edmund Fanning!" He whirled to face Fanning and Tryon, so swiftly that the shackles about his feet almost caused him to fall. As he turned David could see his arms behind him jerking spasmodically, and he leaned forward, as if to gesticulate with his head. "Yes, you won't have the rule always! There'll come another day. I won't be here, but there'll be those here who will see an end of your oppression, Bill Tryon, and an end of your stealing and robbing and seducing of good women, Edmund Fanning, you damned dirty bastard! There'll come a day—"

But James Few's impassioned speech had ended. Edmund Fanning, his face crimson with rage, had rushed forward, struck the horse a vicious blow on the rump, the horse had bolted—

At the end of the rope, his feet three feet from the ground, the Hillsboro carpenter spun—

"Troops!" The Governor had stepped forward. "Present arms!"

The muskets came up smartly and rough hands whacked wooden stocks.

Tryon whirled upon Fanning. "You take too much authority upon yourself—"

"I'm sorry, Your Excellency. The fellow made me mad!"

"You'll never make a soldier, Fanning. You have no control of yourself. The poor devil, I'm bound, was half right as far as yourself was concerned."

David was sick. By force of will he was able to keep his feet, to look upon the spinning body out there before him. Slowly the spinning stopped, and the kicking, gurgling body came to rest . . . A convulsive shudder that started at the shoulders and seemed to run downward ended with a twitch of the shackled feet, and James Few, tongue drooling and bulging sightless eyes staring out over the heads of the soldiers standing stiffly erect, had squared his accounts . . .

The Governor stepped forward again. "Order arms!" The muskets came down with a clatter. "Captain, march the troops and the prisoners back!"

When night came the prisoners were herded together in a tent at one side of the Governor's encampment. A guard was posted at the front and rear and sentry outposts were established at intervals about the grounds.

But the prisoners were late getting to sleep. Their arms and legs ached, though the officer in charge had permitted their hands to be shackled in front so that they could more comfortably lie down. They were sore and half sick and several were suffering from slight injuries received in the battle. But more disturbing than everything else were the visions of James Few winding and unwinding at the end of a rope—

But after a while physical exhaustion brought sleep to David Barksdale. The hard ground upon which he lay sank from under him, fell away. He wandered in a nebulous intangible shapeless void out of which gradually began to evolve confused images of places and persons . . .

He was dancing with Belinda out at Mr. John Davidson's. Many people had come to Rural Retreat. There were fiddles and a banjo and a harpsichord . . . And Lovelace in a pretty little gown with a breast-knot of blue ribbon . . . And Governor Tryon bowing and talking, and sniffing snuff up his nose and sneezing . . . And Colonel Fanning with a sneer . . . And the yard was full of soldiers. The soldiers were in a sort of square that went up the slope above Rural Retreat and came down the other side . . . Uncle McKnitt and Governor Tryon sat at a table in the center, and the Governor was talking . . . He was looking toward the ceiling, and all around were soldiers. "It's a neat contraption, Mr. Alexander. I'd like to have one in the Governor's Palace at New Bern" . . . David was at the table, too, and he was looking at the swinging fly-brush that Uncle McKnitt was treading, and the cord was moving up and down as he worked his foot . . . He was looking steadily toward the ceiling . . . But there wasn't any ceiling there. There was only a limb, and over the limb hung a rope, for it wasn't just a cord, and his eyes ran down the rope . . . But the rope wasn't moving up and down, only the spinning body at the end, and it was turning and it was twitching . . .

The body jerking at the end of the rope . . . He looked closer. No, it was not James Few, the carpenter. It was . . . He peered down into the darkness at the end of the rope and the darkness was growing luminous . . . It was a younger man . . . It was . . . Heavens, it was David Barksdale. He was looking at himself, and he was feeling himself over there, choking, gurgling, choking . . .

And Tryon was taunting him . . . Or was it Fanning? . . . Bending over, whispering in his ear, in his dead, deaf, spinning ear above his choking throat . . . He wanted to scream, but he couldn't . . . His throat . . .

His shoulders, his hands, his cramped feet, were aching. The ground was hard under him. Yes, the ground it was . . . But the whispering. "Davy . . . Davy." Indistinct, a long way off . . . yet right against him, right in his ear. He could feel the warm breath . . . warm tobacco breath . . . "Davy . . ." Quickly now visions were fleeing, actualities were taking shape . . . But the whispering . . . "Davy, Davy." And a coarse hand across his face, over his mouth.

All at once now he came alive. Jethro! Jethro, for a fact. Whispering to him. "It's me, boy. Don't make a sound. It's me."

"Good old Jethro." David was whispering now, whispering in Jethro's face, good old Jethro . . .

"I'm goin' to cut you loose. Then lie still a little bit 'till yore legs wake up. Then we gittin' out o' here, boy."

Ten minutes later they were in the woods. But not until they had reached the place where Jethro had tied the horses down the road that led off toward Salisbury did they talk.

"How'd you ever get up to the tent, Jethro?" David swung into the saddle. Jethro was untying his horse's bridle. "I knocked hell out o' one o' them sentries what was half asleep, and then I crawled up on my belly. But I was scared as hell you'd holler out and get us both catched."

"You don't know how nigh I came to doin' it." He reached over, slapped Jethro's shoulder. "Good old Jethro."

Jethro picked up the reins. "Hit's time we was gittin' started back to Mecklenburg."

Behind them in the east a thin finger of light was pushing upward.

And a bugle blew.

XIV

ONCE AGAIN the troops of Governor Tryon, drawn up in a hollow square, faced the big oak tree. And beneath the outthrusting limb stood the cart, and down from the limb hung a hemp rope, a noose in the end.

Slowly, to a measured tread of solemn drums into the square marched two files of soldiers escorting between them a shuffling line of miserable men, a line shorter by two than the one that yesterday had marched to this same spot.

At the head of this line, his head up, his chin thrust forward, walked Captain Messer.

From his place at the foot of the tree Governor Tryon stepped forward a pace. To his right and a step behind stood Edmund Fanning, and others of the Governor's staff were grouped around.

"Prepare for the execution."

An officer from the escorting files stepped forward, saluted, motioned to Captain Messer. The captain, with the officer, moved toward the cart . . .

Almost unnoticed a woman had followed the soldiers and the prisoners into the square. Screaming, her hair flying wildly, she came running to the Governor, dropped upon her knees in front of him. "You can't! You can't hang my husband, sir! He has done nobody any harm! He is a good man, a good Christian man. Be merciful, sir! Be merciful. Oh, sir, I beg you, spare him!"

"Madam, I cannot grant your petition. Your husband has been tried by a fair court-martial, and has been found guilty of rebellion against His Majesty the King and against His Majesty's govern-

ALEXANDRIANA

ment in North Carolina. I am sorry, Madam, but I cannot rescind the verdict of the court-martial."

Wildly she looked from one officer of the Governor's staff to another, seeking a sign that someone might offer some slight encouragement, might dare to intercede. But they would not look into her face; they were staring straight ahead. And upon Edmund Fanning's bland soft face there was the shadow of a scowl, a half-sneer . . . The woman, turning, saw her husband. Screaming, she fell upon her face. Her body shook . . . Impassively, William Tryon stood above her. Convulsively, her shoulders began to jerk, and the shrill cries slowly gave way to incoherent moanings . . .

Governor Tryon turned half to the right, nodded to the officer. He and his prisoner walked to the cart, and the officer helped the bound man clamber into it. Then he stepped up into the cart himself, reached for the rope.

"Wait, sir, please!"

A small boy confronted His Excellency. He had followed the woman into the square, had just now been bending over her, patting her on the shoulder.

"Who are you, boy?"

"Captain Messer's son, sir."

"You should be at home, and your mother too."

"When we heard last night that my father had been caught, we came to see about him, sir."

"I'm sorry, son. But I cannot do anything for your father. He is a rebel, a fomenter of trouble. I can't help him. Now you must be leaving here."

The boy looked the Governor straight in the face. "Won't you hang me, sir, instead of my father?"

"Who told you to say that?"

"Nobody, sir."

"Well, why do you ask that?"

"Because he's needed so much at home, sir. There are a lot of us children and if our father dies, then there'll be nobody to make a living."

"Do you mean it? Are you willing to die instead of your father?"

ALEXANDRIANA

The child did not hesitate. "Yes, sir."

"Then your father shall not die today, at any rate." He signaled to the officer standing with Captain Messer in the cart. "Return the prisoner to the other prisoners."

The officer alighted, helped Messer from the cart. Tears were streaming down the prisoner's face. His wife ran to him, threw her arms about his shoulders, sobbed on his chest. The boy sidled over, and Messer with his bound hands patted his son's head.

The Governor was talking with Edmund Fanning. He stopped, signaled to the officer. "Bring the prisoner here."

"Messer," said His Excellency, when the prisoner faced him, "Colonel Fanning tells me you have much influence with Herman Husbands. I understand he slipped away before the battle and has started north. I am willing to make you this proposition: I shall give you your liberty on condition that you bring Husbands to me. What do you say?"

"I'll try, sir."

"Very well. I shall parole you on your honor to bring me Herman Husbands or to return to me if you are unable to fetch him. Is that agreed?"

"Yes, sir."

"I shall make the necessary arrangements shortly. Now go back to your crowd." He turned to his staff.

"I shall break camp and move westward. I have determined utterly to stamp out this rebellion in the Province of North Carolina. We have made an excellent beginning. But I am moving into the westward settlements where I shall exact strict oaths of all the inhabitants requiring them to bind themselves to be loyal to His Majesty and His Majesty's government and not only not to rebel against it but to bear arms for His Majesty or His Majesty's government in this province in event such should be asked of them." He pointed toward the prisoners. "I shall take these along and exhibit them as examples of the woe that comes to those who oppose His Majesty's rightful rule in Carolina. And I charge you who have them under guard to see that no one else escapes. 'Twas inexcusable carelessness that the young Mecklenburg rebel got away last night. I shall not be lenient if another is permitted to escape."

His Excellency tapped with polished forefinger upon his smooth forehead, gazed thoughtfully above the heads of his staff officers. "Yes, I was about to forget. I plan to issue a proclamation pardoning all those who were engaged in the recent insurrection who will come into camp, lay down their arms and take the oath of allegiance, with the specific exception of the prisoners here, Herman Husbands, Rednap Howell, James Butler and others whom I shall list, and those damnable ruffians who blew up my powder the other night over in that God-forsaken Mecklenburg. The orders will be posted. But I here and now offer to pay a thousand acres of land and a hundred pounds in money to anybody who will bring me that traitorous Husbands, that insolent writing-fellow Rednap Howell and some others whose names I'll list."

His Excellency, having with evident satisfaction delivered himself of this oratorical effort, pulled forth from his waist-coat his silver snuff box, and proceeded to enjoy the prompt sneezings that followed one upon the other the properly placed pinches.

XV

MOSES ALEXANDER answered the rap at his door. "Come in, Josh. Come right in."

"Much 'bliged, Colonel. Could I see you a little bit on—" He hesitated—"on a little business?"

"W'y, yes. Yes, indeed, Josh. Come right in. I haven't seen you in a long time, Josh. Where you been keeping yourself?"

"Well, sir, it's that I was wantin' to talk to you about." He was twisting his hat in his hands. "You see—well, it's to do with the blowin' up o' that powder over to Mr. Phifer's."

"Oh, I see." The colonel led the young man to the door that opened from the hall into the sitting room. "Walk right in and have a seat, Josh. We'll talk about that. You see, Jim Ashmore was just now talking to me about the same thing."

Another young man was seated in a chair near the window. As Josh walked into the room, this other youth's face flushed deeply And Colonel Alexander, watching Josh Hadley, saw a flame mounting in his cheeks.

"You done told him, Jim?"

"Yeh, I done told him."

"You never told me you was comin' over here to tell."

"You never told me you was a-fixin' to come neither."

"Don't start to fighting, boys. It's no use now."

"No, sir, I'm not a-fixin' to." Josh Hadley was twisting his hat in his hands nervously. "I reckon 'taint no need o' me sayin' nothin' about it then."

"Well, if you were planning to give away your gang that blew up the Governor's powder, Jim's already told me the whole thing."

"And he put me in it, too, I reckon?"

"Yes, he said you were one of the crowd."

"And I reckon that will let him out?"

"The Governor offered to pardon anyone who would turn the King's evidence."

"That's what I was a-fixin' to do, Colonel."

"Well what do you want to tell? I'll listen to you."

"I was jest goin' to tell who was mixed up in blowin' up that powder."

"All right, if you want to, go ahead, Josh. It was the Governor's offer. It's not mine. But you might tell what you got to say and I'll see how it checks up with what your half-brother's just told me. Jim, you step outside a minute, will you?"

When the other boy had left the room, Colonel Alexander closed the door. "All right, now. Go ahead."

"Well, sir. I jest wanted to git out of it, and when I heard tell the Governor would pardon anybody that told on the others I figured that was my chance. And I come over to see you."

"I supposed Jim figured the same thing. Well, what you want to say?"

"Well, I was in it, though I do say it was sorter agin my will. And Jim was too."

"And who were the others?"

"Well, them White boys was in it—Jim and Bill and John White, and their cousin William—over Rocky River way, and Bill Alexander from Sugaw Creek was the leader, and Rob Davis was one of them, and Bob Caruthers and Ben Cochrane, and me and Jim. We blacked up so's we'd be took maybe for Niggers. And when I heared about the Governor offering to let off anybody that would tell about it I figured maybe I'd better come tell you what I knowed about it."

Colonel Alexander stepped to the door. "Come back in a minute, Jim."

When Ashmore returned the colonel closed the door. "Boys," said he, "by virtue of the proclamation of Governor Tryon, I must tell you that you are pardoned for your part in blowing up the powder over at Phifer's. You have turned traitors, violated the solemn oath I understand you all took when you planned that scheme, and revealed the names of those who were engaged in it. You are free to go—" He opened the door— "and nobody will bother you, but I want to tell you that I think you ought to be the first two to be hung. And now you can be getting on your way."

He slammed the front door behind them.

XVI

McKNITT ALEXANDER, his forehead furrowed in thought, sat slumped in his chair before the crackling flames of the big fireplace at Alexandriana.

"My dear, stop scowling so. There're a million wrinkles in your forehead." Jeanie, sitting on the other side of the fireplace from him, let her knitting drop into her lap. "You'll be an old man afore your time, McKnitt."

Her husband straightened up, smiled. "I didn't mean to be scowling, Jeanie. Maybe it was the fire so bright in my eyes."

Jeanie laid the knitting on the small stand beside her, came over and sat on the arm of his chair, smoothed with her fingers the lines in his forehead. " 'Tisn't the fire in your eyes, my dear; 'tis the thoughts, the dark gloomy thoughts in here." She tapped gently upon his forehead. Seriously she looked into his eyes. "Must you always be thinking so much, McKnitt? Must you always be solemn and serious, must you so soon be getting to be an old man, and you not nigh forty yet?"

"In these days, my dear, how can a man keep from thinking dark thoughts? With so much wrong abroad in the land, Jeanie, and the future so full of doubt—"

"But the future has always been full o' doubt, Honey, till we came to it. And don't the Scriptures admonish us to have faith, and don't the parsons tell us the same? And aren't you a good Presbyterian, McKnitt, and the ruling elder in Hopewell—"

"Yes, the Scriptures admonish us to have faith and we Presbyterians believe what's to be will be, I guess, Jeanie, and so did

ALEXANDRIANA

Preacher Craighead and Preacher Caldwell and the others tell us, but still in such times—"

"It's been the same always, McKnitt. These times are no worse, perhaps, than other times. Think of the days of the poor martyrs in Rome eaten by lions and burnt for the sport of cruel people—"

"But these are modern days, Jeanie, civilized times. We've had almost eighteen hundred years of Christianity. And yet the world seems to be slipping back, and the future looks mighty doubtful what with such people as Lord North and Tryon—"

"But bless your soul, Honey, Tryon's been gone since the first o' June. He's not our worry any more. Let the people in New York worry about him now."

"Yes, and he came mighty nigh hanging Davy."

"But he didn't hang him, Honey."

"He hung a lot of good men, though. He hung that poor Captain Messer after his little boy had saved his life one time, and Captain Merrill and those others, Jeanie. That was savagery, Jeanie, that show he put on at Hillsboro after he got back from dragging those poor devils all over the middle settlements in chains. And I'm greatly afraid, my dear, that there may be bad times ahead for us in America." He sat up straight in his chair, leaned forward, his head against her side, his arm about her waist as she sat on the arm of the chair. "You see, Jeanie, those Tories in England can't seem to learn anything. Lord North and his crowd and that German fathead of a king are determined to make slaves out of us. They can't see that we are free men just as they are. They can't seem to understand that our fathers and a lot of us came over here to get away from that mess of politics and wars and continual fighting that they have in Europe one generation after another." He paused, looked into the blazing fire. Jeanie stroked his hair, mischievously pulled his ear.

"Well, we got away, didn't we? What are you quarreling about? Wanting to go back?"

"No, but they may be coming over here."

"What you mean, McKnitt? You mean the English may come over here and try to make us pay their old taxes on tea?"

"Not just that. But things are getting worse all the time between us. Look at the way things are going in the North. British soldiers stationed in Boston, and already trouble between them and the citizens. Sam Adams writing letters around urging the colonies to organize for their common protection. Virginia alarmed. It looks bad, Jeanie."

"But they'll get that all settled. And besides, they'll never come down here into these backwoods settlements to bother us. They'd lose their way and starve, my dear."

"Let's hope not, you little optimist." He stood up, bent down and kissed her. "At any rate, they won't be here before next week. But, say, where's that rascal Davy? He's so big and grown-up I hardly know him any more. And Ephraim Brevard says he's smart as a fox, Jeanie, and'll be ready for Princeton College 'gainst another year."

"He's upstairs primin' and primpin', my dear, and so should you be your ownself. Had you forgot we were going to John Davidson's tonight whilst you were thinking about that silly old Lord North and his politics?"

"I had indeed nigh forgot it, Jeanie. Who all will be there, you reckon?"

"Well, 'twill be a pretty big turnout, I'll vouch. Ephraim will be there if'n he can get away from his books that long, and Thomas Polk, no doubt, and William Lee Davidson and Mary and Waightstill Avery—"

"Ah, so it's the dashing Lawyer Avery and his fine clothes and clever speeches that's interesting you in hurrying me up? Why couldn't you let me stay here and let Davy take you?"

"I could, silly." She pinched him on the cheek. "Except I just don't want to."

McKnitt pulled her to her feet, held her cheeks between his big hands, kissed her lips. "Run along," he said, releasing her, "and dress up, and I'll have Cato see to getting the horses ready, and then I'll see what I can do to improve my own looks. Maybe I'll be able to hold a candle to Waightstill my ownself." He changed his teasing tone. "You know, Jeanie, that's a fine boy, Waightstill. A little wild and he likes his toddy a little too much, I'll vouch, but he's got principles, and he's got sense. He's going to make Mecklenburg a fine man afore many days if'n I'm not badly wrong."

The sun was still high when they mounted their saddle horses and started westward toward Hopewell. But it had set and night had closed upon them when they turned in at the gate to Rural Retreat. From the house down at the foot of the slope came the sound of fiddles scraping, the shrill raucous cadenced cries of the figure-caller, the muffled measured stampings of the dancers. Light streamed from the windows.

Eleven years ago twenty-four-year old John Davidson with his sister Mary had come southwestward from Rowan, leaving his mother, who had married the schoolmaster Henry Henry after their father Robert Davidson had died in Pennsylvania and she had followed her Brevard kinsmen South. They had struck out to establish a home in Tryon County, but on the day they had reached the Catawba River rains had turned it into a raging stream that barred their crossing.

And when they found three springs at the foot of a knoll from which they could look out to the west and see the great river rolling southward, they had decided to stay there and await the receding of the flood waters. That was eleven years ago. John Davidson had decided to stay on the Mecklenburg side.

In his explorations during the next several months he had come upon the home of a neighbor, Samuel Wilson. And the next June he had married his daughter Violet.

Violet met them at the door.

"Come in, Jeanie, and warm your fingers. You must be half-frozen, my dear. And how are you, McKnitt? Come in. And here's Davy. My, boy, but you're well growed. A man a'ready. You come along with me, Jeanie. McKnitt, you and Davy'll find a place to put your things in the room at the other end. You know where. And there's a fire burning." She led Jeanie around the fringe of dancers to the big fireplace. "Warm yourself, Jeanie, and then we'll go let you take off your things."

Jeanie pulled off her mittens, warmed her fingers. "The fire feels

ALEXANDRIANA

good, Violet, but we didn't get very cold. We were well wrapped." She straightened up. "Violet, can I see the baby? I won't wake her."

"Of course, Jeanie. If you've warmed enough, come along with me. She's in the back room. I hope the little rascal's asleep."

"I don't see how she sleeps with all this going on."

"The partition's pretty thick, and—well, she's used to it."

They skirted the circle of dancers again, slipped down the little hallway, tipped into the small room at the back.

"Violet, she's precious," whispered Jeanie, as Violet Davidson pulled back the little blankets and edged the candle nearer. "She's perfectly adorable. I do believe she's the prettiest baby you've had. I wish I could pinch those pretty little pink cheeks." The baby stirred, stretched out a little clinched fist. Jeanie moved the candle back, pulled up the covers. "We must be going. We'll wake her up." They tipped toward the door. "Violet, I do think little Violet's a dear. Won't you give her to me? You'll still have three, and you'll be having a lot more yet."

"I don't know about that, Jeanie. I'm twenty-nine a'ready. And how about your ownself? You're no old woman, Jeanie."

"My dear, I'm all of thirty-two."

Violet Davidson squeezed the little waist of Jeanie. "Just a poor, broke down old woman." She squeezed a little harder. "But you don't look it, my dear. I'm so glad you came tonight, Jeanie. Somehow we don't get to see enough of each other."

"We don't, at that, Violet. Seems like there's always something at home to do, and what with preaching at Hopewell just now and then, it's not often enough we get together. To think, that's the first time I've seen little Violet. And I still want her. But I tell you what I'll do. I won't insist on taking her home with me if'n you'll promise to save her for my Bill."

"But, my dear, William Bain's a big boy. Isabella or Polly would suit him better."

"He's just seven. He's not too old for her."

"But Isabella is seven and Polly's five." She laughed. "Here I am trying to bargain off my daughters."

"They are both beautiful children, Violet, and so is Rebecca—"

ALEXANDRIANA

"Rebecca's a young lady. She's nine. She wanted to stay up for the dance tonight."

"Why didn't you let her?"

"Jeanie, you know she's too young. She should be getting her sleep."

"I suppose so. But I still want little Violet for Bill. I'm serving notice on you, Violet, that she's reserved for Master William Bain. And I want her to bring a big dowry, too." Laughing, they closed the door and returned to the big room where the dancing was in full swing.

William Lee Davidson and Mary had come down from Centre Church and had brought Mary's sisters, Nancy and Rebecca. And Ephraim had left his work at the new Queens College to join them. He had come up to Rural Retreat from Charlottetown with Captain Tom Polk and the captain's little daughter Mary, and two of Pat Jack's daughters, Charity and Lillis had come with them. David Wilson, Violet's brother, was dancing with Hannah Knox, but she had eyes only for his brother Sam. David danced a set with Larissa Sample, but young Andy Barry wasn't letting her get far out of his sight.

Jeanie missed very few sets. Abigail lacked but a week now of being a year old. But Violet Davidson sat out much of the time. "Violet's not three months old until next week," she explained to Charity Jack. "I don't feel strong enough to dance every set, and besides, it might upset the milk. But don't let me throw a damper on things. There's hardly enough men anyway, I'm afraid."

"There's enough, all right, but they're in there talking politics. That's all you hear nowadays, Violet," Charity Jack replied. "That's all they're talking in Charlottetown and when Brother Jim comes down to see us that's all he talks, too. I'm thoroughly sick of it. They talk as if the British might even come over here and fight us. The very idea."

During the pause at the half-set, John Davidson came into the room. "For Heaven's sake, John, why don't you men come in to see us, at least? Were it not for Davy and these younger men, I know the girls would have to be dancing with their ownselves."

ALEXANDRIANA

"How about Waightstill, Violet? Looks like he's doing his part." He pointed toward the young lawyer, who was talking animatedly with Lillis Jack.

"Yes, but what about Ephraim and McKnitt and Tom Polk and William Lee? Why, he's simply deserted Mary. And what about your ownself, John Davidson? You've forgotten you had a wife, I'll vouch."

He pinched her cheek. "Naughty girl. You know I haven't forgot you. But, you see, we haven't all been together in a long time and there's weighty matters to be talked. The situation in the North—"

Violet clapped her hands to her ears. "I'll not hear it. There you go again. Politics, politics, Boston harbor, tea, British. Every time two men in Mecklenburg get together it's politics." She stamped her little foot, dropped her hands. "I didn't hear it," she declared, triumphantly. "Now you go in there and get those men. And bring Pa along too and Mr. Barry. They're not too old to dance. They could dance till daylight had they a mind to. Tell 'em if they don't come in here and dance with these girls, I'll give 'em no midnight snack and I'll make 'em all sleep at the stables."

XVII

"LOOK A-HERE, Jethro, you got your musket all greased up and ready for those Redcoats?"

"I most'n generally keeps her greased, Mr. Patton. And if'n any of 'em ventures down here in these woods I can dang well let 'em have some hot lead. But do you reckon there's goin' to be any shore 'nough trouble?"

"Well, Jethro, I'm hoping 'twon't be any. But it's looking mighty bad in the North. It's been looking bad for a long time, in fact, and it's not getting any better as I see it. Looks like those Britishers are set on making slaves out o' us."

"T'other day Mr. McKnitt got a letter from Davy. You know Davy. He's up at Princeton College learning how to wear pink coats and green britches and sniff snuff up'n his nose and sech-like. Well, a feller what was on his way down through the Valley and headed to Camden fetched the letter to Mr. McKnitt and in the letter Davy said things was lookin' pretty bad up that a-way. Said 'twas lot o' talk 'bout the way things was goin' in Boston, and Philadelphia fokes and them in New York was right smart hot, too. And likewise in Virginia when he went through there."

Jeremiah McCafferty, cutting a strip of blue calico spread out on the counter, paused, laid down the scissors. "But it aint likely to get way over here to us, is it, Ben, even if it comes to actual war?"

"Well, I don't know. It's hard to tell. We're on the way down the Valley into South Carolina and Georgia and we're likewise on the road that leads into the West. Fact, we're in a sorter crossroads—"

"But we're too far back. 'Twouldn't any soldiers come way over

ALEXANDRIANA

in here. They'd do their fighting around Wilmington or Brunswick or Charles Town looks to me like."

"That's what some folks thought about Tryon. But he sent Waddell all through here making the folks take that oath after that fight with the Regulators over at Alamance. The British might do the same."

"You're right, Mr. Patton, as shore as hell. And didn't that damn bastard do his damndest to git them Rocky River boys what burnt up his powder catched and hung? By the way, what's come o' those boys nohow?"

"They're still in the bushes, Jethro. It aint quite safe yet for them to come out o' hiding. It won't be long though, the way things are going now, before they can stop lying out, I'm bound."

"I hear they mighty nigh catched Bob Davis t'other day. How 'bout that?"

"Well, it was a crowd got after him and they thought they had him when they hemmed him up down on the Rocky River. But Bob jumped his horse down a high bank—some says 'twas thirty feet high—and swum him across the river and got away. But whenever any gang gets after those boys we make up another gang and take after them."

"What's ever happened to them two bastards what turned on 'em and gived 'em up?"

"Nothing. But don't anybody have anything to do with 'em. They won't come to any good end, Jethro."

"They should a-come to their end at the end of a rope."

Jeremiah McCafferty finished cutting the cloth, wrapped it in a brown paper. "That'll come to fourteen shillings and three pence, Ben, the way I figure it. It's eight shillings a yard, and it's just short o' two yards."

Ben Patton pulled out a long purse, counted out the coins. "Calico's powerful high."

"Yes, it's a heap higher than linsey-woolsey, but the womenfolks likes it mighty well. What's your wife going to do with this piece?"

"I think she's figuring on a Sunday dress for the girl. She said she was measuring it out pretty close. I reckon it'll be enough."

ALEXANDRIANA

"Need any thread, needle, pins, buttons, or such-like?"

"No, I b'lieve that'll be all today."

"By the way, Mr. Mac, my old woman told me to bring her a needle. Danged if'n she didn't lose her needle t'other day and she put all the chaps to huntin' it but 'twon't to be found. Hit was a plumb good needle, too. She'd had that needle ten year or more, I'm bound, and then she had to up and loss it. Women's danged careless like sometimes."

McCafferty wiped his hands on his apron. " 'Taint none o' my business, Jethro, and I don't mean to be meddling in your business, but I was just a-wondering if'n your old lady was fixing to do some sewing for another little Jethro." The storekeeper smiled, winked at Ben Patton.

"Well, sir, that's right. Hit's supposin' to be mine, 't'any rate."

"How many will that make for you, Jethro?"

" 'Twon't be but 'leven," he spit a stream of amber juice into the dead ashes of the fireplace, "unless'n it's twins."

The two men laughed loudly. "Jethro," said Ben Patton, "you're a good one. But look a-here, if'n you don't mind by the time you quit you'll have a houseful."

"I reckon so. But I like kids and so does the old lady. And besides, hit keeps her peaceable and contented-like." He aimed another stream of tobacco juice at the fireplace. "And I done found out that the best way to manage a woman and keep down trouble is to keep her bigged and barefooted."

When he had paid for the needle, Jethro turned to go. But at the door, through which he saw the log courthouse in the intersection of the two roads, he paused.

"Seein' the courthouse settin' out there jest brought to my mine what I mainly come to Charlottetown for, Mr. Mac. And that was to pass the word around that they's figurin' on having another meetin' Friday evenin' down at Queens Museum. Mr. McKnitt said to tell anybody what come in 'bout the meetin' and I'm goin' down to Joe Nicholson's, and Duncan Ochiltree's store and Pat Jack's and tell them to pass the word around, too. And I'll step over to Waightstill's and tell him. Do you know if'n he's at his office?"

ALEXANDRIANA

"He rode in this morning from 'Squire Hezekiah's. I guess he's over there."

"He mebbe knows 'bout it. Mr. Hezekiah'd tell him if'n he'd been told his ownself. And how 'bout Cap'n Tom Polk? Reckon he's out at the mill, don't you?"

"I guess so. But he'd know a'ready."

"That's right, he would. I guess him and Mr. McKnitt's the ones what set the time. But I'll be gittin' along. You tell ever'body, Mr. Mac, and you tell ever'body over Rocky River and Poplar Tent way, Mr. Patton. And don't fergit that there young Preacher Balch, and Mr. Phifer, and Dave Reese and Zack Wilson. And let me see. There's Richard Harris, too. Well, you know who. They want ever'body they can git to come, he said."

Jethro stepped from the store porch, turned to the right to enter Waightstill Avery's office. But Waightstill wasn't in. He found him later in the taproom at Jack's.

"But I tell you, Uncle Pat," the young lawyer was saying as Jethro pushed up to the bar, "it would be mighty bad if we had to fight the British. The British, you see, are such fine fighters—"

"I tell ye the British are no fighters—" Old Pat Jack, his arm upraised, was shaking his clinched fist; his face was livid. "I tell ye they are a race o' blasted tea-drinkers! They won't fight us, they'll be afeared, I tell ye!"

"But, Uncle Pat, we have got soft. You see, our forefathers were Scotch and they were great fighters back in the old days in Scotland. But on their way over here they stopped off in Ireland a few years and they forgot how to fight, they got soft and flabby, they got so they would run at the sight o' their shadows, they—"

"Git out o' here, ye blasted, dressed-up, dudish lawyer. Git out, I tell you, ye blasted lyin' young blather-skaite. Tellin' me to my teeth the Irish, by Patty, won't fight. Put down that there grog and take yore money you gived for it and git out!" The old man was shaking his fist under Waightstill's nose.

"I'll take it all back, Uncle Pat. I was just teasing. Fact, you knew it all the time, but you're just so full of that good old fighting Irish blood—"

ALEXANDRIANA

Pat Jack's leathery old Irish face softened into a myriad of little wrinkles under his eyes and about the corners of his mouth.

"Now ye're talking better, me lad. Go ahead and drink ye grog and have anither if ye like on the same money. And if'n them blasted Britishers come a-sneakin' round these parts we'll fill 'em so full o' hot lead they'll think they're tendin' hell's fire fer the Devil his ownself!"

But though the Redcoats did not come as the months went by and alarming reports from the North found their way slowly into the western settlements, anxiety increased in Mecklenburg and candles burned late into the night as leading citizens of the county gathered at Queens Museum two hundred yards down the muddy road from the little courthouse in the crossroads, or out at Alexandriana, or at Tom Polk's mill, or in the Poplar Tent neighborhood, or at Richard Barry's house on the Beatty's Ford Road, or at Hezekiah Alexander's or John Davidson's.

And often when the magistrates came together in Charlottetown to form the General Court the adjournment of the court session found serious-minded Mecklenburgers remaining to discuss the newest developments in the North, the voting in Parliament, the fight between the English liberals and their obstinate, unyielding opponents encouraged in their stand by His Majesty George III himself.

And they discussed too the rule of the new Governor, Josiah Martin.

"He's about sech a feller as old Tryon," Jethro observed one day to McKnitt Alexander as they were preparing to make a run of liquor down at the stillhouse on the spring branch. "Mebbe he aint got as much sense, but he's the same stripe. All he's studyin' is lookin' out for them Englishmen on t'other side. He aint givin' a two-penny 'bout us in Carolina, I'll vouch."

"He's a soldier, but he's likely not as good a soldier as Tryon. Tryon's gone and we're well rid of him, Jethro, and he caused us a lot of trouble, but he was a good soldier. You'll have to hand it to him."

"Well, he blowed a lot o' holes in them Regulators' hides, but

ALEXANDRIANA

they didn't know how to fight. They was jest a bunch o' sheep. And what he done after that there fight over at Alamance was what made me mad, Mr. McKnitt. Him a-hangin' them fellers and paradin' 'round over the settlements showin' off his prisoners and makin' fokes swear oaths that warn't noways to their likin' neither. And he dang nigh got Davy."

"Yes, had it not been for your ownself, Jethro, Tryon likely would have hung Davy too." McKnitt Alexander put his hand upon Jethro's shoulder, looked him full in the face. "It never likely occurred to you, Jethro, but it's men like your ownself that must preserve us from men like Tryon. It's men like your ownself that will make us some day, in the Lord's own good time, a nation, a great nation o' God-fearing free men. There's got to be men like Dr. Franklin and Sam Adams and Virginia's Colonel Washington to lead us, but what's going to save us is men like you—like you saved Davy."

XVIII

THROUGH THE doorway to the parlor David Barksdale could see himself in the full length gilt-framed mirror on its low pedestal in the front hallway. The candles upon the dropleaf walnut table nearby shone full upon him and he saw with satisfaction that Jeanie had well folded his new blue coat and breeches so that now only a few wrinkles showed after the long ride from Alexandriana.

He and Jethro had put up at a tavern in Cross Creek. They had arrived at sunset, had seen to the horses before having their own supper, and then David had stripped off his hunting shirt and heavy riding breeches and brought forth from his bag the clothes he had purchased shortly before leaving Princeton College. A bath and the fresh clothes had transformed him, and he had ridden out to the McNeills in high spirits.

The last time he had looked into this mirror, he recalled, he had seen a gawky country boy from the back settlements, his hair tied with one of Jeanie's ribbons, his big hands and big feet thrust out from the new suit bought at Duncan Ochiltree's store, his new black shoes and silver buckles, his clean white shirt.

Now he saw that same country boy, but taller by inches, his same broad shoulders covered by blue broadcloth, his throat engulfed in white stock above a blue and silver waistcoat, his blue coat flowing down past slim hips over blue breeches with silver buckles at the knee, his straight, muscled legs encased in cream-colored stockings above black shoes with silver buckles. And as he looked into the mirror and lifted a lacy wrist to smooth a wrinkle at his left elbow, he thought of that other night he had danced here in this house.

There was a little girl in a pretty dress. A little girl in a cream-colored quilted hoop-petticoat with a light blue silk gown open in front and drawn to the sides in billowing folds over the tight bodice . . . And the bodice was cut low and the deep-cut V at the neck was revealing. He remembered the little breast-knot and the tiny bouquet of flowers between firm little breasts pushing upward . . .

And as he flicked a bit of wool-lint from the sweeping skirt of his coat he remembered another girl. Here in the other end of this room had sat the musicians . . . And here, right over here, the girl had squeezed his hand and he had wildly crushed her to himself, had felt her laced little bosom swelling against his chest . . .

In the mirror he could see the last half dozen steps of the stairway that began its ascent a pace back from the parlor door. He caught his breath as he saw on the steps another image . . .

Lovelace stepped through the doorway, paused, her hand upon her chest. "David Barksdale!" She stepped quickly toward him, her hand out-stretched. He grasped her hand, bent forward, pressed his lips to it.

"I'm so glad to see you again," he said, and his smile covered his tanned face.

"But you have grown! I'd hardly have known you!"

"Exactly the words you said when I was here the last time," he said, with a laugh. "Yes, I reckon I'm well growed. I believe those are the very words I said then, too."

She stepped back, looked him over from head to foot. Then she motioned him to the chair. "Pardon me for staring at you so, David, and forgetting my manners, but, you see, I haven't had a glimpse of you since the night we had our dance here, and your letters didn't say much about how you looked, and they were precious few besides."

She sat down, spreading her skirts, and crossed her feet.

David pulled the chair nearer her, sat down. "The passing was slow, Lovelace, and oftentimes I had no way to send letters. And then, too," he paused and Lovelace saw little crinkles appearing under his eyes and wrinkles crossing his smooth forehead, "I had to study so hard—"

"Yes, but what were you studying, my dear sir? I well know my ownself. 'Twas the ladies, I'll vouch, the ladies around Princeton College and New York and Philadelphia and Trenton and—and—"

"Seems that would be enough to keep one poor man fair busy, I'm bound. But, 'tis a fact, Lovelace, I had to burn a candle a night with my books. And I had precious little time to think of the ladies, only one, and she was so far away—"

"Yes, and she's married, too. You stayed away so long, David, that she gave up hope and—"

"But where's your husband, my dear lady, if you're married? And why are you allowing me to come to see you tonight if you have a new husband around some place? Now answer me that?"

Lovelace laughed, bent over and tapped lightly the back of his hand on the arm of the chair. "You still say such clever things, David. Did they teach you that at Princeton College too?" She was serious again. "But 'tis a fact that Belinda's married."

"You wrote me that, my dear young lady—" he hesitated, "in one of the precious few letters you spared time enough to write from receiving the attention of the young swells of this aristocratic Scotch country. Had you forgot?"

"Maybe not, David. But I do so love to hear you make such pretty little speeches. P'r'aps I'm just vain, but—" she paused, looked at the floor. David moved his chair nearer. She looked up, brightly. "But did I tell you all the details, where she and Angus are living, and all that?"

"No, only that she married that stiff-neck who was with her that night at the dance here."

"Well, Mr. MacDougald gave Angus a big place down on the Cape Fear in Bladen County. It's a terribly big place, David, and a fine house. The house is in a grove of great oaks and they named it Pleasant Grove. Isn't that an attractive name?"

"It really is. But what about Belinda? Is she still haughty? And

ALEXANDRIANA

is she happy? Seems that she would be, with a great place and a snobbish husband."

Lovelace puckered her lips into a pout. "You shouldn't think that about her, David. You shouldn't hold a grudge for—for what she said that day at the muster-ground."

"About my being a bound-boy, you mean. Well, I was a bound-boy, and I shall always be a bound-boy to Uncle McKnitt and Jeanie, bound hand and foot in heart even if not legally."

"Now you are saying nice things, David, lovely things. But you were asking if she is happy. I don't know. I don't see her very often. And sometimes I wonder. Angus is hard to live with, I suspect. And—and I'm certain, David, she—she hasn't forgot you. She liked you a lot, David."

"I don't suppose it was any more than a childish fascination for my big muscles and tanned face and back country clothes and back country talk."

"No, I don't think so. And you were fascinated by her, too, and you can't fool me, even if you have been to Princeton College and sharpened your natural ability at clever talk, Mr.—I was about to say Master—David Barksdale." She shook her finger under his nose.

David laughed. "Well, whatever it was, it was years ago. And I was fascinated then by someone else, too—if you count Belinda—and I still am. I wonder—" Lovelace was looking at her hands clasped in her lap. He leaned forward, lifted her chin until he was looking straight into her eyes. "I wonder if you—"

"Mr. Barksdale!"

Lovelace's father stood in the doorway. They had not heard his steps in the hall. David stood up. Mr. McNeill walked quickly toward him, hand extended.

"Come in, Father," said Lovelace, face flushed in the candlelight.

"Pardon my intrusion, but I heard you were here when I came home and I wanted to welcome you, young man." He shook hands warmly. "How have you been, sir? It's been a time since I saw you and you have turned into a man."

ALEXANDRIANA

"Very good, sir. And how have you been?"

"Quite well, thank you. And how are my friends, Mr. Alexander and Mistress Alexander?"

"They are both quite well, sir."

"I'm glad to hear it. They are fine persons. They treated us royally when we were at their home."

"A lot has happened since then, sir."

"Yes, indeed. Governor Tryon's gone to New York. And—oh, yes, Lovelace told me that you wrote her that you almost got in trouble during the Regulator trouble over in Alamance."

"Why refer to that again, Father?"

David laughed. "That's all right, Lovelace. I don't mind now. Yes, sir, I was in a little trouble, Mr. McNeill. I just escaped getting hung."

Mr. McNeill laughed heartily. "Well, so long as you didn't, I don't suppose there's anything to worry about now." His face clouded. "Governor Tryon didn't handle that affair in the best way, I'm convinced. I think he should have required the submission of the Regulators but he should have been more lenient after the battle. I think the affair that followed at Hillsboro was little short of disgraceful."

"I think it was entirely disgraceful, sir."

"Father," Lovelace, seeing the trace of a scowl on David's face, interposed, "that Regulator trouble was years ago, and Tryon's gone, and why talk about it now?"

"My daughter," observed Mr. McNeill, "doesn't like politics, as you observe, Mr. Barksdale."

"So has she indicated to me every time I have offered to mention something to do with it, Mr. McNeill. Politics is not yet one of the virtues of the fair sex, I'm bound."

"No, but it's one of the failings of the men, I'll vouch." Lovelace gave a toss to her head that misplaced a curl at her ear. "Every time two men get together they start talking about Governor Tryon or Governor Martin or tea or King George or the Regulators or something equally boring. I've a notion times would be better if there wasn't so much talk of the country going to the dogs."

ALEXANDRIANA

"There may be something in that argument, Lovelace," her father agreed. "But 'twould be right difficult not to talk about such things. By the way, Mr. Barksdale, how do you find things in the North?"

"Very threatening, Mr. McNeill. The whole section's alarmed at the apparent efforts of the British to force a condition upon us that would amount almost to slavery."

"Do sit down, you two." Lovelace stood up. "You're started on politics and that means a long discussion, I'll vouch."

"No, I'm going in just a minute, Lovelace."

"Sit down, Father, and you, David. And excuse me a moment while I step out to the kitchen."

"I suppose," said Mr. McNeill, as they sat down, "that conditions are not improving in the North, either?"

"That's right, sir. I fear they are getting worse all the time."

"It's a pity, a great pity, Mr. Barksdale. The Government in London, I suspect, have embarked upon a short-sighted policy. I am for the King, sir. I have sworn an oath of loyalty to His Majesty. After Culloden, you know. And I trust I shall be true to it to my dying day. But I can see how the people of the colonies feel aggrieved. They feel they are being taxed without right."

" I feel that way myself, sir."

"Yes, my boy, I can see how you would. The people in Mecklenburg are wrought up, no doubt?" He smiled.

"Yes, sir, very much so. They are fully expecting to wake up some morning and find Redcoats all over the place." David laughed. "In fact, they're half-way hoping to, I'm bound."

"I suppose Captain Polk and Mr. Alexander and the others are very much interested in the situation in the colonies?"

"Yes, sir, they're having meetings every few weeks down at Queens Museum—that's the new school, you know—"

"I know about it. I was over at the General Assembly the year we met in the Governor's Palace just after it was finished and that's when that school was chartered. But I heard later the King and the Council had refused to allow the charter."

"That's right. The charter was amended the next year and passed but the King still refused to approve it."

ALEXANDRIANA

"Why was that? I should think the fact that it was named for the Queen would have so flattered him that he would have hastened to grant the charter."

"The King doesn't like our politics in Mecklenburg—or our religion. Too many Whigs, and too many Presbyterians."

"I suspect that's it young man. Mecklenburg, I'll vouch, isn't exactly to the liking of His Majesty or the Government in England."

"Yes, sir, and it's mutual, too."

Lovelace entered, carrying a tray. David stood up.

"Sit down, David. Keep your seat, Father. I'll set it right here." David helped her. "It's just some tea and little sweet cakes. If you're through talking about King George and Lord North and the tea tax—and let me hasten to explain, David, that no tax was paid on this tea. It came in after the tax was repealed, if that'll make it taste any better to you."

"Much better, in fact, it'll make it drinkable." David laughed.

Mr. McNeill stood up. "Tax or no tax won't make it all right for me at this time o' night. I wouldn't sleep a wink if I tasted it. But you two go ahead. I've got to be going to bed. I had a hard ride from down in Bladen, and I'm tired." He extended his hand to David, and they shook hands. "Glad to have seen you, Mr. Barksdale, and please present my compliments to Mr. Alexander and Mistress Alexander, and to Captain Polk when you see him and any other of my Mecklenburg friends you may see. And come back to see us, young man, any time you are in these parts."

"Thank you, sir."

Mr. McNeill smiled. "Now you two drink your tea. And I'll not trespass again." He walked toward the door, turned. "Goodnight." Lovelace ran over, kissed him. "Good-night, Father."

They heard him climbing the stairs. "He's the sweetest father in the world."

David reached for her hands. "And he has the sweetest daughter in the world."

"Beautifully said. But didn't I seem to suggest it?"

"Would you take credit for my very infrequent bright remarks?"

ALEXANDRIANA

"No, Mr. Barksdale. I do so like to hear them, even though they're lightly said."

"But they aren't. They're as true as the Scriptures."

"Still the flatterer." She withdrew her hands from his. "But let's do sit down, David."

"The couch looks so much more comfortable. And couldn't we pull the table over to it? I'm just about dying for some of that—that damned tea." There were devilish litle wrinklings under his eyes.

"You don't like tea?"

"Well, I'm not exactly what you'd call a tea-drinker."

"But you do like a cup now and then? Try it; it's already sweetened, but there's more sugar if you want it. And cream."

He took a sip. "It's right good, for a fact, Lovelace. You know —" he placed a finger on his lips, "don't tell anybody, but I do like tea. I like tea but I don't like the principle of drinking the damned stuff. Maybe that's it."

Lovelace laughed. "Men are such strange creatures. Almost as strange as—"

"Women."

"Yes, I suppose so."

David held aloft in his big right hand the dainty cup. Across his knee was the tiny lace doily. "If only Jethro could see me now."

"Who's Jethro? Oh, yes, I believe I remember. He's that funny man that lives on your Uncle McKnitt's place, isn't he?"

"Yes, he's that funny man. He wears rough clothes and he chews tobacco and he talks rough and—and I don't suppose he's ever tasted any tea, and he lives in a cabin with a houseful of young'uns—" David set down his cup. "But he's my friend and he's about the finest American I've ever seen unless 'twould be Uncle McKnitt."

Lovelace patted the back of his big hand. "Of all the pretty things you've said David, I think that's the prettiest, and I don't mind saying I overly admire you for saying it."

He pressed with his free hand the little hand that was patting his. "There are a lot of men the like of Jethro and they're what makes these colonies strong. You got to have men like General Washington and Dr. Franklin and the men of Boston and New York and Philadelphia and Charles Town and like your father and Uncle McKnitt and John Davidson at home—men to lead and do the planning, but you've got to have men like Jethro, too."

"Where is he? At the tavern at Cross Creek?"

"Yes, I left him there."

"You should have brought him along." She drew back her hand.

"Do you really wish I had?"

She laid her doily on the tray, leaned back against the needlepoint suspended beneath the carved pomegranates that formed the arch of the sofa's mahogany woodwork. "No—I don't—really."

Her hand next to him lay inert upon her knee. With his left hand he picked it up, placed it in his right. He was sitting close to her; he thought he felt a little tremor run along her body. And he was conscious, too, of a warm ecstatic sensation coursing through his own frame, coming to center itself along his leg that pressed against hers outlined in the candlelight beneath the smoothness of her rose-colored gown. Her hand was hot in his, he knew it, her eyes beneath the long lashes were upon her lap. A candle burning low sputtered and went out.

"Perhaps," she said, withdrawing her hand, "I'd better get another candle." She sat up.

"We don't need another one. Those three are enough, aren't they?"

"Maybe so." She leaned back against the needlepoint.

He took her hand again. The back of his own was touching lightly her knee beside his. The silk was smooth to the back of his hand. Beneath that silk, and other silks—he wondered how many—would be the velvet white of her skin, creamy pink beneath the weight of their hands. With his head against the upholstery of the sofa, and the fragrance of her hair in his nostrils, the fragrance of her head touching his shoulder ever so lightly, he closed his eyes. The whiteness, the smooth velvet of her skin . . .

But there was no wild surging of hot blood racing through him, no tempestuous urge to clasp her to himself, to possess her, no itching of palms or fingers to caress . . . He remembered Belinda and her squeezing his hand back there on the stairway at Alexandriana, here at the dance at Mr. McNeill's . . . He remembered the frantic burning desire . . . No, this was not that . . . This was something else.

He was conjuring up another picture as he sat here beside this girl in the flicker of candles burning low . . . Pleasant Grove. An old mansion looking down to the Cape Fear moving lazily to the sea. A bedroom, the master bedroom. He felt a sneer curling at the corners of his mouth. The master bedroom, indeed. A high carved four-poster, soft silken covers, damask sheets . . . He closed his eyes, toyed with this illusion . . . Angus MacDougald at one side of the bed, his head, no doubt, tucked into a night-cap, his weak face half buried in his pillow. He had no right to be there. No, by the heavens, that was no place for a weak man. He dismissed Angus, and as a child slyly tastes his syllabub before the whole table has been served, nibbled at the edges of this new imagery coming to focus out of the nebulous cloud of his imaginings . . . Now it had emerged, sharp, distinct, real, as real as the escritoire over there across from him. This moment. Perhaps some sixth sense had transported him to Pleasant Grove. He was standing there looking down upon this bed, this sumptuous bed, upon the lovely shapeliness more revealed than concealed by the filmy night-dress twisted about her in restless turnings . . . Her hair fanned out upon her pillow, her eyes, under the fringe of heavy lashes, looked unseeing upon the canopy of the four-poster, her mouth was half open . . . His eyes traveled the length of her body, now loosed of gown and bodice and petticoat, now freed of the torture of lacing, of the constriction of many garments. He fancied he was bending low above her, was feeling her warm hot breath upon his neck . . . She was tossing . . . And at the other side of the bed Angus snored . . .

"A penny for your thoughts."

He patted her hand. "I guess we had sort of wandered off, hadn't we? It's so nice and cozy and—well, I could sit here by you and never say a thing and be having the best time imaginable—well, forever, I know."

"You have waked up, Mr. Barksdale. Now, sir, I know it."

"But I could. Honestly, I could." Yes, Lovelace was different. He could see visions while sitting here beside her, while holding her little hand in his own, and the vision, the unreal, the conjured-up, would affect him when the real, the present, did not. It wasn't that she wasn't feminine, lovely, muchly to be desired. But she was to be protected, cherished, loved, and Belinda—well, Belinda was to be conquered, to be cooled, Belinda was a challenge, Lovelace a trust. Perhaps that was it . . .

"David, it's getting late, and Father—"

"I haven't been here long."

"But you came late. And Father is rather old-fashioned in his views on such things as young ladies keeping company late hours. And I'm just turned eighteen."

"But so is Belinda, and she has a husband."

"But I haven't, you see. I'm likely to be an old maid."

"Not if I can help it."

"David, you are quick on the comeback. But I always seem to invite your gallant remarks." She sat up. But he continued to loll against the cushions. She stood up, grasped his big hand, tugged upon it. "You must be going, David. We can talk more tomorrow night. But here I go again. You hadn't even asked me if you might call."

"But I haven't had time." David, standing up, held to her hands. "Here I am being pushed out precipitately into the night, almost being thrown out bodily, for no reason other than that it's getting late. And it's been getting late on millions of nights before this. And my horse in the midst of his pleasant dreaming out there at the post, too."

"And still you haven't asked me to let you come tomorrow. Perhaps you'll finish your business and get away in time to spend the night at some tavern up the road a way." She tossed her head.

"Still haven't had time. But before you interrupt again, may I? I do have business that will keep me at Cross Creek all tomorrow.

ALEXANDRIANA

And it's important business. It's the business of waiting until night when I can come back to see you—if I may."

She tapped him lightly on the cheek. "David, you do say the most adorable things. And I too will have business, the business of hoping how fast the clock moves until night, and then how slow."

She walked with him out upon the veranda. When he had stepped down one step her head came up past his shoulders. "I don't want to go." He was holding her hands, extended downward before her. He lifted them to his lips, buried his head against her bosom, felt her lips lightly brush his hair. "I want to stay with you, I want to take you with me." He snuggled against her, turned to look up into her face. "You're so sweet." He slipped his arm about her waist. But she caught his arm. "You mustn't, David—you mustn't—now." Out at the hitching post his horse, sensing his nearness, whinnied. "He'll be waking Father." She gave his hand a squeeze, dropped it, fled across the veranda. At the door she paused. "Tomorrow night. Don't forget." The door closed behind the swirl of silken skirt.

David stared a moment at the closed door, turned, walked down the steps. "Damn that horse." A scowl clouded his face. But he was walking upon air.

XIX

JOHN DAVIDSON cleared his throat. "Gentlemen, we've done a lot of talking here today but not much acting. And it's getting late. Some of us have a lot of riding before we get home. It's a good twelve miles up to Rural Retreat and it's quite a way to Alexandriana, McKnitt. And you men who come from Rocky River and Poplar Tent have a long ride ahead of you. And it's plagued hot, too." He pulled his handkerchief from the inner pocket of his coat, mopped his forehead, ran the handkerchief around the inside of his stock.

"You're right, John," agreed Richard Harris. "We've been doing a parcel o'talking and mighty little else. And there's some of us here from Poplar Tent that's got to be getting on home pretty soon."

"Well, what I was going to say is this. We've talked about all there's any need of. We've been here pretty near all morning. We've discussed everything and everybody from Boston to Georgia and back. We're all familiar with the situation, as familiar as we can be with the news we've had. It all comes down to this, the way I see it. The port at Boston's closed and the British are trying to starve out the folks there to make them come across and pay for that tea they dumped in the water and the tax on the rest they want to bring over. And Boston's called for help and is getting it."

"We'll send 'em clothes and meat our ownselves. We can send it with the stuff that's going up from Charles Town."

"That's right, Zach, we got to do it. But here's what I was going

ALEXANDRIANA

to say. Governor Martin's trying to keep the Assembly from meeting. You know he wouldn't approve anything we did last year and he dismissed us after only a few days. Well, we authorized John Harvey to call another meeting any time he thought it proper to do so. Now he's called one. Martin's poppin'-mad, I reckon, but it makes no difference. What I'm proposing to do is to send a representative to New Bern to this meeting."

"How about your ownself and Martin Phifer? You all did all right last winter. You got along pretty well together."

"Wait a minute, Richard. You're getting ahead o' me."

Richard Barry laughed. "Go ahead, Neighbor."

"Well, I think we ought to send somebody to New Bern to back John Harvey and those other fellows from Perquimans, and Willie Jones from Halifax and Caswell and those men from Dobbs County and Joe Hewes from Edenton and Cornelius Harnett from Wilmington and the rest of 'em. They'll need support. I've a notion Martin will try to get ugly this time."

"But, Mr. Davidson," interposed Hezekiah Balch, "You've been before. You are experienced. You know the leaders. You've just named some of the principal ones. And they know you. I think you'd be the man to represent Mecklenburg again."

"Thank you, sir. I'm flattered by what you say and more by who said it. But I think someone should come from over Rocky River way or from your own Poplar Tent section. You see—" He hesitated. "I hadn't meant to say anything about this but it looks like I'll have to protect my ownself. It's this way, as I see it. You know we've been having a little trouble here in Mecklenburg about where we'd have the county town and put the court house and jail." He cleared his throat again, wiped his forehead. "It's plagued hot," he interposed. "Parson Balch, you folks over at Poplar Tent and Rocky River were much nigher the center of the county than the Hopewell and Charlottetown and Sugaw Creek folks. That's a fact. But we pulled a little political trick on you and built this courthouse before Charlottetown had really been selected as the county town. That sort of gave us an advantage over you fellows." He stopped, looked around the group assembled in this same little courthouse. They were listening closely. "Well, eight years ago when Martin Phifer introduced his bill to let the commissioners lay off Charlottetown into squares and streets and lots and to build a courthouse and the jail and stocks, nothing was said about making Charlottetown the county town and the place for holding the courts, and—well, you know what happened. Tom Polk got the bill killed."

"That's right, John Davidson. That's exactly why we got it killed. We figured maybe there was a political trick in that bill." Tom Polk laughed. "That's the truth, all right. But there was another reason, too, John. And it's already been borne out. We figured that although Charlottetown wasn't then in the center of the county, it would come nigher being in the center later than would Rocky River. It's growing to the west, and they'll likely be cutting us up again on the east. You see, I've been busy surveying boundary lines between us and South Carolina and I'm sorter acquainted with the way the folks are settling these parts."

"That's all so, gentlemen, as Tom Polk says. But to get to the point. When Martin Phifer got through his bill setting up Tryon County—they ought to change it's name right now—and likewise we ought to change the name of this street out here—"

"That muddy road won't ever be called by any name, John."

"Well, we ought to change the name anyway. But as I was trying to say, when Martin put through his bill for cutting off Tryon county Tom Polk got a rider on it providing for holding Mecklenburg's courts in this house for seven years, since we had already built the courthouse. And when the seven years were about to run out last year I put in a bill to build a permanent courthouse here and it was passed but the Governor vetoed it. Martin Phifer didn't fight me on it. Last December Tom Polk put in the bill again, but the Governor ran us off and so it didn't pass. But this past March Tom got it across. I think it's settled for good now. And right here I want to say I think the Rocky River and Poplar Tent folks have acted mighty reasonable about it. And that's what I'm leading up to by reminding you of all this. I think somebody ought to go to New Bern from the eastern part of the county. And so I move Mr. Chair-

ALEXANDRIANA

man, that we name a citizen from Rocky River or Poplar Tent to go to New Bern this August—when's John Harvey's call for?"

"The twenty-fifth." Ephraim Brevard took off his glasses, mopped his forehead, wiped gingerly around the circle of his sightless eye, polished the glasses, replaced them.

"I move we name a citizen from the eastern section of the county to represent us at the Provincial Congress beginning at New Bern August 25 and I move you that we instruct him to vote with the other leaders of this Province for all measures designed to preserve for Americans their rights of freedom and security."

"Well, you all heard the motion." 'Squire Abraham Alexander stood up. "Is there a second?"

"I agree with John Davidson." McKnitt Alexander twisted around in his seat. "I'll gladly second it, though I think John would do to send back."

"Is there any discussion?"

"Question," someone spoke up. A chorus joined him.

The motion carried.

"And now who is the delegate you want to send?"

Benjamin Patton was nominated. "He's the man," Hezekiah Alexander agreed. "He'll make us a good representative."

"But—" Benjamin Patton was rising to his feet.

"You're out of order, Ben," said the chairman. "If I hear no objection—" he paused. He turned to Patton. "Ben, you can be gettin' ready. It's a long way over to New Bern, nigh on to three hundred miles. Maybe more."

XX

"Come in!"

The door opened. Waightstill Avery jumped from his chair, walked around his desk, his arm extended. "Well, Will Kennon! Come in, Will. I'm right powerful glad to see you, man!" A tall young man who had been talking with Waightstill Avery arose. "This is my friend Hezekiah Balch, Will. Have a care about your speech. He's a preacher. But—" he added as an afterthought, "he's a pretty damned reasonable one."

The other two men laughed. William Kennon stepped forward, shook hands with the young minister. "I know Mr. Balch, Waightstill. I'm mighty glad to see you again, sir, though I must say I'm a bit disappointed to find you in such company."

Mr. Balch laughed. "I'm glad to see you again, sir. And now that we've caught each other in such a place, perhaps neither of us will tell on the other."

"It's a fair bargain, sir."

"You'll both improve your standing by publishing it everywhere that you've been here." Waightstill pulled a chair out from the wall. "Sit down, Will. And you too, Hezekiah. Will, you look a little hot and dusty. Maybe we should step down to Joe Nicholson's or Pat Jack's and get a little cooling nip. It's making me hot to look at you, Will. Looks like you might have come all the way from Salisbury today. But I don't reckon you did."

"No, that's too big a trip. Spent the night at Phifer's Mill."

"Still running the Black Boys over that way?"

"Not much, they say. The temper of the people's about got to the

ALEXANDRIANA

point where they won't permit any harm being done those fellows. Most anybody you'd see would be ready now to burn up some more of the Governor's powder. And that's what brings me over to see you, Waightstill. I—" He hesitated, glanced toward the young minister.

"Don't worry about Hezekiah, Will. He's the wildest revolutionary in these parts. He's about ready to chase George off his throne. You can tell him anything you could me."

"Well, it wasn't any secret. But still I didn't know. You got to be sort of cautious nowadays, you know."

"What you got on your mind, Will?"

"We've got a Commitee of Safety in Rowan, as you may have heard."

"Yes, and you're chairman."

"That's right, but unimportant—the chairman part, I mean."

"I don't agree. But go ahead, Will."

"Well, we've just had a meeting and passed a set of resolutions. I brought along a copy to show you. And I'll be glad for you to see it, too, Mr. Balch. I wanted you folks over here in Mecklenburg to be acquainted with what we're doing." He reached into an inner coat pocket, pulled forth a sheaf of papers, handed them to Waightstill Avery. "There's lively times ahead, gentlemen, frantic times, maybe. We've got to keep informed on what each other's doing. Fact, we ought to have some central organization even over in these western settlements."

Waightstill Avery opened the papers. "You got a long document here, Will. Maybe we'd better get a drink before we go into it."

"No, I'd rather you looked it over before we went to the tavern." He smiled. "We might stay down there too long."

Waightstill shrugged. "Just as you say. You're the fellow who's tired and dusty." He glanced at the first sheet. " 'Resolved,' he read aloud, " 'That we will at all times, whenever we are called upon for that purpose, maintain and defend, at the expense of our lives and fortunes, His Majesty's right and title to the Crown of Great Britain and his dominions in America, to whose royal person and government we profess all due obedience and fidelity.' " He turned to Mr. Kennon. "Well, you didn't throw George overboard, at any rate. When we write ours, Hezekiah," he looked toward Pastor Balch, "we're going to throw that fat German out the window, eh?"

"Right now that would be a bit premature, wouldn't it, Waightstill?," the minister replied with a question.

"Perhaps so. But I certainly wouldn't object. Nor would you, my good fellow." He turned to the paper again. "You say the right to impose taxes, though, is peculiarly our own, that the British have no right to impose a tax on tea, you give them hell—pardon me, Hezekiah—for their conduct toward Massachusetts Bay and Boston. 'Resolved,' he began reading aloud again 'That the cause of the town of Boston is the common cause of the American Colonies.' I heartily agree with you there, Will. Let me run down these resolutions, and then I'll turn them over to Hezekiah for his scholarly perusal. Hezekiah's a scholar and a gentleman, Will. I'm a lawyer." He began scanning the paper, turned a sheet. " 'Resolved, That the African trade is injurious to this colony, obstructs the population of it by freemen, prevents manufacturers and other useful emigrants from Europe from settling amongst us, and occasions an annual increase of the balance of trade against the colonies.' That's not going to sit so well with those slave-traders in the North that are starting a good business of selling 'em down here, will it?"

"Maybe not, but it ought to be stopped before it gets started too strong."

Waightstill Avery continued to read the resolves of the Rowan Committee of Saftey. "This is good, Will. I'll read it to you, Hezekiah. Listen: 'Resolved, That at this important and alarming crisis, it be earnestly recommended to the said deputies at their general convention'—That's provided for in the resolve above, Hezekiah, which names Will and Sam Young and Moses Winslow as Rowan's deputies to a meeting on the twentieth at Johnston Court House—'it be earnestly recommended to the said deputies at their general convention, that they nominate and appoint one proper person out of each district of this province, to meet such

ALEXANDRIANA

deputies in a General Congress, as shall be appointed upon the part of the other Continental Colonies in America, to consult and agree upon a firm and indissoluble union and association for preserving, by the best and most proper means, their common rights and liberties.' That's good Will. I'm strongly for that. The only thing in it I would have changed would have been the very first resolve—maybe. But it was probably the politic thing to do at this stage of the situation, at any rate." He handed the paper to Rev. Mr. Balch. "Here, Hezekiah, you read it. Then we'll walk down to Joe Nicholson's and get some refreshment for Will. And the parson will likely find several of his sheep down there. Fact, you could likely make a pastoral call by visiting Joe's or Pat Jack's either."

"Wait a minute, Waightstill. We want Mecklenburg to be represented at this meeting, and also at the meeting at New Bern on the twenty-fifth. The same three are going to New Bern from Rowan."

"We've already got a man named to represent us at the Provincial Congress at New Bern."

"Who is he?"

"Ben Patton, from Poplar Tent."

"When's he leaving?"

"He's already gone."

"Why'd he start so early?"

"Well, he's walking."

"Walking?"

"That's right. He's already gone. But I didn't know it until he'd been gone a couple of days, or I'd got him a horse. You see, Ben's horse died this summer about the time he got his crop laid by and he was so damned independent he wouldn't ask anybody for the loan of one to go to New Bern."

"Man, that's three hundred miles."

"Well, it's two hundred and fifty on a bee-line. And there are a lot of rivers and creeks to cross and swamps to dodge. He'll be walking three hundred or more. But Ben'll get there. He's a good man, Ben Patton."

"He's bound to be. I'll vouch."

"Ben's all right. And now, Hezekiah, put that paper in your pocket. You can study it tonight. Where's your manners? Here we've got a visitor from the city of Salisbury and we're not showing him proper entertainment. And the poor fellow's well nigh famished, I'm bound." He walked over to his desk, picked up a small placard with a string tied at each top corner. Will Kennon glanced at the printing on it. "Come In and Sit Down. Out on Business. Will Be Back Soon."

"I have one like it at my office in Salisbury."

Hezekiah Balch put the resolutions in his pocket. "That sign," said he, "covers a multitude—"

"Of sins, yes. But come on, Hezekiah. You'll likely be needed down at Joe Nicholson's to pull some devout parishioner out of a beer keg in which he's fallen head first." Waightstill Avery shooed the two out on Tryon Street, pulled the door shut, hung the sign on the knob.

XXI

"WELL, McKNITT, they're still talking war."

"Yes, that's pretty much all you hear nowadays. It looks serious."

"I believe my ownself that there's too much war talk. It's not good for business. The only thing folks want to buy now is powder and flints. O' course, that's stretching it a little, but if it keeps up like it's going, that'll be all they'll want to buy. I tell you this war talk's mighty bad for the merchants."

"I wasn't thinking so much about you merchants, Duncan, as I was about all of us. It looks bad for the whole province, for all the colonies, in fact."

"I tell you, McKnitt, I don't think much of this Continental Congress. Those fellows up in Philadelphia's getting us closer to war every day. That kind of stuff is bound to make the King mad, McKnitt."

"I suppose it is. But I don't think that should be our guide, what the King thinks."

"Well, I hate to cross him. Those folks up in Massachusetts Bay have got themselves in a tight jam, all right, but it was their own doing. I say it's not up to us to get them out or to go do the same way and get our ownselves in the same fix. I believe in going ahead with our own business. We're one province and they're another. So's Virginia and Pennsylvania and the rest of 'em. I don't believe in all this tying up together."

"What are you going to do if the British decide to enforce their demands on us if we don't stand together?"

ALEXANDRIANA

"That's foolish, McKnitt. People are so quick to get scared, get hysterical. The British don't figure on coming over here fighting us. How'd they ever get away down here in these back settlements?"

"They're already in Boston—"

"That's just for policing purposes. They wouldn't have been there if the Boston folks had minded their business. And we're fixing to get right in the same trouble. Look at that Continental Congress last September. All that resoluting and carrying on. It's bound to make the King and the government in London sore at us. And that hurts business. I figure we should stay out of it and not send anybody up there to the next session and—"

"And just crawl in our shells and try to protect our own necks by letting our brothers in Boston and anywhere else where the King threatens them—"

"Call it crawling in our shells if you want, but I call it just good sense, good business."

"I don't see it that way, Duncan Ochiltree. I'm not interested in saving your business of selling calico and buttons while the rest of the country is going to the devil and we are doing nothing to help them. I figure if we want to save our ownselves we'd best organize with them and fight alongside them if it comes to that, God forbid. I'm for sending Hooper and Joe Hewes and Caswell back to Philadelphia and instructing them to work shoulder to shoulder with the other delegates toward protecting us—all of us, I mean—from the aggression of those selfish interests that seem to have the upper hand in Great Britian just now. And you can tell anybody that's my view, Duncan. And now I'd best be going before I say more. Good day, sir." McKnitt Alexander stalked from the store.

At Waightstill Avery's law office he found Tom Polk.

"Damn that fat bastard!" said Waightstill, when McKnitt had recounted to them the conversation he had just had with the merchant. "He'd sell his soul for a shilling, I'll vouch. He's the sort of fellow we got to watch, men. There aren't many of them in Mecklenburg, thank God, but there's some. And we better get

ALEXANDRIANA

our fingers on 'em so we can put them in their places if things start getting hot. Anybody—any patriot, too, I mean—that thinks we can let Boston and Massachusetts Bay go to hell while we sit by and take care of our own little affairs is crazy as the devil. To hell with that argument! I'm for putting an end to that sort of talk wherever it's found. In fact, I'm way ahead of a lot of folks, good Americans too."

"I'm with you, Waightstill. But you're a little indiscreet in talking too openly what we're all beginning to think is the only solution."

"Maybe so, McKnitt. But what I believe, by heavens, I believe. And I don't give a damn who knows it."

"That's all right, Waightstill. But some times it's best not to let your enemy know just what you think."

"You're right, McKnitt. You and Colonel Polk here probably believe about the same thing I do but you've got more sense about talking. That's so. You're right. But I'm beginning to get mad, and it's hard for me to keep my own counsel with things going like they are in Boston. I'm getting ready for action."

"Well, we all are. We've been meeting at Queens Museum and the courthouse and out at Alexandriana and Rural Retreat—all about the county, in fact, and a lot of times—and I don't know but what it wouldn't be a good thing to have a general convention of the county. And that's what I came here to talk about. What do you think about the idea, Waightstill, of giving the job to our friend Polk here to call a convention whenever he thinks the time's right?"

"Why not your ownself, McKnitt?" Colonel Polk asked the question.

"No, McKnitt's right, Colonel. I see his point. You are the colonel of the Mecklenburg militia and you live here in Charlottetown, too. You're the logical man for the job."

"That was the way I felt about it. Waightstill's expressed it exactly."

"How should the delegates to the convention be named? Should everybody who comes constitute the convention? That would be sort of unwieldy and it might not be entirely representative."

"You're right, Colonel," agreed Avery. "How would this do, McKnitt? Let Colonel Polk call the convention and instruct each of the nine militia companies to name a delegate, or two delegates, or whatever number would be agreed upon?"

"I think that would be proper, Waightstill. And now we'll talk this around and you call the meeting when you figure the time comes for it. And I'll get Ephraim Brevard and Preacher Balch busy on drawing up a paper to be presented. How'll that do?"

"First rate, McKnitt, that is, about the paper. And I'll serve if you all want me to. It looks like it's getting to be time when we're going to have to take a stand." Tom Polk picked up his hat. "Boys, I got to be going out to the mill. I left Bill out there looking after things and I'd better go see if anything's happened to him."

A few minutes after Colonel Polk left, Hezekiah Alexander and John Davidson came in.

"Waightstill," said John Davidson, after the greetings had been finished, "Hezekiah here's been telling me about his house out in Sugaw Creek. Sounds like it's going to be a fine place."

"It is, for a fact, John. 'Twon't be anything finer in Mecklenburg than the Rock House. Isn't that right, Landlord?"

Hezekiah laughed. "Waightstill's a little overly enthusiastic, or maybe, being a lawyer, he just likes to do a lot of big talking. It's going to be a good house, I think, though't will be just a plain square house. And it'll have a big wide front door so's Waightstill'll be able to get in on these nights when he's been overly long at Pat Jack's." The men laughed, but Waightstill Avery stood his ground. "Well, it takes a big door for a big man. Were it but for these long stringy Alexanders the cat hole would suffice as a door."

John Davidson slapped Hezekiah Alexander on the back. "Damned if he didn't get you there, Hezekiah. That was good, Waightstill. Some day, boy, you'll make a lawyer. And talking about houses makes me want to get started on my house."

"What's wrong with Rural Retreat, John?"

ALEXANDRIANA

"Well, it's all right. But I built it down at the foot of the hill for a purpose, Hezekiah. I planned all along some day to build myself a fine brick house at the top of the hill from where I could look off to the Catawba and maybe see the houses of my children scattered about over the place. And I've already named it. Violet's agreed, too. We're going to call it Rural Hill."

"That'll be fine, John," said Waightstill. "But when are you going to start?"

"It'll have to wait until after the war."

"The war, John?" Hezekiah set down one of Waightstill's law books he had just picked up. "You think so?"

"It's coming, boys, yes, sir, it's coming. Just as sure—just as sure as that court house sits out there in the crossroads."

"God forbid. But you may be right, John."

"That's the way it looks to me, McKnitt, and that's the way you feel, too, I'm bound."

"I'm afraid you're right."

"I was talking the other day with Ben Patton," John Davidson continued. "I saw him over here at Duncan Ochiltree's store—"

"Damn that tight Scotchman!" interposed Waightstill Avery. "I don't like him. He'll be one of the first to sell us out. Mark my words."

"Well, he does like his shillings. But as I was going to say, I saw Ben Patton at Ochiltree's and Ben gave me a sort of inside view of the way things were at the Provincial Congress over at New Bern. Ben walked over there and back, you know, which shows his interest, I'll vouch. Well, Ben said that although officially they tried to smooth things over with England, on the quiet there wasn't so much smoothing. They expressed their regard for the Constitution and the King but they bore down pretty heavy when they came to the place where they pointed out that the British had no right to tax us when we had no say in it, and they rapped on them pretty rough about closing the Boston port and providing for sending Americans to England for trial of offenses done in this country. Well, none of that will sit so well in England with that Tory crowd that's running things right now."

ALEXANDRIANA

"No, it won't, John. Neither will such things as that affair up at Boston winter before last when those men dressed up like Indians and threw that tea off those ships in the harbor—"

"Nor those women folks at New Bern last October signing that paper backing up the delegates in their resolves and deciding not to use any more tax-paid tea."

"That's right. Everything is heading one way, boys, and unless something happens to put that Tory gang out of power in England they'll be forcing a war on us as sure as we're sitting here."

"That's what we were saying just a little while ago when Tom Polk was in here, John. Tell them what we took it on ourselves to do, Waightstill. Then if you fellows don't like it, we can get it undone. But it struck us as a pretty sensible thing to do."

"Well, McKnitt could just as well go ahead and tell the rest. But this is what we did. We told Colonel Polk to call a convention of representatives of the nine militia companies in Mecklenburg to discuss the situation and possibly take action, and he is to call it when he thinks the time is right."

"That's a good idea, boys. Tom Polk's colonel of the militia and he's here in Charlottetown where the folks generally meet up with each other from time to time. He can sort of gauge things, I reckon, and know when it would be best to have such a meeting. At least, that's my idea. What do you say, Hezekiah? You could take off time from finishing your house—"

"It's as good as finished. And that wouldn't make any difference anyway. I think it's a good idea. And I wouldn't be surprised at hearing almost any time that Tom's called the meeting. Things are beginning to move mighty fast, too fast, I'm afraid, boys, too fast."

"Well, we haven't been fast about getting a drink." Waightstill Avery lifted his hat from the peg on the wall. "I'm not rushing you off, boys, and you can come back with me, but get your hats and let's step down to old Pat Jack's. I'd like to devil him some more, anyway."

XXII

DAVID THREW the rein over the hitching post at the uppin'-block. As he walked toward the house he could hear Venus singing to the baby.

"Where's Uncle Mac, Venus?" he asked, as he stepped inside.

"Lawdy, you scairt me, Mas' Davy. Come steppin' in here all unbeknownst to me. And you done woke up dis baby." She bounced the baby up and down in front of her swelling bosom. "Dey's gone—him and Mis' Jeanie—over to Marse Davidson's to see de new baby."

David stuck out his forefinger toward the baby. "Go 'long wid you, Mas' Davy. I got to git dis baby-child to sleep." The baby clutched Davy's finger in his fat little hand.

"That's the boy, Joe, grab it. That's the way he'll hold a musket, Venus. He'll be a general in the army. General Joseph McKnitt Alexander."

"Go 'long wid you. He aint goin' to be no sojer fer to kill fokes. This here child's goin' to be a doctor; he's goin' to cure fokes o' what ails 'em. Aint you, Honey?" The baby cooed. "See dar, Mas' Davy. He say so his ownself."

"You say they've gone over to Cousin John's to see the baby? Cousin Violet's sure keeping up with Aunt Jeanie, eh, Venus? Fact, she's one ahead, if I haven't lost the count."

"Go 'long from here. Mis' Violet started two years ahead o' Mis' Jeanie. She aint got but six and Mis' Jeanie jes' got five."

"One every two years as regular as the clock ticks—"

"'Taint no sich, Mas' Davy. You well knows yore ownse'f dis

ALEXANDRIANA

here child come 'long four years after little Abigail lackin' five or six months. You was here when they was both fetched."

"Yeh, I was here when they were fetched, all right. And they fetch 'em pretty regular at Alexandriana and Rural Retreat, too."

"Look here, Mas' Davy—" Venus stopped rocking, gave David her most disapproving scowl. "Honey, you oughtn't talk lak dat. Dat's the Lawd's will you makin' fun of. De Lawd sends babies to fokes—"

"Well, I reckon Uncle Mac and Cousin John might have helped the Lord a little, didn't they, Venus?"

Venus set the baby down in her lap, shooed with her fat arms. "Go 'long, Mas' Davy. Gwan 'bout yo' bus'ness. I aint goin' listen to no sech talk. Don't you know de Lawd likely to strike you down daid, Honey?" She picked up little Joe, began singing loudly as she rocked back and forth.

Davy strode through the hallway, out the front door, laughing. At the hitching post he swung into the saddle, turned westward toward Hopewell Church and the Beatty's Ford Road. An hour and a half later he rode through the gates at Rural Retreat.

John Davidson and McKnitt Alexander were sitting under a tree in front of the house. "Tie your horse and come on over, Davy," John Davidson called to him.

David hitched his rein in the ring of the post, loosened the saddle girth. Then he walked over toward the two men. John Davidson stood up, shook hands. "How are you, son? Getting on to the doctoring business pretty well? Know as much about bleeding and blistering as Ephraim Brevard a'ready? And you got a plentiful stock of leeches?"

"No, sir, not that much." David grinned. "Ephraim's a good doctor. And he's always studying the newest things in medicine. But I'm doing all right, I guess. It's sorter hard to get much interested in it right now, though."

"It is for a fact, Davy. Times are looking pretty bad. It's hard for anybody to plan much ahead, a young fellow just starting out, especially, I'm bound."

"That's what I rode over here for. I saw Colonel Polk in Char-

ALEXANDRIANA

lottetown and he told me to tell Uncle Mac—and I figured you ought to know too, so I came right on over—that he had called that meeting of the militia representatives for the nineteenth. He said there was a lot to be done in the meantime."

"Well, so that's that, John." McKnitt Alexander threw down the stick on which he had been whittling, closed his knife, put it in his pocket. "I'm glad you rode on over here, Davy. I'm glad John knows about it today. There's not much time to be lost. Today's the first day of May, isn't it? That's less than three weeks." He turned to face David. "I wonder why he decided to call the convention, son. Did he say?"

"Nothing especially. He talked like the news from the North was getting worse all the time. There's been fighting between the people and the troops at Boston and the Continental Congress is meeting again at Philadelphia pretty soon, next week, I believe he said. Up around Boston the people have organized so that if anything happens they can be called out on a minute's notice. And I reckon Governor Martin's dissolving the Assembly over at New Bern had something to do with it too."

"McKnitt, the war's coming, just like I told you all down there at Waightstill Avery's office the other day. It looks like there's got to be some blood-letting before those thick-headed, selfish Tories that run the government in England learn any sense."

"You may be right, John, God forbid. But in the meantime we've got a lot to do. We ought to have in mind what we want to do when we meet in convention. We ought to have the proper resolutions already framed. If we don't get things lined up ahead of time it's likely to turn into a speech-making affair with everybody giving his views and the meeting agreeing on nothing. That would be bad. We should study the situation carefully, select our course, and follow it straight through."

"Why not start working on some proposed resolutions, McKnitt? You're the man to do the job your ownself."

"No, we should have a committee. It should be studied carefully. It oughtn't to be the work of one man. And then it should probably be changed somewhat after the convention has debated

ALEXANDRIANA

it thoroughly. But I tell you what I'll do. I believe I suggested it the other day. I'll get Ephraim Brevard—he's a scholar and a level-headed fellow besides—and Preacher Balch, who's likewise got plenty of practical sense even if he is little more than a boy, and we'll start drafting something. I'll sort of sit in with them but they can do the drafting. How's that, John?"

"Sounds first rate to me. But there oughtn't be any time lost. And the militia companies will have to meet to name their representatives. How many is each company to have, Davy?"

"Colonel Polk said each militia district would send two."

"That would make eighteen delegates to the convention. Not very many."

"Well, details like that can be worked out later, John."

"Yes, that's a fact. The thing to do now is to get to work on what we should do at the meeting."

McKnitt Alexander stood up, stretched his long legs. "Tomorrow, Davy, you can ride up to Centre Church and notify Ephraim— or is he in Charlottetown this week?"

"He's at home."

"Well, you ride up and tell him to come to Alexandriana day after tomorrow, without fail. Tell him what we're planning. I'll send Jethro over to Poplar Tent to notify Hezekiah Balch."

"Now, we're getting somewhere, McKnitt. What do you suppose will be the nature of those resolutions, the general tone, I mean?"

"I've a notion they'll be pretty strong, stronger than those Rowan resolves they passed last August. In fact, I'm pretty certain the Rowan folks would pass stronger ones now were they to have another meeting."

"That's right, I expect they would. And by the way, we ought to invite Will Kennon over from Salisbury to our meeting. He'd likely be a lot o' help. He was the ramrod of the Rowan committee."

"Yes, we must get word to Will. He's got plenty of sense and plenty of nerve, to boot. We'd better speak to Tom Polk, though, and see what he thinks about it. He'll agree we ought to ask Will, I'll vouch."

XXIII

At THE DOOR Jethro O'Flannagan stopped, pulled the quid of chewed tobacco from his mouth, threw it aside. Then he rolled his tongue around the inside of his mouth, spit over his left shoulder into the thick dust of Trade Street.

"By damn, Bedent," said he to his companion, who pushed through the doorway behind him, "I don't know whether I'd ruther have a shot o' Uncle Pat's toddy or keep my 'bacco." They pushed their way through the milling crowd in the taproom, ranged themselves alongside the bar. "Rustle us up a couple o' them slings o' West Indian rum," he commanded the fat barkeeper confronting him.

"All gone, Jethro."

"All gone? What sort of a damned tavern is this? Why don't you keep stuff in stock as much passin' as they is 'tween here and Charles Town?"

"Too big a crowd in town today. Drunk us out. How 'bout a stiff swig o' stewed wine? Got claret and Madeira in it, and it's good and hot."

"Well, fix us up a couple. We ought to go 'round to Joe Nicholson's though."

"Joe's nigher drunk out than us. He's closer to the court house."

"Is they a big crowd up at the court house? We aint been up there yet."

"They say there aint no place to set down and the crowd's swarming around outside. But I aint been up there neither. Hell, we been so busy I aint had time to scratch." He swung the steaming drinks in front of Jethro. "You can pay me now. They's such a damned bunch in here it's hard to keep up." Jethro set down his drink, pulled from his hunting shirt a small coarse bag drawn together at the end. He fumbled with the rawhide drawstring, pulled the bag open, selected a coin, dropped it on the bar.

"Hell, Jethro, you got money, boy. Where'd you git this half-Joe?"

"Charles Town. And here's some South Ca'lina money if you'd ruther have it, and North Ca'lina proclamation money too."

"I'll take the hard money any day, Jethro. This here half-Joe's all right. Here's yore change." He counted out the shillings and pence, handed them across the bar.

"Bedent, this here stuff's pretty good. Tastes like it mought'a come from Joe Nicholson's." He drained the last swallow, slid the empty mug across the polished board. "Here, fill this here thing up again. Hurry up, Bedent, and git another." Bedent gulped down the hot liquid, shoved his mug toward the barkeeper.

"Jest a drap more. Not too much. This here stuff's pretty stout."

"That's what you need on a day like this, Bedent. Hell, this here's a big day in Mecklenburg. Charlottetown's danged nigh a city today, man. And hit's hot, too. They's nothing calculated to keep a feller cool on a hot day like drinkin' something hot and sweatin' the heat out o' yore hide. That's the way them Chiney-men does."

They finished their stewed wine, turned to push their way through the crowd. A young man across the room threw up his hand. "Hey, Jethro, how you making it, fellow?"

Jethro spotted him. "Hello, George. How you coming on yore ownself?" He recognized Humphrey Hunter seated beside George Graham. "Hello, Hump. Poplar Tent's come to town, eh?" He walked over toward their table.

"How you getting 'long, Jethro?" Humphrey Hunter finished his drink. "Where's David? Did he come down here today?"

"Yeh, he come down with his Uncle McKnitt. You all aint seen him? I guess mebbe he's down burning out his gullet at Joe Nicholson's. Look a-here. What you boys doin' here? If yore

ALEXANDRIANA

mammies knowed you was here swilling Jim Jack's toddy, danged if they wouldn't give you a proper hidin', when they got you home."

"We're growed men, Jethro. Hell, I'm twenty a'ready. Was twenty five days ago past. And George is seventeen."

"Hell, aint neither one o' you dry behint yore ears. You done paid for yore toddy?"

"Paid for this one."

"That's enough fer you. Come on, let's mosey up 'bout the court house and see what's goin' on."

They drained their mugs, got up. "Maybe we'll run into David up that way, George. Let's go 'long with Jethro and Bedent."

Horses switched their tails at hitching-racks along the road up to the court house. "Man, it's a lot o' people in town today," observed Jethro, as they trudged toward the court house at the crossroads. "Danged if this place don't sorter look like Salisbury today."

"Yeh," agreed Humphrey Hunter, "but when they ride back to Hopewell and Poplar Tent and Centre Church and Providence and Steele Creek and Sugaw Creek 'twon't be nothin' left. But look a-here, with all this crowd, we ought to be able to get up a big match o' long-balls."

"It's likely to be enough happenin' at the court house to keep you pretty well entertained, Hump, I've a notion. They goin' to do some pretty straight talkin' to King George, I'm bound."

They pushed their way up the narrow steps that led to the courtroom. "Hit's so many fokes in there I can't see nothin'," said Bedent Spraggins. "I'm goin' to slip back down and set down out there under that tree. Hit's too hot in there, I'm bound."

But Jethro and the two boys squeezed their way just inside the door. Jethro nudged Humphrey Hunter. "Listen to Lawyer Avery. I told you they was goin' to give the King hell today, didn't I?" The three squirmed and pushed until they had gained a place along the back wall from which they could see 'Squire Abraham Alexander presiding over the assembly from the low platform at the opposite end of the room.

In the little cleared place in front of the platform Waightstill Avery was addressing the perspiring convention. By craning their necks and peeking over and around a solid phalanx of coonskin caps and cocked hats held shoulder high to prevent their being crushed, they could occasionally get a look at the earnest flushed face of the young lawyer.

"——can no longer be tolerated," Jethro caught a phrase. "Nor should we stand idly by and permit our brothers in Boston to suffer because of this tyrannical government across the seas." Jethro nudged his elbow into Humphrey's side. *"He's gittin' right, aint he?"*

"Mr. Chairman, we are free men. We came into this wilderness—many of us here came, and the rest are the second generation of those who came—to escape this very evil that is rearing its ugly head in Britain, this Tory serpent that is seeking to stick its fangs into our free life in America. We must not permit it. We must stand behind our brothers in Boston, in Massachusetts Bay. We must not permit these Tories in England, who against the good advice and athwart the will of their own liberal members of Parliament, are attempting to impose a foreign government, a foreign idea of government, upon us free men in America, in Boston, in the Carolinas, in Virginia. Mr. Chairman, I move you, sir, that you name a committee to draw up appropriate resolutions stating in unequivocal terms our views of the situation and our determination not to abide the further wrongs of the Tory element that now has Great Britain under its heel!"

A loud handclapping, accompanied by a nodding of heads in agreement, followed Avery's motion. When it had somewhat subsided, 'Squire Alexander banged his gavel upon the table. "The chair had planned to appoint such a committee, Mr. Avery. In fact, a committee has been working for some time on resolutions to be presented to this convention. But before I name such a committee to make further study of the matter and give a report, I think 'twould be a good idea to have some more discussion."

A stocky bald man raised his hand. "Mr. Chairman, Mr. Chairman!" The chairman saw him, nodded his recognition. "Get quiet, please. Mr. Ochiltree wants to speak." The squat man pushed into the little cleared space. "You all know me. Duncan Ochiltree."

ALEXANDRIANA

He was panting from the exertion of making his way forward. "I want to say a few words. All you men are my friends. I like you all, and I hope you all like me. I aint got no axe to grind. But I want to caution moderation. We mustn't go too far, gentlemen. Now Lawyer Avery here is a fine young man, but he's a young man, and he's got a lot of things to learn. He's full o' fire, which is all right, but old heads should study this thing and we must take our time." He paused for breath, wiped his perspiring forehead with a big handkerchief he had pulled from the tail of his coat. "Yes, sir, men. We don't want to be too rash. We don't want to make the King mad at us nor the Government of England neither. It'll hurt us. It'll hurt business, men. After all, Boston's a long way from Mecklenburg—" Jethro strained forward, his head turned to catch every word. "We aint got no business messing in Boston's affairs. We ought to leave the care o' Boston to the Lord and look after our ownselves. If we tend our own business, we needn't be scared o' the British coming way over here in these backwoods after us. It's a long way, men, from England to us. All that water to cross, and all these long miles after they get to our coast. We're safe, if we stay quiet-like and mind our own knittin'." He paused for breath, wiped his forehead, his red neck. In that instant hands flew up about the room. "Mr. Chairman!" A man a few steps in front of Jethro was trying to get the floor. Another one across the room was calling for recognition. "Mr. Chairman!" Over in the jury box a man in hunting shirt jumped to his feet.

"Just a minute!" The chairman turned to Duncan Ochiltree. "Have you finished?"

"I reckon that's all I want to say."

"It's too much!" A fellow at the back of the room shouted out angrily. "We don't like no such talk!" Heads were nodding approval. A buzz of talk was threatening to swell into a roar of denunciation. But Chairman Alexander banged his gavel. "Quiet, please. Everybody's got a right to his say." He pointed to one of the men who had asked for recognition. "Mr. David Reese has the floor."

ALEXANDRIANA

"I just wanted to say, Mr. Chairman, that I agree heartily with Mr. Avery and I disagree just as heartily with Duncan Ochiltree. I want to say that I don't give a ha'-penny about business when my freedom's being threatened. I want to say that I'm not in favor o' leaving it to the Lord to look after our brother Americans in Boston and elsewhere where they are being oppressed. The Lord has got a lot to do besides that, and I think it's our business to help out the Lord in such matters. And I guess that's 'bout all I want to say." He sat down.

The chairman banged his gavel. "Is that 'bout what you other gentlemen wanted to say?" He looked about the room. They were all nodding. "I thought maybe 'twas. And I want to say that I agree with Mr. Reese, too. But I believe there's been enough discussion and maybe it's time we were getting down to business. I'm going to name that committee and they can retire and draw up resolutions. Then they can come back and report and after that we can discuss the proposed resolutions. That'll give chance for anybody that wants to to have his say. How does that course strike you, Mr. Davidson?"

John Davidson, seated at the right of the platform, nodded. "I think that's a good idea, Mr. Chairman."

"Well, I'm going to appoint to this committee Dr. Ephraim Brevard of Centre Church, Rev. Hezekiah Balch of Poplar Tent, and our good friend from Salisbury, Lawyer Will Kennon. Mr. Kennon is a leading man in Rowan and we're right happy to have the benefit of his counsel here today. You got their names, didn't you, McKnitt? Very well, then, and the committee may now retire and bring in its report when it is ready." The members of the committee filed soberly from the room. "What shall we do now?" asked the chairman.

"Mr. Chairman, I move you we have further discussion. There's much talk going the rounds of declaring strongly in favor of actual independence from England. There's some as favors and some as opposes. We might do well to discuss it."

A man in hunting shirt and leather breeches stood up over in the corner toward Waightstill Avery's law office. "Mr. Chairman,

I'm in favor of the rights o' free men bein' preserved for 'em. I showed I was in favor of it. I'm one o' those who fit agin Tryon at Alamance Creek. And you all know what happened. You all know that Tryon he sent Waddell over into these settlements and made us swear an oath to uphold the King and the royal government in Carolina. Well, I took that oath and there's others in this room who took it. We aim to stand by our oaths, Mr. Chairman. We daren't swear to an oath before God and then go back on it. And I ask you, Mr. Chairman, how can we declare ourselves agin the rule o' the King, whether we like it or not, after we took that oath? I ask you that, Mr. Chairman."

Many persons in the hall had been asking themselves that same question, Jethro knew. That oath sworn to after the battle at Alamance had been forced upon them, he knew, but it had been taken, nevertheless. And an oath is an oath.

In the room now there was subdued talking, the wagging of many heads. Jethro could see McKnitt Alexander seated at the table in front of the platform. He was the convention secretary. He had been scribbling notes. But now he had laid down his pen. He was looking out the window, down along dusty Trade Street toward Pat Jack's tavern. And his face was serious.

Another man had taken the floor. "Mr. Chairman, our neighbor's right. We took that oath. We swore to support the King, to defend him, to uphold his reign in this Province. We cannot go back on that oath. To do so would endanger us to worse than the King. It would endanger us to hell fire itself. We cannot, however much we may wish to, declare ourselves free of the shackles that bind us to King George and Great Britain. We cannot—"

"Mr. Chairman!" A man had arisen near the window that gave a view along the other side of Trade Street that straggled down the little slope crowned by the courthouse itself. 'Squire Alexander, turning toward the man who had been speaking, saw he had sat down. He recognized the man who had called to him.

"Mr. Chairman, these gentlemen are right. We did take that oath. I took it, even though it was forced on me. And I have kept it. But these good men have forgot one thing, and one most important thing. We took an oath to uphold King George and the King's government in this Province. That's right. But the conditions under which we took that oath no longer apply. That oath applied so long as the King and the government in Carolina gave us protection. Now that protection has been withdrawn, and that nullifies our oath. That absolves us from it. Do you understand, men? The King has sent his soldiers to enslave our brothers in Boston. There has been bloodshed in that city. The soldiers have assaulted free and law-abiding citizens. There is no royal protection in Boston this minute. There is none in these colonies. The King has chosen to turn upon us, to assault us rather than protect us. Our oath did not contemplate our upholding a King who was assailing us. It was binding only as long as he gave us royal protection and support. Don't you see, men, it is a mutual thing—it's like—" He paused. The stuffy, hot little courtroom was still. Earnest faces focused upon his. "It's like—" The speaker now was looking out the window at his left. Suddenly his face lighted up. He pointed with lean brown forefinger. "Look, Mr. Chairman, and gentlemen, it's like this. See that oak tree out there? It's full of green leaves. This is May. Today we take an oath. It is a serious, solemn obligation. We swear with our hands upon the Holy Scriptures to uphold this oath—to uphold this oath, Mr. Chairman, as long as the leaves stay upon that oak tree. Do you see now? Today and tomorrow and through June and July and August and September that oath holds us. We cannot deny it, we cannot default. But when the wintry blasts of winter come and the leaves fall from that oak tree, what then, Mr. Chairman? Then we are absolved of our oaths. We become free men again. We are no longer bound by God or man."

From his place in the rear of the room Jethro could see heads nodding approval. The mumble of low voices was attaining volume. "He's right!" A man in the far corner, ignoring parliamentary procedure, waved his coonskin cap, shouting. "He's right, men. That oath is dead. The King he killed it his ownself!"

"Mr. Chairman—." The man who had arisen was the same man who had reminded the convention of the oath many of the

ALEXANDRIANA

delegates had taken after the Regulators' battle. 'Squire Alexander with a nod recognized him.

"Mr. Chairman, I thank my neighbor for what he has said. He is everlastingly right, men. He has made me see the light, too, I took that oath. Many of us took it. And we kept it. We kept it long after the conditions under which it was taken had ceased to be in effect. It is just as if we kept it until death. He's right. The oath is dead because the conditions under which we took it, the provisions of that oath, we might say, no longer exist. Gentlemen of Mecklenburg, we are free agents again. We are free to do today what our judgment and our conscience dictate. I most sincerely thank my neighbor for this great load of doubt he has lifted from my shoulders." He sat down.

In the rear of the room another man was waving for the chairman's recognition. "Mr. Chairman," he shouted, when 'Squire Alexander had given him the floor, "I think we should send somebody to our committee to instruct them about what has just been said, and I think we ought to instruct them to write up articles declaring ourselves a free country, and I think—" But his voice was drowned out in a swelling chorus of cheering and stamping.

"I might tell the delegate," declared Chairman Alexander, when his vigorous gavel-pounding had restored quiet, "that Dr. Brevard and Reverend Mr. Balch have been working on resolutions for the last several weeks and I'm of the opinion Mr. Kennon will be of the same mind about the set they'll bring in, which I'm pretty sure will be powerful strong words."

"Well, sir, Mr. Chairman—" The delegate was still on his feet. "I think, sir, that the time has passed for any more attempts at reconciliation with England. That seems to be what the Continental Congress is trying to do. But I think there's no need trying any longer. The bunch that's in control in England is determined to make slaves of us. They aint willing to compromise. And I for one, Mr. Chairman, aint willing to be nobody's slave. I aint willing—" He paused, for there was a commotion at the door, and the delegates, packed in their seats, were twisting about to learn the cause.

ALEXANDRIANA

A young man, holding aloft a paper, was pushing his way forward. Behind him a crowd was surging up the high narrow steps and shoving through the doorway. "Let 'im through! Let 'im through!" the crowd in the rear was yelling.

'Squire Alexander stood up, banged with his gavel. "Please make way for him. Make way. Let him through. Step right over here, sir."

The paper still held high, he pushed into the little opening immediately in front of the platform. "The chair recognizes Mr. Barksdale!"

"Mr. Chairman, I'm not a delegate to this convention and I ask your pardon for rushing into this meeting. But I have here a message that I thought should be placed before you in all haste." He turned to face the delegates. McKnitt Alexander at the secretary's table was staring at him. So was John Davidson. So were all the men in the courtroom, for now a dead calm had fallen upon the house. "Shall I go ahead, sir—" He turned to the chairman, "or shall I give this paper to the secretary to be read?"

"Go ahead, David, go right ahead."

"Well sir—" He turned to face the delegates again, "an express has just fetched this hand-bill. He would have borne it himself to you, but he was dog-tired and they have taken him off to Jack's Tavern for refreshment and rest. He asked me to bring it to you. It has come swiftly south from Massachusetts Bay. Relays have spread the news over the provinces. Southward to New York and Philadelphia and Annapolis, over the Potomac at Mount Vernon, through Williamsburg to New Bern and Wilmington, into the western settlements—"

"Read it! Read it! Let's hear it!"

"Just a minute. This message left Lexington in Massachusetts just one month ago today—April 19. It has traveled with unbelievable speed. And now I'll read it."

The delegates strained forward in their seats, many hands cupped to ears. David began reading: "This day the blood of Americans has been spilt in defense of their homes and their freedom. On the common at Lexington the British soldiery has slain inoffensive citizens who sought only the protection of themselves and their families, their liberties and their honor." He read on, as the hand-bill described the fight at Lexington, the battle by the little bridge at Concord, the determined, deadly chase by the minute-men as they pursued the British retreating toward Boston.

The delegates were talking now in low tones. Feet shuffled on the rough boards of the floor. "That's enough!" shouted a man in a hunting shirt, as he raised his coonskin cap high in clenched fist. "We've heared enough readin.' I'm ready for actin'!"

The chairman banged his gavel. "Let him proceed."

"There isn't much more, Mr. Chairman," said David. He turned again to the paper: "Friends of liberty everywhere, Americans all! We conjure you by all that is dear, by all that is sacred; we beg and entreat, as you will answer it to your consciences, to your country, to your hearts, above all, to God Himself, that you will hasten and encourage by all means possible the enlistment of men to form an army to fight for freedom, and that you send them forward with all expedition. The war is on, citizens of America. The die has been cast! Let us stand together, let us fight like freemen to protect our liberties!"

He concluded, handed the paper to the chairman. There was a momentary silence. A man jumped to his feet. Another, another. They were popping up all over the courtroom.

"Mr. Chairman!"

"Mr. Chairman!"

"Mr. Chairman!"

'Squire Alexander recognized a man at his right. The others stayed on their feet. "Mr. Chairman, I move you, sir, that we recall our commmittee, inform them of what we have just received by express from Massachusetts, and instruct the committee to listen to further discussion—if there is any desire for it—before going any further with their report."

"Mr. Chairman, I second that motion!"

A squat bald man jumped to his feet. "I protest, Mr. Chairman. I don't think we should be stampeded into going to war—"

"There's a motion before the house, Mr. Ochiltree."

"—getting our ownselves involved. It'll hurt us, I tell you. We're sorry the British soldiers killed those folks up in Massachusetts. But that's not our business, after all, that's not—"

"Throw 'im out! Throw 'im out! The damned fat British-lovin' bastard!"

Chairman Alexander whanged on the table. "We must have order! There's a motion before the house, Mr. Ochiltree. You're out of order, sir."

"He's worse'n out o' order!" Jethro could restrain himself no longer. "He's goin' to be out o' his pants and in a nice suit o' tar and feathers if'n he don't shet his damned mouth!"

The crowd roared its approval. The chairman banged his gavel again. "We must conduct this convention in good order." He waited until calm had been restored. "Now you have heard the motion just made by Mr. Mathew McClure. So many as favor the motion say 'aye'." Thunderous approval greeted his putting the motion. "And so many as oppose say 'no'."

All eyes were now upon Duncan Ochiltree. But, his cheeks flaming, he kept his silence.

"The committee will be recalled. But before we do that, gentlemen, I think we should recess a while. We've been in here a long time, and it's mighty hot. I'm tired myself and I know you all are. And it's getting late, too. We'll recess to get ourselves refreshed and we'll come back after a bit. We've got a lot of business ahead of us. And I want to caution you that when the crier calls for you you should come back to the court house at once." He picked up his gavel, smiled. "I've a notion the taprooms at Pat Jack's and Joe Nicholson's are already full up. And now this convention stands recessed." He banged the gavel.

XXIV

"Is THE COMMITTEE ready to report?"
"The committee's ready, Mr. Chairman." Hezekiah Balch handed a document to John McKnitt Alexander. He turned to face the chairman again. "May I say just this word for the committee, sir?" The young minister's face was drawn and haggard, his light brown hair clung in damp ringlets about his ears, stuck to his forehead. But from his clear eyes the fire still blazed.

"Go ahead, Mr. Balch, this convention is alway happy to hear anything you might wish to say."

"Thank you, sir." He turned to face the delegates. "Gentlemen of the militia districts of Mecklenburg: Your committee has worked long and faithfully in the preparation of the document the secretary will shortly read to you. For some weeks before this convention assembled yesterday Dr. Brevard and I, with the able counsel of Mr. McKnitt Alexander, your secretary here, and other leading men of our settlement, have been working on the preparation of a tentative document for your consideration. We have had since the beginning of the committee's official work the strong and patriotic counsel and aid of Mr. Kennon of Salisbury." He pulled a handkerchief from his coat pocket, wiped his forehead and ran it around inside his wilting stock. When he resumed speaking it was with a new intensity. "Gentlemen, the document you will hear read to you in a moment is couched in strong words, in understandable, clear words, words that will permit of no misinterpretation. We caution you, gentlemen, the moment this document is made known, the moment the tidings of its passage—in

ALEXANDRIANA

event you adopt it—are made known in these colonies, the eyes of America, aye, the eyes of Great Britain will be upon us." He paused. "We have worked hard to make it as we thought you would want it. We have prayed for divine guidance. We think it a good and proper paper. We ask you to give it your approval." He sat down.

"The secretary of the convention will now read the resolutions."

John McKnitt Alexander cleared his throat, arose, held the paper so that the light from the candles was full upon it. "Resolved, first. That whoever directly or indirectly abets, or in any way, form or manner, countenances the unchartered and dangerous invasion of our rights, as claimed by Great Britain, is an enemy to this country, to America, and to the inherent and inalienable rights of man.

" 'Resolved, second. That we, the citizens of Mecklenburg county do hereby dissolve the political bands which have connected us to the mother country, and hereby absolve ourselves from all allegiance to the British Crown and—"

His reading was drowned in a tumult of yelling, scraping of feet, handclapping, raucous shouting. About the room men were throwing up their hats, their coonskin caps. Those standing up about the walls stamped their feet. The chairman was wielding his gavel viciously. "Order! Order! The house must come to order!" Now the noise, the shouting, the stamping of feet began to subside. "Let us hear the resolutions before we evidence our feelings. Get quiet, please."

McKnitt Alexander raised the paper, resumed his reading. " 'That we, the citizens of Mecklenburg county, do hereby dissolve the political bands which have connected us to the mother country, and hereby absolve ourselves from all allegiance to the British Crown and abjure all political connection, contract, or association, with that nation, who have wantonly trampled on our rights and liberties, and inhumanly shed the blood of American patriots at Lexington.

" 'Resolved, third. That we do hereby declare ourselves a free and independent people—" A man in a homespun suit in the rear

ALEXANDRIANA

of the room clapped his big hands together. "Amen! That's it! We're through with England and old George!" It was the signal for another burst of shouting, stamping of feet. David Barksdale, standing at one of the windows that opened on Trade Street toward Jack's tavern, saw that the shouting had brought the throng still congregated outside running toward the courthouse.

"What's up?" a man yelled to him. "What they doin'?"

David stuck his head out the window. "Reading a resolution calling for independence from England."

"Hooray! Give 'em hell!" The man grabbed off his cap, threw it high into the air, caught it as it sailed down into the light from the window, the tail streaming behind.

Again 'Squire Alexander restored order.

"Proceed, Mr. Secretary."

" 'That we do hereby declare ourselves a free and independent people; are, and of right ought to be a sovereign and self-governing association, under the control of no power other than that of God and the general government of the Congress; to the maintenance of which independence we solemnly pledge to each other our mutual co-operation, our lives, our fortunes and our most sacred honor.

" 'Resolved, fourth. That as we acknowledge the existence and control of no law, or legal officer, civil or military, within this county, we do hereby ordain and adopt, as a rule of life, all, each, and every one of our former laws; wherein, nevertheless, the crown of Great Britain can never be considered as holding rights, privileges, immunities, or authority therein."

He paused, cleared his throat again.

" 'Resolved, fifth. That it is also further decreed that all, each, and every military officer in this county is hereby retained in his former command and authority, he acting conformably to these regulations. And that every member present of this delegation shall henceforth be a civil officer, viz., a justice of the peace, in the character of a committeeman, to issue process, hear and determine all matters of controversy, according to said adopted laws; and to preserve peace, union and harmony in said county; and to use every exertion to spread the love of country, and fire of freedom throughout America, until a more general and organized government be established in this Province."

He stopped. "That is the end of the resolutions, Mr. Chairman. I move their adoption by this convention. I do so with the full recognition of the solemnity of such action."

The delegates, a moment ago jubilant, wild, unrestrained in their enthusiasm, were now silent. The chairman, looking upon them from his place on the platform as the light from the candles flickered in their faces, observed the quick change, the deadly seriousness of their expressions. "This is indeed a momentous decision, gentlemen, you are about to be called upon to make. Is there any discussion before I put to you the motion?"

Not a man stirred. For a moment a silence had dropped upon the assembly. Only the noises of the crowd outside disturbed the deep sudden quiet.

"Question." John Davidson sat upright.

"Question." From across the room another delegate spoke.

"Question." Over the assemblage ran a chorus.

The chairman arose. "Gentlemen, you have heard the motion. Are you ready for the question?"

"Question. Question."

"Question."

"Very well, are you all agreed?" Silence again. "So many of you as favor the motion will say 'aye.'"

One long, deep, throaty "Aye!" swelled to the ceiling.

"So many as are opposed will say 'no.'" No person spoke.

Rev. Hezekiah Balch, his eyes blazing, stood up. "Mr. Chairman," he said, when he had been recognized, "for the committee and for myself I thank you for the adoption of the resolutions." He paused. Every man was looking upon the intent, serious face of the young minister. They saw a tear well in his eye, overflow, run down his cheek. With a flick of his hand he brushed it away. A sudden bright smile flooded his face, shone out through the mist in his eyes. "Gentlemen, you see tears in my eyes. They are not tears of fear, let me assure you, though we have just done a fearful thing; they are not tears of sorrow, though our deed today may bring us and all our loved ones into the deepest shadows of the valley of sorrow. No, they are tears of pure joy. Though I live a thousand years, men of Mecklenburg, I shall never experience a more thrilling moment than your action has just given me. I am weeping, indeed, with joy. Something has struck the deep down fountains within me and they must overflow." He paused again, But not a man moved. "I wonder if you realize what you have done today, this moment, this tremendous moment in our destiny. I am sure we have all caught some sort of a vision, have seen from afar off a distant gleam. For me it has been a glorious vision, a vision that has stirred and shaken me, a vision that for but a moment's seeing has repaid me countless times over for the work I have done on this document we have just given to history.

"Mr. Chairman and gentlemen, do you realize that here in this little backwoods courthouse in this far away settlement, under the kind ministration of rough knotted hands, the hands, if you please, of pioneer men beneath whose coarse hunting shirts beat warm kindly hearts, has just been born a new nation? Do you realize that here in this small room almost at the beginning hour of this twentieth day of May you have delivered an infant whose life, God grant, may extend long past our going into the dim remote days of the unheralded future? Mark you well this day, gentlemen. It shall be a bright day on the calendar of the ages." He stopped again. Little beads of perspiration running together on his forehead coursed down his temples, clotted in the warm wet hair curling above his flushed cheeks. And not a man stirred.

"You may call me a sentimentalist, my friends. Perhaps I am. Perhaps I am given to seeing visions. But this day I have been profoundly stirred. I have seen visions, indeed. Two visions. The first is sunk in the deep wells of doubt, despair, death. Slowly to the beat of muffled drums we mount the steep steps of the scaffold, we men of Mecklenburg. Strangling in the noose, we pay the price of our folly and our lack of faith. We die the death of the revolutionist who ventured one step but having ventured lost his courage." He had spoken quietly, with deadly calm.

ALEXANDRIANA

But now over the face of the young pastor of Poplar Tent spread anew the warm brightness of a smile that transfigured him. And the new fire in his eyes flashed out intense and burning through the film of waters coming up from deep within him. "But there is another vision, my friends. It is a vision whose utter magnitude may startle you. Perhaps it is but the vain foolish visioning of youth. But I think not. I see this new nation, this infant nation born here a moment ago, moving with childish faltering steps through the dark woods and the deep waters toward the doom that seems to await. But as it moves it grows stronger, its steps attain purpose and direction and vigor. It turns aside from the doom ahead and moves onward to a new and glorious destiny. In a word, Mr. Chairman, I see the enemies of freedom, the strong mad foes of democracy and the rights of the individual man, I see them maddened to a new fury by the action taken here today. I see a new assault upon America, upon our ideals, our beliefs, upon our very shores. And for a time, gentlemen, these enemies will be successful. Despair may seize upon us, but we must overthrow despair. We shall have to fight for our liberties, I doubt not. And we shall see our brothers slain, our homes desolated. But we must fight on. We must fight and fight yet again.

"I see a new day, gentlemen, and a new world. Out from this little courthouse will go the message of freedom. Today, gentlemen, we are free. We are the first in all this broad America to be free. We have thrown off the yoke. We shall fight and we shall die ere that yoke is shackled again around our necks. Our action shall inspire our brothers. Along this seaboard and back into these remote settlements will penetrate this message of freedom. Up and down this land, this scattered, divided land we shall see and see shortly a great fusing, gentlemen, a fusing of ideas and ideals, a fusing of good red blood. The blood of our brothers in Boston will be mixed and fused with the blood we are yet to shed, the blood of our brothers in New York and Virginia and Georgia and South Carolina shall run red with our own blood.

"But in the end, my friends, if we keep the faith, if we keep our courage, if we keep steadfast our claim upon our Father's care—

in the end, we shall conquer, and out from the walls of this little house will have come a mighty nation whose course will shape gloriously the destiny of our earth."

He sat down at the secretary's table. In all the room not a man stirred. McKnitt Alexander, facing the delegates, saw through tears washing his own eyes streams of tears flowing unashamed down the bronzed cheeks and wiry beards of the men out there in front. He reached across to pat the young preacher's knee. "God bless you, my boy. God bless you. God bless you." Hezekiah Balch gripped the hand on his knee.

"Jethro, you're cryin'." The man standing beside Jethro O'Flannagan was dumbfounded. "I aint never seen you cryin' before, man."

"Hell, man, you aint never heard no speech like that before neither. Damn you, you ought to be cryin' yore ownself. That boy there—he's the finest damned preacher I ever set under. How'n the hell—" Jethro was whispering, but they could hear him back there in the rear corner where he stood in the center of a mass of sweating men—"could a feller help from cryin' at a damn fine speech like that boy just put up?"

'Squire Alexander had arisen. "I can add nothing to that, my friends. We have been powerfully touched. I can say nothing more except to thank God for such young men as our friend here. And now, gentlemen, we have adopted the resolutions. I think it proper that it should be read to the concourse of people on the outside. If I hear no objection, I shall appoint Colonel Polk to read the resolutions from the courthouse steps, and I'll ask the crier to go out and announce it. I'd suggest that we take a recess and all go out and get a little fresh air. It's mighty hot in here."

Waightstill Avery arose. "Mr. Chairman, it is getting late. We have been in this room a great while. There is much yet to be done by this convention. And although there are quite a number of the faithful of Mecklenburg still outside, others have long since sought their slumber. I move, therefore, Mr. Chairman, that the reading of the resolutions to the people be deferred until noon. I believe that would give opportunity for a great many more persons to

ALEXANDRIANA

hear them read. And it would give us an opportunity to obtain sorely needed refreshment and sleep."

"Lawyer Avery's right, Mr. Chairman." Richard Harris of Poplar Tent stood up. The light from the candles on the secretary's table played on his tired face. "We're all wearied. We ought to recess a while and get some sleep. I second the motion."

The chairman put the motion. It passed without opposition.

"But before we leave, Mr. Chairman—" Ephraim Brevard, seated near John McKnitt Alexander, stood up and faced 'Squire Alexander, "we should sign the resolutions."

"That's right, Mr. Brevard. The secretary will call the names of the delegates and as each is called let him come forward to the table and sign. Do you have ink and quills ready, McKnitt?"

"Yes, sir."

"The secretary will proceed to call the names."

"The chairman of the convention, Abraham Alexander."

'Squire Alexander stepped down from the platform, picked up the quill, dipped it into the ink, signed in meticulous strokes.

"I suppose the secretaries come next. Ephraim Brevard."

"I'm just your assistant. You sign next. I'll follow you."

McKnitt Alexander in bold strokes wrote his full name. He handed the pen to Brevard, who signed.

"Rev. Hezekiah J. Balch."

The young minister, who had been sitting quietly facing the delegates, added with a flourish his signature.

"John Phifer." Out in the center of the hall the Rocky River man stood up, pushed his way forward toward the table.

"James Harris."

"William Kennon." The Salisbury lawyer moved out behind Harris.

"John Foard."

"Richard Barry."

"Henry Downes." The procession was moving out and back as the men added their signatures.

"Ezra Alexander."

"William Graham."

ALEXANDRIANA

"John Queary."

"Hezekiah Alexander." From his place near one of the windows on the left McKnitt's brother fell in behind the others.

"Adam Alexander."

"Charles Alexander."

"It's a damned sight o' Alexanders in this bunch, aint it?" Jethro whispered to the man beside him. "Thick as 'possums on a dead hoss."

"Zaccheus Wilson."

"Waightstill Avery."

"I bet you Lawyer Avery'd give a half-Joe for a good drink," suggested Jethro. "He's been here 'bout all day and night, and I bet he's drier'n hell. Fact, I am my ownself."

"Benjamin Patton." The secretary was still calling the delegates.

"Well, if'n you're so dry why don't you go git yoreself a nip? You aint no delegate. You don't have to stay here."

"I don't want to miss nothin'."

"Matthew McClure."

"Neill Morrison."

"Robert Irwin."

"John Flenniken."

The men were moving forward, signing their names, shuffling back to their seats.

"Duncan Ochiltree."

The men moving forward to sign hesitated, turned to watch the merchant. The eyes of everybody in the little room suddenly were upon him. He leaned forward, as if to arise, sat back momentarily, then scrambled to his feet, pushed out into the aisle. "Sure, I'll sign it," said he, and his low voice indicated he was talking more to himself than to those about him, "though I'll probably hang for it."

"David Reese."

"John Davidson." The squire of Rural Retreat stepped forward, waited as those ahead signed.

"Richard Harris."

"Thomas Polk."

ALEXANDRIANA

"Gentlemen of the convention—" Chairman Abraham Alexander arose. "I am sure we all realize what we have just done. This is but the beginning. Let us look to Divine Providence to see us through to the end. And now this convention stands recessed until noon, when we shall reassemble to hear the public reading of the resolutions by Colonel Polk and complete the business of this body."

He banged down the gavel.

XXV

NEVER HAD a game of long-balls or even a gander-pulling brought together so many of the young blades, the beaus and belles, the older folks, even the children of Mecklenburg.

They filled the intersection in front of the courthouse. From Hopewell and Centre Church, from Poplar Tent and Rocky River and Sugaw Creek, from Providence and Steele Creek, from every one of the two dozen or so houses in Charlottetown, they had converged at the courthouse. And when Colonel Polk finished reading the declaration from the high steps, they shouted and yelled their approval, clapped their hands, threw their hats and coonskin caps into the air.

"Look a-yonder!" Susan Barnett pointed toward the courthouse George Smart, who had had eyes only for her while the Colonel had been reading, looked. "See, that man threw his hat up so high it lodged on the courthouse. However will he get it down?"

"He'll more'n likely have to lay a ladder up 'side the wall, I reckon. Serves him right anyhow."

George Smart sidled over to the girl. "Look a-here, Honey, this is a big day. It would be a good time—"

"Silly boy. Not now. It's too much excitement. I could never stand all that in one day. Besides—" she spoke lower, for her parents were only a few paces away. "Mother and Papa don't think I'm old enough."

"You're already fourteen past, Honey. You're started on being an old maid a'ready. If'n you don't hurry up and—"

"Hello, George, still hangin' 'round, Susan, eh!" A big man coming up from down along Trade Street slapped George Smart on the back. "Well, can't say that I blame you, boy. But Susan now, I don't know about her taste, eh?"

"Oh, hello, Cap'n Jack. Didn't know you were anywhere 'round. It's so many people here. I was jest tellin' Susan she couldn't do any better in this whole crowd. How 'bout it, Cap'n?"

Captain Jim Jack laughed. "She could do worse in this same crowd, all right, George, that's a fact."

John Barnett turned around at the sound of the Captain's voice. "Hello, Jim, how're you? Big crowd, aint it?"

"It's a big day, John. Mecklenburg's done challenged England. That's a pretty big day, I'd say." He spotted Mrs. Barnett. "Hello, Ann, how are you? You're looking mighty good to be standing around in all this crowd with old John here. Old man Tom Spratt's daughter is still the best looking woman 'round here, I'm bound, aint she, John?"

"Go 'long with you, Jim Jack. How's Margaret? I've seen Charity and Lillis but not your wife."

"I told Margaret to come on up here, Ann, but she wouldn't do it. She's stopped going out much. Can't much blame her. She's big as a barrel. She's figuring on being down by September."

Susan, who had been listening, blushed, turned away. "Look a-yonder, George, that man is trying to climb up the side o' the house to get his hat."

"Yeh, and he'll like as not break his neck."

As the delegates returned to their deliberations inside the courtroom the throng outside began to disperse. Soon the taprooms at Joe Nicholson's and Jack's were filled. On the commons down in front of the courthouse children had begun to play, and here and there in groups under the trees the women had paused to exchange the community gossip.

Inside Waightstill Avery was addressing the delegates. "We have declared ourselves independent of England, Mr. Chairman and gentlemen. The fourth and fifth articles attempt to provide for the carrying on of the affairs of the county by the adoption

ALEXANDRIANA

of the laws of Great Britain as our own and the retaining of military officers in their commands and authority, along with the constitution of each of the delegates here as a justice of the peace to handle civil matters." He paused to wipe with his handkerchief his perspiring forehead.

"But that isn't enough, Mr. Chairman. We've got to do more. We don't know what is ahead. There may be war. Do you think that the King will do nothing to prevent us from maintaining the freedom we have this day declared? I for one do not think he will permit this action to go unchallenged. For that reason and to provide in some degree for the exigencies of this county in this alarming time, I think we should name a committee to draw up a specific plan of government under which we will be able to work for the maintenance of our freedom, and I do not think we should long delay such action."

"What do you propose? Will you make a motion on it?"

"Yes, sir, Mr. Chairman. I move you, sir, that such a committee be named and that we meet again—say within two weeks—I move that we meet again May 31 to hear the committee's report."

The motion was carried by acclamation. "I appoint Dr. Brevard chairman and instruct him to obtain to aid him in drawing up the document any persons he may desire."

"There is another thing that we should attend to before we adjourn," John Davidson reminded the chairman. "I think that we should dispatch an express to the Continental Congress at Philadelphia apprising our representatives in that body of the action we have taken in Mecklenburg."

"I agree, sir. What do the delegates think of Mr. Davidson's proposal."

"It's the thing to do, Mr. Chairman," said a man in the rear. "Maybe it'll snap them fellers up there in Philadelphy up a little."

"Whom shall we send with the message?"

"Cap'n Jack's the man if he can go." There was a general nodding of heads in agreement.

Captain Jack was sent for, informed of the mission proposed for him, and agreed to go. And the convention adjourned.

ALEXANDRIANA

The shadows were pushing out from the courthouse toward Waightstill Avery's office when John McKnitt Alexander, David and Jethro swung into their saddles for the long ride up the Great Road to Alexandriana. Ephraim Brevard, starting the twenty-five miles to his home at Centre Church, rode down Trade Street with them, past Jack's Tavern, out into the country.

"You look mighty tired, Ephraim." McKnitt pulled up beside the doctor. "You'll spend the night and tomorrow at Alexandriana."

"I am tired, McKnitt. We've had a full two days."

"Yes, and I've a notion there are fuller days ahead of us."

"You're right, McKnitt, I'll vouch. And sometimes I wonder—I wonder if we can see 'em through. There'll be days of work and toil, days of trouble and deep gloom and much pain."

"But they'll be great days, Ephraim—soul-stirring days."

David, riding a few paces behind, said nothing. And for Jethro the attempt to talk would have been too difficult, for he had just inserted between his jaws half a twist of tobacco.

XXVI

THE NEGRO tapped David lightly on the shoulder. " 'Scuse me, Mas' David," he said, apologetically, when David turned to face him, "but it's a lady back there said tell you to step over there where she's at." He pointed toward a small room partitioned off from the taproom at the rear.

"A lady? Who is she, Solomon?" David set down his mug.

"I don't know who she be, Mas' David. I aint never seed her befo'. She's a powerful fine lookin' lady, though; looks like the quality."

David gulped down the remainder of his drink, wiped his lips. "I wonder who in the world—Much obliged, Solomon."

He walked across the room, pushed open the door that stood ajar, stepped across the threshold. He stopped.

"David!" She dropped her fork, gulped down the food she had been chewing. With her doily she dabbed at her lips.

"Belinda, I'm bound!" He walked across, took her extended hand, bent low and kissed it. "However in the world do you happen to be at Jack's Tavern?"

"On my way to Camden, David. My, but you're a man now, indeed!"

"I suppose I should be." He laughed. "It's been a long time since you've seen me and the last time you saw me you said I was well growed. And you're married since then, too. Where's your husband?"

"He's not with me. I'm traveling with father. But do sit down, David, and tell me about yourself."

ALEXANDRIANA

"There's little to say." David sat down. "And I'd much prefer to talk about your ownself."

"There's certainly nothing interesting about me. I'm—I've settled into obscurity."

"That's not what I understood. I wouldn't think being the mistress of a great estate like Pleasant Grove would mean settling into obscurity."

"That's what Lovelace was telling you. She told me about your visit down there. She could talk of nothing else for weeks."

"How is she? When have you seen her?"

"I saw her two or three weeks ago. She was fine, and as pretty as a picture."

"Not married yet?"

"No. And I fancy you know why, David." He thought he saw something—he couldn't explain just what—in the flash of her eyes as she said it. Could it be a bit—just a touch—of jealousy? He wondered. And he hoped it could.

"It's been a long time since I was down at Cross Creek. A lot has happened since then. I didn't know but what she had followed your lead."

"Well, she hasn't. And I hope she—" Belinda stopped, her sentence unfinished.

"You hope she won't? Why wouldn't you want her to get married?"

"Oh, I didn't mean that. You said maybe she had followed my lead—" She broke off with a sudden sharp little laugh. "Oh, I don't know what I was trying to say. It was nothing anyway."

"How's Angus?"

"He's very well, I suppose. And he's a long, long way off. I presume he's all right. He was the last time I saw him."

"You don't mean—"

"Oh, yes, I'm still living with him, if that's what you mean."

"Still?"

"And I suppose I'll keep on. I'm not planning to divorce him, if that's what you're maybe thinking."

"I wasn't trying to pick you. I'm sorry. I—"

ALEXANDRIANA

"It's all right, David. It's no secret in the Cape Fear country that Angus and I are not especially happy with each other. But I'm not blaming him; I reckon it's as much my fault as his. We were married too young perhaps, certainly before we knew each other well. And we're interested in different things. There's little of mutual interest we share. But I didn't call you in here for sympathy. I heard you talking out there at the bar. I couldn't resist seeing you again."

"I'd never have forgiven you if hadn't called me. But where's your father? I presume he's already eaten." He pointed to the soiled dishes and silver across from her.

"Yes, he was very tired. We rode all the way today from Torrence's Tavern at Centre Church and—"

"And you came right by Alexandriana and didn't stop?"

"Yes, we did stop. But only the children and some of the Negroes were there. They said Mr. Alexander had come to Charlottetown and Mistress Alexander had gone over to the Davidsons."

"And did you ask about me?"

Belinda looked up at him from beneath long dark lashes. "Of course, I did, David. They said you were down here too. And I ate my dinner ever so slowly in the hope that you might come in. And you did and—" she stopped. "And here we are."

"And—" David took up her words. "And Angus is a long, long way off." But his laugh was unaffected.

"I wasn't thinking of Angus."

"I was just trying to be clever."

She ignored the reply. "David, would you order us a drink, and couldn't we sit here a while longer and talk? Or must you be going?"

"Of course." He tapped lightly on the table with the handle of a knife. "And I have nothing to do and no reason to leave. I could stay all night."

She laughed. "I wouldn't ask you to stay all night."

"That would be perhaps—well, irregular."

"Yes, I should think so. But it will be all right to sit here, won't it? We won't disturb anybody?"

ALEXANDRIANA

"We could shut the door if you—"

"No, no, David, we mustn't—I wouldn't want—we mustn't close the door."

The Negro appeared in the doorway. David ordered the drinks. In a minute Solomon returned with them. She tasted hers. "It's good," she said. "I like it."

"It'll pick you up after your long ride."

"Perhaps—" David saw she was looking out from underneath her eyelashes again—"I shouldn't be picked up too much."

David reached over, patted her hand. "Belinda, you haven't changed much with the years. You're the same—

"The same coquette who squeezed a bashful boy's hand on the stairway at Alexandriana, and who herself got squeezed at Lovelace's dance. Yes, you're right, David, I'm still that same coquette, always making advances, never perhaps quite carrying them through."

"Never *perhaps?*"

"Yes, perhaps. I don't know. Maybe I lack courage. I didn't know. I can never be sure until—"

"Until?"

She laughed, but David felt that there was little mirth in it, rather a suggestion of frustration. "All my life I have thought of situations, and what would happen were such situations actually to confront me. I have dreamed dreams and they have seemed real enough. It may be that I have had the courage in dreaming that I perhaps lack in waking hours. The center and core of my dreaming, of course, have been men, big, strong, masculine men." She sipped her drink, swallowed, blinked. "And I married Angus MacDougald." She took another sip.

"But, my dear, after all, you married. That's more than I have done. That's more definite, I'd think, than the most realistic dreams."

"No, it isn't. Dreams are more real than life, David. And being married to—to— Oh, why am I saying all this to you? I have no right to burden you. You're not, you shouldn't be, interested, perhaps. After all, I'm a married woman—"

ALEXANDRIANA

"Look here, Belinda, you're working yourself up over nothing, it seems to me. This stuff about dreams and all that. I've had dreams, too. I've dreamed about you, and you were very real, I'll admit, in those dreams I had." He saw her eyes begin to warm. "But you're a damn sight more real sitting here beside me right now than you ever were in the most realistic of those dreams." He edged nearer to her. "There's nothing wrong with you that can't be remedied. You're still young, God knows you're beautiful. It certainly does not appear that matrimony has gone hard with you. If Angus has been neglecting you, if you have not been permitted the—the joys, say, of matrimony, then Angus must be a—a—must be blind."

She laughed again, but there was a trace of bitterness, of cynicism, in it. "Listen, Mr. David Barksdale, I did not call you in here to seduce you. As I said before, I might want to but I haven't the courage. That's that. As for Angus, he is a weakling. I have tasted the joys of matrimony, as you described it. Angus hasn't been altogether blind. But I have been a side interest with him. Not exactly a plaything, for he hasn't had much time for playing. He's too much of a damned Scotchman. He's been interested in expanding his acres. And I too have been uninterested in him. I have been dreaming of other fields when I should perhaps have been cultivating him. I have resented his weakness and have failed to see my own. I have lain sleepless beside him at night resenting his—"

"I know it. I have seen you."

She sat up, set down the glass. "You have seen me?"

"Yes. In every detail. In every delicious detail, my dear."

"But I—I don't understand."

"No, you didn't know I was there. But I was. I was watching you twist and toss while Angus snored." He smiled, and there was a devilish light in his eyes.

"I see now." Belinda was smiling too. "It's funny, isn't it? I was seeing you at the same time, seeing you in bed with—with some tavern wench."

"Your visions were deceiving."

ALEXANDRIANA

"How do I know? Yours were true enough. Why shouldn't mine have been too?"

Her glass was empty. He tapped on the table again, ordered another round. "Would you go up to my father's room and see if he is coming back down, please?" she asked the Negro when he returned with the drinks.

In a moment he was back. "I listened outside his do', Mist'ess, and I heared him snorin'. I guess he must done went to bed."

She thanked him, he slipped out. "Father's worried these days. Politics, you know. Always politics. There's right much division of opinion down in the Scotch country. He's for the King, you know. But there's difference of sentiment."

"There's none up this way. We're all against the King."

"Yes, if father knew I was down here talking with a rebel, he'd probably come down and order me to bed. Poor father. He's very tired. He'll sleep like a log tonight. I'm glad. He needs the rest."

"I'm glad, too."

"You're glad, too? Why?"

"Why shouldn't I be glad at the prospect of your father's having a good night's rest?"

"Well, there's no reason you shouldn't. It's just the way you seemed to say it."

He patted her hand, squeezed it in his other one. It was warm; he was conscious, he thought, of its warming further to his touch. "Where is your room, Belinda? Is it comfortable? Jack's isn't the most comfortable tavern on the road, you know."

"It's the corner one that looks out toward the courthouse, the one fronting on the road. Father's is across the hall."

"It's a good room. And there's a back hall that it opens on, too. Did you know that?"

"I believe I saw a door, but I hadn't investigated. How did you know?"

He laughed at the tone of her question. "Oh, I know all the rooms and halls and back stairways in this whole tavern."

"Yes, I suppose so. And I'm quite sure my dreams were correct, too, in every detail—in every delicious detail."

ALEXANDRIANA

She shook her glass, watched the beads forming as the golden liquid whirled. When it had stopped spinning, she took a sip, set down the glass. "I must be going to bed soon. It's getting late, and I'm tired."

"Tired of me?"

"No, David."

"After all, I haven't seen you much. That day at the muster-ground, that night at Alexandriana, another night at Lovelace's dance, a million nights in my dreams."

"A million nights are a lot of nights."

"But they were dreams. I prefer the realities."

"For instance?"

"This night, this thirty-first day of May, 1775, this day on which Mecklenburg County has set up her government, has adopted her resolutions for the conduct of the government independent of Great Britain, has set up her courts—"

"Politics. Always politics."

"But I was leading up to something else. I was merely stating realities."

"I'm sorry; go on."

"This last day of May in this tavern, in another half hour, hour, say, in a room that looks out toward the courthouse and fronts on the road, on Trade Street—"

"No, David, no, not now—" Her eyes were faltering.

"I remember those were the very words you said that night at Lovelace's."

Her eyes beneath the dropping lashes watched the liquid beading in her glass. "No, no, I haven't—I don't—" She stopped. Then she picked up the glass, downed the remainder of her drink in one swallow. "I really must be going, David." She stood up, dabbed with her doily at the few crumbs that had fallen in her lap. "I'm so glad I saw you again. And I'm sorry I have been so—so—"

"So unresponsive."

"So unpromising, maybe."

"Well, Belinda, the night's young."

"I only wish it were, David, but—"

ALEXANDRIANA

"It could be."

"No, no—" She hesitated. Then she held out her hand. "I just must be getting to bed. We're going to try to make it down to the Waxhaw Settlements tomorrow, and that'll be another long ride."

He took her hand. "But I'll go upstairs with you, Belinda, and see to your windows. I'd bet a half-Joe old Pat Jack's put 'em all down. He doesn't like the night air."

"Oh, you needn't mind, David. I can handle them."

"But maybe you can't. They might be wedged."

"Then I could call that Negro."

He ignored her remark. "Are all your things up in your room?"

"Yes, but—Oh, David, you mustn't go up there. I—I—oh, you mustn't."

He was walking beside her toward the door. Outside the stairs went up to the chambers above the taproom. "But do you want me to sleep here in the taproom?" he said, laughing. "Don't you want me to go up to my room?"

"You mean you're—?"

"My room is just down the back hallway a couple of doors from yours."

Now they were on the stairs. "Belinda," he said, as they neared the top, "for old time's sake—" he reached up and caught her hand— "won't you give my fingers just a little squeeze?" He was laughing, but she caught the quality of tenseness in the question, of eagerness . . .

"I don't dare." She broke away, ran into her room. But he was inside too before she could shut the door. He walked over toward the window.

"See, I told you old Pat would have the windows down. And it's as hot as the devil in here." He flung up the window, let it back down until it tightened upon the stick he placed at an angle in the opening. Then he opened the other one. "Pat's scared o' distempers coming in with the night air. There's more inside than on the outside, I'm bound." He walked over to the stand of drawers. "You'll have to be going to bed soon, young lady, else you'll be needing a new candle. This one's about gone."

ALEXANDRIANA

"I'll be in bed in a jiffy if you'll run on now to your room. Thank you for opening the windows for me. It'll be cool soon." She stood at the door. "Perhaps I'll see you in the morning before we leave, at breakfast, maybe?"

But he sat down on the chest near the bed. Through the closed door across the narrow hallway they could hear the rhythmical coarse snoring of Belinda's father. "For heaven's sake, Belinda, come sit down. I'll be going in a minute. You've got all night to sleep. And why be afraid of me? I'm just a bashful backwoods boy. I'm none of your coast country gentry with fine clothes and gay manners going around robbing married women of their virtue."

Belinda laughed. "You always did say the cleverest things, David, the—the most disarming things. And I'm not afraid of you." She sat down on the bed opposite him. "It's that I'm—I'm afraid of myself."

He leaned back against the wall. "You seem to have taken pretty good care of yourself, my dear lady. You—"

"But you weren't around." She laughed, a merry little teasing laugh. "Forgive me, David, but you gave me such an opening. And now jump up and run to bed. We're both tired, I'm bound. Me with my riding and you with your politics."

"I'm going in a minute." He sat up. "It's been a busy day for me, all right. All day at the courthouse listening to speeches and hearing the committee's resolutions and all that, and tonight—"

"Tonight must have been unusually tiring for you—"

"Hah! On the contrary, it's been the most exciting part of the day, the most exciting time in many a day, in fact. I could just sit here and talk the rest of the night, and look at you. Belinda, you don't look tired. Have you been riding all day in those stays? Seems to me you would be choked to death riding side-saddle in a tight corset."

"David, you do talk with such frankness. If you must know, I only tightened them before I went down to eat. I thought I might see you, you see."

"There was no need lacing yourself up that way for me. It hurts me to look at your waist all squeezed in that way."

ALEXANDRIANA

"Well, if you'd just run on to bed I'd loosen up, and get to sleep, too."

He sat still. "Why don't you loosen up anyway. You'd be more comfortable. And you may need me to untie a hard knot in the strings."

David sensed a certain tremulous note in her laugh despite her apparent effort to be calm, composed. "David Barksdale, if you think you are coming in here and undress me, young man, you are very badly mistaken."

He continued to sit on the chest. "I had no such thought, Mrs. Angus MacDougald. I merely was offering my services to a lady in possible need of help. I have been told that unlacing a corset may be at times extremely difficult, especially if by mischance the strings become tied in a hard knot."

"Thank you, sir," she answered, in mock seriousness. "I appreciate your kind offer, but I shall manage it quite well my ownself, and if perchance I cannot, I shall sleep in my clothes. And now—" she stood up, and David arose from the chest—" you must be going, David, and I'll see you in the morning, won't I?"

She held out her hands. He took them, pulled them up to his lips, pressed his lips hard against them. Just as quickly he released them. "Good-night," he said, and turned toward the door opening upon the back hallway.

"Good-night, David," she said.

He opened the door. The draft rushing through the room slammed shut the door opening upon the other hallway. And it blew out the candle.

She was still standing beside the bed. The yellow light of the candle gone, she stood in the edge of the soft square of white light from the moon hanging high above the courthouse. He saw her raise her hand in a swift, spontaneous gesture. "Oh, David, don't—"

In one instant, one unheeding moment, he was upon her, crushing her lithe young body against his big chest. Her hot breath swept up into his face bending to her half-open mouth. He could feel her fingers pressing hard against the back of his neck. Her lips were warm, soft, fleshy. His teeth grated against hers. The contact released a surcharge of sensation . . .

She was standing close to him, pressed against him along the swelling contour of her body. The first rushing wave of passion subsiding within him, the first gush of hot blood draining back into his body from his inflamed brain, had left him more conscious of these individual and separate contacts. The delicate fragrance of her hair mingling with the flavor of her lips, the scent of her breath, enveloping him, the sharpness of her nails pushing into his neck, the hard hot push of her round firm breasts against him, the pressure of her soft sinuous leg between his own . . .

He felt again the hot blood rising, up from his toes, running out to his fingertips, racing toward and into his brain. He felt a sudden slight paroxysm passing over the girl in his tightening embrace . . . "Oh, David—uh—uh—" She was panting weakly, as she clung to him— "be—uh—be—"

David felt her go limp. He let her down upon the bed, sat beside her, pulled her gently down upon his lap.

In the moonlight she opened her eyes, looked up into his face bent toward hers. "I'm such a—a fool," she said, now calmer. "I—I tried, but I couldn't help it." She smiled, lowered her eyes. "Now I don't care."

His right arm hooked beneath her neck and shoulders, he raised her face toward his, bent low to meet her lips . . . And now only the old clock of Pat Jack, ticking its inexorable intervals upon the stairway landing, recorded time in all this darkened quiet tavern. In the still silvered haze of the chamber above the taproom time was standing aside . . .

She lay inert. She seemed oblivious to the big hand fumbling at the tiny bow of her breast-knot. She appeared not to know when the right ribbon-end had been found, had yielded to the clumsy pull, when even the slipping drawstring of her tightly-laced corset was giving release to cramped white flesh. Eyes closed under dark curved lashes, mouth open, breath coming and going in short quick measured pants, she seemed not even to be conscious when delicate lace gave way and white and firm and erect in the soft moonlight, her breasts stood revealed and bare beneath hungry eyes. Nor did she stir as he bent forward to seek with famished lips, as his clumsily gentle hand stole along yielded bodice to cup a hot and eager palm . . .

A sharp, staccato rapping of hard knuckles on the door. The girl leaped to her feet. He stood up, stepped noiselessly across toward the other doorway. As he moved through it into the little back hallway he saw her white hands in the moonlight working fast at her bodice. She shut the door behind him; he heard her throw the bolt.

Through both doors in the stillness he heard the rapping renewed. "Daughter! Daughter! Belinda!"

"Yes, Father." She said it sleepily. "Just a minute. I have no way of lighting the candle, and besides, I think it has burnt out."

"Don't bother, child. Are you all right? I—I hadn't heard you come to bed. I—I must have dreamed something about you. I—"

"Yes, Father, I'm all right. I've been hearing you snoring. But if you'll wait just a minute I'll slip on something and let you in."

"No, no. Don't. I'm sorry I disturbed you, I reckon I was dreaming. Go back to bed, and I'll see you in the morning. I'm sorry."

"That's all right, Father. I—I—"

"Good-night, Daughter."

"Good-night."

He heard her father's door close. He walked down the hallway, turned into his room. "Damn that old man. Damn him to hell!" He flung himself across the bed. He knew there was no use stealing back along the dark hallway. That bolt had dropped with a click of finality. "The gates of heaven ajar, and then they slam in your face!" He got up, walked over to the window. The moonlight flooded the stable behind the tavern. "Hell, I can't sleep here tonight!" He tipped from the room, picked his way stealthily down the back stairway, moved across the moonlit yard to the stable, bridled and saddled his horse.

"It'll take a lot of riding to settle me down to sleeping." He swung easily into the saddle, moved quietly around the tavern to come out upon Trade Street, turned west toward the Great Road and Alexandriana.

ALEXANDRIANA

Straight behind him stood the little courthouse, high and quiet upon its stilts, lighted by the moon now swinging lower over Duncan Ochiltree's store. But he didn't see the courthouse or the store. The quick glance over his left shoulder revealed only Jack's Tavern, silent and squat, and the corner chamber above the taproom, silent, too, and dark and still in the cold moonlight.

XXVII

"WILL, YOU have uncommonly good whiskey here at the Mansion House. It's not often we get this good a stuff at Pat Jack's or Joe Nicholson's." Waightstill Avery sloshed the golden liquid in his glass, watched the beads forming.

"Well, we're a city, Waightstill. Salisbury's no Charlottetown." Will Kennon laughed. "We're another Williamsburg. Why, man, we're growing. Some day we'll be another Charles Town. We're no back country settlement."

"That's right. We'll never catch up with Salisbury, Will." He sipped his drink. "We'll pick up a little as time goes along and the people keep pushing west, but we'll never be more than a crossroads village, I'll vouch." His eye caught the clock behind the bar. He downed the remainder of the liquid. "Look here, Will, it's late. We'd better be getting back to court." He turned around.

A man carrying saddlebags was entering the taproom. "Well, if it isn't Captain Jack himself, by George! Come up to the bar, Jim. I'll bet you're famished for a drink. Will, you know Captain Jim Jack, don't you?"

"Why, of course, I know Captain Jack." Will Kennon advanced to meet the newcomer, shook hands cordially. "Haven't seen you since the convention in Charlottetown."

"That's right, Mr. Kennon. I haven't seen you since then."

"You're on your way to Philadelphia, Jim, with the copies of the declaration and the resolves, I'm bound."

"Yes, that's where I'm headed, Waightstill. I've got a long ways to go though."

ALEXANDRIANA

"When did you leave Charlottetown?"

"This morning before day. I've been riding pretty steady. My horse is pretty well lathered."

Waightstill turned to glare at the bartender. "Look here, fellow, don't you see the Captain here's practically burning with thirst? Rustle him up a good heady nip." He looked at Will Kennon. Kennon nodded. Waightstill turned again to the bartender. "You might make it three of 'em. It makes me dry to look at Jim."

"Say—" Will Kennon set down his glass. "I was just thinking. I'll bet you got those papers in your saddlebags there, judging by the way you've been keeping your eye on 'em, Captain. I was just wondering, Waightstill. There's a bunch up there at the courthouse that would like powerful well to hear those papers read. John Brevard's there, and I don't think he was in Charlottetown when they were read out, and I doubt if Ephraim's shown them to him, and there's Moses Winslow and Grif Rutherford, and Bill Sharpe and Matt Locke—and some others, Sam Young, Jim Brandon, Adlai Osborne, John Dunn and Ben Boote—"

"Dunn and Boote, from what I hear of 'em from your Committee of Public Safety bunch, wouldn't care to hear 'em read."

"No, likely they wouldn't, Waightstill. But the others would, and it won't do Dunn and Boote any harm to hear a little good American doctrine read to 'em." He turned to Jim Jack. "Say, Captain, I don't want to rush you, but I'd like powerful well for you to go up to the courthouse with me and Waightstill and let those men hear those papers read out to 'em. We've just about got time before court adjourns. The sun's beginning to get pretty low."

Captain Jack finished his drink, opened the saddlebags and took out the papers. "That'll be all right, Mr. Kennon. Won't it, Waightstill? I reckon the more that hear about it the better, eh?"

"That's my idea, Jim. That's what you're carrying it to the Continental Congress for, I'd say. We're not trying to hide it. We want all the provinces to adopt independence as their course."

At the courthouse Lawyer Kennon explained the documents before he proceeded to read them. "The set of resolves adopted by the committee a few days ago—" He glanced at one of the papers—

ALEXANDRIANA

"May 31, I see here— was decreed by the men of Mecklenburg in pursuance of and as a result of this other paper. The resolves set up a government for that county now that it has thrown off and denied allegiance to the government of Great Britain. This other paper, approved on last May 20 and signed by a large group of citizens, of which I have the honor to be one, is the actual declaration itself. Now I'll proceed, with the permission of the court, to read them."

As Will Kennon read, Waightstill Avery studied the faces of the men of Rowan. Griffith Rutherford and Moses Winslow were following his every word with eager attention; John Brevard, his eyes upon Kennon, drummed with noiseless fingers upon the arm of his chair. John Dunn fidgeted in his seat, his angry eyes darting from one solemn, rapt countenance to another. Matthew Locke and Adlai Osborne never once took their eyes from Will Kennon's face. Nor did James Brandon. But Benjamin Boote sat slumped in his chair, his eyes upon the floor, his cheeks flaming.

When Kennon concluded, there was silence. Carefully the lawyer folded the papers, stepped over to Captain Jack and returned them. The Captain placed them in his inside coat pocket.

John Dunn was on his feet. "It appears that this assembly approves the sentiments expressed by these papers. I want to say that I do not." He slapped his right fist in his cupped left palm. "In my opinion these are treasonable documents. In my opinion—"

"Mr. Dunn's opinion was not asked." Moses Winslow cleared his throat. "I might say that these papers were passed by the men of Mecklenburg. They didn't seek the views of Mr. Dunn. They had the aid of Mr. Kennon here, and I want to say that Mr. Kennon in signing that paper represented me as I would have wanted to be represented."

"No, my opinion wasn't sought. But I'm giving it anyway."

Benjamin Boote raised his eyes from the floor. An angry scowl crossed his face. "I agree with you, Mr. Dunn. Mr. Kennon certainly did not represent me in signing that treasonable paper."

"Treasonable! That's the word for it! That's the word for the damnable action of these backwoodsmen from Mecklenburg. I

ALEXANDRIANA

oppose this paper, the sentiments it expresses. It will bring upon its authors—and justly so—the fury of the King. I want it distinctly understood that I'm not of any such company—"

"That appears without saying." Waightstill Avery, turning toward the man who had interrupted Dunn, saw a flush spreading over the bronzed cheeks of John Brevard of the Centre Church community. "Mr. Dunn does not need to tell us that he stands without the circle of upright, patriotic citizens." He was looking straight into the teeth of John Dunn. But Dunn had finished speaking, had taken his seat.

"Mr. Brevard may cast aspersions upon my friend Dunn if he likes," now spoke up Benjamin Boote, "but he is only putting himself upon record as being among the enemies of His Majesty, and when this rebellion—"

"I am happy and honored to be so numbered, Mr. Boote."

"When this rebellion is overthrown, it may be that you gentlemen will remember and rue what you say here today in support of this rebellious document. I think for your own good, gentlemen, you should disavow any connection with this Mecklenburg rebellion. I think you should detain this man and forbid him from going farther with these seditious documents—"

"And I think that when news of these remarks by Mr. Boote and his friend Mr. Dunn get back to Mecklenburg, as they will, I assure you, gentlemen, they will be waited upon by a delegation from Charlottetown."

John Dunn sprang to his feet. "You may threaten me, but all this will be set straight in good time. I want it understood that I am demanding that this fellow be detained, his seditious papers destroyed—"

James Jack jerked his pistol from the holster at his belt. "I'll kill the first man that offers to lay a hand on me!"

"Put up your gun, Captain," said John Brevard. "It won't be needed." His laugh was mirthless, cold, as he faced Dunn and Boote. "A small horse-whip would be more fitting, and 'twould be all you'd need to run all the damned Tories in Rowan clear to the other side o' the Yadkin."

XXVIII

At a small table in a little private chamber partitioned off from the taproom of the Inn of the Golden Cock in Philadelphia sat three men.

Two appeared to be in their middle forties, the other in his early thirties. The more youthful of the three was of slight stature and more delicate than robust, and his occasional drumming with sensitive fingers upon the table and his twisting in his hard chair plainly disclosed a nervous restlessness. But his sharp clear eyes betrayed a quick intelligence. He was quietly but elegantly dressed.

It was easily evident that one of the other men was a frontiersman. His dress showed it, his speech, his every action. But it was likewise evident, even to the most casual lounger at the bar of the Inn of the Golden Cock, that he was a man of strength, of rugged courage and capacity, of determined will.

The third of the trio was talking. He sat relaxed, he paid not the slightest attention to the persons passing the open doorway that led into the taproom, he was speaking quietly, carefully, with calm assurance. He, too, showed himself to be a man of innate strength, of clear perceptive powers, of quiet assurance.

"We have studied the papers carefully, Captain Jack. We have been very busy with committee assignments and a thousand and one matters that have been pressing upon the Congress. But we took the necessary time to read them and digest them. All three of us—Mr. Hooper here and Mr. Hewes also. By the way, Will, where is Joe?"

"I understand he was unable to get away from an important committee meeting."

ALEXANDRIANA

"Yes. You see, Captain Jack, that's the way it goes. We are very busy. It's a tremendously hard working Congress."

"Yes, sir, Mr. Caswell, I've seen that in the little time I've been in Philadelphia. I know you all are mighty busy. We appreciate your taking the time to bother with us."

"That's what we were sent up here for, Captain. That's our job. If we can't handle it, then we should go home and let somebody else come up here from North Carolina. Isn't that right, Will?"

"Exactly, Dick." William Hooper's intelligent young face lighted with a quick, engaging smile. "We're up here to serve the dear people, Captain. Sometimes I wonder if we don't serve them better by lining the rails of the taprooms than by lifting the rafters of the chambers of Congress with our oratory."

"Will's a mere youth, Captain, and he craves action, always action. He's one of the brightest young men Harvard College ever turned out, but he isn't prone to weigh matters from every angle. But he'll calm down and make us a conservative member some of these days."

William Hooper laughed. "If the British don't hang him first. But don't let me interrupt you, Dick. Pardon me. Go ahead with what you were about to report to Captain Jack."

"Yes, yes. We were getting a bit off the subject. But as I was saying, Mr. Hewes has also studied these papers and he agrees with us. We are heartily in sympathy with the sentiment expressed in them, Captain. We admire tremendously the courage of Mecklenburg in decreeing its independence from Great Britain. That was a very courageous thing to do, more courageous, I suspect, than some of you men realized when you were placing your names to this paper. It certainly marks your section as the first in all the colonies to defy England. And it may—" he paused— "it may light the way for the future course of the Congress. But just at this time, Captain, we feel that submission of this declaration of independence to the Congress would be premature. Isn't that our view, Will?"

"That's right, Captain. Personally, I agree with Mecklenburg. In fact, we all three do. Dick here says I'm young and rash. Well, he's a hoary-headed old man of forty-six while I was thirty-three

215

ALEXANDRIANA

only last Saturday, and Joe Hewes is half way between us at forty, and Joe agrees with Dick. But we'll all three, and you, too, Captain, live to see, and see very shortly, I suspect, that Mecklenburg has shown the way in our course toward Great Britain. Just now, however, the attitude of the Congress is one of reconciliation, and the submission of this paper, as several other members with whom we have discussed it have pointed out, would not be calculated to promote the advancement of such a policy."

"But, gentlemen—" Captain Jack sat up in his chair. "How does the Congress reconcile that position with its organization of an army and its appointment of Colonel Washington of Virginia to command that army?"

"There, Captain Jack, you have posed a significant question, my dear sir, you have placed your finger upon the crux of the matter." There was a trace of sarcasm in the smile that lightened the sensitive face of young Hooper.

"That is a somewhat anomalous position, I'll concede you, Captain. But—"

"Can you fight England and still be an English colony? You are a soldier, Mr. Caswell—Colonel Caswell, in fact. You were one of Governor Tryon's main leaders at Alamance—"

Young Hooper laughed, leaned forward to strike the table an easy blow with his fist. "Again, my dear Captain, you have placed your finger upon an exceedingly sore spot, sir, a most touchous spot, when you speak of His Excellency, the former Governor of North Carolina."

"I'm sorry. I didn't mean to, sir. You did what you conceived to be your duty then and you are doing it now. That nobody doubts. But I was just wondering how the Congress can reconcile its action in making plans for raising an army and at the same time seeking to be reconciled with England. Just how does that work out?"

"That's a sensible question, Captain. I'm not so sure whether it's my view. But I'm a member of the Congress and I must go along with that body for the time being, at any rate. At any time we may part company, or the Congress may change its policy. But right now the Congress feels that we have been assailed by England,

ALEXANDRIANA

that we have been reduced to the alternative of submitting to a harsh and uncomprehending government in London or resisting by force. We are declaring that we have a just cause, that we are being forced to fight, and that we will and can fight. We are resolved to fight and die as free men rather than live as slaves of the mother country. We are not raising armies to rebel and tear ourselves away from England but simply to defend our freedom. We shall lay down our arms when we win this freedom, and not before it, Captain."

"I don't believe we can ever be free and at the same time continue to be the colonies of England. I see the position of the Congress, Mr. Caswell, but I don't believe that such a position can be followed very long. Before so many months the Congress, I'll vouch, will be doing what we've already done in Mecklenburg. And whether the Congress does it or not, Mr. Caswell, Mecklenburg's already free from England. And I'm a notion the British will have to kill out every man, woman and child before they'll get us back."

"Captain, I have a feeling you're right." William Hooper stood up, stretched his legs. "But for the time being I think it would be the politic thing not to present to the Congress this declaration of Mecklenburg's. That is the view of several of the other older heads—" he nodded almost imperceptibly toward Richard Caswell and smiled broadly— "of the other provinces and I presume I am in agreement with it—for the present, at any rate. But I plan to discuss the proposition further. There are several others before whom I shall lay it. There's this young red-headed Tom Jefferson from Virginia, for instance, though he's even younger than I and as strong-willed and independent as they make them."

"Well, gentlemen, I suppose there's nothing left for me to do now except start back to North Carolina. It's a mighty long ride, you know. Maybe it's better the way you have figured it out, though we folks in Mecklenburg did want a little support." He grinned. "We'll be a mighty little country over there in the backwoods all by ourselves, you know. But I'll leave these papers with you all and you can show them around as you think best. Maybe they'll get something started. It might be a good idea to let the Virginia dele-

ALEXANDRIANA

gates see it, and that Mr. Jefferson. They say he's a pretty lively young fellow."

"We'll do that, Captain. Tell your friends in Mecklenburg—I know some of them, two or three of the Alexanders—McKnitt's one of them—and Waightstill Avery—How's that young rapscallion, Captain? He's a great boy, Waightstill. True blue. Yes, sir. Tell them that we greatly respect their action but hold it to be a little premature and that we'll—"

A man stuck his head in the door. "A big parade's going by. If you fellows want to see it, you better step to the door." He darted away.

"He's had a little too much grog, no doubt. Tell them, Captain—"

Through the door came the sound of fifes and drums, the cadenced thump-thump of men marching over cobblestones. "Wait! That fellow was right. I remember now. Let's get to the door!" Richard Caswell pushed back his chair. "That must be General Washington leaving!"

The handclapping and shouts down the street grew steadily into a roar as the parade drew abreast of the Inn of the Golden Cock. In the front marched the drum and fife corps and behind them came officers of the militia stepping smartly, their swords slapping against their legs.

"Look!" Richard Caswell pointed through an opening in the crowd that had swarmed across the sidewalk to the edge of the street. "There he is! General Washington, the big man. There! See him?"

Captain Jack saw a stalwart man, broad shoulders filling out the blue uniform, handsome three-cornered hat evenly upon his head, riding along ahead of the company of light-horse in uniform. From time to time he turned to one side of the street and then the other to acknowledge the plaudits of the crowds. But his face remained glum, serious, impassive. Behind the light-horse marched in uncadenced step the Massachusetts delegates, delegates from Virginia, New York, Pennsylvania, Georgia . . .

"Poor fellow. He's got a tremendous job ahead."

"Where's he going, Mr. Caswell?"

"He's on his way north now. Going to Boston to take charge of the American forces. There goes the commander of the American army."

But the eyes of young William Hooper, who had said nothing as the procession had approached and passed, were still upon the big silent man up there ahead. Now he spoke, and there was no trace of affectation in his voice.

"Dick, you're wrong. There goes *the* American army."

XXIX

THE CROPS at Alexandriana lay parched and lanquid under the still dead heat of early August. In the field behind the barns across the Great Road from the house corn blades curled and twisted on long stalks, and the tobacco in the patch up the slope from the spring was burning to a deep brown crisp.

"If it doesn't soon rain, Cato, Jethro'll have to chew rabbit-tobacco this winter and we'll have to eat acorns." He dismounted, handed the reins to the Negro.

"Yas, suh, Marse McKnitt, hit's powerful dry. I aint worryin' 'bout Mist' Jethro chewin' and spittin' rabbit-'bacco, but a-corns they'd be powerful po' fare."

"Maybe we'll be glad to get acorns after the British get here."

He stalked on tired legs into the house, sat down in his big chair.

"You're all tuckered out, McKnitt." Jeanie ran her fingers through his damp hair, across his perspiring forehead. "I'll get you a drink, and after you rest a bit you can take a good bath and put on fresh clothes and you'll feel a lot better. What do you want, hot coffee or a toddy? I can heat up the coffee in a jiffy."

"It's not worth while heating the coffee, Jeanie. Just fetch me a little toddy." He leaned back in the chair, opened his waistcoat.

"Well, Jeanie," he began, when she brought him the drink, "I've got to be starting off again in a few days."

She did not appear surprised. "Where to this time? Politics, I suppose?"

"Yes. Hillsboro. The Assembly. Samuel Johnston's called it to meet on the twentieth."

ALEXANDRIANA

"And you're to go from Mecklenburg?"

"That's right."

"Why must you always be the one to go, McKnitt?"

"I'm not the only one, Sweet."

"Well, I can name them, I'll vouch."

He pulled her down on the arm of the chair. "Well, who?"

"Tom Polk, and likely Waightstill."

He laughed. "Yes, you're right, by George, Jeanie. But there'll be three others, too—John Phifer and Sam Martin and Jim Houston."

"Why is the Assembly meeting this time? They just met last August and again in April."

"Well, there's no legally constituted government in the province. You see, the Governor dissolved the Assembly in April and then he threw up his job and ran off to Fort Johnston and now they say he's aboard a ship in the Cape Fear River. So it's necessary to set up a legal government. But there's another reason that to my notion's more pressing and—" He hesitated.

"The war?"

"Yes, getting ready for it."

"Is that what they are saying in Charlottetown?"

"A lot of 'em are. Some don't think so. Figure it won't get down this far. Think we're safe if we just lie low and don't do anything more to rile the English."

She took his empty glass, set it on the little table near his chair. "What do you think, McKnitt?"

"Well, I hardly know what to think, Jeanie. But I do think we should get ready for 'em in case they do come. And I think we should send help to the folks in the North. Jim Jack told me—"

"Is he back from Philadelphia?"

"Yes. I talked with him a long time today. He's convinced there's going to be a hard war ahead for us. You see, he talked with our men at Philadelphia—Mr. Caswell and young Hooper—and several of the other delegates, and he was able to feel out the temper of the Congress pretty well. He said they were still hoping and working for reconciliation with England, but few of the delegates were very hopeful about it. There's already been a big fight up at Bunker Hill and more fighting's expected. And, Jeanie, he saw General Washington."

"He did, for a fact?"

"Yes, he happened to see him as they were escorting him out of the city on his way north to take command of the army. He said he was a big, fine-looking man; said there was something about him that sort of got you when you looked at him, sort of the look of quiet strength and power—"

He sat silent a moment, nor did Jeanie speak. "I wonder, Jeanie—" Still he seemed unable to frame the thoughts struggling within him. "We are so terribly unprepared for war, Jeanie. We are a young country. We have been working to build a civilization in a wilderness. In fact, we are no country at all. We are just a group of scattered, disconnected provinces strung along the coast, savage Indians on our west, the English coming on our east. I wonder if there isn't something about this man, Jeanie, this Washington, around which we can build a united country, something that will tie us together, inspire us to fight as one man." He broke off. "Oh, I don't know. Sometimes I have hopes. But it's a big job ahead, Sweet. It's hard to face the days ahead—"

"Wait till they come, McKnitt. Maybe they'll be easier when they really get here. And now you've rested a bit. Jump up and get your bath. I'll have Venus carry you some hot water. Then you'll feel better and we can have supper."

XXX

THE SUGAR MAPLES flamed red in the soft calm haze that had settled upon the dead fields and still woods of Alexandriana on this afternoon late in September. More restrained and modest were the silver maples with their lacy leaves washed in pale yellow and crinkling to show the silver underneath. But bolder, more brash even than the sugar maples were the black gums with their blood red leaves and the sweet gums in the reds and greens and browns and yellows of a gypsy's dress. And above the somber green mass of cedars that ringed the spring at the foot of the slope shot up in yellow glory the slender gray stalk of a giant poplar.

"It's good to be home again, Jeanie." McKnitt Alexander in one impulsive sweep of his arm embraced the maples, the gums, the cedars, the red bare fields, the quiet unstirring woods. "To be here with this. I'm a rich man, Sweet, a man rolling in wealth. I know not how to count my riches."

"Then why do so?"

"There you go again, my little philosopher." He reached down, grabbed her under the knees and about the waist, swung her in one motion to a seat on the uppin'-block, leaned his head against her. "You are so practical, Jeanie."

"And you?"

"I'm an impractical dreamer, a man whose dreams and realities are forever mixing into one another. Most of the time I'm living in the past or the future, so much so that I somehow don't see the present. And that makes me fearful that life will be over before

ALEXANDRIANA

I've really had a chance to enjoy my wealth. Here tonight as the sun is dropping low and the smell of autumn is in our nostrils—"

"McKnitt Alexander, you are positively a poet." She held up her right hand, spread her fingers. "A surveyor." She counted the little finger. "A tailor." She counted the second finger. "A farmer. A magistrate. A legislator." She counted her thumb. "An elder in Hopewell Church. A lot of other things. And now a poet. McKnitt, you are a remarkable man."

"You left out one, the very best."

"What?"

"The husband of the finest, most attractive woman in the world." She counted another finger. "A diplomat."

He laughed, slapped her gently on both cheeks, pulled her face down and kissed her. "Oh, Jeanie, you are clever and smart with all your other virtues. You know what I wish? I wish I could go on living here with you and the children at Alexandriana forever."

"Wouldn't it be wonderful?"

His face was serious now. "Everything's so peaceful. So beautiful." He sniffed. "Smell those muscadines down by the spring? And the smell of the woods now that autumn's coming? Can you pick 'em out? I can. And I love it. Wouldn't it be nice if it could keep on just like this?"

"Maybe we can. Maybe things will clear up."

No, Honey. It won't stay like this. It can't. Even if we escape fighting—actual fighting right here in Mecklenburg—it won't be the same. War is a destroyer. It tears down. Nobody wins a war. And we'll lose even if England loses. It will take a long time to repair the damages. We likely won't live to see things settled again as they are—as they look to be here tonight in the peace and quiet of Alexandriana."

"Let's don't talk about it any more now. It's so depressing, and it doesn't help to talk about it. We'll be ready for 'em when the time comes, I'm bound. We'll—" The clanging of the dinner bell from the kitchen house interrupted. "Venus has supper ready. Let's go eat. John and Violet will be here before long and you and John can get started talking all the earlier."

ALEXANDRIANA

The Davidsons drove up as they were finishing. They came on out to the kitchen house. "Go ahead and get through eating," said Violet. "We've already eaten, Jeanie, and you and I are in for a night of it by our ownselves, I'll vouch. John will want McKnitt to do over for him every single thing that was done in a month's time at Hillsboro. It's a great pity we hadn't heard earlier so we could have planned to get ourselves a beau apiece for tonight. But John wanted to come over the minute he heard McKnitt was back and that's why he sent to see if you all would be home tonight."

Night was rolling in from Poplar Tent, pushing back relentlessly the light hanging low over Hopewell and Rural Retreat, when they took their split-bottom chairs out into the yard and sat down under the big oak. They lighted their pipes, puffed for a few moments in silence disturbed only by the chirpings of insects in the trees and a solitary whippoorwill's calling from the woods below the spring.

"Well, McKnitt—" John Davidson shifted the pipe in his mouth, "did you have any trouble getting back from Hillsboro?"

"No, not the least bit. I was pretty tired when I got here—was tired when I started, in fact—but I made the trip by easy stages and everything went along first-rate."

"I know you were tired. Must have been a busy session of the Assembly. A lot of important things before you, I know."

"Yes. I expect it was about the most important session the Assembly's ever had, John. We sort of burnt the bridges behind us."

"That's what I gathered from what I've already heard." He puffed in silence as he leaned back in the chair; the burning tobacco glowed in the pipe-bowl. "It's war, isn't it, McKnitt?"

"It's bound to be. I can't see any way around it. Unless the government in England yields, and it won't, I'm bound."

"Will we be ready?"

"That's what's worrying me, John. What do you think?"

"We're not prepared for war, McKnitt. In the first place, we're not even a nation. We have no unity. We are just a bunch of colonies. What do we know about Massachusetts, for instance? What do they know about us? What do we care for each other?"

ALEXANDRIANA

"Yes, that's true. But already in the face of danger from England we seem to be getting together. That fighting up at Lexington, for instance, struck fire way down here in Mecklenburg."

"Well, you're right there. And that's our hope. But if England cuts loose her full strength against us—well, you and I and the rest of us who signed that paper back in May will be hung, along with most of the Continental Congress."

"I'm hoping England has her hands pretty full on the other side already. And not all the English people are against us, either. Many of them are following Pitt. And I'm hoping that if worse comes to worse and they send a big army over here, we may be able to show them some new brand of fighting. You know what happened to Braddock. Well, maybe we can give them some more of the same medicine. I don't know, John. I hate to think about it. But, plague it, a fellow can't help but think about it."

"Did you all get much done at Hillsboro except talk?"

"Yes, it would surprise you, John, just how much was done. We did so much that there'll be no chance of back-tracking now. For one thing, we wiped off accounts with Governor Martin—"

"I heard he'd run out."

"Yes, he sent us a proclamation from his ship out in the Cape Fear. He denounced our Mecklenburg convention and the action it took last May, and he denounced the Assembly itself—called it 'one of the black artifices of falsehood and sedition.' But we gave him as good as he sent. We pronounced his proclamation 'a false, scurrilous and seditious libel' and we directed that it be burnt by the public hangman."

"Good for the Assembly! That's the way I like to hear men talk. I'm tired of this effort to smooth down everybody—the Governor, the King, the English government. I don't believe we'll get anywhere with this mealy-mouth attitude."

"That's my notion, too, John. I think the Continental Congress should have followed Mecklenburg's lead and declared independence. I believe the Province of North Carolina is nearer to that view, too, than the Congress. The Assembly, at any rate, took for granted that war's coming and laid plans for it."

ALEXANDRIANA

"What did you do in that respect?"

"Well, we set up a civil government for the State and we made plans for raising two regiments for the Continental Line. There'll be a provincial council for the whole province, headed by Samuel Johnston of Edenton—he became moderator of the Assembly after John Harvey died, you remember—and then there'll be two members from each of the six districts. Waightstill and Sam Spencer were elected from the Salisbury district. It's the main governing body of the province. They are to meet every four months and they have a lot of authority. They can call out the militia, they can suspend officers, they can draw on the treasury for whatever money they may need for the military service. In fact, John, they can do just about anything they think necessary to protect the province."

"Well, that's a couple of good men from this section. I'm certainly glad you put Waightstill on it. He's young and he's got energy."

"An he's got sense, too, John."

"You're right, he has. And courage. He's a good boy. Who were some of the others?"

"Well, Cornelius Harnett and Samuel Ashe from the Wilmington district, as I remember—"

"Good. Who else?"

"Abner Nash from the New Bern district, and, well, the Joneses from Halifax and Thomas Person from Hillsboro. I can't recall all the members."

"They're all right, those you named. And who'll be under them? What sort of a supporting group, I mean?"

"There's a Committee of Safety for each of these six districts, and then there are town and county committees of safety under the district committees. They all sort of dove-tail together, you see."

"That's good, McKnitt. That's a good arrangement, it seems to me. Who are some of the Committee of Safety for the Salisbury district?"

"I doubt if I can name them all, John. There are twelve for each district in addition to a chairman. Hezekiah's one, and John

ALEXANDRIANA

Brevard and Grif Rutherford, Maxwell Chambers, Ben Patton—let me see, John Crawford, Charlie Galloway, Bob Ewert—there's one or two more."

"Good men, too. How about the county committees?"

"They are to be elected by the freeholders. Twenty-one members in each county, I believe I'm correct in the number, and fifteen each for Wilmington and New Bern and Edenton, and seven for each of the other towns. Each committee will select seven of its members to act as a committee of correspondence. They'll keep in touch with the Provincial Council and their own district committee. Their job will be to examine all suspicious persons—"

"They'd better be looking into some of our Mecklenburg folks—"

"Ochiltree?"

"Yes. You remember how he carried on at the convention last May. I wouldn't want to risk him if the British got down this way. He'd sell us out, McKnitt."

"Maybe not, John. Duncan Ochiltree likes his money. He's Scotch, but—"

"And he'd starve a Jew to death out-trading him."

McKnitt took his pipe from his mouth, knocked out the ashes against a rung of the chair. "There's a lot of 'em in Mecklenburg would do that, John." He laughed. "You're no slouch at trading your ownself."

"I'll never get good enough to skin you, McKnitt." He stood up, stamped his legs. "My leg had 'most gone to sleep." He sat down. "But, say, McKnitt, how about those regiments? I guess I'm more interested in that somehow than the civil end of it. I've a notion if the war comes, I'll be getting in it. But don't you be telling Violet, or Jeanie either, for that matter."

"Violet might be glad to get rid o' you, John. She'd make a powerful pretty widow."

"Look here, McKnitt, don't you be talking like that, man. She just might be one before this business is over, by George."

"Yes, and so might Jeanie. It's serious, John. But about those regiments for the Continental Line. They named James Moore colonel of one and Robert Howe colonel of the other. George Davidson's a captain in the first regiment and George Graham's an ensign. I don't believe any of our folks were named officers in the second. Then each district is to raise ten companies of minute men, fifty men to each company. Thomas Wade of Anson is colonel of the Salisbury district battalion and Adlai Osborne is lieutenant colonel. That's the set-up so far. But the Provincial Council's set to meet in December and they'll likely name more battalions of minute men. We just sort of got the thing started, laid the framework."

"Yes, it'll take a lot more men, McKnitt, a lot of money, too, and hard work and planning, a lot of grief and blood, too, I'll vouch, before it's over."

XXXI

"CHRISTMAS GIFT, Bedent! Wake up over there, man. Christmas gift!" Jethro sat up, combed hay out of his hair and eyes with extended fingers, felt in his shirt for his twist of tobacco.

A pile of hay over in the corner of the loft stirred vaguely, heaved, and erupted to bring forth a sleepy-eyed bearded individual. "Damn, Jethro, this here's Christmas shore'n hell, aint it?" He twisted shaggy head on the stem of a long red neck and his Adam's apple pitched violently as he swallowed. "But I don't see no sign o' Sandy Claus nowheres, or breakfas' neither."

"Hell, man, you didn't hang up yore sock."

"Well, this here stable aint got no chimley."

"No, and you wouldn't a-took off yore socks if'n it had a-had. I bet you aint had off'n them there socks since we left Charlottetown, Bedent, and it's a damn good thing we're sleepin' in a stable over stock."

"Well, I aint seen you washin' yore feet yore ownself, Jethro."

"Me and the Sergeant did take off our shoes and let our feets air out. But I'm glad you kept yore'n on, Bedent." Another mound of hay stirred and up from it arose a third man, shaking hay and chaff from his head and shoulders. His eyes looked out from a week's growth of beard.

Jethro, sitting in the hay, saluted smartly. "Sergeant Barksdale, at yore orders, sir!"

David saluted. "Corporal O'Flannagan, sir. I am now ready for breakfast. You may fetch me a couple of poached eggs, a nice slab of fried ham, some quince preserves, a slab of butter and hot biscuits. And coffee. And don't forget the damask doily, my dear corporal." He saluted again.

Jethro saluted. "It'll take me jest a little time to rustle up that there order, Sergeant. And I may have to change it a little. I can maybe sarve you up a nice slab o' gray mule if you'd jest as soon have it raw and some snow-cream if'n that cow there ain't dry and if'n you don't care fer it bein' sweetened. And fer a doily I can offer you Private Spraggins's shirt-tail, sir." Jethro threw back his head and guffawed. "Damn, Davy, here we all's hungrier'n hell and you talk 'bout poached eggs and fried ham and coffee—"

"It aint nothin' to be laughin' 'bout." Bedent scowled. "We got to be figurin' on eatin'. My stomach's stickin' 'ginst my backbone. Hit thinks my throats cut, I'm bound. And the damn snow two-foot deep—"

"Hell, it's Christmas, aint it? Don't you know Christmas and snow's supposed to come together?"

"Not way down here in the middle o' South Ca'lina."

"Aw, hell, Bedent, a little bit o' snow aint gonna hurt you. Hit'll keep old Colonel Tom from drillin hell out o' us."

"But I'd ruther drill than lay here in this barn and freeze and starve. That there sorry commissary's al'ays slow 'bout gittin' our rations issued out."

"Bedent, this is Christmas and the commissary's got to sleep a little late. We'll git something t' eat pretty soon. Time we git out in that snow and stir 'round a bit they'll have breakfast ready. 'Taint no use a-growlin'. I'd like to be home my ownself and playin' with the young'uns. I hope the old lady she got their Sandy Claus all right. My little Flossie Belle she was all set on Sandy fetchin' her a rag doll—"

"Aunt Jeanie saw to that, I'll vouch."

"More'n likely Mis' Jeanie done that very thing, Davy. She's a powerful woman to think about all sech like."

"I'd like to be home, too. What in the devil did we come way down here in South Ca'lina for nohow? They said we was comin' down here to whup hell out'n them Scuffleites. I aint seen a Scuffleite since I been down here. What in hell is a Scuffleite nohow?" Bedent turned to David, his lack of understanding evident in the puzzled expression on his whiskered face.

"Well, Bedent, there was a villain down in these parts several years ago named Scoffel. He was some such a scoundrel as Fanning. Jethro remembers Fanning—"

"Yeh, and I reckon you 'member him yore ownself."

"This Scoffel was a crook who led a gang that preyed on the Regulators down this way. Here lately they've sort of bunched all the folks down in this section who are against the American cause under the name of Scoffelites. I reckon that sort of explains it, doesn't it?"

"Maybe so, but still I don't see no sense to comin' way down here. Look at that damn snow, and my stomach's as empty—"

"The King's men in these parts were rising up. There was some talk that they were trying to turn the Cherokee's 'gainst us. On the other hand, a lot of them thought we were fixing to turn the Cherokees on them. It was mostly misunderstanding fanned up by folks like Scoffel, but there are a lot of the King's men in this section of the back country—"

Jethro spit toward a big knot-hole in the plank just below the eaves. "I was talkin' with one of them prisoners they catched over at the Big Cane Brake on Reedy River. That's what he said. Said them rich stuck-up fokes in the Low Country wasn't givin' them no share in the runnin' o' things nohow. Said the King hadn't never done nothin' to them and they didn't give a damn 'bout no tea and they wasn't gittin' no rep'esentation in Charles Town nohow. He seemed to be a pretty good kind o' feller, Davy. Wonder what they goin' to do with them fellers they catched."

"Hang 'em, more'n likely, Jethro." Bedent shook out one leg, then the other. "I aint seen a real good hangin' since they hung that feller in Charlottetown last spring fer stealin' that there hoss."

Jethro grinned, winked at Bedent.

"Don't speak o' no hangin' 'round the Sergeant here, Bedent. Hit'll give him the cold shivers. He aint never got over that there time over at Alamance Creek."

David shrugged his shoulders. "That's the truth, Jethro. I thought my jig was up when you slipped in that tent and untied me. I can still feel that rope around my neck. But as for these fellows, I don't think they're figuring on hanging any of 'em. They're in sort of the same shape the Regulators were. All it'll take to make them good loyal supporters of our cause is consideration and fair dealing, I'm bound. We've got to show them the power of the Congress and the mercy of the officers of our side, and I've a notion most of them will join up with us after this." He poked about in the shadows where the rafters came down to the loft floor and located his three-cornered hat, set it jauntily on his head. "But look here, boys," he said, as he clambered to his feet, "we got to be foraging around for a little breakfast."

XXXII

WITH ONE upward jerk McKnitt Alexander turned the log in the fireplace at Alexandriana. Sparks crackled and roared up the chimney. He bent forward, leveled out the coals under the burning wood.

John Davidson hunched back his chair. "McKnitt, you'd run a man out in the winter air with all this heat, chunking the fire up like that. This corn liquor's hot enough without any more fire."

"That's the trouble, John. I thought you knew McKnitt's liquor was the hotest stuff this side the Yadkin. I told you to take Scotch."

"Probably it's not the quality so much as it's the quantity, Colonel, that's heating up the 'squire. But that fire, I'm bound, is powerful hot." Ephraim Brevard pushed back his chair. "I think I'll back up a little myself. Waightstill, how about you? Aren't you a little warm, old man?"

"I've been over here in the corner where it doesn't hit me straight in the face. And as you all well know, I don't drink liquor."

The group laughed at the lawyer's quip. "I'll have to take up for Waightstill, gentlemen." Hezekiah Balch at the other side of the fireplace pushed back his chair. "He's cutting down on his whiskey. And I'm glad to testify for him."

"Getting in politics. Can't do much of it. Politicians don't drink liquor, as you all can testify."

When the laughter had subsided, McKnitt Alexander, who had taken his seat, spoke up. "Waightstill's joking, of course, but he is in politics and in it in a big way. And he's doing a good job on the Provincial Council—"

ALEXANDRIANA

"You're right, McKnitt. Didn't I help appoint Tom Polk here colonel of one of our minute men regiments in the Salisbury district? And didn't he go right off down to South Carolina and get that Tory trouble straightened up in spite of all that snow?"

Thomas Polk clapped a big hand on the knee of the young man seated beside him. "David here is the boy who licked that Scoffelite crowd—"

"Colonel, you forgot Jethro." David grinned, continued to stare into the roaring blaze.

"Yes, that's a fact. Old Jethro's a hell of a fine soldier." The Colonel turned to confront David. "By the way, son, I hear the girls in Mecklenburg are on the warpath, too. I hear they won't receive the company of any young buck who refused to serve with us down in the Snow Campaign. I reckon you're glad you went." He thumped him on the chest.

"That's right, Colonel." Waightstill leaned back in his chair. Mr. Hezekiah's Will told me all about it. The girls wrote themselves a paper and signed it."

"Another declaration of independence, by George!" Ephraim Brevard pushed his chair back another two feet.

"I understand, Colonel Polk, that Ephraim ought to know. I hear the doctor has been visiting your house frequently and not always on the business of the county or on a professional call."

"You're correct, Waightstill." Dr. Brevard spoke up without hesitation. "The Colonel's daughter had already apprised me of that document. She explained that we weren't the only ones who could write a declaration. And she said they were going to send copies to Salisbury and maybe other places and ask that the young ladies in those communities take similar action."

"Well, it's a patriotic move, and it's likely to be an effective one, gentlemen, for when the women folks take out after you they generally get results. And that's what we need, that's what we badly need."

"It's looking pretty bad, isn't it, McKnitt?" John Davidson's face was serious now. So was Waightstill's. So were all the faces that ringed the big fireplace at Alexandriana. Outside, the wind of a dark February day whistled around the eaves and plowed little furrows in the boxwoods.

"Yes, I think so. This report that Clinton's coming south from Boston and that Parker's coming across from England with an army under Cornwallis may be wrong, of course. We get a lot of false rumors. But then it may be right. And if they land at Wilmington they'll naturally head right this way. They will move up the Cape Fear, I've a notion, and the Scotch around Cross Creek will join with them. And they'd likely move right on up to Hillsboro and on back this way through Salisbury. What's to hinder them, men?"

"Well, there's a regiment at Wilmington under Colonel Moore—"

"But what's a regiment, Waightstill? They're brave men, don't misunderstand me. Man for man, we'll give them more than they send. But we aren't trained, we don't have the equipment. I doubt if there's a dozen rounds of powder and balls for Moore's men. And where are our cannon?" He shrugged his shoulders. "We don't have them, that's all."

"But what about Washington? Couldn't he send us help, McKnitt?"

"Why, Ephraim, Washington's in sore straits his ownself. He's got little equipment and he's got few men. They're not disciplined. They've enlisted for only a few months at a time. Congress isn't supporting him, the different provinces are bickering about their rights and Washington's generals are quarreling among themselves. That fellow Lee—"

"McKnitt's right, men." Colonel Polk leaned forward in his chair, stood up, turned his back to the fire. "The situation in the north's bad, very bad. And it's not so much better down here. Of course, we cleaned up this Tory trouble in the back country of South Carolina. But that won't last. The British have agents back there stirring up the people, telling them the supporters of our side are planning to put the Cherokees on them, and all that sort of stuff. And those folks haven't anything against the King or the government in London. They don't know anything about the issues,

ALEXANDRIANA

They're good folks, a lot of 'em; but they're ignorant and they've been living back there by themselves, even more than we have here in Mecklenburg. And they don't have leaders to tell them the straight o' things."

"Colonel," said Dr. Brevard, when Tom Polk paused, "it looks like we've got Tories all around us—"

"And some right here in Mecklenburg," added Waightstill.

"Yes, Ephraim. But not many here, Waightstill. You could count 'em on your two hands, I'll vouch. But over east in the Cape Fear country they're thick as fleas on a dog's back. And that's our big danger, I'm thinking." He sat down, jumped up quickly to shake his breeches legs behind. "That fire's hot, all right, McKnitt." He sat down again.

"Look here, McKnitt—" John Davidson's forehead was furrowed and little wrinkles webbed about his eyes, "we ought to find out for certain about this report of the British coming south. We oughtn't to sit here like an ostrich with his head in the sand and tell ourselves nothing's going to harm us. By George, we'd better find out what's what and do something about it."

"Well, we're doing something, 'Squire. Colonel Polks' men are getting equipped better all along and learning to drill better and—"

Hezekiah Balch interrupted Dr. Brevard. "Mr. Davidson's right, Ephraim. We have been working. I've been preaching, trying to warn my people, trying to tell them that death itself is better than being enslaved. I have been riding around visiting and talking, trying to put more spirit into them—"

"You have, indeed, Hezekiah," McKnitt Alexander interposed. "You have been a flaming spirit, and you've been over-exerting yourself."

"No, I haven't, Mr. Alexander. I haven't done enough. And that's what I was going to say. We must all do more to prepare. We must not permit the enemy to come upon us unaware. We must all be ready to venture everything, as we have already done in signing that declaration. And we must all remember to be unceasing in our prayers."

"I want to say to you men that I agree with our young parson here, and I want to say that all Mecklenburg is proud of him. If we all follow his example, we'll never yield our country to any enemy." John Davidson, surveying the half circle about the fireplace, saw they were all in agreement. Hezekiah Balch was leaning back in his chair. The firelight played upon his tired pale face, but the reflection of the flames danced in his burning bright eyes. "And now, what we've got to do is this, according to my way of thinking. We've got to find out what they're doing down around Wilmington, what Colonel Moore is planning—I understood he was going north with the Continental Line—" He turned to Waightstill Avery. "And that reminds me, Waightstill, I want you to look out for me when you have your next meeting, and so does William Lee. As I was saying, we must get in contact with Moore and find out where we stand. Waightstill, when's your next session of the Provincial Council?"

"The last day of this month, at New Bern."

He turned to McKnitt Alexander. "When do you go to the next meeting of the Provincial Congress, McKnitt."

"Samuel Johnston's called it for April 4."

"They're both some time off. And Waightstill likely won't be home before McKnitt leaves. Where's the Congress meeting this time, McKnitt?"

"Halifax."

"And you won't be back until the middle of the summer, likely. We must find out the situation before then. We're bound to."

"You're right, John. I could send one of my men—"

David, who had been leaning back in his split-bottom chair, straightened up, and the front legs of the chair banged against the wide boards of the floor. "Colonel Polk, let me go, sir. I know all that country down that way. I can start tomorrow, and it won't take me long. I'll get the information for you, I'll—"

"How about it, McKnitt?"

"He knows the country, and he's one of your soldiers." McKnitt smiled. "And he's his own man."

"And a pretty good man, at that, McKnitt. What do you men think about it?"

ALEXANDRIANA

"You'll have to watch out when you hit the Scotch country around Cross Creek, David."

"I know that, Parson. But I know all the pig-paths down that way. I'll swing around the Cross Creek country and dodge the Tories."

"He'd better take Jethro along, Thomas."

"Yes, you'd better, David. You and Jethro make a good team."

"Well, Colonel—" David's broad grin evidenced his delight at the new assignment, "—I'll be glad for Jethro to go along. We've done a good bit of soldiering together already."

It was agreed that it would be best for the two to strike straight east from Charlottetown, cross the Peedee either at Haley's Ferry or above the ferry at the point where the road turned directly eastward toward Cross Creek, and follow that road to the crossing of the Lumber River. Here, Colonel Polk advised, they should swing toward the south and east and leave Cross Creek miles to their left. "Even then you'll be right in the middle of the Scotch country, David, and there'll be Tories on every side. Be careful. Don't get into any arguments. Don't wear your uniforms. And McKnitt might give you some hides or some liquor to carry along as if you were going down that way trading. But if you take a pack horse along be sure he's a plug you wouldn't miss if you had to run for it and leave him."

"At the last meeting of the Council there was a lot of discussion, as you all know, of the likelihood of the Scotch around Cross Creek rising up for the King." Waightstill Avery stood up, his back to the fire, hoisted his coattails to let the heat to his back. "We were concerned about it. We understood that Governor Martin was trying to lead a movement among those Highlanders and that he had in mind commissioning Donald MacDonald, who is one of the leading men in that country, to raise an army for the King. We recommended that all communications between Martin and any of the loyalists be opened by the committee of safety. I don't know what's happened down that way lately, gentlemen, but I wouldn't be surprised if Martin hasn't succeeded in getting something started around Cross Creek. He's a persistent devil."

ALEXANDRIANA

"That's just it, Waightstill. We may think a lot of things. But we don't know. And that's why I think it's a good idea for David and O'Flannagan to slip down that way and find out. I've a notion my ownself that the Scotch will get up an army and try to move down to the coast and meet the British and then they may try to cut the Carolinas in two sections by marching along the boundary, and that would bring them right here. And they're no fools, those Scotch, and no cowards either. They're on the wrong side but they are following their consciences just as we are following ours, and they're good people, and resourceful. There's that Flora MacDonald and her husband. We've all heard how they fought for Prince Charles and now they'll likely be fighting just as much for old George, I'll vouch. Aint that a fact, Tom?"

"You're right, John. And the bad thing about it is that we are fiddling around and doing nothing about it. Moore's in Wilmington and Caswell's got a few hundred minute men at New Bern, but what would they be if MacDonald should get to Wilmington with a thousand or more men and tie up with Clinton's crowd, and then there's that fellow Cornwallis to figure with—"

"Well, David'll bring us the news." John Davidson got up, stretched. "I think we've had enough talking for a while. Look a-here, McKnitt, this Scotch is getting a little low."

"There's plenty more in the bottom o' the sideboard. I'll call Cato to fetch it. That'll hold you till it gets here."

"It'll hold me—" John Davidson stepped over to the little table, picked up the whiskey, started pouring it into the glasses, "but this'll be a powerful small nip for Waightstill."

Waightstill glanced at the glass in John Davidson's hand.

"You said it, 'Squire," he agreed.

XXXIII

"WE DONE played hell!" Jethro slowed his horse to drop back alongside David. "Look a-yonder. Soldiers. And over yonder. All 'round us."

"Just act natural, and don't talk too much. Maybe it's our crowd anyway. And just keep riding—till they stop us."

In another instant they were halted. "Where you fellows going?" A young man of about David's age asked the question. He was riding a big bay mare. Four or five men with him blocked the road.

"We were heading down Wilmington way."

"What's your business, friend?" The young fellow was genial enough, David admitted to himself. But he apparently wouldn't stand to be trifled with either.

"Traders from Mecklenburg." David's tone was casual.

"Mecklenburg? You're a hell of a ways from home. What's your party?"

"We aint got no party, Mister." Jethro casually turned his head, spit a stream of amber over his horse's rump. "We're by ourselves."

The man laughed. "I mean what's your politics, who do you stand for?"

"You got me there, Mister. I most'n generally stands for my ownself and plenty o' good liquor."

The young fellow's face was beginning to cloud. "I've a notion you're trying to put me off. Are you Scotch?"

"Me Scotch, and my name's O'Flannagan, Mister? What do you think?"

ALEXANDRIANA

"I think you'd better damn soon answer my questions. Are you our friends?"

"What's your party, sir?" David had turned questioner.

"Hah. You beat me to it. Well, I don't mind saying. We're on the American side. We're against the King."

"Damn, Mister, and I don't mind tellin' you you shore scared hell out o' us." Jethro spit again. "We thought maybe you was some o' them blasted Tory fellers."

"Well, I still don't know about you two fellows. You may be all right, and then again you may be damned Tories. You'll have to go along with us and see what the Colonel thinks. Things are getting tight round here. We can't take any risks with stray fellows."

"That's fair enough. We'll go. Who's your colonel?"

"Colonel Aleck Lillington, and he's a damn good soldier, too."

"Then your bunch is the Wilmington minute men?"

"That's right. How'd you know?"

"Well, that's sort of our business."

"Hell, you all spies?" The soldier evidenced a new interest. "I'm damned certain now I'll have to take you along."

"We're looking for information. I've a notion Colonel Lillington's the man we want to see, eh, Jethro?"

"You're right, Davy. Go ahead, friend, lead the way. We'll fall in behind you and these other fellows can ride behind us if you're a-feared we'll try to run."

They rode silently toward the east through the pine woods, and after a while they turned north. The leader of the detachment from Colonel Lillington's minute men dropped back alongside David. "How does it happen that you two fellows were down here below the river if you were headed to Wilmington? Why didn't you come through Cross Creek?"

"We figured the Scotch Tories would be pretty thick at Cross Creek. We were figuring on swinging around south and east of them. And it's a nigher route besides if you know how to find your way."

"You couldn't have been heading down toward Governor

ALEXANDRIANA

Martin, could you? You couldn't have been swinging out from Cross Creek to dodge us?"

David saw the direction of his questioning. "No, we've got no business with Martin. He's not on our side."

"Well, you look all right and you tell a pretty straight story. But you were right in the spot to be headed Martin's way."

"How's that?"

"You either really don't understand or you're putting up a good face. But you can't do us any damage now either way, and I just as well tell you. You see, Martin some time ago gave old man Donald MacDonald a commission to raise up an army for the King and he collected a big bunch of Tories at Cross Creek and marched for Wilmington to meet up with the British who are supposed to be due there pretty soon from the north and from England. He stopped on the Cape Fear four miles below Cross Creek, and Colonel Moore, who marched his regiment up from Wilmington when he heard that the Tories were coming together at Cross Creek, set up his camp on the Rockfish about twelve miles below old man MacDonald. That's where we joined him. And it's been our business to scour around over this country and break up all passing between MacDonald's bunch and Governor Martin. And we picked up you two fellows just about on a line between 'em."

David ignored the minute man's imputation. "How does your force compare with the Tories?"

"Well, now that's certainly the sort of question a spy would ask."

"If I had been much of a spy, I'd already have found that out, wouldn't I?"

The young soldier laughed. "I reckon so, at that." He rode on a little way. "I guess he's got some sixteen hundred," he answered, evidently after some thought, "and I guess we got some thousand or a little better. There's Colonel Moore's men, and Lillington's got some hundred and fifty, and there's the militia from Duplin, maybe two hundred, and a hundred or so of Ashe's rangers, and Colonel Caswell, they say, is coming down with the minute men from New Bern."

"That looks like there might be some fighting."
"I wouldn't be surprised. How would that strike you fellows?"
"Well, it wouldn't be our first."
"How's that, friend?"
"That fellow back there and I were in the fight five years ago at Alamance Creek when old Tryon jumped on the Regulators. They caught me and had me waiting to be hung, but that fellow back there slipped me out."
"Well, I do say." The young fellow's tone was frankly admiring. "I wouldn't a thought you'd already been in a war. You're that much ahead o' me. This is my first enlistment."
"Maybe you'll see a plenty o' fighting yet."
"I will, I'll vouch."
A half hour later they rode into the camp at Rockfish River.

XXXIV

JETHRO O'FLANNAGAN lay on his back under a little scrub oak fifty paces from the eastern end of the bridge over Widow Moore's Creek. The flickering light from the campfires on the other side of the creek played upon the naked branches above him but it did nothing to repel the damp coldness that arose out of the swamps to stab at the marrow in his bones. Up from his face with the regularity of his breathing arose little columns of white vapor. His head pillowed upon the curled tail of his coonskin cap, he watched the firelight dancing.

But when the accumulating amber made it impossible for him to lie still longer, he raised himself upon an elbow and shot into the cold night a stream of tobacco-juice that sprayed and shattered the dancing light beams along the swift true arc of its flight.

"I was just lyin' here a-thinkin', Davy," he observed, now that his heretofore submerged vocal mechanisms were released for speaking, "that it do beat all how me and you can git ourselves into scrapes. You mind how we walked right in on that fight at Alamance Creek and dang nigh got you hung, and now we're all set for another fight way down here in the swamps nigh to Wilmington. Here we done rid two hundred miles from Mecklenburg to git ourselves in a fight with these here Scotch country Tories. And we're not hardly got back from that scrap down in South Ca'lina."

"Well, do you want to saddle up and start for home? The horses are tied up back there, you know."

"Me go home?" Jethro's grin crinkled the grizzled beard on his

ALEXANDRIANA

leathery face. "Don't you know I'm scared to ride through the woods in the night time, Davy? One o' them Jack-o'-lanterns down here in these here swamps might take after me."

"More'n likely it'll be one o' MacDonald's Tories."

"If'n don't more'n one take after me, damned if'n he hadn't better watch his step. Look a-here, Davy, when you reckin we're likely to have some fun?"

"Well, I wouldn't be surprised if they don't try to slip up on us some time before daylight. That's what Colonel Lillington thinks."

"Let 'em come." Jethro hugged his musket. "Me and Flossie Belle here—I named my gun fer my baby, Davy—me and Flossie Belle'll blow hell out'n our part o' them damned Tory fellers."

"MacDonald's bunch is just six miles away. It wouldn't take them long to get here if they don't get lost in a swamp or something. And you knew one of their fellows came into Colonel Caswell's camp over there this afternoon with another message from MacDonald claling on the Colonel to declare for the King? Well, I've a notion that fellow was a spy. MacDonald ever since he left the camp at Cross Creek and swung out around Colonel Lillington has been trying to beat Caswell before all our bunch could get together. And with Caswell on the same side of the creek with him and us on this side, it sort of sounds like to me that MacDonald may try to jump Caswell tonight, and if he does—"

"If'n he does, by damn, we'll all be a-sittin' here waitin' fer him."

Men were crossing the bridge now, fanning out to take up positions along the bank of the creek. A man with a shovel in his hand and his musket slung by a cord about his shoulder nudged Jethro gently with the toe of his heavy shoe. "Hey, friend, how 'bout movin' over a ways and let me throw up a little dirt here in front of the bridge. It'll give us something to duck behind if things starts gittin' hot."

"Sure, pardner—" Jethro clambered to his feet, spit over his left shoulder. "If'n you'll git me a shovel I'll help you, or I'll take turns with that there one. Say, though, how come you fellows comin' 'cross the creek?"

"Colonel Caswell's fixin' to fool hell out'n them Tories, friend.

ALEXANDRIANA

He's lookin' fer 'em some time after midnight and they'll be lookin' fer us on that side. We'll be over here with you boys so you won't be shootin' hell out'n us, and we'll knock 'em off when they try to rush the bridge. Old Caswell he's slick as hell. MacDonald's been tryin' fer a week to catch us and whup us afore we could join up with you fellers, but Caswell's too damn slick."

The men were filing across the bridge, the loose boards of the bridge clattered under the impact of heavy shoes. The eastern bank of the stream was thickening now with militia men, minute men from the coast country up around New Bern come now to join Lillington's men from down Wilmington way, from over in Duplin. But on the western bank other men were piling branches from dead pines, scrub oaks, long dried grasses, and the flames were leaping high to throw dancing light upon men silently taking their places.

"Look a-yonder!" Jethro pointed a lean brown finger toward the bridge. The man raised up, leaned on his shovel handle.

"They're taking the planks off the bridge," he explained. "So the damned Tory fellers can't git acrost. Caswell's slick, I tell you, friend, slicker'n hell. They's likely to be a lot o' drowned Tories when they come flying down to cross that there bridge." He resumed his shoveling gray dirt.

Through the long hours after midnight the cold air gnawed the stiffening fingers and toes of the minute men sprawled back from the bridge. Non-commissioned officers moved quietly among them, here and there awoke dozing soldiers to inquire about their muskets. "Keep your powder dry and see to it you've got wadding a-plenty. If you run out o' paper, this gray moss ought to serve. Don't let this dampness foul your powder."

David sat hunched against a stubby pine. Ten feet away Jethro, his mouth open, was snoring, his musket clutched in the crook of his right arm. But David had no thought for sleeping. Unlike his companion from Mecklenburg, he did not have the ability to close the door upon the visions that persisted. Not that he was fearful, that he was alarmed, that he was giving thought to what the next hours might bring. For he was looking forward to the coming of

ALEXANDRIANA

MacDonald's Tories, he was even relishing the expected encounter, the shock of man upon man, the rough wild savage symphony of battle . . .

He was thinking of two houses that sat back there along the Cape Fear, and two women . . . Lovelace, and her father and her mother. She knew little of this clash of ideas, she called it all politics, she wanted desperately to dismiss it, to live gently and happily and with good will to all men. Why should men fight and kill each other and pour out their blood in forests and along the banks of streams, men who were essentially the same, men who lived alike, who saw the same stars and watched the same sun pushing back the death of the night, who felt the same cool wind, the same hot sun upon their cheeks, who loved life, and their wives and the cooing of their babies. Why should men fight each other and slay and kill and murder? How could one explain it to a girl like Lovelace? He wondered about Mr. McNeill. He remembered that tiny scar upon his wrist, that symbol, that reminder, of the Blood Oath . . . There had been much fighting around Cross Creek, he had learned from Colonel Lillington's men, mean fighting, the desperate cruel bitter battling of brother against brother. How had Mr. McNeill fared? How had Lovelace? Instinctively, he swept his cold hand across his eyes, striving to wipe away the terror that was threatening to envelop him.

Consciously, purposely, he sought to bolster another vision taking shape . . . He thought of a night in the summer, the last night of May, the night of the day on which the resolves were drafted and passed, the night in Jack's Tavern. Here in this cold clammy darkness before the dawn of a February day he traced with ecstatic delight the details of that night's adventure. Belinda was a flame, a hot, searing, burning delightful fire that warmed and promised and beckoned . . . "Damn that old man!" He said it half aloud, but Jethro was asleep, snoring, his mouth open to the thick settling miasma of the swamps. Belinda and her Tory husband, Angus MacDougald . . .

"Who goes there!"

The challenging shout came from down at the bridge. In the

ALEXANDRIANA

stillness it cut sharply through the cold air. David realized he had been deaf to the night sounds, to the stealthy approach of men slipping toward the bridge.

On his all-fours he crawled over to Jethro, shook him roughly. "Wake up, Jethro! Wake up!" Jethro sat up, rubbed his eyes. "Wake up, fellow! I think maybe the Tories are about ready to come after us."

"Damn!" Jethro was instantly awake. "Where 'bouts?"

From the end of the bridge the challenge was renewed. "Who goes there!"

"A friend!" The answer on the other side of the bridge was clear. Minute men all about now were stirring, seeing to their muskets.

"A friend to whom?"

"To the King."

A dead stillness. Then from the other side came a jumble of words. "What's that? What's he saying?" Jethro's face in the reflection of the firelight was furrowed in a deep scowl; he was staring across beyond the bridge, into the black rim of the woods beyond.

"Must be some of that Scotch talk. I can't make it out."

Now the officers were moving along the front of the minute men faced upon the Widow Moore's Creek. "Ready, men. They're gettin' ready to come at us. Hold your fire till they're down to the edge of the creek. And watch out for your powder. Steady now, steady."

The sharp report of a single musket cleaved the cold still air. Then a command, and the rattle of muskets along the creek's edge. Bullets whined; a dead stick from the scrub oak struck David on the shoulder.

Out from the shadows into the glare of the fires a group of men made toward the bridge, and down from the woods came others with a rush. Two men raced along the bridge sleepers, reeling to keep their balance as they came.

"Fire!" The shout was almost in David's ear, and the crash of muskets along the bank of the creek crackled and spurts of flame

ALEXANDRIANA

jabbed the shadows. The two men on the logs, David could see through the smoke, were about to reach the bank. The light from the fires shone full upon them now. And as he peered toward the bridge, one man threw up his arm, his musket shot out and down into the waters of the creek, and he twisted on one foot, stepped crazily forward, and fell to the ground. The other man, now across the sleeper, turned, beckoned to the men on the other side, and in that instant pitched forward on his face.

On the other side the first rush of the Tories had struck the plankless bridge. Men raced out upon the sleepers, lost their balance, fell into the black water. Others, carried off their feet by the impact of bodies rushing down upon them from behind, were shoved down to disappear, some with screams as hot bullets plowed into them from the eastern bank.

The man who had first fallen pulled to his feet, waved an arm aloft. "Come on, men! Come on! King George and broadswords! Come—" Now he was down again, flat on his face. Men were pushing out along the sleepers. But they were dropping off, and the muskets crackled . . .

Another man, David could see as he stepped from behind the low dirt embankment, had reached the eastern bank, was headed straight toward him. He was startled as Jethro's gun went off almost in his ear. But through the smoke of Jethro's weapon he saw the man spin crazily, throw out an arm that cut a swift half circle, and sink to his knees, roll out flat upon his stomach. From the other side jabs of flame were spitting out, and bullets whined. David aimed his musket across the sleepers, pulled the trigger. A roar, his shoulder snapped back, he felt the flame sear his face. "Too much powder in that one."

Calmly Jethro poured powder into the muzzle of his gun, dropped shot behind it. Calmly he removed from his mouth the wadding he had been chewing, dropped it into the muzzle, chunked his ramrod down upon it, pulled the ramrod out.

Now he was raising the musket to his shoulder. David peered through the smoke. A man had got across the sleeper, was on the bank. The leader who had first crossed it had pulled up on his elbow. He raised an arm. "Come on, men! King George and—" But he didn't finish it, for he had tumbled over on his face.

The man who had just crossed turned for an instant to glance behind. In that moment David looked squarely into his face, now lighted by the blaze on the western bank. "I wonder—" He saw out of the corner of his eye Jethro's musket leveling upon the young man, now coming on a run away from the bridge, straight toward him. In a flash he shot his arm out, struck the musket an upward blow. The gun roared.

"Hell fire!" Jethro's eyes, David saw, were blazing. "I had a bead on 'im. Another second and he'd a-bit the dust."

"That's why—" David stopped. The young man, now not more than thirty paces out there, screamed, dropped his gun, sagged slowly in the middle, fell in a heap.

"Somebody else got him anyway," said David.

Down by the bridge the fallen leader of the Tories twisted over on his side, slowly pushed himself upward until he was almost in a sitting position again. Weakly he raised his left arm, and David saw by the light from the fires across the creek that the sleeve was clotted with blood and dirt. "At 'em, men." The command was weak. "King George—" He fell back.

"He's a brave man." David nudged Jethro. "That man down by the bridge. Do you suppose that's MacDonald?"

"Maybe so. He's nervy, all right. But that young fellow over there. How come did you knock my gun up fer him?"

"You'll find out. Look, Jethro, they're running!"

Back from the plankless bridge the Tories were pushing in panic as bullets plowed into them from across the stream. They were spreading out now, running to gain the cover of the scrubby woods behind, the cover of the lifting darkness unlighted by deceitful campfires. Down towards Jethro and David a man was racing. "After 'em, boys!" he yelled. "Over the creek! Run 'em down!"

"Who's that fellow, Davy?"

"Must be Colonel Caswell."

The minute men were swarming across the creek. Some raced along the smooth sleepers, some gained the shore and others fell off with loud splashings to reach the western side with curses that they had lost their weapons or drenched their powder. Others plunged into the dark waters to thresh and swim across, holding their guns aloft. Jethro raced for the bridge. David, stopping beside the crumpled young man, looked up to see Jethro step off the other end of the sleeper, plunge after the fleeing Tories.

He turned the wounded man over on his back. His eyes were closed. "It's him, all right." David bent down, his ear to the young fellow's chest. "He's still alive." But in the flickering light, now fading out as the fires burned low, his face was ashen. "But he's losing a lot of blood."

Quickly David sought the wound. From his waist to his knees his clothes were soggy with blood. David fumbled at his belt, got it unbuckled, pulled his breeches down, tore at the drawers dripping with blood. He found the wound. A bullet had torn a hole in his right leg half way between the knee and the hip; the blood was still oozing from it. He ran his left hand under the wound, with his right pulled the leg at the calf. He heard the bones grating.

"Too bad." He shook his head. "Now Dr. Barksdale will have a chance at showing whether he's learned anything under Dr. Brevard. Damned if I don't wish Ephraim was here."

The blood was still oozing from the wound, and he had already lost much blood. "I've got to stop that blood in a hurry and I haven't any bandages." He stood up, stripped off his hunting shirt, threw it on the ground, then pulled off his under shirt, began tearing it into strips. With strong sure fingers now he wadded up a small piece of the cloth, pressed it down firmly above the wound, slipped a longer strip under the leg, brought the ends together above the wad and tied it tightly. The wadding was coloring, growing dark in the little light that remained. He wrapped another strip around the leg, and another and another. "And now for splints. That'll be a job to find, I'm bound." Back at the scrub oak he cut off several branches, some dead and stiff, others alive and pliable, and quickly whittled them into rough shape. And having scooped out a little hole in the sandy soil underneath the wounded man's foot, he banked the dirt on each side of the foot to hold it in proper position while he applied the splints and wrapped them about with other strips from the torn under shirt. "Well, Dr. Barksdale, that's a pretty fair job considering what you had to work with, if I do say so. And now if I just had a good shot o' Uncle McKnitt's Mecklenburg corn liquor I believe I'd have the patient in pretty good shape." He stood up. For the first time he realized it was cold. His teeth were chattering. He reached down, recovered his hunting shirt and put it on "Fact, I believe a shot o' Uncle McKnitt's corn would help the doctor."

Some of Caswell's men were straggling back to the fires, he could see. "Hey, over there!" he shouted. "One o' you fellows fetch me some fire over here, will you? I got a wounded man I'm working on."

One of them brought a burning stick and started a fire. After a while the young man opened his eyes, stared a moment at David, closed his eyes again. In a few minutes he opened them again, flung out an arm in an impulsive gesture.

"Steady, old man."

The young fellow grimaced as he pulled up his uninjured leg, pushed it back slowly.

"Steady. Be still. You've got a bad leg, fellow."

The injured man looked with unblinking eyes at David. Slowly a half-smile, half-scowl spread over his haggard pale face. "Fancy seeing you here. Are you the fellow that plugged me?"

"No, Angus. I'm the fellow who doctored on you. It was a sort of makeshift job but I think it will serve. But you must be quiet; you've lost a lot of blood and you got a nasty fracture."

"I know it. I'm done for. But it don't make a damn."

"Oh, no. You'll be all right. But go to sleep and rest. I'll get a blanket and fix you up."

"Listen, Barksdale, I've got something to say to you—"

"No, not now. You're too weak, Angus. You've got to be quiet. Then you can talk."

Angus MacDougald closed his eyes. In a few minutes he was sleeping. David found some bedding and a blanket. It was daylight now. Down at the bridge the two Tory leaders lay cold and stiff. The man who had risen to wave an arm and call upon his men would never call again. He lay crumpled and broken and David, standing silently looking down upon him, saw that every stitch of his clothing was clotted with his blood. At the very edge of the creek bank lay several stiffened bodies, and in the creek and across on the other side he saw others.

Groups of Caswell's and Lillington's men were coming up now, many of them herding together Tories whom they had overtaken in their flight. Several had crossed the sleepers of the wrecked bridge to see in the light of early morning the place where they had been fighting in the hour before dawn. "Bring one of the prisoners over here," David called across the creek. "I want to find out who these two men are. I think maybe this one is MacDonald."

A young Scotchman was brought across. "It's not General MacDonald," he said, as he came up. "He was too sick to be in the battle. That's Colonel Campbell over there, and this—" He turned the dead man over gently so that he could see his face, ghastly in a smear of dirt and dried blood. "This is Colonel MacLeod. They were our leaders." The boy stood silently looking down upon the dead face. "Could I get something and cover them up?"

"Of course, son." David said it without hesitation. "And I'll help you. You have every right to be proud of them. They were brave men; their King never had braver. This man here must have been shot a dozen times."

Toward mid-morning Angus MacDougald aroused. "I want to talk to you." His voice was weak, and there was a feverish brightness in his eyes.

"Wait a while, Angus. We'll talk after you get stronger. You're too weak now."

"I'm not going to be any stronger. I'm—I'm getting weaker. I'm—"

"Oh, no, you aren't. Just wait here and let me get you a drink—"

"Listen, Barksdale, why didn't you kill me? Why didn't you let me go on and bleed to death? God knows, I wouldn't've given a damn. And I'd a shot the hell out o' you if I'd got the chance—"

ALEXANDRIANA

"Steady, fellow. Let that talking wait a while—"

"God knows I didn't like you, David Barksdale. I hated you. I may still hate you. I don't know. But I've been lying here thinking. I haven't been sleeping all the time—"

"Angus, shut up that talking. You're too weak. You've got to—"

"God knows Belinda wanted you, and still does, I'm bound—"

"For God's sake, Angus—"

"Oh, yes, I know all about it. I haven't been as big a fool as you two thought. I found out about that night at the tavern in Charlottetown. Fact, Belinda got in a rage and told me. She wanted like hell to sleep with you. She always has. By God, she still does. She still—does. She—still—" Angus stopped. But his eyes were burning, bright, glassy, staring.

David put his hand on the wan forehead, under the chin. Angus was hot, the fever was mounting, the exertion of his wild talking had already had its effect. "Go to sleep, Angus. Don't think about anything. Just rest."

"I'll have plenty of time to rest, all right." A tired smile played for a moment over his face now drenched of all color. "I'll be gone before night. And then you can have her. After all, you two were meant for each other, I'm bound. I didn't fit. She thought I was no man—"

"Listen, Angus, you got farthest across the bridge—"

His face lighted. "Did I? Tell her that, will you? That'll be enough. But you'll tell her that?"

"Sure, I'll tell her. But you can tell her yourself."

"No, I'll never see her any more. I'm done for as sure as hell." He closed his eyes. "But you'll tell her that? By God, I'd like for her to know that. I'd like for her to—" His voice fell away.

Colonel Moore and a detachment of his men rode up during the forenoon, and as the hours passed more and more Tories were brought into the camp on the Widow Moore's Creek. Jethro, his boots caked with mud, came in about noon. "Them damned Tories could run like rabbits. We had a hell of a time catchin' 'em but we shore catched a sight of 'em. We comed up on that fellow MacDonald a-sittin' on a stump sicker'n hell, and he had a right to be, I'll

ALEXANDRIANA

vouch. And we catched that fellow Allan MacDonald too, and a sight o' other Tory officers. And guns and wagons and hosses and swords, man, you never seen the like o' the stuff we catched. And even a big box of money—gold, they said it was. I'm tireder'n hell. If'n I could jest get a good nip of liquor—"

"Hell, Jethro, get out and find some. Whoever heard of you not being able to locate liquor? I want a shot for this fellow over here. He's in a pretty bad way."

When Jethro came back with the liquor, Angus MacDougald lay unmoving beneath the blanket. "He's dead," said David.

"Who is he?"

"He's the fellow I wouldn't let you shoot. He's a fellow named MacDougald; he's the husband of Belinda. You know, one of those girls that came to Mecklenburg with Tryon that time."

"Yes, I know, the one that had fire in her eyes."

"That's right." He paused, considered a moment. "Look here, Jethro, we've got to be getting back to Mecklenburg. And we've got to get him home. I'll tell you what. How about your riding along ahead to Pleasant Grove—that's their home up the river in Bladen—and notifying them that I'm coming with him? You might give it out that he's badly hurt instead of saying he's dead. It's lucky we've got the horses, and the pack horse to carry him. And we can get a little sleep and start before day tomorrow. And I'll stay a little way behind you. You can find the place. Everybody up the river knows where Pleasant Grove is."

Jethro was waiting outside the gates of Pleasant Grove when David rode up in mid-afternoon. "She's pretty certain he's dead," he reported. "But she's taking it pretty good. They sent out and got some neighbor men and women to come in. You can go up to the house and I'll stay here with him. We've done made it up for some of the men to come down and take him to the house when you show up there."

David rode up the lane to the house, tied his horse at the hitching-post, mounted the steps and crossed the piazza to lift the brass knocker and let it fall gently.

Belinda opened the door. Her eyes were red, but she was com-

ALEXANDRIANA

posed. "Come in, David," she said quietly. She led him into the parlor at the right. In the room across the hall he could hear the hum of low conversation. "I know you are very tired and cold. Stand over by the fireplace, and I'll have you a drink brought." She tapped a little bell on the escritoire, spoke in low calm tones to the Negro who appeared in the doorway. "It was good of you to—to bring him home, David. He is—dead?" David turned from warming his fingers, swallowed, hesitated. "Yes, I know he is dead." She said it calmly. "I have known it all along. Your friend tried to leave a little hope, but he did not deceive me." She was looking at him, now, and her very look seemed to be pushing into his flesh, paining him. "You killed him yourself, perchance?"

"No, no, Belinda, no." He was speaking now without difficulty. "No, I tried to save his life. I—"

"I'm glad you weren't the one who killed him, David, though I suspect he would have killed you had he had the chance."

"He said so himself. But I don't think he would have."

"Then you talked with him? He wasn't killed outright?"

"Yes, I bandaged his leg and made splints for it but he lost too much blood and the shock—"

"Did you all talk about me, David?"

"Yes."

"What did he say? Did he speak of that night at the tavern in Charlottetown the last time I saw you till now?"

"He said you had got sore and told him about it."

"Yes, I was rotten to do it. But I did. And what else did he say?"

"Belinda, we shouldn't talk about that now, should we?"

"Yes, we must. I cannot rest until I know. I cannot—Oh, David—" tears were welling in her eyes. "I can't put him away until I am at peace with him, until we at this late moment somehow understand each other. Do you see?"

"He said that you had always liked me—I don't like to be saying this, Belinda—"

"Please go on."

"And that you hadn't liked him very much. That you had never thought him much of a man, and I told him that I'd tell you that

ALEXANDRIANA

of all MacDonald's men he had got closest to us before he fell. I told him I'd tell you that and he said he hoped I would."

"I only wish he had. But it was nice of you to tell him that."

"But he did, Belinda. I was telling him the truth. He was farthest across the bridge. He was so close to me that I recognized him and knocked up Jethro's gun when he was about to shoot him."

The girl smiled. "That means much to me, David. That makes me almost happy. And now I must go back and rest. Mother is with me. I'll send someone in to keep you company. And they are seeing about—about Angus, I know. You must spend the night at Pleasant Grove. I know you are so tired." She took his hand. "Thank you, David, more than you can ever know."

"I must be going, Belinda. I'm—I'm so sorry it—it happened."

"But you must spend the night somewhere, David, and—"

"We'd figured on stopping at a tavern at Cross Creek." He patted her hand. "Be brave, keep up your spunk, Belinda."

"Lovelace will be glad to see you. She's coming here in the morning." She moved toward the door, turned, smiled through tearful eyes. "Good-bye, David."

XXXV

On a dark morning late in March John McKnitt Alexander swung into his saddle, bent down low to kiss Jeanie again, and rode quickly through the gates of Alexandriana toward Poplar Tent Church. At the crown of the little slope he turned in his saddle. Jeanie was standing on the uppin'-block. She waved and threw him a kiss. He waved gaily, threw a kiss, waved again. When he faced eastward and swung down the slope he saw the road ahead through a blur . . .

His thoughts were as dark as this gray dispiriting morning. He turned up the collar of his greatcoat to shield his throat from the damp, cold air; but by no such simple act could he shield his mind from clammy cold thoughts. Back there behind him lay warmth, security, happiness, everything. Back there were Jeanie and the children and pleasant rolling acres and barns well filled and a smokhouse and cribs pushed out with a summer's store.

He was leaving it. Soon now, in an hour's steady jogging, he would be past the boundaries of Alexandriana, tonight he would rest at Phifer's, in another day he would be in Salisbury perhaps. And after Salisbury a week's hard riding to Halifax for this fourth meeting of the Provincial Congress.

But he refused to think that far ahead. Behind him now, over the hill behind, out of sight already, out of sight behind the wet foreboding woods around which this Tuckaseegee Road was twisting its way, lay Alexandriana and a pleasant way of life. Before him lay hard riding and cold whistling winds and stabbing sleet perhaps, but before him lay more unpleasant things than winds

ALEXANDRIANA

and sleet and long roads that stretched interminably ahead, or even lurking Tories.

Before him lay fateful decisions to make, before him were hours and agonies of debate and study and the burning of many candles. There would be at Halifax able men, but able men would be needed and the prudence and judgment and patriotic zeal of able men might not suffice. There would be Cornelius Harnett from Wilmington, mild, gentle, with a smile of womanly sweetness, Cornelius Harnett whose slender frame and courteous, kindly dignity concealed the strength and fire of deep conviction and unmeasured, immeasurable courage.

Joseph Hewes, back from the Continental Congress in Philadelphia, would be there from New Bern; and Richard Caswell, fresh from his victory over the Tories at the Widow Moore's Creek bridge, would come up from Dobbs; and Abner Nash from New Bern would add his counsel and his courage; Wilie Jones would need to do no riding, for his home was at Halifax. David Nesbit had been named to go over from Salisbury, for Salisbury, being a city, had a representative of its own, and Grif Rutherford and Matt Locke from Rowan.

John Phifer and Robert Irwin had been named from Mecklenburg as his colleagues. If Tryon County was sending anyone, McKnitt hadn't heard, he reflected. Nor would John Harvey be there, with his flaming devotion to the cause, for John Harvey had been dead now almost a year; but from Perquimans would come other Harveys, no doubt, for they were of the leading men in the north coast country.

It would require men of brains and courage, for great were the problems ahead. Armies to be raised and equipped, for although the rout of the Highlander Tories had saved North Carolina, McKnitt Alexander knew that it was but a respite against that day when the British would strike. A civil government to be set up for the province. And that always pressing question of independence, of casting away every anchor. Well, he knew how he would stand on that question, indeed . . .

When he should reach Halifax, however, and plunge into the

ALEXANDRIANA

work of the Congress there would be no time for gloomy forebodings, he knew.

And so he found, when after many days of weary travel he rode into Halifax and took his seat in the Congress. From the lighting of the candles until past midnight, sometimes until the dawn of a spring morning was breaking, they labored with the problems of the province, and McKnitt Alexander rejoiced when on April 12, but eight days after they had convened, Cornelius Harnett with shining bright eyes stood before the assemblage and read the document his committee had evolved out of study and reflection and prayer and much sweat.

It had a familiar ring, this paper, and something about Cornelius Harnett, older and wiser with more years and much thinking, reminded McKnitt Alexander of the boy preacher back at Poplar Tent, who a year ago in the little log courthouse at the crossing of the roads in Charlottetown had stood up with shining eyes and sweet glowing face to speak of his faith in America.

"Resolved," read Cornelius Harnett, "That the delegates from this Colony in the Continental Congress be empowered to concur with the delegates from the other colonies in declaring independence and forming foreign alliances; reserving to this colony the sole and exclusive right of forming a constitution and laws for this colony."

Samuel Johnston put the question. And from the moment of the rising throaty roar of acclamation, McKnitt Alexander went about his tasks with a new heart, for now North Carolina had joined Mecklenburg.

The Congress named Wilie Jones to the new Council of Safety. The delegates from the Salisbury district elected Hezekiah Alexander to displace Waightstill Avery on this body, for another task had been decreed for the young lawyer from Charlottetown. His was to be the important work of aiding in the framing of the new constitution.

But first in the minds of the delegates was military defense. Clinton was nearing Brunswick and Sir Peter Parker with Cornwallis any moment now might be sailing into the Cape Fear. And

ALEXANDRIANA

the arrival of the Redcoats might revive the Tories of the Scotch country.

"We are woefully unprepared! We've got to get ready to meet the British when they come! And they are coming, gentlemen." McKnitt listened as the delegate spoke, for the man was expressing his views, the views, in fact, of virtually every delegate in the Congress. "We argue and orate and discuss and plan and all the time where are our soldiers, where are the weapons to place in their hands, where is the powder, where the balls, the flints? We can't fight the British with words, men. They are powerfully trained and organized, excellently equipped and supplied, they are a war machine, they are not to be stopped by words. You say that we are free people, that we are pioneers, strong, hardy, straight-shooting. Yes, gentlemen, but a bullet from a British musket will kill a hardy pioneer just as quickly as it will a soft ballroom courtier. And how are our men to shoot straight if we give them no guns, no powder, no flints and balls?"

Now a new army was in the making. Four new regiments for the Continental Line were created, with Thomas Polk of Mecklenburg colonel of the fourth, James Thackston lieutenant colonel, and William Lee Davidson major. Six brigadier generals were named, and Griffith Rutherford of Rowan was one of the six. Already Colonel James Moore of the first regiment of the Continental Line and Colonel Robert Howe of the second had been named brigadier generals and now Francis Nash was advanced to the command of the first and Alexander Martin to the command of the second.

Hezekiah Alexander was commissioned paymaster of Colonel Polk's fourth regiment. From each district the Congress named officers to raise new battalions; it named officers for three companies of light horse, and appointed field officers for each county. Adam Alexander was advanced to be colonel of the Mecklenburg militia, John Phifer was made lieutenant colonel, and John Davidson became first major, with George Alexander second major.

Late in April the Congress granted a parole of honor to General Donald MacDonald and his son, to Allan MacDonald and other

ALEXANDRIANA

officers captured after the battle at Moore's Creek, who had been brought to the jail at Halifax. By showing kindness to the prisoners and their families, the delegates felt they would advance the cause of the independence they had just now declared. "In our power," declared the manifesto the Congress published, "their errors claim our pity, their situation disarms our resentment. We shall hail their reformation with increasing pleasure, and receive them among us with open arms . . . We shall bless the day which shall restore them to us, friends of liberty, to the cause of America, the cause of God and mankind."

And as May opened the Congress named young William Hooper, the Wilmington lawyer born in Boston, and Joseph Hewes, the New Bern merchant born in New Jersey, to return to the Continental Congress, and with them in the place of Richard Caswell, now become the treasurer of the province, thirty-six-year old John Penn, Granville County lawyer born in Virginia.

The Congress adjourned on May 14, but already Henry Clinton had reached the Cape Fear and was scourging the country roundabout, including Robert Howe's plantation in Brunswick, with fire and sword.

And Hezekiah Alexander was nearing Wilmington for the meeting of the Council of Safety as his brother finished packing his saddlebags and began the long trip westward.

It was late on a June afternoon when McKnitt turned in at the gates of Alexandriana. "I would have stopped at Poplar Tent to see Hezekiah Balch if it hadn't been getting a little late and if I hadn't been so anxious to see you all," he said to Jeanie, after he had kissed her and the children and given them the little trinkets he had fetched from Halifax.

"I'm glad you—" Jeanie hesitated. McKnitt saw her face pale as if a sharp pain had stabbed through her temples.

"My dear, what—"

"McKnitt—" Now she was composed again. "Hezekiah is gone."

"But—"

"He's dead. He—he died while you were away."

McKnitt Alexander stood speechless. "But—but he can't be, Jeanie. He was just a boy. And he was so needed, so beloved—"

"Yes, but he's gone. And they've buried him in the very center of Poplar Tent graveyard, for he was in the center of their affections."

"Oh, this war. These damnable British. They killed him, Jeanie. They killed him just as certainly as they massacred those people up in Boston. They—"

"Hezekiah wouldn't have talked that way, Sweetheart."

"No—I'm sorry. But I loved that boy, Jeanie. I'll miss him. And we need him so much, God knows we need him. God knows—"

"Some time we'll understand it, dear. Haven't you said it yourself many times?"

"Yes, some time, I suppose. Some time we'll understand even this war, this struggle to live, these sacrifices, this eternal waiting for doom to strike us down—"

He sat down in his big chair.

"Don't worry, McKnitt. Sit there and rest. You must be powerful tuckered out, I'll vouch. And I'll run fix you up a drink."

XXXVI

LITTLE CLOUDS of red dust puffed up from the horses' feet. Lined up roughly with their riders along a sagging front here on the muster-ground at Charlottetown, they stamped their legs to dislodge the stinging flies. Under the hot summer sun tramping men and horses had worn down the grass and weeds and beaten the red soil into a dry hot pulpy dirtiness.

From the shade of a tree at the edge of the muster-ground several members of the Mecklenburg militia were watching the light horse of Captain Charlie Polk assemble for the roll-call. The captain and his two lieutenants, William Lindsay and John Lemmond, sat on their horses facing the company. The clerk, William Lemmond, was calling off the names.

"Sergeant John Montgomery."

"Here!"

"Sergeant William Galbraith."

" 'Ere!"

"Hugh Lindsay, drummer."

"Here, sir." The youngster's reply was an effort at imitation of the deeper voices of the two sergeants.

"Humphrey Hunter."

"Heigh-o!" The raw-boned young Poplar Tent militiaman yelled it out.

"Jonathan Buckaloe."

"Hy-o-o!"

"James Hall."

"Here!"

ALEXANDRIANA

Jethro O'Flannagan hunched David in the side with bony elbow. "That there feller's a preacher. Jest got his preachin' papers here this spring from Orange Presbyte'y. And he's got a hell of a gang to be chaplain over."

"How'd you know he was a preacher?" Bedent Spraggins shifted the cud of tobacco in his mouth. "And how'd you know Rev'end Hall had got preachin' papers this spring?"

"Hell-fire—" Jethro spat through his fingers to spray the dust. "I go to church. I heared him preach at Hopewell. He's a damned good preacher, too. But if'n he keeps Charlie Polk and Hump Hunter and them Maxwell boys and them other fellers straightened out, he'll shore keep busy as hell."

"Aint nothin' wrong with them fellers, Jethro. They's rough, but they's good-hearted. Hell, Hump Hunter might make a preacher hisself some day."

Jethro laughed. "Damned if I wouldn't go a long ways to hear Hump preach. But he could, by damn, if'n he put his mind to it. And o' course, them fellers is all right. They'll give them Cherokees hell, too, if we don't git 'em all killed out afore Charlie and his crowd gits there."

The clerk was monotonously singing out the names.

"Thomas Shelby."

"Hyo-o!" Shelby sang it back to him.

"John Stansill."

"Here!"

"Robert Harris, Junior."

"Here, sir."

"John Foard."

"Heigh-o-o!"

Horses were cantering over the dusty road from up toward the courthouse at the crossing. Jethro turned. He pointed a lean forefinger. "Hell's bells, Bedent, look a-yonder. Look at that big feller with Cap'n McKnitt and Dr. Brevard. Damn! That there's the biggest damn man I ever seen. He ought to git down and let that there hoss ride. Wonder who—"

"That's Colonel Ben Cleveland, Jethro," David said, "from up

ALEXANDRIANA

in Surry. He's got a bunch going over into the Cherokee country too. You'll be seeing a lot of him over past the Quaker Meadows. He's one of General Rutherford's best men."

"I reckon we ought to be seein' a lot o' him. Damn if he aint one o' the biggest bastards I ever seen. He must weigh bettrn'n three hundred."

The roll call was completed now; Captain Polk was conferring with the officers who had just ridden up. "We'll be startin' afore long," observed Bedent Spraggins. "You better come go 'long with us, Davy."

"I'd like to get a crack at those Indians, all right, but I'll have to be heading the other way, Bedent. I'm signed up to go with Colonel Davidson—"

"Well, he's a-goin' after the Cherokees, too."

"I'm not talking about Major John; I'm going with William Lee and Will Polk to join the Continental Line. The brigade's forming at Wilmington. We're likely to be sent north to help General Washington."

"Well, 'cordin' to what I hear, the General's needin' all he can git."

"Yes, it's looking pretty bad, Bedent. But, say, I've got to be starting back to Alexandriana. Take care of yourself, Bedent, and look after Jethro. Don't let any of those redskins get your scalps, boys. I've got to be getting ready my ownself to start down to the coast—"

"He's got to stop on the way, Bedent. Got a little business down 'bout Cross Creek." Jethro nudged David, spat through his fingers. "He's got to show off that there new uniform Cap'n McKnitt and Mis' Jeanie's a-makin' fer him."

XXXVII

ONCE AGAIN David Barksdale saw himself in the long gilt-framed mirror in the front hallway of the McNeill home at Cross Creek. Once again the light from the candles on the dropleaf walnut table shone full upon him and his image smiled back. The buff that lined the dark blue of his uniform stood out in the light from the candles and the light sparkled in the buttons down the front.

Years ago he had stood before this mirror a gawky, big-knuckled boy from the back settlements, his hair tied behind with one of Jeanie's ribbons, awkward and self-conscious in his store-bought clothes. And that image had yielded to another, that of a tall young man with broad shoulders fitted to blue broadcloth, throat swathed in white stock above a blue and silver waistcoat, coat dropping past slim hips in blue breeches with silver buckles at the knee, muscles bulging in cream-colored stockings above black shoes and more silver buckles. The gay young blade home from Princeton College . . .

Tonight the broadcloth, the black and silver waistcoat, had faded out, and David saw again with satisfaction that his clothing was unwrinkled, that the image was tall, the shoulders broad, that the candlelight danced and played upon the insignia of a lieutenant in the North Carolina Line.

"David!" Lovelace came quickly down the stairs, and he met her at the bottom, and took both her hands. "But how did you know that Father was not at home?"

"I didn't know it. I just came on out. Why?"

ALEXANDRIANA

"Well—But let us sit down in the parlor first." She led him by the hand through the doorway. "Would you rather sit in the chair there or on the couch?"

He laughed. "On the couch, of course—with you. Don't you remember it took me several hours and all my wits to progress from the chair to the couch the last time? Would you want me to start again at the beginning?"

"David, you are your same old self, I'm bound. And I'm so glad to see you." She sat down, spread her skirts, crossed her feet. He sat down beside her.

"And I'm so glad to see you, too. It seems forever since I've seen you. So much has happened and things have been moving so fast."

"Yes, so much has happened." She seemed to say it with a meaning beyond the perfunctory. He sensed it.

"Is that what you meant by asking me how I knew that your father wasn't home?"

"Well, yes. Father has changed. He has been rather badly treated and he even feels that you are among his enemies."

"But—"

"He heard about your being at the battle down Wilmington way. He found it out when the story got abroad in these parts that you had brought Angus home. That was a noble thing to do, David. It—"

David interrupted. "But, my dear girl, I had naught against your father. Was he, by any chance, in that fight? I was only in it by accident, though I'm glad I got a crack at those Tories."

"No, he wasn't in the battle. But since then he has suffered much at the hands of sorry rascals who call themselves patriots. They have given him ill treatment, stolen from him, burned his property, handled him so cruelly that they have made him even stronger for the King."

"That's bad. I'm sorry. But that is the way with civil war. I had hoped he would be on our side."

"You didn't know Father. You see, he took the Blood Oath."

"Yes, but—"

"He would never have gone against the King. But had they left

ALEXANDRIANA

him alone he would never have been active in support of him. As it is, he hates those on your side and he's given me orders not to—"

"Not to let me come to see you?"

"Yes, David."

"Well, you didn't let me. I just came."

"And he's gone, too."

"I would have come had he been here."

"I believe you would. And I'm—I'm—"

"Glad?"

"Yes. I'm glad. I've missed you so much. I've wanted so long to see you."

"Bless your heart, Lovelace. Bless your sweet little heart." He lifted her hand, kissed the back, turned it over, kissed the palm. "And I've missed you so much, too. And I'm sorry your father feels the way he does about me. I wish he could be on our side, too. We need good men on our side. We need all the good men we can get. Sometimes I even wonder if we have enough. I can't see why good men wouldn't be fighting along with us."

"But not all the men on your side are good men, David. There are many rascals. It may not be that way in Mecklenburg, but it is that way down here. There are good men and bad men on both sides and the bad men are causing the trouble. They burn and steal and plunder. It's been terrible. Father has suffered much at the hands of rascals on your side—"

"On *our* side, my dear."

"I don't know that I can say that, David." Her face was serious. "Naturally, I've been doing a lot of thinking. And I've been trying to ignore the fact that Father is for the King and you are against him. I've been trying to think it out for myself. That's something you haven't had to do. All the people you love are on one side—"

"I don't know that yet. You just said you weren't sure which side you were on—"

She looked into his face, and a quick bright smile lighted her own. "That's a rather indirect way to say a thing."

"But I can say it other ways, by George. If it's directness you want—"

"No, David." She was serious again, and she eased her hand from his big palm and turned half way on the couch so that she could face him. "As I was about to say, though, you have had no test of loyalties. You can see only one side. But I can see two. And that's the tragedy. I don't believe it would be so hard to fight if all one's friends were in one camp and all one's enemies were in the other. Or even if one's beliefs and disbeliefs were separated. But I can see good and bad on both sides—"

"You're right, Lovelace. I can understand what you are saying, all right. After all, there are even many people in England that are on our side. They believe in the principles we are fighting for—"

"I'm not sure that I do, David." She said it deliberately, quietly, without feeling. It caught him unprepared.

"But surely you—"

"Yes, I knew it would shock you, David. But it's true. And I've thought much about that, too. I don't know that all the good principles, the right thinking, are on the side of the colonies. I don't even know whether they outweigh the good principles on the side of the King."

"But my dear girl—"

She laughed. But there was little mirth in it; David was certain it had a new quality, a new tone, a mettle he had never heard in her laughing. "You are surprised that I have even been thinking, that I am even capable of thinking. Yes, I can see the amazement plainly written on your face. You can't yet understand how a sweet young clinging vine is capable of thinking about anything beyond pretty clothes and coy smiles. Can you?"

"Now your smile is coy enough." He hesitated. "I'm glad to say."

The girl was amazing him. She had described his feelings. Yes, he had never suspected it. She was presenting a new side, an entirely unsuspected quality. A most interesting quality, he was discovering, a most intriguing one.

"But I'm not a Tory, David. No, you can depend upon me; I'll not turn you over to the Highlanders to be hung. Nor am I a Whig. I'm just, well—I'm sort of standing off trying to see the whole picture, to weigh the thing, to balance the principles of one side

ALEXANDRIANA

against those of the other." She stopped, turned quickly to face him directly. "You had never even thought that the other side could have any, had you, David?"

"I don't suspect I had."

"I wonder if you know what principles you really stand for. You've heard a lot of talk, a lot of oratory about liberty and freedom and the rights of the individual, a lot of abstract things, things like that Patrick Henry up in Virginia has been saying, and Hooper and Cornelius Harnett and a lot of other lawyers. When the Americans win the war there'll be freedom for everybody, they say, and the individual citizen will be king." She laughed again and David didn't like to hear her laugh that way. "I wonder if you've ever thought what that would mean. There'd be King George Washington and Hancock and Franklin and Jefferson and King Uncle McKnitt and King Cornelius Harnett—yes, a lot of kings like that. And that would be all right. They'd at least have three-cornered hats and clean shirts if they didn't have golden crowns and ermine robes. But how about King What's-His-Name—"

"Jethro O'Flannagan?"

"Yes. King Jethro."

"He'd make a damn good one. A damn sight better one than King George." He said it with a little warmth. Lovelace noticed it.

"Perhaps he would. I didn't mean to offend you, David. I just happened to think of him because of his hunting shirts and his coonskin cap and his tobacco—"

"And you forgot he saved my life, and his willingness to risk his neck for his friend, and his utter bravery, and his sound common sense, and the fact that under his rough exterior he's one of the finest gentlemen in this province—"

"I'm sorry, David. I apologize. I—"

"I see your point. But you got the wrong fellow for an example. You think liberty for the individual is all right as long as the individual has on a white shirt and a clean stock and perhaps knee breeches and silk stockings and silver buckles and—"

"No, I don't think that exactly." She patted the back of his hand. "I didn't mean to rile you. I don't believe, though, that you

ALEXANDRIANA

can turn the government of a country over to just everybody in it. I think the educated, high-born people should direct it for the benefit of themselves and the others. And that's why I don't know whether your principles are sound, my dear."

"Well, I believe in liberty for everybody and I believe that if you give all the people the right—I don't mean if you give it to them, for I believe they already have the right, in fact—I believe they'll in the main do the right thing. That's the views, as I understand, of this young fellow Jefferson up in Virginia, and he's as high-born and blue-blooded as they get." He paused. "But look here, we're getting ahead of things. We've got to win this war first, and then after that we can argue political principles and set up the sort of government we want."

"Yes, we're getting ahead of ourselves. We should be talking about your plans."

"About my plans for you?"

"For me?"

"Yes, for you."

"But we must win the war first. You've just said those very words."

He sat up, turned to face her. "Now you are talking as you should. I don't mean about winning the war first. But like that. You know. Not politics and theories of government—"

"You didn't think that I ever thought of such things, did you?"

"You used to say you despised politics and you always tried to stop your father and me from talking about the Regulators."

"Yes, but then the issue wasn't so sharp; it didn't mean so much to me. Now I have to think of such things. I—I can't avoid it. But here we've started it again." She patted the buff trimmings of his uniform sleeve. "Pretty," she said, and she smiled. "I bet it's like General Washington's."

"His probably has a little more gold braid. And stars."

She fingered the insignia, smoothed the fringe on the epaulette next to her. "Lieutenant Barksdale. Maybe some day you'll be a general."

"Maybe if the war lasts a hundred years."

"But I hope it doesn't."

"I hope it doesn't, too. I hope it's over by next June."

"Why June?"

"Because that's a nice time for a wedding."

"She may be married before then if you don't watch out."

"Who? Belinda, I suppose."

"Yes."

"Has she started setting her cap again?"

"Well, I believe she could be prevailed upon to set it. She's a pretty gay widow. But you'd better watch out, David. She's quite a Tory, they do say."

"I haven't seen her since we brought Angus home, and then for but a minute. Did she take his death very hard?"

"At first, yes, I think she did. She and Angus hadn't gotten along very well. But after he was dead she seemed to fall in love with him. Perhaps it was because he had died fighting. She probably saw him for the first time as a sort of hero in her own eyes, something he never was while he was living."

"Do you suppose she'll marry again?"

"She'd marry you, David, even though you're a Whig, I'm bound."

"But I have other plans."

"Oh, please excuse me."

"This one time. But if you ever suggest again that I marry Belinda, if you ever try to marry me off again—"

"Maybe I just appeared to be suggesting it, maybe I was really suggesting—"

"That I am planning to marry you?"

"Yes."

"I am."

"Perhaps I've been planning to marry you, too." The dancing light in her eyes, her quick, merry little laugh, the casualness of the tap she gave his knee beside her own outlined beneath the smooth silk of her gown, relieved the mounting tenseness of the moment. "Perhaps some day I'll succeed in wheedling a proposal out of you, Lieutenant Barksdale." Just as quickly she was serious again.

ALEXANDRIANA

"Please forgive me, David. But we must keep our heads, you know. We couldn't get married now with you heading off to join General Washington." Her quick smile flashed again. "You might find a girl up there in New York or Philadelphia somewhere—"

"I've found the girl—"

"You think so now, perhaps. But there's the war. War—you said so yourself, as good as said it, anyway—war changes things and we must win the war first, and then we can talk—politics."

"But this wouldn't come under the head of politics." He laughed. "You're a clever little rascal, Lovelace, and that makes me love you all the more. And as soon as we get Cornwallis and Clinton in the bag, my dear young lady, I'm going to invade Cross Creek and capture you. And you needn't be building any defense, either."

The candles on the walnut dropleaf table in the hall were burning low when he arose. She walked with him into the hall, lifted his hat from the folding wall-rack. "It's nice looking," she said, "crimped up in front and behind."

"Like General Washington's," he said, laughing.

"When you come back you'll be a general."

"No, just a private—for you to command forever."

Out on the veranda she smiled up into his face. And when he took her in his arms and kissed her, her lips were warm and sweet and eager.

After a while he released her. "You must be going, David." Quickly she walked to the door, turned. "Hurry and come back, Darling. And remember I'll be thinking of you and praying for you—and loving you!" She paused, smiled. And even in the moonlight that cut across her face through an opening in the tree that shaded the veranda he saw that her smile was different now, sweet and tender and earth-removed. And in the instant that he saw this she was gone.

XXXVIII

W HEN DAVID reached Wilmington Hezekiah Alexander had gone with the other members of the Council of Safety to Halifax, and the Council was busily engaged with measures to put down the Tories when a horseman galloping southward from Philadelphia brought the news on July 22 that the Continental Congress had declared the American colonies free from Great Britain.

On the first day of August sleepy little Halifax was overflowing with people. The taverns were overrun, the shops were filled. From the farms roundabout the people had flocked to town, for the Council had set apart the day for the proclaiming of the new declaration.

At noon Cornelius Harnett, escorted by soldiers and fifes and drums and flying flags, stepped from the procession to mount the improvised stage in front of the courthouse. And now the crowd was quiet, and in the bright heat of the midday sun they turned up sweating faces to the slight gentle man standing there before them reading from the paper that had set a new nation upon its course . . .

And when he had concluded and with his handkerchief had mopped his perspiring, reddening face, the crowd broke into a tumult of cheering, a little cannon boomed its saluting, and the soldiers rushed upon the platform to bear away upon their shoulders the protesting, smiling president of the Council of Safety . . . And Hezekiah Alexander of Mecklenburg's Sugaw Creek, watching this spontaneous pageantry of a proud people, put aside

ALEXANDRIANA

his taciturnity to wave his three-cornered hat and cheer . . . Captain Jack's ride to Philadelphia had borne fruit. The free boundaries of Mecklenburg had been pushed outward to embrace a new vast land up and down the seaboard from the mountains to the rolling ocean.

But back in the center of this expanding circle of free country, back in little crossroads Charlottetown, the news of this great day at Halifax had not yet reached, nor had it overtaken the men of Mecklenburg moving westward in pursuit of the Cherokees, pushing through Swannanoa Gap to the French Broad along the valley of Hominy Creek past Pisgah and beyond Pigeon River up Richland Creek and across Tuckaseegee River to Cowee Mountain. Nor did David, joining the Third Regiment of the North Carolina Line under Lieutenant-Colonel William Lee Davidson, know that the colonies had united with Mecklenburg . . .

In the late fall Jethro was back at Alexandriana to help with the harvesting, delayed because of the expedition against the Cherokees. And at Alexandriana and Rural Retreat, down at the Rock House in Sugaw Creek, at Centre Church and Poplar Tent and Steele Creek and Providence, at Hopewell and up from Charlottetown along the Beatty's Ford Road, candles burned late into the night as nimble fingers worked with spinning wheels and looms and needles and thimbles . . . The war was on in earnest now, and men who fight must have uniforms.

Hezekiah Alexander had gone back to Halifax, and with him Robert Irwin and John Phifer, returned now from the campaign with Grif Rutherford against the Cherokees, and Zack Wilson and Waightstill Avery. Seven days before Christmas they joined their colleagues of the Provincial Congress in approving the new Constitution. And when under the provisions of this new instrument they elected Richard Caswell the first Governor of the new State of North Carolina, the delegates chose Mecklenburg's Avery as the first attorney general.

More and more, as the warm days of a pleasant Indian summer gave way to winter and Christmas came and passed and long cold nights brought the burning of many candles, the management of

ALEXANDRIANA

Alexandriana fell to Jeanie. For McKnitt's days now were spent in the saddle and his nights in taverns or the homes of patriots with whom he was laboring to give strength to the new government of North Carolina now that he was the first State senator from Mecklenburg.

There was much for Jeanie to do. The children were growing. William Bain, now thirteen, was a dependable boy and much of the farm work he was able to direct. Peggy was a young lady of eleven and Polly was nine, and little Abigail was a big girl of seven. Joe McKnitt was hardly a baby any more; he was three.

Much of the time Jethro was away from the place, for he was a member of the militia, and with Tory uprisings in the southwest and frequent drilling at Charlottetown he was subject to call.

And nothing had been heard of David for months. The North Carolina Brigade had formed at Wilmington and had been doing duty down in South Carolina and along the border where the Tory influence was still strong even though the British had been driven away from Charles Town after their vain attempt to batter down Fort Moultrie.

One day when warm days had come back to Alexandriana and the bees were droning in the flower garden out beyond the kitchen house McKnitt returned from Charlottetown and Jeanie knew in her quick intuitive way that he was bearing grave news.

"What is it, McKnitt?" She met him out by the boxwoods. "News from—from David?"

He kissed her. "Yes, I heard it today in Charlottetown. It was fetched by a man on his way over into the western country from down Wilmington way."

"Is it bad news, McKnitt?" She said it quickly, fearfully.

"No, Sweet. Only that the North Carolina Line has been ordered north to join General Washington."

"Have they gone?"

"Yes; by now they're no doubt at Philadelphia."

"And was there any word of David?"

"No. Nothing of David, or William Lee or the Polks, nothing direct about any of the Mecklenburg men."

ALEXANDRIANA

"Well." It was a sigh, a release of fear long carried silently. She smiled, and then the tears burst from her eyes, and she fell into his arms. "Oh, Darling, do you suppose they'll ever come back again?" And she was crying now, and McKnitt was patting her shoulder.

"Of course, dear girl, they'll be back and the British will be gone and everything will be quiet again and we'll all be happy. General Washington's a great man and a great soldier; he'll look after David and them. Everything'll be all right and they'll be home again in the spring."

She was calming now, and she smiled. "McKnitt, you are powerfully afraid your ownself."

"Yes, I am, Jeanie. I can't deceive you, of course. But we mustn't think about such things. We must think of only one thing now, and that's winning this war."

"But what would a free country be like, what would freedom here in Mecklenburg be like without David, and William Lee and Tom Polk and his boys, and the others, McKnitt? Answer me that?"

"There's no answer to it, my dear. It's just something to be faced and borne."

Late in October came news to Mecklenburg that there had been battles in the north. Young Bill Polk, major in the Ninth Regiment, had been wounded at a place on the Brandywine River up near Philadelphia. Susan Polk was greatly distressed. The message had said that his injury had been slight, but Susan Polk was fearful that her boy was in great danger. She had visions of William lying in some dirty bunk, his leg or arm shattered, gangrene eating its horrid way.

Another Christmas passed. It was a cold winter in Mecklenburg. Some times McKnitt Alexander, sitting before the open fire of a January night, would look into the dancing flames and see soldiers in thin uniforms trudging through the snow . . . Strange how one could vision snow and sleet and ice and hungry thin men in the leaping hot flames from hickory and oak and ash. Strange how visions could plague and molest and terrify . . .

ALEXANDRIANA

And then on a cold dark day came a man southward on his way to Camden, and stopping at old Pat Jack's Tavern for a warming drink of stewed wine he told how the British had taken up winter quarters in Philadelphia, where there were food and warmth and women and dancing and soft downy beds, and how General Washington and his men were freezing and starving at a place some twenty miles west, a little place in the bed of a creek running northward into the Schuylkill River, a place they called the Valley Forge.

"There's but one thing to do," said Jeanie, when McKnitt had told her. "We've got to send Jethro up there to take David and our other men something to eat and some money and maybe clothes."

"But Continental money's no good, Jeanie. It would take a saddlebag full to buy a ham. And it's a fearful hard trip in the dead of a winter like this."

"But David may be fearful hungry, my dear."

"Maybe Bedent Spraggins can go along, and they can take a couple of pack horses. You can be figuring on the stuff to take, and I'll see to the arrangements for them to start right away."

Three days later Jethro and Bedent, leading pack horses loaded down with hams, shoulder meat, a leg of mutton, a big side of dried beef, bags of flour and meal, and bulging jugs from last fall's run at the still, and socks and sweaters newly knitted and woolen drawers and under shirts, rode through the gates of Alexandriana and turned left up the Great Road. Ahead lay Centre Church, and farther ahead lay the Moravian Settlements, and beyond the Moravian Settlements lay the Valley of Virginia mantled in snow, and on beyond and beyond, somewhere up there, was Pennsylvania and in a little valley huddled in the deep snow was an encampment . . .

"Hit's a long trip we headed out on, Bedent." Jethro settled himself in the saddle.

"You said it, Jethro. A hell of a long trip. But we'll git there, I'm bound."

XXXIX

Through the snow that sucked at their tired horses' feet they had mounted a slow rise that now dropped away before them. Down the slope and in the valley on this dark cold day smoke ascended in thin gray columns from innumerable fires. In the distance beyond the smoke ran a large stream.

Jethro stopped his horse, pointed toward the valley. "That's it, Bedent, as shore as hell—Valley Forge. Aint it?"

Bedent slapped his mittened hands together. "It is, I do believe, for a fact. And I'll be glad to git there and git a smell o' smoke. It's plague-taked cold, Jethro."

"It's colder'n hell, Bedent, all right. And I'll be glad to git there too. But I've a notion if'n we don't scheme a little right here when we git to where David's at we won't have nothin' to give them fellows from home. Jedgin' by all reports, these soldiers is oncommon hongry and they wouldn't stand back on takin' this stuff away from us, I'm bound. Git down off'n yore horse and le's do a little fixin' afore we ride down to the camp."

A half hour later they had descended the slope past a house on the left in front of which a cadaverous looking sentry was pacing with sluggish steps. At the bridge over a creek they came upon a detachment of men. "Look at 'em," said Jethro, under his breath. "Starved, naked. They look 'more like beasts than men, Bedent. They look—"

"Hold up, over there!" He was a long, spare fellow with a hawk-billed nose thrust out from matted beard that divided into the bluish-red slit of his mouth when he called out, and his dialect was

ALEXANDRIANA

unmistakably Pennsylvania Dutch. "You fellows looking for somebody?" In a moment they had surrounded the four horses.

"We was a-lookin' for the brigade from North Ca'lina, Mister, and we'd shore be powerful 'bliged if'n some of you mens would point it out to us."

"What you got there? You fetching them rations?" A young man with a thin red mustache and long hair that hung down to his shoulders was feeling with blue white hands the pack on the horse Bedent had been leading.

"Well, now, we did fetch 'em a little snack which we'll 'preciate if'n you'll—"

"Food!" The fellow was tearing at the pack. "Food, men. Hams, meat, meat, meat!" He was screaming now. "Red meat, I tell you!"

"I'm sorry, Mister," said the man who had first called to them, "but we'll have to borry this stuff you fetched." Already the men had torn away the bindings that had held the packs in place, were clawing and clutching at the red meat. The Pennsylvanian dived into the center of the fighting group, came out with a big hunk of beef. With the meat clutched securely under his left arm, he motioned off toward the right with his other. "Go on down along this road which runs beside Valley Creek and just before you come to the river you'll find yourself in front of the dugouts of the Carolina troops. That'll be out in front of General Washington's headquarters." He bit into the meat, and his lips and teeth were red when he spoke again. "Good-bye, Santa Claus. Sorry we had to take your stuff. But you're lucky anyhow. A month ago and we'd have eat your horses, too."

After another half hour of inquiring, they knocked at the door of a low dugout around which earth had been banked and from which a thin wisp of smoke curled into the freezing air.

"Beg yore pardon, Mister," said Jethro, when the door was opened and a man ageless in thick heavy beard and untrimmed hair stood before them, "but we was looking a-lookin' for Sergeant David Barksdale—"

"Well, I'm damned if you'll have to look any farther for Captain Barksdale—"

ALEXANDRIANA

"Captain?"

"That's right, Jethro. You and Bedent come on in. It's too cold to be keeping the door open."

"Look a-here—" Jethro turned to Bedent, turned back to stare into the bearded face of the man before him. "Is this here Bill Polk?"

"It's what's left of him, as sure as hell, Jethro."

David had heard the talking at the door. He met Jethro just as they stepped inside. "Jethro, how in the devil—Oh, boy, I'm glad to see you." He grabbed Jethro, gave him a powerful squeeze. "And how're you, Bedent? Damn, we're glad to see you fellows. Come up to the fire. It's not much, but it'll help warm your fingers a little."

They pushed toward the smoldering fire, took off their mittens, warmed their fingers, turned around to let the heat strike their backs.

"A pretty pair of gents, nice and fat and greasy looking, a likely pair of soldiers that knows how to look after a woman." Jethro wheeled about. Over on a bunk in the corner a woman lay hunched up on an elbow, her legs across a man who snored rhythmically. "Hello, Sweetheart," she said to Jethro.

"Shut up, damn you, you dirty slut! Aint I told you to keep your damned mouth shut?" A man on a bunk over in the other corner stuck a shaggy head out from under a dirty, torn quilt. "Don't you see they's company?"

"If Amos was awake you wouldn't talk to me like that, you filthy blue-gummed bastard. Aint nothing wrong with you except you're just mad 'cause I won't sleep with you." She laughed and her laugh sent new chills along the marrow of Jethro's frozen bones. It was a high shrill starving laugh, a shrill mirthless bitter laugh that ran out through the dugout's chinkless cracks to lose itself in freezing winds now beginning to whirl the snow over the darkening flats of Valley Forge. She pointed a grimy finger at the fellow, pulled up her skinny legs and swung around to confront him. The tattered overcoat with which she had been covering herself fell from her shoulders, leaving her nude from her waist up, revealing flabby white breasts that swung out as she turned. "Look at him!" she screamed, pulling the coat back across her sunken shoulders. "Aint he something to be telling a lady to shut her mouth? Look at his damned feet. Rotten, stinking clods o' dead meat. Hell's fire, Jason Hornbeck, you couldn't get over here if I was willing to let you sleep with me—"

"I wouldn't walk over there if my feets was well and you was the only damn woman in the world, you damn bad-smellin' Philadelphy whore. Now shut yore mouth and lay down if'n you don't want me to tell Amos to beat hell out'n you when he wakes up."

The woman sprang up from the bunk, the coat clutched about her shoulders. Jethro saw she was wearing a tattered pair of old homespun breeches. "Damn you, Jason Hornbeck, I'll—"

"Sit down, Nellie. Save your strength." The woman slumped back on the bunk. David laughed. "Don't get alarmed, Jethro, you and Bedent. We're all good friends together. That's just a little exchange of friendly greetings between Nellie and Jason over there. We have a rather informal atmosphere here at Valley Forge; we don't conform strictly to conventions."

The woman was looking at Jethro again. "Look here, Sweetheart. You and that other fellow look mighty fat and greasy looking. You must have been eating pretty regular. Aint you fetched your friends nothing?"

"Come to think of it, Jethro, you two are fat. How'd you all pick up all those stomachs? When I left you all that day at the muster ground in Charlottetown you were both skinny as a rail."

"We come up here to fetch you all some stuff to eat—hams, mutton, beef, shoulder meat—"

"Where's it at, Friend?" The fellow with the lumpy feet showed a sudden interest.

"Right up the road here some fellows stopped us and took it away from us, some soldier fellows. They—"

"That would be them damned Pennsylvania Brigade fellows, unless'n it was them damned Virginians. That was likely Wayne's men, damn 'em. Ham! Man, when has I eat any ham? Mutton and beef and shoulder meat. The devil take them damned Pennsylvanians, or else them damned Virginia boys. Ham! Damn me. When has I ever tasted a nice slab o' ham!" Jason rolled back in his dirty bunk, moved cautiously the two sore feet cloddy in their frayed wrappings, through which the blood had soaked and dried in soiled brown splotches. "Ham! We had ham a-comin' and them damned Wayne's Pennsylvanians stole it." He pulled up the tattered quilt, twisted his head beneath it.

Jethro was grinning. "You think we's fat, do you? Well, I 'lowed some o' these hongry fellers was likely to take our stuff, so we pulled a little trick on 'em." He pulled off his overcoat, motioned to Bedent. "Take off yore'n, too, Bedent." His small coat was bulging about his middle. "Fat, aint I, David?" He unbuttoned the coat.

"Meat! Look there, David. Do you see what I do?" Will Polk was laughing, and tears were welling in his eyes as he laughed. "Meat. Ham. Mutton. Look, David." The bearded young soldier put out his hand to touch the ham, fondled it, smelled his greasy fingers, tasted the grease on his fingers. "Mecklenburg ham, David, boy! Mecklenburg meat!"

The pockets of Jethro and Bedent yielded woolen socks and from under their waistcoats came more socks and sweaters. And soon the smell of frying meat was mixing with the smoke curling above the dugout close by the point where Valley Creek emptied into the Schuylkill.

"I'm going out to find my father and Colonel Davidson, David. You watch that meat and don't let it burn," said Will Polk. "And save a bite for them. They haven't tasted any meat from home—and damned little from anywhere else, I'm bound—in many a day. I won't be gone long. I think I'll find them over at the General's headquarters, or else with some of that Masonic crowd in the Pennsylvania bunch. By the way, Jethro, I don't reckon you'd heard tell we'd formed ourselves a Masonic lodge—"

"No, I hadn't. Fact, we haven't heard much o' anything from you fellows up this a-way. That's how come me and Bedent come up here a-huntin' fer you all."

"Well, we have. Our charter's from the Grand Lodge of Penn-

ALEXANDRIANA

sylvania. Our lodge's name is the Phalanx. We're figuring on adding a lot of members when we get back to Charlottetown and get things settled again. Likely my father's off with some of that crowd now. I'll be fetchin' 'em soon. Save us all a bite, David. I hate like hell to go off and leave that stuff." He pulled back the door, pushed out through it as the snow swirled in.

David was busy with the frying meat on the hearth. "Here, Nellie," he speared a piece of the sizzling meat from the coals, waved it a moment to cool it, held it out to the woman. "This'll put you in a better humor, make you love Jason more."

The woman clutched the hot meat, slipped it from the knife eagerly, devoured it quickly, licked her lips. "Give me some more, Cap'n David. That's good; that's the best eatin' I've had since I been in this damned hellhole." She laughed, a shrill high cackle. "Give Jason a piece too; he's weaker'n hell. He needs a little filling in his belly to give him strength. He needs a little—"

"I got enough strengt' to handle you, you stinkin' slut, if'n I wanted to, which I don't." He sat up on his bunk, moved gingerly his lumpy feet. "But that stuff do smell powerful good, Cap'n David. You might reach me a piece over here anyhow."

Nellie was tugging at the man in the bunk beside her. "Wake up, Amos. Wake up. Here's meat, Honey, meat. Do you hear, meat!" The fellow closed his mouth and his snoring stopped. He threw out an arm and his hand fumbled at the woman's waist. "Cold—still cold. Cold. You don't—warm me—any more." He was half asleep, mumbling. "You're cold, skinny. 'Taint any fat on you no more—just a damn cold skinny slut. I hadn't ought 'o took you from them Pennsylvania fellers nohow." He slapped her on her hip next to him. "Lay down. You got the kivers off." She snuggled down. In the light from the fire Jethro saw his hand fumbling at her waist, moving up her skinny stomach to fold sleepily upon a sagging breast. He opened his mouth, the snoring started again.

She sat up, shook him. "Wake up, Amos! It'll soon be your turn again. Get up. And here's meat, Honey—ham, and beef and sheep."

"He thinks it's some more of the same stuff you been a-givin' him." Jason dragged his arm across his greasy lips, snickered. "He don't want no more o' that. And I can't blame him neither."

Nellie shook her fist at him. "Damn you, you damned toothless bastard! I'll remember that when he goes out to take his turn at the sentry post and you start begging me to crawl over there and lay with you, you and them stinking, rotten feet. Damn you, I'll see you in hell 'fore I'll lay over there in that lousy bunk alongside o' you. You can stay there and wait on your damned Virginian whore—"

"Hell fire," interrupted Jason, "damned if'n 'taint 'bout time that there woman was a-gittin' here. My back's gittin' colder'n hell a'ready."

XL

DAVID PULLED open the dugout door. The skies were dark and heavy but the snow had stopped. "It's warming up a bit," said David. "There'll be slush before long."

"Yes, and it's a fit day for von Steuben, a fair fit day."

"Who's he?" Jethro inquired of Will Polk.

"He's the German officer who's been drilling us. You'll see him."

"I want to see General Washington."

"You'll see him too, likely."

David stepped back to the door. "Look after Jason, Nellie. Keep the fire going. Looks like his woman's left him for good."

"And who in hell'd blame her," Jethro heard the woman yell back. "But I'll watch out for him, Cap'n David. He'll be all right."

David pulled the door shut. "We'll walk up the Gulph Road." He pointed. "Straight up that way eighteen miles is Philadelphia and the British are quartered over there." When they came out upon the Gulph Road and turned to the left, David pointed off toward his right. "Over that way's how you all came into camp. That's the Valley Road and Valley Creek running along beside it. Across over there's Stirling's headquarters. You passed it yesterday. Down there's the Virginians' encampment. Up there—" he pointed ahead and a little to the right, "is the hospital."

"Hospital, hell," said Will Polk. "It's a hell-hole if I ever saw one. Men stacked three deep all over the place, dying faster'n flies. God help anybody that goes to that hospital. Leeching and bleeding and chopping and sawing. All the tools they got up there are saws and butcher knives. You remember poor old Malachi—"

ALEXANDRIANA

"I don't believe they ought to've bled Malachi. He'd already lost a lot of blood, what with his feet and nothing to eat but that damned parched corn and a damned little bit of it."

"But he was out of his head, David. They say you have to bleed a fellow till he comes back to his senses. And Malachi came into his right mind—"

"And he died, too. And damned quick."

They trudged through the snow. "These here are the New Jersey huts across over yonder—See?" He pointed to his left. "That's Varnum's headquarters over there on the road this side of the redoubt. This is Knox's artillery here on the right and straight ahead is Wayne's headquarters, and beyond it are the dugouts of his Pennsylvania Line. The Massachusetts Line's across the road from him. And here's where we turn off the road. This is the parade ground."

"It's a big place, by damn," said Bedent. "Bigger'n the muster ground at Charlottetown."

David laughed. "Yeh, it's pretty good sized, Bedent. I guess it's a mile and a quarter straight across from here to the river."

They trudged on another quarter of a mile through the thinning snow. "It's the Pennsylvanians he's giving hell this morning, Wayne's Pennsylvanians," said Will Polk, pointing. "Look, Jethro, you and Bedent. See the short, squatty man in the white cocked hat and the white breeches? Leastways, they were white when he came early in the spring. That's von Steuben. Man, but he can handle a musket. Watch him. I guess we'll catch it this afternoon, or else the Massachusetts Brigades or the Virginians."

Over at one side stood a group of women watching. Suddenly the column wheeled and started marching toward the group, thrusting forward their legs stiffly, splashing them down hard in the snowy slush. Von Steuben was moving on short fat legs out beyond them, counting. "Vun, doo, t'ree, vore,—vun, doo, t'ree, vore—vun, doo, t'ree—" He raised his eyes, looked toward the head of the column. "Out der vay! Out der vay, you vimmen! Everyv'ere at dis blagued blace dere is vimmen. Out der vay!" The women scattered, giggling, as the column moved toward them.

ALEXANDRIANA

The stocky Prussian in the dirty white breeches and blue coat and black high boots brought the column back. "Vun, doo, t'ree, vore—vun, doo, t'ree, vore—" Out in front sat officers on horseback. One, tall, large, broad of face, serious, sat a few paces in advance of the others. David nodded, spoke quietly. "That's General Washington, boys, and that's Nat Greene on his left, and Wayne, and Colonel Hamilton. And I can't make out those other two from here."

"Damned if'n he aint a fine lookin' man," said Bedent.

"He is a damn fine man," declared Jethro.

"The finest," agreed David. "He's been through hell this winter. All of us, in fact. But he's suffered the most, because his has been the greatest responsibility. But we're getting an army, boys. Old von Steuben's been giving us hell but he's making an army out of a bunch of ragged scare crows. Wait till you see them doing the manual of arms."

Von Steuben ran on short stiff legs toward the big man on the horse. "See, mine General, dey imbrove—mine children. Dey learn vat I have teached dem. Soon, mine commander, dey will be ready. Soon, ve vill make der British fly; ve vill make dem eat der baynets, soon."

General Washington nodded, von Steuben wheeled, came charging back. "Halt dem!" he yelled. "Now, mine poys, you vill vatch me v'ile I makes for you der manual of arms." He ran over to a tall Pennsylvanian, snatched his musket, looked at it a moment, flung it from him into the slush. His red round face was flaming. "It is dirty. You have not clean it. You have hold it over der fire for to cook vit it. Now pick it up. Ven you have finish der drill you vill clean it. Ja. You vill not stick meat on it. It is not for meat cooking. It is not for sticking meat—" A big grin overspread his angry face—" only British meat. Ja. Now, mine children, you vill vatch v'ile I makes der movements vit der baynet."

So passed the days and the weeks and warmth crept again into the valley along the Schuylkill. Men pushed out from evil-smelling huts, threw wide dugout doors to let in clean air, unwound soiled bandages from knotty blue feet, gingerly picked scabs from healing

ALEXANDRIANA

sores. In the Valley Creek and along its sun-drenched banks men lay naked, and in the chilly waters of the Schuylkill they swam and splashed. On bushes and the roofs of low huts were spread tattered breeches and shirts and pieces of coats, torn and bedraggled but clean. Everywhere thin white bodies sought the sun.

The women, too, washed themselves in the Valley Creek and patched and cleaned their thin garments. In little groups they splashed in the cold clean water of the creek and giggled and squatted down when the men came by and tossed sticks at them and made bawdy observations about their revealed feminine charms.

And after a while May overspread the little valley where once stood a forge at the meeting of the Valley Creek and the Schuylkill River, and with May came rumors that soon the Continentals would take the road toward Philadelphia and the British.

The troops were reorganized. Shattered regiments were consolidated. In his headquarters up beyond the Carolinians General Washington wrote feverish letters to the Continental Congress asking for supplies, shoes, clothing, guns, powder, balls, flints. Into the valley rumbled wagons with provisions, and on the parade ground von Steuben labored as long as men could see to perfect the work with the bayonet, to show them how to charge.

One night Colonel Tom Polk came into David's dugout. "Our brigade is being reorganized, David. We've lost a lot of men. We had ninety-four hundred at Wilmington; we'll have less than twelve hundred when we are reformed into four regiments. General Washington needs more men. I'm resigning my commission here, David, and I'm going back to North Carolina to help procure more enlistments. William Lee is staying. There are officers here a-plenty." He smiled, hesitated. "David—"

"Yes, sir."

"Things are much better for us—"

"Yes, sir, General von Steuben—"

"Yes, but that's not all, David." He clapped a big hand on David's shoulder. "We've made an alliance with the French."

"You don't mean—"

ALEXANDRIANA

"Absolutely, David."

The younger officer smiled broadly. "That fellow Lafayette—"

"Yes, he had a hand in it. But so did old Ben Franklin. So, you see, things are looking considerably better. But the General needs more men, and I'm going back home to help roust 'em up."

"Yes, sir, Colonel. But about this French alliance—"

"You'll hear about it at the parade tomorrow."

Men lined the parade ground. Over here the Pennsylvanians, regiment after regiment, company front upon company front. Over there the Maryland men, and beside them the regiments from Jersey. Here the Carolinians, there the Virginians. Straight they stood and clean-limbed. Gaunt, yes, and spare and bony. But clean, and straight-standing.

In front, facing the men, sat General Washington, and by him sat a slim beardless young man in a sparkling uniform. Jethro, standing a little way over from the position occupied by the Carolinians, nudged Bedent. "That must be Lafayette, that young fellow over there beside the General. I'd a thought he'd a-been a older feller. He aint nothin' but a boy."

Von Steuben rode forward from his place just behind and to the left of Washington. "Mine children," he said, when he had neared the Pennsylvanians, and he raised his voice until it was a shout for all the troops to hear, "Mine children, mine fine poys! Today we have der grand parade for der General. Der General is vatching, mine children. Ja! He is vatching der movements, der manual of arms, der drill, der charging. Ve vill make der formations now. And ve must make a fine showing, ja. A fine showing for der General, ja."

He gave instructions to the brigades, placed them as he wanted them, shouted orders, screamed commands. The troops performed for him. They ran through the movements, they lunged forward, their bayonets gleaming in the spring sunshine, thrust, parried, thrust again, wheeled, chased imaginary Redcoats back along the great parade ground. Von Steuben was shouting, crying, pleading, throwing back his head and laughing, cursing and pleading, pleading and cursing.

ALEXANDRIANA

Back toward Washington he raced. "Mine commander, see?" he shouted, and there were tears running down his cheeks. "Mine fine poys. See, mine commander? A great army. See? No more are dey scarecrows, what? No more are dey men behind der bushes. See dere faces, mine commander? Clean and shaved, what, and brown in der sunshine. And dere baynets, dey shine; no more are dey for der meat cooking. Dey are ready, mine commander. I give dem to you, dis fine army, dese prave poys, dese mine fine children." He raced back toward the columns, shouted more commands. Soldiers wheeled, marched forward, turned, formed a great hollow half square in front of General Washington. "Now, mine children," said von Steuben, and there were tears on his round red face, "I give you to your General and he has somet'ng for to tell you." He turned, gave General Washington a stiff salute, which the General returned, and moved around to the rear of the commander.

George Washington rode forward a few paces, reined in his horse. Jethro and Bedent slipped as far as they dared toward him through the crowd of Valley people come out to watch. The commander, they saw, was also wet-eyed. From deep sad eyes he looked upon his men, up and down the straight lines, back and forth until he had surveyed them all, before he opened his mouth. And then he spoke. His voice was even, calm. But it carried out to the farthest ranks. And not a man but gave him an eager ear.

"I wish first to thank Baron von Steuben. He has made us an army. He has worked a miracle. And I wish to thank you, my men. You have wrought a miracle too. We have endured, you and I, through this terrible winter. The valley is dotted with graves, my men, where lie our comrades. They gave their all to our sacred cause. But you and I have endured. We have come through. We are ready for the tasks yet ahead. I wish humbly to thank you." And now across the calm serious broad face of George Washington passed the quick light of a smile. "I have welcome news for you. Now we have an ally. The great nation of France, land of our young friend here who has come to join our cause, fights with us against the common enemy. Soon we shall be taking the battle to the British. Soon, if it be God's will, we shall have the victory."

ALEXANDRIANA

The commander had finished speaking. A wild exultant roar swept along the ranks. For this silent great grim man upon a horse it was a symbol. Up from tautened gaunt stomachs it rose, up past stout determined hearts, out through deep coarse throats. It rose and swelled and swept along through the warming air of early May. It stirred and vibrated a million blossoms white and pink upon a thousand fruit trees of thrifty Dutchmen squatted peacefully in the valley. It was the wild joyous release of a myriad caged emotions, the melting away of a winter's compounding of frozen shoutings. And listening silent and calm and confident, George Washington heard above the deep throaty roar a high sharp note of anger and exultation and terrible challenge . . .

XLI

"Jeanie, you shouldn't have waited up for me." McKnitt Alexander bent down to kiss his wife's upturned lips. "And you shouldn't knit so much, Sweet. 'Twill ruin your eyes, and you must be so tired."

"I was just wanting to finish these socks for Davy—" She dropped her needles in her lap, smoothed out the sock upon which she had been working. "And, see, they're finished. I'll send them north by the first chance." She laid them on the little sewing table beside her chair, stood up, stretched, smiled. "I reckon I am a little tired. But, Honey, you must be tireder, after all day in Charlottetown and then the long ride home through the night. Sit down, and I'll fetch you something to drink, and a little bite—"

"I'm not hungry, Jeanie. We had a big supper. I ate with the Governor and the Council of State at Waightstill's—"

"Well, now—" Jeanie's interest was evident. "I bet you did have a fine supper. Tell me, McKnitt, is Waightstill's wife a good hostess?"

"Fine. She's an uncommonly clever woman. Old Waightstill did a good day's work getting her, if I do say."

"I hear good reports of her. Violet Davidson said she likes her first rate. And they do say she's rich. Was the money from her husband?"

"I don't know about him. He was a Mr. Frank from down New Bern way. But her father was wealthy—a rich merchant from Maryland. He left her a lot of money, they do say. But you'd never know it from the way she acts. She's a clever young woman."

ALEXANDRIANA

"Is Waightstill sort of settled down like, too? I've hardly seen him the last two years. Has matrimony sort of clipped his wings?"

"He's calmed down, for a fact, Jeanie. But I don't think 'tis so much matrimony as 'tis the weight o' these times. And he's busy, Jeanie, mighty busy, what with his duties of helping set up a state government, with no money and little credit and with troops to raise and equip. 'Tis enough to settle men down, my dear girl." He stretched out his long legs, and the sigh that came up from deep in his lungs betrayed his feelings as well as his fatigue. "It's causing us all worriment, Jeanie."

"But we mustn't think too much o' the war, McKnitt. 'Twill do none of us good and 'twill not help whip the British. After all, things could be worse. Didn't General Washington chase them up there at that Monmouth place and isn't he still holding out in the north? And Will Polk's well again and David's so far escaped—"

"Yes, things could be worse, my dear. But they're mighty bad. In fact, I don't see how they could be much worse without meaning we're whipped. I reckon we do think about it too much, Jeanie, but how's a man to keep from thinking, how's a man to keep from dreaming, from always worrying and studying and fearing?"

"But we just must, Honey. We must pray and work and do our best, and then leave it with the Heavenly Father—"

"Yes, Jeanie, we must pray and never cease to pray, and always hope. Jethro said David and Will Polk and the others told him General Washington prayed in the snow up there at Valley Forge, and kept on working and hoping. He said sometimes they'd come on him out behind a little shack on his knees in the snow—"

Jeanie's eyes were beaming. "He must be a wonderful man, McKnitt, General Washington, a God-given man sent for a time like this. Oh, he must be."

"Yes, he must be." McKnitt with unseeing eyes stared at his dust-covered boots. "He's about all we have left, Jeanie. General Washington is the American army."

"But there's Davy, McKnitt."

"Yes." His quick smile lighted his grave face. "We must never

ALEXANDRIANA

forget Davy, Sweet, and there are a lot of other Davys, too, with General Washington. But he's the only symbol of America. I guess that's it. He's the only thing around which we can rally, Jeanie. He stands for what little unity the colonies have. It's a certain thing that the Continental Congress does not. Congress is a group of bickering, jealous politicians, Jeanie. Massachusetts wants to dominate, Virginia wants to dominate, the Carolinas want to dominate. The delegates—most of them, I'm bound—see the war from the standpoint of their own states." He fumbled in his waistcoat, found his pipe and tobacco, filled the bowl, lighted it. "Yes," he went on, after he had puffed a time or two, "that is our one great trouble, as I see it, and I'm back here away from everything, Jeanie, and I see few papers and the news is slow coming. But we aren't united. The states have too much authority. Fact, there's no real central authority, as I see it. The Continental Congress can call upon the states to do this or that thing, but how can the Congress enforce what it enacts?"

"But after the war, McKnitt, the states can organize better and make themselves into a common country better and set up a stronger government—"

"If we aren't all British slaves, or hung." He smiled grimly. "There's no need fooling our ownselves, Jeanie. We are in a bad fix. Congress debates and argues and orates while that little army we have is fast going to pieces. The soldiers enlist for only a few months and when their time's up they go home, and how can you blame them when you think about their families suffering and they getting no pay, and when they get it the money is as good as worthless? In the north they figure the war's about over, I hear, and some of the merchants and business people have already given up and are now trying to make money. And the politicians are busy trying to set up state governments when none of that will be any good if we are defeated." He stopped speaking, puffed slowly upon his pipe. Nor did Jeanie say anything. She appeared intently interested in watching a tiny upthrust finger of wax melt in the candle's flame and run down in a thin stream to the bowl of the pewter candlestick.

ALEXANDRIANA

"Was Ephraim at Waightstill's tonight?" she asked.

McKnitt sat upright in his chair. "Yes. You knew he was going with the troops tomorrow, didn't you, as their doctor?"

"Yes. You'd already told me. And was he cheerful?"

"As much as a man could be with his grief, I reckon."

"I feel so sorry for Ephraim. Mary's going was a great blow. But he has the baby. I guess she'll stay with Susan Polk. Poor little motherless thing."

"The poor boy was hardly married, it seems, before his wife was taken. I guess that's one reason why he decided to go to Charles Town with the militia. It'll help get his mind off Mary. And I feel mighty sorry for Tammas and Susan. They set right much store by their daughter."

"Yes, I do too. I'm worried about Ephraim, McKnitt. He's not strong. That trip over into the Cherokee country weakened him, and then he'd already been with those Queen's Museum boys—"

"It's not Queen's Museum any more, Jeanie. It's Liberty Hall now, you know."

"Yes, but it's hard to stop calling it Queen's Museum. But as I was saying, the trip down into the Scotch country after those Tories and then the trip with Griffith Rutherford over to the Cherokee country—all that and his grief over Mary, too, has sapped his strength, I'll vouch, and now this trip to Charles Town. I'm afraid for him, McKnitt."

"Yes, so'm I, but he's set on going, and I admire him for it."

She was quiet again for a moment. "Do you suppose there'll be bad fighting at Charles Town, McKnitt?" she asked, as she picked up the knitted socks and rolled them into a ball.

"Yes, I reckon so, Sweet."

"But we'll win again, won't we? The British got chased off when they tried it two or three years ago."

"It's different this time. And Clinton's got blood in his eyes now. He'll do his best to make up for the other beating he got."

"But won't General Washington send us aid, McKnitt?" Her face was beaming now. "Maybe David will be sent, and William Lee and Will Polk."

ALEXANDRIANA

"He will if he can spare them. But they're dropping out fast, they do say." He knocked the ashes from his pipe, threw them from his cupped palm into the cold fireplace. "But look here, Sweet, we've got to be getting to bed. It must be past midnight a'ready."

"It's a fact, Honey. But I forgot to ask one thing. Did you see the Davie boy, and is he going to Charles Town? I heard tell he was organizing a company to go."

"That's right. I saw him. He's been practicing law in Salisbury since he finished at Princeton College after being in the army of the north for a while. Governor Caswell commissioned him a lieutenant the other day. Light horse. William Barnett's captain."

"Is he handsome, McKnitt? He was a fine looking boy when he was a student at Queen's Museum. You mind he came home with David one night and they went hunting the next day?"

"Yes, I mind, Jeanie. And he's a fine looking young fellow. And smart, too. But we'd best be going to bed." He picked up the candle. "I'll light the way."

The next day from the muster ground at Charlottetown seven hundred troops moved southward under the command of General Butler and in the forefront of one of the companies of light horse, smiling and clear-eyed and stiffly erect in his saddle, rode newly commissioned Lieutenant William Richardson Davie.

XLII

"YES, SIR, Uncle Pat, this here's right smart chilly weather all right, but you should ought o' seen that there snow up at Valley Forge last spring." Jethro O'Flannagan set down his mug of stewed wine, hoisted his foot to the bar rail.

Uncle Pat Jack poured himself three fingers, downed it with a gulp. "You do say, Jethro," he observed, with some emphasis. "I been hearin' tell that it was damnacious cold up there in Pennsylvany, but I didn't know just how much to b'lieve o' those stories."

"Well, sir," Jethro sipped his grog again, set down the mug, "you could o' believed dang nigh anything you heared. I mind one morning—you see, Uncle Pat, the North Ca'lina troops' dugouts was out in front o' General Washington's headquarters, right perninst 'em, in fact—and I mind I walked out early to catch some fresh air. It was powerful smelly and tight in them dugouts and I walked out to git a breath o' good air. The snow it was waist deep and I was wallowin' round out in front of our dugout when I walked right smack up to a big solemn lookin' man in a cocked hat and a blue coat with green trimmin's. And damme, Uncle Pat, if'n it wasn't General Washington his ownself—"

"The General his ownself, Jethro?"

"The General his ownself as shore as hell, Uncle Pat. Well, I saluted big like, and damme if'n the General didn't salute back."

"He did, Jethro?"

"Yes, sir, Uncle Pat. He knocked me off a snappy salute, and he looked so friendly like I raised my hat and passed the time o' mornin' with him and 'lowed it was damn cold weather."

ALEXANDRIANA

" 'Yes, sir, Major O'Flannagan,' he says, 'it's damned cold, sir; you're right about that, Major O'Flannagan.' "

Uncle Pat Jack poured himself two fingers, downed it, wiped his lips. "You're the first man I ever heard say he really talked with the General. There's been them that's seen him. My boy Jim seen him when he was up in Philadelphy that time, but he just seen him when he rid by; he didn't pass no words with him. What else did you all say to each other, Jethro? And look a-here, did the General really cuss?"

"Well, that wasn't to say cussin', Uncle Pat. It was damn cold."

Uncle Pat lifted the liquor bottle, set it down, reflected. "Look a-here Jethro, did you say he called you 'Major O'Flannagan?' Damn if'n you didn't get to be a major mighty quick, and he shore learned yore name in a powerful hurry."

"Well, Uncle Pat, I gits 'round pretty well and tries to be neighborly like and—"

"What else did you two friends say to each other?" Uncle Pat poured another finger, tossed it off.

"Not much, Uncle Pat. It was too cold. I think I said somethin' about wishin' I could get a-hold o' that feller Clinton over 'bout Philadelphy and the General he 'lowed that's jest what he was wantin' to do his ownself—"

"Look a-here, Jethro O'Flannagan." Uncle Pat was squinting out of one eye as he slowly surveyed Jethro. "You are either drunk or tellin' a damnacious big lie."

Jethro slapped old Pat Jack a resounding whack on the back that almost dislodged the old gentleman's octagon-shaped spectacles. "Both, Uncle Pat!" he guffawed. Old man Jack, his eyes merry in their frames of tiny wrinkles, whacked Jethro across the shoulders. "You and General Washington, by Patty! You and the General. Wouldn't that be a pair for ye? You and General Washington! A-standin' out in the snow a-talkin'. You and the General—"

"But it was colder'n hell up there, Uncle Pat. It was so cold—"

"It was, for a fact. I'll swear to that my ownself!"

The two whirled about to face a tall spare young man in the blue and buff of the Continental Line.

ALEXANDRIANA

"Davy!"

In an instant Jethro was beside David, had his arms about the younger man. He released his grasp upon him, stood back to survey him. "Wherever in the world'd you come from, Davy? You been to Alexandriana yet? Man, you're looking pretty thin. Must 'a' had hard travelin'."

David laughed. "One at a time, Jethro. And how're you, Uncle Pat? Haven't surrendered to the Britishers yet, have you?"

"Not yet nor the next time you see me, Davy, boy. Step up and let me rustle you up a little grog. It's pretty cold out there; you likely need a little stomach warmer." He walked around the bar, selected a bottle, poured a big drink. "That'll jest about fix you up, Son."

David sipped the drink. "That's good, Uncle Pat. Haven't had much lately either." He took another sip, set down the glass. "Good old Jethro. How you been gettin' along, boy?"

"Pretty good, I reckon. Aint no Tory nicked me yit, and we been a-runnin' a powerful lot of 'em. But when did you git home, Davy?"

"Last night, Jethro. I got to Alexandriana, but Uncle McKnitt wasn't there and I came down here looking for him and you and anybody else I might run into. They've sort of thinned out, eh?"

"Yeh, Davy, it's a lot of the boys gone off down Charles Town way and others is off down in the Scotch country and over west on the border line runnin' Tories. They's pretty well scattered. And Mr. John Phifer he's dead. But you'd heared that, hadn't you?"

"Yes, I'd had word of that."

"What you doin' home? You aint deserted the General?"

"No, but General Washington's sent us south to try to help General Lincoln hold Charles Town. The troops have already gone on, but Colonel Davidson and I got furloughs to come by home for a little visit. We'll be going on down that way pretty soon. Want to go 'long, Jethro?"

"I might do it. But these Tories is mighty bad down below the Waxhaws. We have to keep scatterin' 'em now and then or they'd take the country worse'n wild onions. But where's Colonel William Lee?"

ALEXANDRIANA

"He stopped up at Centre Church. He hadn't been home since our regiment went north to join the Continental Line. But look here, Jethro, where's Uncle McKnitt?"

"He's likely still up at the courthouse. He's sittin' on the General Court lately. He's 'bout the busiest man in these parts, what with runnin' his farm and entertainin' all the preachers what comes through here and bein' treasurer for the synod and sittin' on the court and raisin' money to pay the militia and helpin' git recruits and marryin' fokes and readin' all the papers he can git his hands on—"

"Uncle McKnitt's always got to be doin' something, all right. Let's go up to the courthouse and see if we can find him. Or maybe he'll be at Mr. Avery's office, or at Ochiltree's store—"

"Not there. No, sir. Not at that there damned Tory's hole, not yore Uncle McKnitt, Davy."

"Ochiltree's still up to his old tricks, eh? Well, we'll find Uncle McKnitt somewhere up about the crossroads." He gave Uncle Pat a tap on the shoulder. "Thank you for the grog, Uncle Pat. It warmed me up just right. And I'll be seeing you again before long."

A week later Colonel William Lee Davidson joined Captain Barksdale at Alexandriana, and they rode southward toward Charles Town.

"They have gone again," said Jeanie, as she stepped down from the uppin'-block from which she had waved to them as they rounded the bend in the Great Road and disappeared beyond the gaunt woods. "Many times has Davy gone away since the war started, and many times has he returned. You know, McKnitt, I've a feeling they'll both be back in the spring."

"I hope so, Jeanie. But I fear there are black days ahead. I don't see how we can hold back the British at Charles Town, and if they take Charles Town then they'll sooner or later be heading this way." His face was serious. And then he smiled. But even in his smile Jeanie saw the flash of a fierce earnestness. "But if they do come this way, we'll give 'em trouble and a-plenty."

XLIII

COLD WINTER marched through the Carolinas, and the Carolinas lay cold and desolate and fearful beneath the tread of its invasion. In Mecklenburg candles burned and spinning wheels whirred and looms clacked late into the night and the tired sore fingers of weary women carded cotton and wool and urged on knitting needles and sewed endless seams.

Requisitions called for clothing for the Continental Line and for the men and boys with the militia. Twelve dozen pairs of shoes and stockings, six dozen hats, twelve dozen yards of woolen or double-woven cloth, hundreds of yards of linen for the binding of wounds —there was never an ending to those calls. And the burden, as does the burden of every war, fell upon the women. The men had only to march and fight and some times to lie hot and feverish and bleeding upon a frozen field and die. The women had to work and plan and lie sleepless and unarmed before formless and frightening apparitions that returned relentlessly to plague their pillows.

And the winter deepening in Mecklenburg brought stories of horror below the border in South Carolina. Soon the garrison at Charles Town must fall, soon the Redcoat hordes must be released upon the suffering land. But worse than the Redcoats of Cornwallis were the Tories that scourged and robbed and burned and raped.

One night McKnitt stumbled into the house, cold and weary and wet and muddy, and slumped into his big chair before the fire. "Things look bad, Jeanie, mighty bad." He sighed and his sigh was half a moan. "Sometimes I wonder if the Almighty has forsaken us, if He has turned His face away from us."

ALEXANDRIANA

"But you must never wonder such, McKnitt. 'Tis doubting the Scriptures, indeed."

"Yes, I should not doubt. You're right, Jeanie, as you're always right. A hundred years from now, perhaps, 'twill not be known what we endure now. But 'tis powerful hard upon the generation that lives to endure it."

"What's troubling you tonight unduly, Honey? Have bad reports come from down Charles Town way?"

"No more than all the time, Jeanie. They're always bad from Charles Town. I cannot understand why General Lincoln doesn't get out of that trap while he can. He should well know he cannot defend Charles Town with a handful of troops. He should refuse to listen longer to the Charles Town officials and get out while there's a chance. In another few weeks he'll likely be cut off, if he isn't a'ready. He can't hold out against Clinton, and there's talk that another British army under Lord Cornwallis is coming from New York—"

"Was there any news today in Charlottetown of the Mecklenburg men at Charles Town?"

"Not a word, Jeanie." McKnitt, still slumped in his chair, watched the flames leaping to surround the crane in the big fireplace. "I do wish General Lincoln would leave Charles Town to the British and get to the open country where he'd have a chance—and where he'd do some good. It's these Tories, Jeanie. They're ruining the land."

"You must have heard something today?"

"Some more of the same sort of stories. Old Bill Cunningham and his bunch and nobody knows how many others. They're out stealing and plundering and burning and doing worse things even, Jeanie. With the men gone to Charles Town the country's open to the Tories and the Indians. It's terrible, sickening, the stories you hear nowadays. They do say you can trail these Tory bands by the smoke from burning houses they set afire. Something's got to be done. I wouldn't be surprised to wake up some morning and find them here at Alexandriana—and such thoughts, Jeanie, makes a man's blood boil."

ALEXANDRIANA

"And there was no word of Davy or William Lee or Ephraim Brevard—none of them?"

"No, they've just disappeared." He hunched his shoulder, threw out his hands, palms upturned in a gesture of resignation, despair, perhaps. "They may all be dead. We may never hear of them again."

"McKnitt Alexander—"Jeanie looked him full in the eye, "they'll be back—back in the spring. And just let a Tory come prowling about Alexandriana, and I'll—I'll—"

McKnitt laughed. "You'll do what, my dear?"

"I'll pour a kettle o' boiling water on him!"

"I believe you." He got up, turned his back to the fire, smiled. "And I believe the boys will be back in the spring too. I only hope they'll get here ahead of the British."

And so cold winter, marching through the Carolinas, began to falter and after a while spring, pressing relentlessly forward, overtook winter and winter died upon the warming winds of April. And one day in May a weary horseman rode up to the hitching rack at Jack's Tavern, dismounted, walked inside. "Charles Town's fell," he announced. "Cornwallis's likely to be headin' this way any day now. You fellow's better be gettin' ready." And he called for a drink.

A week later David rode through the gates at Alexandriana. "We never did get to Charles Town," he explained, after the excitement caused by his unexpected arrival had somewhat subsided. "The British had the whole place surrounded and we couldn't even slip in. We hung around until the surrender, and then we headed back this way. Colonel William Lee's gone up home."

"How'd you all come home? By way of Camden?"

"No, sir, Uncle Mac; we came up the coast to Georgetown and from there we came along the Haley's Ferry Road to the crossing of the Peedee, where we headed straight north to the Little Peedee, and we followed it on up."

"That would bring you out in the Scotch country around Cross Creek."

"Yes, sir. You see, we got news that Cornwallis was heading out Camden way and we figured it would be safer if we swung around

ALEXANDRIANA

him. There's a young fellow Tarleton with him, a colonel of cavalry, who's got the name of being the most merciless devil in the British army and we didn't want to run the risk of falling in with him."

McKnitt Alexander grinned. "Yes, I understand." Little crinkles furrowed out from under his eyes. "That was a good reason for coming home by way of Cross Creek. But not the main one. How was she, Davy?"

Now David laughed. "She was first rate, Uncle Mac. Only I didn't get to stay there hardly any time. Didn't see much of her."

"How about her father?"

"He came home while I was there. But he behaved pretty nicely. He's still for the King, but he appeared to be weakening. The way the Tories have been doing has sort of cooled his feeling for that side, I'm bound. At any rate, he didn't order me out the house. But I left pretty soon, anyway."

"Well, Davy, when'll it be?"

"Go 'long, McKnitt, let the boy be. Don't you see he's tired out, and you asking him all these questions that don't exactly concern your ownself anyhow." Jeanie took him by the arm. "Come on, Davy, come talk with me whilst I fix you up a nice cooling drink. Then you can tell me all about Lovelace—or was it Belinda?"

Davy gave Jeanie a big squeeze. "What do you think? he asked, laughing.

"Lovelace."

He nodded. "You're right."

"I'm glad," she said. "But did you see Belinda?"

"No'm. I did run by her place, but they said she had gone to Wilmington. Then I went on to Cross Creek."

"And you hurried?"

"Yes'm."

"I don't blame you, Davy. She's mighty sweet."

He bent down and kissed her. "So're you."

"You're quite a soldier, Davy," said Jeanie, "and you're quite a man with the ladies, I'm bound."

He asked her about Jethro.

"He went off with a crowd to try to catch a bunch of Tories down below in South Carolina," she explained. "Said he might go on to Charles Town. We haven't heard anything of him since. Haven't you, by any chance, run across him anywhere?"

David shook his head. "No, I've hardly seen any of our crowd. I haven't seen Ephraim even. But I heard tell that he was captured when Lincoln surrendered. He'll probably be paroled home pretty soon."

But in the days that followed Ephraim Brevard did not come back to Mecklenburg, nor was there any word of Jethro. And then on the last afternoon in May, Jethro, his left arm in a sling, came shuffling through the gates at Alexandriana, gaunt, his tired eyes set back deep in the matted beard of his wan face.

"I've had rough travelin', Davy, boy," he said, after he had downed the whiskey David brought him. "But danged if'n I wasn't lucky gittin' here at all."

He had struck southward past Camden and was well on the road to Charles Town when he had heard of the surrender of the Americans, he explained. Cornwallis, said South Carolinians fleeing northward, was pushing fast toward Camden, and so he turned and started back. After a few days he had fallen in with some troops from Virginia. "They was under Colonel Buford," Jethro added. "They had started to Charles Town to help out General Lincoln, but they was too late gittin' there and so they turned around and started back towards home. We had got as far as up here to the Waxhaw Settlements and wasn't thinkin' o' no trouble when this devil Tarleton come on us day before yistiddy and gived us hell and a-plenty. The Colonel and some o' those that had hosses and about a hundred infantry fellers got away; the rest gived up quick and asked fer quarters but them Redcoats didn't give them no chance. They jest hacked and slashed till they got tired o' killin'. They do say they killed more'n a hundred and chopped up that many more or more'n that many so bad they couldn't git away, and them that was able to walk they carried off to Charles Town."

"And how about your ownself?"

"Well, I managed to git away. But one o' them Redcoats on his hoss struck at me and I guess he'd danged nigh chopped off my

ALEXANDRIANA

head if'n I hadn't th'owed up my arm, and as it was he give me a good slash."

And now South Carolina lay under the tread of Redcoats and despicable Tories who pillaged and laid waste the land. The property of the landed people was confiscated, their plantations ravaged and overrun; families fled from their burning homes, roving bands of marauders now licensed to carry on their rapine in the name of the King whipped and hanged men in the back country because they had not enlisted in the armies of His Majesty, drove their wives and their children into the deep forest or left them huddled over the smoking ruins of their homes. Fugitives pushed across the border into North Carolina, tramped along the Nation's Ford Road into Charlottetown, fleeing the terror that came swiftly upon them in the day or in the night.

One day down at his brother Hezekiah's, John McKnitt Alexander encountered a freckled, big-knuckled young fellow in ill-fitting clothes. He was certain he hadn't seen the boy before. "Hello, Son," he greeted him. "You are new around these parts, aren't you?"

"Yes, sir. We aint been up here long. We're staying at Mr. John Wilson's house, Ma and me. My Pa's dead and my brothers they're in the army agin the British. I'm a-goin' to join up my ownself pretty soon."

"You're not quite old enough—"

"I'm thirteen, Mister, this March past. I aint so old but I'm pretty tough, and I'll give them British hell and a-plenty, Mister." The awkward youngster grinned, pushed his big-toe into the hot dust. "You'll be hearin' 'bout me yet, Mister."

"Well, you're game, Son. What's your name?"

"Jackson. Andy Jackson."

XLIV

GENERAL GRIFFITH Rutherford sat upon his horse at the western edge of the muster ground at Charlottetown. Quietly, his face an impassive mask, he faced the militia assembled before him. "Boys," he said, after a while, "I'm no speech-maker. I'm a man of few words. Sometimes I wish I could talk—like Dr. McWhorter has just now been talking to you fellows. But he's the president of Queen's Museum—I mean Liberty Hall Academy—" He hesitated, and a smile that indicated his slight embarrassment lighted his bronzed face. "He can make speeches, and good ones. That was one hell of a good speech he just now made you boys, and I want you to remember it. It was a fighting speech, calculated to make a man want to fight to defend his home." He stopped. All the men, slumped upon their muskets, were listening.

"And that's all I got to say to you. Just this. We are right up against it, boys. The damned British are down Camden way and they're likely to be on us any minute. They're raiding about the country. You've heard about this Tarleton in the Waxhaws. South Carolina's in a bad fix, boys. The Tories and the British between them have got that country down. We've been hearing a lot of bad reports about hangings and burnings and rapings—a lot of mighty bad stuff, men. And they're heading up this way and we've got to stop 'em." He paused. "We're going to do it, or they'll have to kill every damned man in these parts. Aint that what you say, boys?"

Caps sailed into the air; shouts, halloos, sudden shrill whistlings, stamping of feet in the dust of the trampled muster ground made a bedlam. General Rutherford held up his hand. "That's what I wanted to hear, boys. And now we're going home. We've got nine hundred men here today. That's enough to give those Britishers a lot of hell. Listen, boys. I want every one of you to go home, get yourselves muskets, you that haven't any, and all the powder and balls and flints you can find, and be ready whenever I call on you. And now you're dismissed."

A week later General Rutherford, having had word that General Rawdon's Redcoats had reached the Waxhaw Settlements, sent out his call to the militia to assemble at a farm up in Mallard Creek out northeast of Alexandriana. Quickly the troops were organized. Major Davie, now well of his wound at Stono down near Charles Town the year before, was given command of the cavalry, and three hundred light infantry were assigned to Colonel William Lee Davidson. The other officers were given their commands.

David was appointed by the general as a member of his staff. "I want you to do scouting for me, Barksdale," said General Rutherford. "You know all the country in these parts, and down Camden way. In fact, for a young man you've done a powerful lot o' traveling. And you're a tough young buck besides and can stand a lot o' riding."

When he neared Charlottetown on the march from Mallard Creek General Rutherford had news that Rawdon had moved back to Camden. The general struck west to the Tuckaseegee Ford, sent a message to Colonel Locke to meet him up the river. "There's a big bunch of Tories over in Tryon County up about Ramsour's Mill," he explained to David. "They're getting pretty bold. They figure the Redcoats will soon be here and that we won't dare a fight with 'em. I'm going to surprise 'em."

But the message didn't reach Colonel Locke. And shortly before midnight the next night an officer came galloping into camp with a message from Locke. "We're going to attack the Tories at sun-up tomorrow," said Locke.

By daylight Rutherford was hurrying north, and seven miles below Ramsour's Major David Wilson and Captain William Alexander, their horses foaming, met him. "The fight's already started,

ALEXANDRIANA

General." Young Wilson was almost as nearly winded as his horse. "They've got us badly outnumbered. Colonel Locke's hoping, sir, you can hurry on to help him out a little."

Major Davie's cavalry was off at a gallop up the narrow road to Ramsour's and Colonel Davidson's infantry moved out as fast as they could tramp behind the horsemen. But two miles up the road they met a group of Major Wilson's men. "Hold up, there!" shouted one of Rutherford's officers. "You men deserting? It'll fare hard with you."

"Deserting, hell. We done whupped hell out'n them damned Tory fellers." David, reining in his horse abreast the group, recognized Jethro, and Jethro at the same time saw him. "Hi, there, Cap'n," he shouted, "come here and take this feller off'n us. He's got the all-fired crazy notion that them Tories has runned us off."

Rutherford's men continued to Ramsour's Mill. It was a gory battlefield they came upon. On the side of the ridge they counted more than fifty dead men, and across the ridge toward the mill others lay still, their arms and legs grotesque and stiffening; and over the whole field wounded and dying men called feebly for water. Here lay a Tory, a green twig in his hat proclaiming his allegiance, and over here a Whig with a piece of white paper stuck in his hat, a target for some straight-shooting friend of the King. Many of those dead with white papers in their hats were cousins and friends and even brothers of those lying stiff and cold above or under hats with green twigs.

And after a while came the women and children of the country roundabout to search among the dead and the dying, to turn over cold stiffened bodies, to go suddenly pale and uttering high shrill frightened cries to fall despairingly across unseeing stiff bloody husbands and fathers and brothers.

And so June wore away as the terror from below the border grew and spread and established itself in Mecklenburg upon the lips of women and children and frightened men fleeing northward. For Clinton had sailed for New York, leaving Cornwallis in command, and on his going had reported that from every quarter the people of South Carolina were declaring their allegiance to the King.

ALEXANDRIANA

Many of the best people in every part of the state from Charles Town and Beaufort and Georgetown on the coast to Ninety-Six and Camden in the back country, unable to protect their families, had taken protection of the British. Now, according to the reports coming into Charlottetown, these men were being rounded up by the British and required to enter active military service.

"And if they refuse?" Waightstill Avery, sitting behind his desk in his office across from the log courthouse, where workmen were engaged in bricking in the space beneath the building, turned to question the young man who had ridden up from down below the Waxhaw Settlements.

The man made a swift circular motion with his forefinger pointing toward his throat. "The rope."

"You mean the British are hanging men who have taken their paroles because they will not enlist under Cornwallis to fight against their own countrymen?"

"Yes, sir, Mr. Avery. That's exactly what I mean. That's what they're doing. I don't mean, either, that that's what I've heard they're doing. I've seen it. That's what they'll do to me if they ever catch me. I was in their army. They caught me and marched me off to join up with Ferguson; but I upped and left. And if they catch me, they'll hang me as sure as the devil."

"That's against all the rules of war."

"I don't know about that." The young South Carolinian grinned. "I haven't noticed war having many rules, except to kill or get killed. And that's the reason I'm hoping to stay away from the Redcoats. They'll break my neck in a hurry if they catch me."

"But you're no deserter. You were a prisoner of war."

"I don't know about that. All I know is the fellow who tries to catch me is going to have his hands full, Mr. Avery."

"Did you actually get to Ferguson's crowd before you got away from them?"

"Yes, sir. I was with him a couple of weeks."

"What sort of a fellow does he seem to be? Is he as sorry a knave as Tarleton?"

"Well, Mr. Avery, Pat Ferguson's no friend of mine, o' course.

But he strikes me as being a pretty good fellow, considering he's our enemy. And he aint scared of all hell, you can say that for him. I heard him talking one night and he told something that sort of made me feel a little kindly toward him—if it's so."

"What was that?"

"I didn't catch the whole story. But as I got it it seems Ferguson had a chance to kill General Washington, and didn't do it."

"Well, now, that was something. What did he say about it?"

"He was talking with another Redcoat officer when it came up. I think it was at the battle at Brandywine three years ago this fall. He was lying in the edge of the woods with his riflemen—you know, Mr. Avery, he's one of the best shots in the British army—"

"So I've heard."

"Well, while he was lying there two American officers rode by about a hundred yards away. He said he ordered three of his men to slip up a little nearer and shoot them. But before they could do it, he said, he felt ashamed of himself and called them back. A little while later one of these men rode back by. He was wearing a blue uniform with green trimmings. Ferguson said he stepped out and called to him to stop. The man did stop, he said. But then he turned and without even looking back pulled on his horse's rein and cantered off. Ferguson said he could have put a half dozen balls in him. But he let him go. And later he found out that the man was General Washington. And he said he wasn't sorry he didn't know at the time that it was the General."

"That is a good story," Avery agreed. "You reckon it's so?"

"I don't know about the man being General Washington. But I do know Pat Ferguson must have been a hell of a good shot before he got that bad wound that ruined his right arm—judging by the stories I heard told about him."

"Well, you heard some good stories while you were with the Redcoats, and if they don't catch you again, I reckon the spell with them won't do you any harm." Waightstill laughed. "And now, I judge, the only thing for us to do is to get ready for them and blast the daylight out of Cornwallis before he can get north."

"Yes, sir. You see, Cornwallis has Ferguson in the western

settlements rounding up Tories and drilling them. The British, it looks like to me, are trying to win this war by making the Tories do it. And I'm a notion they won't do it, even if they have played hell with South Carolina. If we can get enough help from North Carolina and Virginia, I believe the Whigs in our state will get their hopes up and rise up against Cornwallis. That's what we're counting on. You see, we aren't all whipped down. There's Sumter and his bunch. And down in the swamps there's Marion. They're fast riding fools, all those fellows. They keep the Redcoats worried all right."

"We've got a fellow pretty much like them, a young fellow Davie. He's got a bunch of fast riding young fellows—"

"I've heard tell of him," said the young man, with a nod. "He works some with Sumter, doesn't he?"

"Yes, that's right. You'll hear more of Davie, too."

XLV

DEAD SUMMER lay heavily across the woods and fields of Alexandriana. The thick heavy heat of early August pressed in upon the green unstirring pines and oaks and cedars and gums, upon the dark unrustling quiet rows of corn, the calm still cold water of the spring at the foot of the slope.

"It's mighty hot, McKnitt, powerful hot. There'll be rain before night, I'm bound."

"Yes, it's too hot to last without rain. But it's dry and the corn's twisting. Rain's needed." He fell silent, looking with unseeing eyes out southward across green still cornfields toward Charlottetown; Jeanie was reading his thoughts, too, and she did not break in upon them, knowing he had not finished speaking. "And in the same way it's too peaceful here at Alexandriana, Jeanie, to last without war and bloodshed. It's been peaceful and happy here and good living, my dear, but like the corn out yonder, we have twisted, we have shriveled in our minds—" He was still looking straight out across the fields with eyes for some far away vision—"we have been blind to the privileges of this land, to the blessings we have enjoyed. Now it may be—" He was talking slowly, as if feeling his way with his thoughts—"it may be that war is needed Jeanie, to—"

"No, no, McKnitt. War is never needed. War's an instrument of the devil—"

"Yes, but perhaps used of the Lord—"

"I think not, McKnitt."

"Sometimes the rain comes in floods and destroys the corn, but can you say for that reason that rain is not needed?"

ALEXANDRIANA

"But that doesn't hold, McKnitt. You cannot mean that a proper amount of war is a good thing while too much war is bad. Any amount of war is bad. There is no right amount of war, my dear."

"No; you're right. I left off logic." He smiled. "But how about war as the Father's manner of punishing us? Could it not be that, Jeanie? Could it not be that we have spent our thoughts on prospering, on filling our storehouses with this world's goods—" He pointed across the Great Road to the barns and granary and cribs— "and have forgot to appreciate the riches that come with being an American, even a poor and unpretending American?"

"But have you ever forgot that privilege, McKnitt? Have you not always been a good citizen, a good elder, and a good father and husband?"

He leaned across to her, patted her cheek. "I've tried, Sweet, but oftentimes I've failed to realize my privileges; I've taken for granted things like freedom and security and the right to go and come as I please and worship in my own way, things that other persons in other lands have died to get, that our own people in this country are dying to keep." He was silent again, and Jeanie saw in his deep still eyes that same far away intentness. And then he turned to her, and there was a smile on his serious face, a smile in which she saw a battle ended, a calm resignation, almost an eagerness for struggle anticipated. "But now, Jeanie, we understand the value of these things as we come to face the test that may take them away from us forever, and from our children and their children—"

"I've a notion we'll be spared in Mecklenburg. I've a notion our men will chase that Cornwallis and his Britishers back to Charles Town and drive them into the sea. Soon General Gates will be at Camden and General Gates is a great general. You said so your ownself, McKnitt."

"Yes, he won at Saratoga. The Continental Congress has great faith in him. They appointed him to head the southern army. But I've since heard tell that General Washington wanted Greene instead, and I've the greatest respect for General Washington—"

"Yes, General Washington has the respect of everybody."

ALEXANDRIANA

"—And somehow, Jeanie, I'm not so certain any more about Gates."

"But there's Griffith Rutherford and the militia, McKnitt, and Governor Caswell. By now they must have already joined up with Gates. And there's David and Jethro and Humphrey Hunter and—"

"Yes, Jeanie, and by the same token, with all those Mecklenburg boys scattered all over South Carolina with young Davie and William Lee and Grif Rutherford and Caswell and the rest of 'em, who'll be here when the British come up this way? Who'll be here to stop them?"

"But I believe, McKnitt, they'll stop them down Camden way."

"No. Jeanie. I've a feeling they won't. I don't know why. I can't explain it. They do say Gates has more men than Cornwallis. But I'm afraid for our boys. Yes, I'm afraid." He was looking off again, off across the Great Road, toward Charlottetown, toward Camden, off across the silent green unmoving corn. "No, Jeanie, we shall not escape the test. I feel it. I know it. The British are coming. The British are coming to Mecklenburg, to Charlottetown, to Alexandriana, I'm bound. But worse than the British, the test is coming to us. We can't evade it, we can't dodge it. We've got to stand up and face it."

"McKnitt Alexander—" Jeanie's eyes were blazing. "I'll never take British protection!"

"W'y Jeanie. Bless your heart, bless your sweet little heart!" McKnitt kissed her, held her out at arm's length to watch the flame in her cheeks, the fire in her eyes. "My little rebel. Bless your heart."

Quickly though he fell back into his serious mood. "No, Jeanie, you won't take British protection. But what of me? What of the men of Mecklenburg? A man will do a lot of things when he has a family that he wouldn't do if he didn't have them. Look at those men in South Carolina. Big men, too. Look at that fellow Pinckney. He was president of the South Carolina Senate. And Lowndes. And Henry Middleton. W'y, Jeanie, he was president of the first Congress. Big men, Jeanie, and good men. And they took protection."

ALEXANDRIANA

"Listen, McKnitt, Ephraim Brevard didn't take British protection. No, sir, he let them take him to one of those rotten prison-ships in Charles Town harbor before he'd seek their protection—"

"Did you know that some of our women have gone to Charles Town to nurse our boys, Jeanie, by the way? Hezekiah told me Widow Jackson had already gone—"

"I'm glad. It must be powerful bad on those ships. But Ephraim Brevard'll die o' that fever before he asks protection. Nor will John Davidson take protection, McKnitt. Nor Richard Barry. Nor Tom Polk. Nor Hezekiah. Nor you, McKnitt Alexander."

Her husband sat unmoving, looking across the fields that stretched onward toward the meeting with the woods that shut off the view of the Great Road where it turned to go. southward. He sat quiet and silent, but in his eyes a flame was building. And Jeanie saw it. And she was glad.

"No," said McKnitt, after a time. "I'll not take British protection, God giving me strength. I'll see this place plundered, all our wheat and corn and cattle and hogs taken, I'll see Alexandriana burnt to the ground first, Jeanie. Nor will Tam Polk, nor John Davidson, nor Hezekiah, nor any of us, I'm bound. We'll see everything go, we'll die first, Jeanie. Yes, I'm bound we will." The flame was mounting. "But they'll pay well and they'll pay hard for every ear of corn, for every pig and chicken and cow and every grist of wheat they get in Mecklenburg. They'll have trouble and a-plenty. We'll fight 'em from every bush and rock and canebrake. They may plunder us and destroy us but they'll pay a dear price, Jeanie. Most of the men may be away fighting but what's left and the boys will give them trouble, and I've a notion they won't find our hospitality to their liking, either."

XLVI

Out of a confusion of strange dreams Captain James Jack awoke slowly to the consciousness of a heavy belaboring upon the front door of the tavern.

He slipped noiselessly from the bed, padded over to the window, peered down upon two dark forms. "Who is it?" he shouted.

"Friends, Jack." A face, white in the dim light, peered upward. "This is Richard Caswell. We are right powerful tired and hungry. We want refreshment—"

"Hold a minute, gentlemen. I'll be right down and unbar the door." He slipped quickly into his shoes, threw his night shirt over his head, pulled on his trousers and shirt almost by the time the night shirt was settling upon the foot of the bed. At the bottom of the stairs that rose from the taproom he lighted a candle on a wall stand, and near the door he lighted another.

"Come in, gentlemen." He pulled wide the door. "Come right in."

The two men stumbled inside.

"Your horses—"

"They're tied at the rack. They're badly worn, too."

"I'm sorry there was nobody to receive you."

" 'Twas a damnably unseasonable hour. Captain Jack, we meet again." He extended his hand. "First, at the Inn of the Golden Cock in Philadelphia. Again, at Hillsboro, wasn't it? Again, when I came here in April to review the troops going to Charles Town. And now, you are shaking hands with a thoroughly defeated and thoroughly discouraged man." He smiled wanly.

ALEXANDRIANA

"But after you have had a drink—"

"No, 'twill take more than liquor, Captain. But pardon me, gentlemen. I have no manners. I can no longer think. General Gates, allow me to present Captain James Jack of the Mecklenburg militia. Captain Jack, General Horatio Gates, commander of the southern army."

Captain Jack opened his mouth as if to say something, swallowed, stepped back, bowed low. General Gates nodded. The three stood awkwardly a moment. Captain Jack recovered himself. "Here, gentlemen, let me pour you all a good stiff drink whilst I roust out my Negro. Then we'll get you all some supper and see to the horses—"

"Breakfast'd be more like it, Captain. It's damnably late, or early, 'twould be more properly said."

Captain Jack was pouring liquor from a tall bottle. He pushed the glasses toward them. They picked them up, and the glasses almost to their lips, then they hesitated, clinked the glasses together lightly. Caswell nodded to General Gates. "To another day," said the General. "And another result," added the former Governor of North Carolina. They downed their drinks.

"Now, gentlemen, sit down there and rest yourselves whilst I get things stirring. I take it you two have had a long tiresome trip from somewhere and would like to get to bed as soon as you've had something to eat. And I'm just hoping you all don't bear bad news—"

"The very worst, Captain. We come from Camden. There was a big battle there this morning. Our whole damned army's killed, wounded, captured or taken to their heels through the swamps—"

"You don't say, Governor?"

"Captain—" General Gates pushed forward his glass. "I wish you'd pour me about three fingers more of that liquor."

"Yes, sir, General." Captain Jack poured a stiff drink. "And how about you, Governor?"

"You might give me another one, too, Captain. But not too big."

"Have you any word of the Mecklenburg men, how they fared, Governor?" Captain Jack poured Richard Caswell another drink.

ALEXANDRIANA

Caswell lifted the glass to his lips, sipped it. "No, Captain, I haven't. I did hear that Griffith Rutherford had been captured by the Redcoats. But I don't know—I don't know anything positively, Captain." He sipped the yellow liquor again, shook it, watched the beads form, sipped it again. "All I know is that Cornwallis gave us a damnably bad licking. The General and I didn't wait long to see just what had been the results. We have come to Charlottetown, Captain, without stopping."

"It's a right smart ride you took, Governor."

"I want a bed as quickly as possible, Captain, and a fresh horse in the morning. I'm going on to Hillsboro. General Caswell will remain here to collect the troops and try to hold back the British until we can make other plans." General Gates wiped his lips with the cuff of his bedraggled blue and buff uniform of the Continentals. "I don't suppose now's the hour to be spending any time rehearsing the events at Camden."

A week later Jethro O'Flannagan, his beard long and powder-blackened, his clothes torn and mud-caked, pushed through the doorway of Jack's Tavern. "You'll have to put me down fer a drink, Uncle Pat," he said, as he trudged up to the bar. "I got cleaned out down the country and I been a whole week gittin' here from down 'bout Camden."

"Step up, Jethro. Damme, boy, where you been this time? You look all tuckered out. Was you in that fightin' down Camden way?"

"Yes, sir, Uncle Pat. I was down there and they dang nigh got me. Fact, they catched me but I got away when they started me with a batch o' prisoners fer Charles Town."

"You been all this time a-comin' home, Jethro?"

"Yes, sir, Uncle Pat." Jethro downed the liquor, pushed his glass back for another three fingers. "You see, I had to lay in the swamps and canebrakes all day and walk at night—"

"That would be pretty damnacious hard travelin', I'm bound, Jethro. But you're lucky to git here at all, judgin' by the reports we got o' that battle. General Caswell—him what was Governor—and General Gates they come here way in the night o' the day they done the fightin' and they 'lowed that dang nigh the whole works

ALEXANDRIANA

was killed or run off. Gates he went a-flyin' off to Hillsboro the next morning like as if a ghost was a-runnin' him. But look a-here, Jethro, what's come o' Grif Rutherford and William Lee Davidson and that young fellow Davie and Hump Hunter and these here boys 'round here? Looks like they's about all left the county. How'd they fare in the fightin'?"

"General Grif and Hump they got catched, 'twas told me. I don't fer certain know. But it was mean fightin' a while, 'fore our crowd broke and run like scared rabbits."

"I guess you seen Cornwallis?"

"Yes, Uncle Pat, I seen him."

"And I guess you saluted him, like you done General Washington up there at Valley Forge, and I guess he saluted you back and passed the time o' day, like the General done, too."

"No, I didn't salute old man Cornwallis. But I seen him. And I guess the only passin' I done with him was passin' him when I was runnin' like hell to git away." He guffawed at his wit, finished his liquor, wiped his lips on his coat sleeves. "Much b'liged, Uncle Pat. I guess that'll help me out so's I can git on up to Alexandriana." He hoisted his cup again, let the last drops trickle on his tongue.

"Want another nip, Jethro?"

"No, sir, not this time. I aint been used to no liquor lately. It'd be too much of a shock on my stomach, I guess. Fact, I aint been use to nothin' much but green roas'in-nyears and they been gittin' hard the last week—roas'in-nyears and branch water and sometimes some knotty apples."

"McKnitt's eatin's'll taste right smart good, eh, Jethro?"

"Right smart, yes, sir. By the way, Uncle Pat, when you seen Mr. McKnitt and Davy or any o' the rest o' my crowd?"

"Well, I see McKnitt every few days. He's always got business down here. He's a busy man, is McKnitt. But Davy went off down into South Ca'lina with William Lee Davidson, I've a notion 'twas, and I aint had no report of him since. I'd a thought you might a-seen him down Camden way."

"No, sir, I don't think he was down there, though 'twas a powerful lot o' Mecklenburg and Rowan and Tryon men down

ALEXANDRIANA

in that country. But I figure he was with Colonel Davidson or else young Davie or Sumter—some o' that cavalry bunch."

" 'Twasn't Sumter."

"How's that? How you know 'twasn't Sumter?"

"Because three days after that fightin' down Camden way Sumter he and his crowd went to sleep down here on Fishing Creek and that damned Tarleton come up on 'em, catched two or three hundred of 'em, took back a big bunch o' Britishers Sumter had catched, and generally whupped hell out'n him."

"But how'd you hear tell o' that, Uncle Pat?"

Old Pat Jack poured more liquor into Jethro's glass, half-filled one for himself, downed it, wiped his lips.

"Because," said he, as he set the liquor bottle back on the shelf, "Sumter rid up to the hitchin' rack out there, without a hat or coat or saddle, mind you, and come in here and I give him a big swig o' my best liquor—the same kind you been a-guzzlin', damn you, Jethro, high-priced liquor from Charles Town before the war—and he stood right there where you're standin' and told me all about it his ownself."

"Sumter must 'a' been in a hell of a hurry, Uncle Pat, if'n he run out of his hat and coat and saddle."

"You'd 'a' been too if'n that Tarleton was on yore tail, Jethro. They do say he's the meanest scoundrel in the whole danged British army. I wouldn't be surprised to find out, if'n what they says about him is any ways nigh the truth, that he's sproutin' horns."

"Uncle Pat, did General Sumter say Davy wasn't in his bunch?"

"Yes, he did. Said he knowed every man in his bunch and wasn't no Barksdale in it. Said he'd heared tell o' Davy from William Lee, but he'd never made his 'quaintance."

"Did he figure the Britishers was a-comin' on up this way?"

"He said he was lookin' for 'em soon as we got our crops pulled and in the barns. Said they'd about et out everything down Camden way and they 'lowed they'd git their stomachs filled up here in Mecklenburg and Rowan."

"Well, that's jest about the way I figures it my ownself. Sumter had the biggest bunch left after Gates and now if they done licked

ALEXANDRIANA

Sumter and sent his crowd a-runnin' there aint much to keep Cornwallis from headin' this way. I guess the next big general you'll be entertainin' will be His Lordship old man Cornwallis."

Old Pat Jack replaced the liquor bottle on the shelf, removed the glasses, wiped off the bar. Having completed his task, he raised a gnarled fist, shook it under Jethro's nose.

"Jest let him come a-messin' around here—" His face was purpling. "And I'll—I'll—"

"What would you do to Cornwallis, Uncle Pat?" Jethro's eyes, back in the brush of his matted beard, were sparkling.

"I'd—I'd fill his lousy hide full o' buck-shot."

"And we'd skin him and tack his hide to the barn door and sell it for shoe leather down Charles Town way come this spring, Uncle Pat."

Uncle Pat whacked Jethro across the shoulder. "Damme, Jethro, if we don't do it, sure'n hell." He reached for the liquor bottle and the glasses, poured the sparkling liquid. "Le's have another wee drap," said he, as he handed Jethro his glass, "and we'll drink this one to—to the damnacious good lickin' we're a-goin' to give them Redcoats if they come a-venturin' up this way."

They clinked their glasses. "The sooner's the better," added Jethro.

And they downed their liquor.

XLVII

DAVID BARKSDALE sprang from his horse, walked with the spraddle-legged gait of a man long in the saddle toward the little group of men near the fire out in front of the courthouse steps.

A tall young man in long blue coat and cavalry breeches jumped to his feet. David saluted him; the young officer returned the salute.

"Colonel Davie—"

"Yes, sir, Captain Barksdale, what did you find?"

"They've camped for the night some few miles down the road."

"Good." He turned his head, motioned with his arm toward several men seated within the ring of the firelight several paces to the right. "Hey, Joe, come over this way a minute."

Another young fellow clambered to his feet, came around the fire. "Hi, David," said he, as he walked up.

David saluted. "How you, Joe—Major Graham?"

Graham saluted. "Fit as a fiddle, David."

"Joe," said Colonel Davie, "Captain Barksdale's been down scouting the Redcoats. He says Cornwallis has camped for the night a few miles below here." He turned to David. "The camp has every appearance of being temporary—just for the night?"

"Yes, sir. Likely he's resting his men to come at us in the morning."

"More than likely. Well, we'll be rested too. We'll need it. We've been pretty much on the run ever since that business at Hanging Rock and that fracas down at Captain Wahab's. Joe, you've got all the pickets out?"

ALEXANDRIANA

"They're all placed. But I'll keep track of them through the night. We got to get these fellows to sleep, though, Colonel. We don't want any sleepy-headed fools when the damned Redcoats get here."

"That's a fact, Joe. Sumter could tell you that."

"Yes, and Tarleton's along with Cornwallis, too. We don't want this to be any Fishing Creek."

"I got word that Tarleton's sick," David interposed. "I don't know how reliable it was."

"Good!" Young Colonel Davie beamed. "That's good news. Tarleton's a hell-cat."

"It's a damned shame he aint dead," Joe Graham observed.

"Maybe he'll be this time tomorrow," suggested Davie. "But say, Joe, we must get our plans laid. Cornwallis is likely to be here early—maybe by sunrise. We don't want to be surprised."

"That's right, Colonel. We should get right at it."

"But before you start on that, Colonel," David interposed, "I wonder if you'll need my services for the next few hours—by daylight, at the latest. I'd like to run up to Alexandriana. I think I can pick up a little help for tomorrow and—"

"That would be Jethro O'Flannagan, I'll vouch," said Joe Graham.

"Yes," David nodded, "and Bedent Spraggins."

"A couple o' good soldiers, Colonel. But I thought Jethro was captured at Camden, David."

"He was, but he got away from them."

"We'll need all the men we can get, I'm bound," said Colonel Davie, "but get back as quickly as you can, Captain."

David saluted. "Yes, sir, I will." He moved toward his horse.

Colonel Davie stopped him with a gesture of his hand. "Just a minute, Captain Barksdale." David walked back to Davie. "Which way will the British come into Charlottetown, do you figure?"

"Up the Nation's Ford Road, I think. And on up along Tryon Street."

"Then they'll come up by Queen's Museum—"

ALEXANDRIANA

"It's Liberty Hall now, Colonel," Joe Graham corrected him.

"Yes, I know that. But that's what we called it when we went to school and I can't get used to the new name. By the way, there'll be a lot of the Queen's boys in the fight tomorrow, I'll vouch. And I expect a lot of window-lights will get shot out. That'll worry old Doc McWhorter, I'm bound. And say, Joe, by the way, how's Colonel McLure that was badly shot up at Hanging Creek? We fetched him there to the hospital shortly after the fight."

"He died a week ago—a week ago today, it was," Joe Graham replied.

Colonel Davie's face clouded. "That's bad. I'm sorry. When we three fellows went to school there we had no notion it would soon be turned into a hospital, did we?" He turned to David. "Well, Captain, you can get going now. And Joe, we'd better get our plans arranged. See if you can't find George Locke, and we'll all talk it over. If Cornwallis is coming up the Nation's Ford Road then he'll come at us up Tryon Street, as Barksdale says, and we can give him hell. We'll post men along both sides the street back from it a little ways, and under the courthouse here. Since they built up this underpinning they've made us a first-rate fort. We'll have to give way, of course, and retreat toward Sugaw Creek, but we can give them a fit before we withdraw."

"General Davidson isn't expecting us to hold Cornwallis here—not with our little handful of cavalry, is he?"

"No, Joe; he wants us to slow him up, worry him, keep nicking him, until he and General Sumner can get farther north and get our forces reorganized. We've been taking some mighty hard lickings lately, you know."

"Yes, that's a fact. How far has General Davidson got now? Have you had any reports?"

"He and Sumner have already passed Phifer's Mill. They cut out to the right and hit straight for Salisbury by way of Phifer's. We'll retreat as slowly as we can until we join up with them."

"I wish," said Joe Graham, "we could knock hell out of the Redcoats right here and keep 'em from going any farther north. If we did we'd save North Carolina."

ALEXANDRIANA

"They got us some fifteen to one," Colonel Davie observed. "That's a pretty big margin, Joe."

Joe Graham shrugged his shoulders. "Damn if it aint." A grin spread over his boyish face. "But those Redcoats aint ever been in Mecklenburg before."

XLVIII

THE CLEAR clean silvery call of a distant bugle cut sharply through the still September morning.

Jethro hunched Bedent Spraggins with his elbow. "There they come, Bedent, as shore as hell. That's them damned Redcoats. I've heared that same damned horn a-tootin' many a time a' ready." He clutched his musket affectionately. "Me and Flossie Belle's heared it all 'bout the country, but I reckon it sounded more scary like down 'bout Camden than anywheres else."

"It don't sound so pleasurable to me right now," observed Bedent. "You oughtn't to be talkin' so big, Jethro; that mought be old Saint Peter a-blowin' fer you."

"Well, here we stand, me and Flossie Belle—" He ran his fingers along the barrel of his musket. "He can git us right here. And the same goes fer that damn Cornwallis—if'n he's able. But I'm a notion he's goin' to git a pretty hot reception in Mecklenburg pretty soon now. Aint nobody invited him up here and these is danged contrary fokes; sometimes they don't fancy strangers inviting theirselves in without bein' asked."

"Jethro, you shore yore hoss's tied?"

"Yeh, back there perninst Lawyer Avery's. Why?"

"Because yo're likely to be needin' him in a hurry. That's mighty clost up, too."

"Ain't no need o' walkin' back a far piece to git on yore hoss. And mebbe we won't need our hosses."

"The hell we won't. Colonel Davie's got 'bout a hundred and fifty men and Joe Graham's got no more'n a dozen or so. How

ALEXANDRIANA

they goin' to stop the whole British army? We better be ready to git out from under this here courthouse in a hurry. What if'n we had to retreat back behint yore hoss? Then you'd be in a bad fix, I'm bound."

"Hell, Bedent, I'd git on him to do my retreatin'. But look a-yonder—"

A solitary horseman came racing up Tryon Street. He swung from the saddle, ran over to a group of officers, saluted, began talking with animation. But Jethro couldn't understand what he was saying.

"I wish I could hear what that feller's a-sayin'," he observed, to Bedent. "I guess he's been out scoutin' the Redcoats."

In a minute Colonel Davie on his horse came galloping up to the courthouse. "The Redcoats are getting close. Remember, men, hold your fire until you get the command. Keep yourself under cover. Keep your heads down behind this wall while you're loading and when you have to clear out, clear out fast. Get on your horses as quickly as possible. Give way, but not too fast. We want to hold them as long as we can. If we have to run for it, we'll reform out at Sugaw Creek Church." He raced back down Tryon Street, calling his instructions to the officers down there below the courthouse.

"He's got the militia lined up behind the houses and garden fenses along both sides the road," Jethro explained. "I reckon when they throw a load o' hot lead into them Britishers they'll think they've rid straight into hell." Over toward Duncan Ochiltree's store Jethro caught sight of young Joe Graham on his horse. He pointed to him. "That kid's already a first-rate soldier if'n he aint but 'bout twenty or so. He's done been in the war two year and he's cool as a cucumber right now. Look at 'im."

But Bedent's eyes were upon a column of cavalry advancing calmly around the curve in the road a half mile or so down Tryon Street. He punched Jethro. "Look a-yonder yore ownself. There they come!"

Jethro looked. "That's them, all right! Look at them uniforms, them red coats and white crossed belts. Here they come, boys.

ALEXANDRIANA

That's that feller Tarleton's men. That's Tarleton's Legions." He clutched his gun. "All right, Flossie Belle—"

"Hold your fire, men." It was young Joe Graham. "Don't get nervous. Don't shoot too quick. Wait till you get a good bead on 'em before you fire. Don't waste your powder and balls. Make every damned shot count for a Redcoat. Steady now, steady—"

A man pushed up beside Jethro, bumped against him. "Hell, feller—" Jethro looked around. The intruder was David.

"You was about to miss the fun, Davy." Jethro grinned. "I thought you'd come and got me and Bedent and then runned out on us."

"I've been out scouting. I had to run my horse pretty hard to get here ahead of 'em. It's a big crowd of those Britishers."

"Where's yore hoss?"

"Tied back there near the end of Tryon Street right where I can get him in a hurry. We'll have to run for it, Jethro. We can't hold all that crowd long." He felt of his gun, noticed the priming. "You all set?"

"Me and Flossie Belle's ready. See that feller at the head o' them cavalry. That must be Tarleton. Watch me and Flossie Belle knock hell out'n him."

"That's not Tarleton, I'm sorry to say. Tarleton's sick. Hanger's commanding his Legion, I think. That must be him. I wish it were Tarleton."

The Legion had stopped advancing. Three hundred yards down in front of the courthouse they were forming. Their front now filled the little narrow street, extended from the low fences on one side to those on the other. Beyond the Legion and on their flanks Jethro could see the British infantry, company upon company. "It's a bunch of 'em, all right. You were right about that."

The charge sounded. Up came Tarleton's Legions, up toward the little log courthouse high upon its pillars in the crossing of the roads at the crest of the rise.

"Hold your fire. Hold your fire, men," Joe Graham was calm, steady. "Wait for the command. Hold your fire."

Across on the other side of the courthouse Jethro could see

ALEXANDRIANA

Colonel Davie, his head back, his eyes upon the advancing Redcoats, steadying his dismounted cavalry, calming them with hands weaving gently.

Still came the British, up the street, their horses stepping high, stamping out little puffs of red dust that blew out into the warm September sunshine. On they came. Jethro could see them now, their faces, round pink British faces, healthy faces, impassive above their scarlet coats, their white crossed belts . . . "Steady now, men. Ready. Ready. Hold it. Hold it. Now then, men." The British horsemen were seventy-five yards from the courthouse. Seventy yards. "Now then, men. Aim." Sixty-five yards. On they came, their horses stepping high, their company front a straight line across little dusty Tryon Street. Sixty yards . . . "FIRE!"

A wall of flame leaped from beneath the courthouse at the crest of the little slope. Hot stinging death flung itself upon those horses stepping high and rhythmically over an alien unknown soil, upon those pink round British faces above the crested arched necks of those proudly marching horses now so suddenly stopped in their marching.

And now what but a moment ago was order and the perfection of British discipline was become a confusion and a shouting and a breaking and running, and the proud horses bearing their round faced British riders were bearing them backward upon the ranks of the infantry down below Duncan Ochiltree's store, as far down as Joe Nicholson's tavern. But onward marched the infantry, in steady cadence, swinging arms and legs in a rhythm that brought them steadily toward the little courthouse from which death was pouring . . .

And now upon the marching infantrymen the Americans from behind the houses and the garden fences and the hedgerows rained hot lead . . . But steadily forward marched the infantry . . . "They'll surround our boys and cut 'em off from us!" shouted David above the rattle of musketry. But the officers down that way had foreseen their peril and now they were withdrawing them, and they were retreating toward the courthouse. And down below in the street the Legion was reforming . . .

ALEXANDRIANA

Here was Joe Graham . . . "They're rallying, men. They'll be back. Hold your fire, and when they get close enough pour it into 'em. Ready, boys. Here they come!"

The leader had rallied them. Now they were charging. Back up the dusty road. Closer now, closer, close . . . "FIRE!"

They reeled again, fled down the street. In the presence of their brothers of the infantry they were rushing madly, wildly, in the disorder of flight, back upon the mass of the British.

But the infantry had been steadily advancing under the cover of the houses and fences, as the Americans dropped back before them toward the courthouse. And now they were threatening to turn Colonel Davie's right flank.

The young commander, who had been covering with quick eyes the whole sweep and spread of the battle, had become conscious of this new danger; quickly and in good order he drew off these threatened companies, and one covering the other in successive withdrawals, they formed at the end of Tryon Street some hundred yards above the courthouse.

"Watch it, men! Here they come again!" Joe Graham was dashing about beneath the courthouse. "Hold your fire until they're close enough. Then throw it to 'em, boys!"

The crackle of musketry fanned out again from the walls underneath the little structure. Flame spouted from long barrels. A Britisher shot out his arm, dived from his charging horse. Another. Another. But the horsemen came on. Past the courthouse they dashed, and from under it the men of Davie and Graham poured forth a blinding hail of hot lead.

Now they broke again, and fled back down the street, the thunder of their galloping, madly flying horses shaking the very ground, the confusion of their flight now becoming quickly a panic of cries and curses and unheeded commands and fast thickening dust . . .

"Damned if'n we aint gived 'em hell and a-plenty, boys," said Jethro, as he raised his barrel and blew away the smoke still curling from it. "D'you reckon we can keep 'em back? 'Twouldn't be possible and yit we—"

"Hold on, Jethro." David, prepared to ram in his wadding, laid his ramrod across the wall, peered down the street. "Look. Down there. The big man, the one over there, coming across on the bay—"

"That's Cornwallis! Yes, sir. That's him. That's Cornwallis shore'n hell. I know that round-faced feller. I seen him down at Camden. I was clost to him when he come up and talked to that French general after he got shot, that feller de Kalb. Yes, sir. I got a good look at him. That there's Cornwallis, boys. I wonder what he's up to now—"

"Maybe we can hear him." But Cornwallis was down the street, too far to be heard in the confusion beneath the little courthouse. David could see him gesticulating, and it appeared that he was talking angrily to Tarleton's Legion. But he disappeared in a moment behind the massed troops.

"All right, boys—" It was Joe Graham again. "All right. they're getting ready to come at us again. Hold your fire. If they don't break this time we may have to run for it. Be ready to head for the horses. We'll give back along the road to Sugaw Creek. All right now, boys, steady. Steady. They're coming!"

Jethro had his musket barrel steadied on the wall and he was squinting along the barrel. "Watch that feller you said wasn't Tarleton. I wish he was. But if'n he aint he'll serve."

"Calm, boys. Steady now. Steady. Hold it. Hold it. All right, now. Aim. Get you a man." Joe Graham's voice was soothing. "Ready now. Ready. All right . . . FIRE!"

The muskets crackled and flame spouted from the underpinnings of the little house in the crossroads. Horses reared, walked backward on their hind legs, squealed as the hot lead bit into them. "Look!" Jethro pointed through the smoke. David saw the leader of the Legion rocking back and forth in his saddle. Slowly he crumpled toward the right, fell to the ground. For a moment his foot caught in the stirrup; as the horse moved to the side, away from the wounded and dismounted rider, the foot slipped out, fell with a thud to the ground. Jethro blew the smoke from the end of the barrel. "I told you Flossie Belle would git that feller."

But the Redcoats continued to charge the courthouse. They

ALEXANDRIANA

swarmed about both sides, plunged their horses across in front of the high steps. And the infantry was about to close in upon the little band of defenders. "All right, boys, we've got to clear out. Back to your horses, and don't waste any time!"

And now Jethro and David were retreating slowly along the little red road that led out to Sugaw Creek and onward to Phifer's Mill and Salisbury. But the British, impressed evidently by the fierceness of the reception they had just met at the courthouse, were following with caution.

Joe Graham rode up, spied David. "We're forming to attack them again, David. That'll give the boys ahead more time to get on up the road." Quickly he lined up a group of his cavalry, plunged down the road upon the Redcoat infantrymen marching stolidly along in the dust of the red road. Quickly, having struck their blow, his men fled back toward Sugaw Creek.

And now the young cavalry leader was forming them again, on the hill across from the church. Major White was helping round up the men. "We'd better hurry and take a crack at the infantry again," Joe Graham was urging him, "and then get away before the dragoons come up. I've a notion those dragoons have blood in their eyes by now, the way we've been belting 'em." But Major White was anxious to get the men together in perfect formation, and he dallied. In a few minutes from below the hill Joe Graham saw the Redcoats, their cross belts shining in the bright afternoon sunshine. The dragoons, having caught sight of the little group of American horsemen on the hill, spurred up their horses.

"We've got to run for it!" Joe Graham sat on his horse, yelling to his men. "Get on up the road, boys. There's too many of them for us. We'll outrun them." He sat calmly, getting his men along ahead of him, as he watched the British dragoons spurring up the road toward him. Then he turned and followed his men.

But they had waited too long. Soon the British were upon them, shooting and hacking with their sabres. The sunlight glinted as the curved blades swung out and up and down. The Americans fought, but there was no end of the dragoons. Out of the corner of his eye David saw a group of Britishers surrounding Lieutenant George

ALEXANDRIANA

Locke. He was on the edge of a little pond. He couldn't escape them. David saw him go down under an avalanche of swift curving blades that flashed and glinted in the sun.

They were swarming around Joe Graham too. But the young Mecklenburger was fighting. Jethro, watching Joe, almost failed to see a curved sabre descending upon himself; in the flick of an eyelash he ducked, and it swished harmlessly above him. Furiously he swung his musket around with a butt stroke that landed the stock squarely across the left ear of a florid Britisher, sent him spinning crazily from the saddle, and his sabre cut a swift arc through the sunshine . . .

Jethro's horse was running. He turned in his saddle. Joe Graham lay in a crumpled heap. A Britisher was charging straight toward him, and Joe lay squarely in the path. Jethro winced, twisted his head not to see the horse crash into Joe . . . But the horse jumped. Straight toward him came the British. Redcoats, crossed white belts, shining, slashing sabres . . . All the Redcoats in the world were coming straight for him . . . Jethro dug his heels in his horse's ribs . . .

Aunt Susannah Alexander's cow didn't come up to be milked that night. Nor could Aunt Susannah blame the poor creature. With all that shooting and running of horses and fighting up there near the church, 'twas a wonder the cow hadn't run clear to Poplar Tent before stopping. "She'll be hard to find, I'm bound," she told her daughter.

They started on the hunt. Horses' tracks and men's tracks. All over the road and all out in the fields. The weeds beaten down, grass scuffed up. Yes, and here and there brown splotches on leaves that must be blood, dried blood. It was beginning to get dark now, and the air was crisp with the crispness of a late September day. It would be hard to find that cow . . .

Over here was a huddled form. Aunt Susannah's eyes were not the best now, and it was getting dark. But that strange huddled clump . . . She called her daughter.

"He's one of our men. You can tell that by his clothes." They

ALEXANDRIANA

turned him over. A low moan. A bloody bubble blew out from his lips, burst. "Merciful heavens, he's alive. Look, I can't see well. But is he not Mis' Graham's boy?"

The younger woman bent nearer, brushed the matted blood-soaked hair from his face. "Yes, 'tis. 'Tis Joe Graham."

"Merciful heavens! We must get him home. He's bad hurt, I'm bound. He'll die 'gainst mornin' if we don't get him home and doctor on him."

They put him on the loft. It would be safest, in event any Redcoats came prowling around. They bathed his wounds, found the places where three musket balls had entered his body, put poultices on the sabre cuts, bandaged them securely. "The boy's fairly cut to pieces," declared Aunt Susannah. "Six bad cuts. That's a terrible slash in his side. And his poor head. If it hadn't 'ave been for that stock buckle they'd 'ave cut off his head, I'm bound."

Through the September night they watched him on his pallet on the loft above Aunt Susannah's big room. Sometimes he mumbled words and phrases that the two women could not fashion into any meaning, jumbles of moaning sounds, of vague and unconnected thoughts. But toward the morning he fought his way up through troubled feverish dreams to consciousness, and when late in the afternoon a strange woman came to the house he was able to follow the talk as he listened above the women in the big room.

She was the wife of an officer, one of the British officers now quartered at Charlottetown, he could make out, though her talk was powerful strange. And she was wanting to buy chickens. She thought this place was a likely one for chickens. The women talked. Strange how they could talk, how they could be polite to the wife of an invading Britisher. Strange, too, that she should be wanting to pay money, good coined money, for the chickens.

The women talked on. And after a while Aunt Susannah told her of the wounded boy in the loft above. Yes, he had been badly wounded, left for dead. Surely he would have died had it not been for the stock buckle. Listening above them, lying sick and feverish and fearful, Joe Graham heard them discussing him.

The British woman was sympathetic. "When I ride back to

ALEXANDRIANA

Charlottetown I shall report the injured young man to Lord Cornwallis. He will send out a surgeon to attend him." After a while she was gone.

The boy thumped upon the loose planks of the loft. "Aunt Susannah, I've got to get out of here," he said, when Mrs. Alexander went up the steep narrow stairs to answer his knocking. "I'll not stay and be carted off to prison. I heard what that woman said. She'll not get me caught."

"But she seemed a fair clever woman, Joey. And she was willing to pay for the chickens, though I had none for her."

"She may be a clever woman and she may mean me no harm, but I'll have no British tending me; I'll die first. I've got to get home, Aunt Susannah."

"But you're in no shape, Joey. You been rough-handled. Only the good Lord has kept you livin', I'm bound."

"I've got to get home. If you'll help me down the ladder and on my horse—"

"I haven't seen your horse, Joey."

"I guess he went on home. I don't remember much. But you'll give me the loan of a horse—"

"But you're in no way to be ridin', Joey."

Joe Graham was persistent. He would not be dissuaded. They got him down from the loft. The boy groaned as they helped him, half carrying him, down the steep stairway, and after a while settled him upon the horse.

"You won't be able to stay in the saddle, Joey."

The boy gritted his teeth. "Hand me the reins," he said.

They watched him as he rode westward into the setting sun.

XLIX

GENERAL CORNWALLIS sat behind a table that had been pulled out into the center of Thomas Polk's sitting room. Before him lay a sheaf of papers, an inkstand, and a pen fashioned of a long goose quill. The scarlet of his coat heightened the pink of his round cheeks.

He slapped a white palm upon the papers in front of him and the lace at his wrist flipped outward from lavishly braided cuff. "You see, Mr. Ochiltree, it's that way everywhere in this plagued—"

A discreet knocking upon the door interrupted. "Come in!" he commanded, a bit sharply.

An orderly entered, stood rigidly at attention.

"What is it, Sergeant? Speak up."

"Major Doyle begs to report, sir, that the patrol 'e sent out this morning is back."

"Well, what luck had it?"

The soldier was standing immobile. "Major Doyle begs to report, sir, that 'e managed to obtain only a few 'ead of very poor cattle, and little corn. And seven men were lost, sir, and thirteen wounded, six of them, 'e said, sir, seriously. They have been taken to the hospital."

His Lordship picked up the papers, slammed them upon the table. "There you see it, sir. I send out a patrol, three times as many as should be needed, and they come back with some scrawny cows and a few bushels of corn and seven of my men killed and another dozen knocked out of service, some of them likely for good." He turned to the orderly. "Very well, Sergeant. Thank you." The orderly withdrew stiffly.

"Mr. Ochiltree, of all the damnably rebellious provinces in America, I believe this is the worst. I had been informed by your Governor Martin, who has been with me in South Carolina, that when I advanced into North Carolina the people would rise to greet me—" His Lordship's serious, intent expression softened into the semblance of a smile. "They rose to greet me, all right, but by the heavens it was an inhospitable greeting. I hadn't crossed the line until these damned Mecklenburg people were shooting at my men, and they've kept it up continuously. I send out patrols to forage and they come back with miserable, scrawny poor cattle—"

"There's plenty good cattle in these parts, General, but they're hidin' 'em in the canebrakes and woods." Duncan Ochiltree fingered his hat nervously.

"I'm willing to pay for the damned stuff. I'm not a ruthless man, Mr. Ochiltree. I've been harsh, 'tis true, but I'm fighting a war. It's the course my government orders me to pursue. I've hanged a lot of men for breaking their paroles. But that's war. I'm willing to pay for the cattle and corn and wheat if the damned people would stay home and get their money when my men come for it." He stamped a clenched white pudgy fist upon the table. "But instead of that, they hide their stuff, burn it up or otherwise dispose of it, and run off into the woods to shoot down my men. Aside from you and Cafferty, Mr. Ochiltree, I've been harshly received in Mecklenburg. Of course—" His face relaxed into a smile again, "Colonel Polk has provided his home as my headquarters, but I have moved in without his invitation and he and his family did not wait to receive me."

"Well, sir, General—" Ochiltree twisted the brim of his three-cornered hat, "I can't complain. You've paid me well. But these people hereabouts is a contrary bunch. They talk a lot about principles and freedom and such like and they'd burn up their stuff before they'd let your bunch have it, though you were willing to pay them well. They're queer that way. But I guess, General, I'd better be gettin' back to the store. I'm likely missin' a lot of tradin'." He

ALEXANDRIANA

bowed his way out and at the door almost collided with the orderly, who stood stiffly at attention.

"Come in, Sergeant," said His Lordship, as Duncan Ochiltree disappeared in the hallway. "More bad news, I presume?"

"News has just been brought into camp, sir, that one of our patrols this morning at a ford due west of here on the Catawba came upon the body of one of Major Ferguson's American Volunteers—"

"Damn!" His Lordship rose from his chair, walked back and forth, his broad forehead crinkled. He turned on his heel. "On which side of the ford was the fellow?"

"On this side, sir, some hundred or so paces from the river."

"He had no message on him, of course?"

"No, sir. Nothing to identify him but his insignia. Presumably he was on his way from Major Ferguson with a dispatch to Your Lordship—"

"Yes, of course. And no signs of his horse?"

"Only the tracks, sir. But they were quickly lost."

"Some of these damnable Mecklenburg guerrillas got him. I wonder about Pat—" He hesitated, his forehead creased in a dozen lines. He whirled upon the orderly. "Find Colonel Tarleton and send him to me."

"Ban," said he, when the young cavalry officer strode in, "I'm worried about Ferguson. He's trying to get a dispatch to me. The messengers aren't getting through. There was another one found this morning—shot dead—just this side the ford of the Catawba—Tuckaseegee or Toole's, I don't know which. It doesn't matter a damn anyway; they get them wherever they cross. I'm worried about Pat."

"I don't believe you need be, General. Pat's over in the western settlements and most of the people over that way are either our friends by choice or they are afraid to oppose us. Pat's put the fear of the King in their lousy hides. Everywhere, according to our last reports, they're flocking to join up with him or else take protection and he's hanging every one that violates his parole—"

"Yes, that's right, Ban. The last reports we've had from Pat were

342

good. But we haven't had a word out of him since we came into Charlottetown. He should be over in the neighborhood of Gilberttown. And he should be making good progress. But I don't like the way we've lost contact with him. Something may have happened. This is damned rebellious country."

"You're right, Your Lordship. This is damned rebellious country." He pointed toward the floor. "This damned Mecklenburg. There's a damned rebel shooting at you every time you stick your head out of camp, and I wouldn't be surprised if they shouldn't even try to raid us here."

General Cornwallis tapped the sheets of paper with the back of his hand. "These tell a bad story, Ban. We had been led to believe that once we got into North Carolina we'd find provisions in plenty. But this tells another story." He picked up a sheet. "Look at the cattle we have been consuming. 'September 27—103 head; September 28—98 head; September 29—107 head'. That's the way it is every day—a hundred head or more. That shows how lean the cattle is we're getting. And we're paying a terrific price for that meat, Ban. The hospital must be about full of wounded men."

"Yes, Your Lordship, it is. And the graves out there beside it are increasing every day, too. We're getting a sizable graveyard beside that damnable Presbyterian schoolhouse."

"By the way, are the wounded men making progress? How about Hanger and Campbell and McDonald?"

"They're getting better, Your Lordship. But there's been a lot of men added to the list since the day we came into Charlottetown."

"I'm glad you were ill that day, Ban. I may need you and that right shortly."

"I'm not criticizing Major Hanger, Your Lordship, but I wish I'd been at the head of my Legion the other day. I don't believe it would have been necessary for you to scold them if I'd been leading them. We'd have given them some more of the medicine we gave Buford at the Waxhaws."

"Ban," General Cornwallis smiled, "you're not what one would call a—a humanitarian. For a very young man you're rather strong in your methods. You're not more than—"

ALEXANDRIANA

"I was twenty-six August twenty-first past. That's pretty damned old, Your Lordship."

Cornwallis walked to the window, looked out, turned around to face Colonel Banastre Tarleton again. "I can't get it out of my head that Pat Ferguson may be in a bad way. That fellow Shelby's been moving around over in the western settlements and there may be devilment afoot. These confounded rebels in Carolina—"

"They're nowhere so bad as they are right here in this county, Your Lordship. This is the center and fountain head of rebellion. It was here they wrote that damned declaration—"

"Yes, I've heard of that paper. A more damnably seditious document there never was."

"These people are damned Presbyterians, Your Lordship. Wherever you find one of the breed you find an enemy of the King. And that damned schoolhouse down there where we have our hospital has been sowing the seeds of rebellion ever since it started. And since we are talking of it, Your Lordship, I want to make a suggestion which I hope you'll consider well, and not hold me insubordinate—"

"What is it, Ban? Speak up."

"I suggest that you make an example of some of these rebels in these parts. I believe that would put the fear of the King and Your Lordship in their rebellious thick heads. I know Your Lordship doesn't believe in pillaging, burning—"

"No, Ban, I don't believe in making war that way."

"Nor do I, under usual conditions, Your Lordship, but—"

The round florid face of the British commander lighted with a beaming smile. "No, Ban, I know you are against it under usual conditions. You have just never run upon usual conditions, have you, where you could apply that rule?"

Tarleton laughed. "I believe in giving 'em all the hell I know how to hand out, Your Lordship. But to get back to Mecklenburg, sir. You are living in the house of one of the greatest rebels in Carolina—this Tom Polk."

"Would you want me to burn down the house over my own head, Ban?"

ALEXANDRIANA

"Oh, no, no, sir, no indeed. Not now. But right over there—" He motioned with his thumb— "is the law office of one of the leaders in that seditious movement to draw up that declaration, a fellow Avery. And right out there is the courthouse—so these back countrymen call it—in which they had their meetings." A scowl clouded his face. "And right down that road a way is a tavern run by a damnable old Irishman named Jack who has sired more damned rebels to fight his King than any one in my knowing, and every day he curses and raves and insults His Majesty's name and His Majesty's soldiers. I say, Your Lordship, they should have the torch set to 'em, the whole blasted lot. 'Twould not be pillaging, Your Lordship. 'Twould be punishment. And they deserve punishment, and not only those here in Charlottetown, but those rebels out in the countryside who are shooting down our men. They should be stamped out entirely. There's a rich rebel up the country a short way, so Ochiltree tells me—"

"I don't like him. He was in here just before you came. I don't like traitors. I haven't any use for Arnold. And no more for this Ochiltree. You can't trust them."

"No, sir, but you can use them as long as they serve you. And then, if you like, you can slit their throats. But Ochiltree does know this country and he'd sell his soul for a couple of pounds—"

"We'd be cheated, at that."

Tarleton laughed. "We would. But he says there's a fellow named Alexander who has laid in a fine crop this year and is well stocked with cattle and hogs. And he's a most knavish rebel. We might pay him a visit."

"Ban, I'll have no pillaging for the mere sake of pillaging. I will not countenance the burning of this little courthouse. It is the symbol of justice and law. It may be law administered in rebellion, but I daresay what law is administered from it is good English law. At any rate, the British army shall not wantonly pillage. I want that understood. I shall enforce that. I shall severely punish pillaging, burning and raping—" He hesitated, looked squarely into the face of the young colonel. "I want that understood by everyone— everyone, sir."

ALEXANDRIANA

"Yes, sir, Your Lordship."

"As for this Alexander, I shall send a detachment to his place to bring in whatever supplies it may find available to our use. But the occupants of the house, if they are at home, shall not be harmed or insulted, and the house shall not be burned. It will require a strong detachment. I shall send either Rawdon or Webster with half our army as a covering party for the foragers. I cannot spare more than half, or I may find myself attacked here. You know they attacked Guyon's picket down at Polk's mill and they've attacked our convoys from Camden and the post at Blair's mill. We must be on our guard every moment."

"Yes, sir, you're right, Your Lordship. I only wish we could get at them on a battlefield."

"But we cannot, Ban. They have us at a disadvantage. They know the country. They shoot from behind rocks and trees and then scurry away into the deep woods. That's why I can't get it off my mind that something may have happened to Pat Ferguson."

"Your Lordship hasn't given any instructions concerning Avery's office or Jack's Tavern."

Cornwallis sat silent. "Ban, I don't like your suggestion. That sounds very near to pillaging to me. And yet, war is no parlor game. There is no plunder to be obtained in a law office. I'm convinced none of my soldiers want law books. And that tavern is no good influence on my soldiers. They have issued to them all the rum they need. I'll have no carousing." He appeared to be arguing with himself rather than with Colonel Tarleton. "And the owners eminently deserve punishment. The destruction of these properties may prove a deterrent to further guerrilla activities against my foraging parties. I'm not well convinced." He looked up, smiled. "I sleep soundly at nights, Ban. I shall give instructions tonight not to be awakened unless we are attacked."

"I understand, sir. Thank you. And now—"

"I shall call you when I want you again, Ban."

"Thank you, sir." He saluted, walked briskly toward the doorway, his sabre clanking against his leg.

His Lordship nodded, turned to look out the window.

L

THE NEGRO ran out to the uppin'-block to meet his master.

"Hi, Cato." McKnitt Alexander swung from the saddle, handed over the reins. "Anything happened while I've been gone?"

"Yas, suh, Marse McKnitt; Marse Davy him and Mr. Jethro come home this mawnin' with Colonel Davie and a bunch o' other mens on hosses."

"Is that right? Well, that is good news. Where'd they come from? Did they say?"

"They come from Mr. Adam Torrence's tavern where they stayed at last night. Come from Salisbury yistiddy. That's what they said."

"Where are they now, Cato?"

"Marse Davy him and Colonel Davie rid over to see Marse Joe Graham. The other mens they rid off back up towards Centre Church."

"Well, they got back pretty soon. They say anything about Colonel Davidson?"

"Mis' Jeanie she asked 'em that same question and they told her Marse Willie Lee done crossed the Yadkin River beyont Salisbury."

"Well, I'm glad Davie's back around here. We'll likely be needing him. Cato, you haven't forgot what I told you about the barns and storehouse—"

"No, suh, Marse McKnitt. I mind it all lak you said. But 'twould be a great pity to have to—"

"Yes, 'twould, Cato. I reckon this is about the best crop we've

ALEXANDRIANA

had in a long time. But I'm determined those Redcoats won't eat any stuff out of those houses out there. The first minute you see any signs o' Redcoats 'rounding that bend, Cato, you run set fire to the whole works. And keep some fat pine handy for torches—"

"Yas, suh, I done got all that fixed. But I shore hopes 'twon't be no need o' doin' it."

McKnitt walked into the house. "Cato said David and Jethro had come back with young Davie. How'd they say things looked, Jeanie?"

His wife took his three-cornered hat, hung it on the folding cross-rack. "Sit down, Honey," she said. "You look all tuckered out. I'll get you a drink. Then I'll tell you."

In a minute she brought the drink. "They were tired from all the riding they'd done. We fed them—there were a dozen or more men on horses along—and they rested a while. Then David and Colonel Davie rode over to Mrs. Graham's to see Joe. They were worried about him. Hadn't heard how he fared in the fighting. The others rode back up towards Centre Church. I think they're going to meet up there somewhere—"

"Yes, we're trying to reassemble a bunch somewhere above here to keep an eye on the British at Charlottetown—give 'em all the trouble we can. I've got a considerable crowd joined up a'ready. Have any Redcoats been prowling about, Jeanie?"

"No, we haven't seen hide nor hair of any Britisher."

"Well, they'll be along. They're getting low on stuff to eat. We've been working on their foraging patrols. Has Cato got the cattle hid out—and the hogs and horses?"

"All except a few, and those we've already sent off for our boys, McKnitt."

"Well, that's what I meant—those our men didn't need. I want that no Britisher eats of stuff growed at Alexandriana." He stopped, stared ahead, "Jeanie?"

"Yes, Honey?"

"You know what I've instructed Cato?"

"W'y, yes."

"And you're agreed?"

ALEXANDRIANA

Standing above him, she lifted his chin, bent down and kissed him. "Of course, my dear. You know it."

"Yes, I knew it. I suppose I was but trying to bolster up my own courage. 'Twould be bad to see the sweat of many a hot day, the struggle of many a cold day, go up in smoke, Jeanie."

Jeanie's eyes flashed. "'Twould be a right smart worse to see it go into Britishers' stomachs."

McKnitt pulled her down upon his lap, snuggled his face in her long hair. "What a woman you are, Jeanie, what a fair treasure you are, what a tower of strength to a poor weak man—"

"You're no weak man, McKnitt Alexander. You're a strong, abidin' man, a man to make proud a woman's heart, a man like—like General Washington his ownself!" As she turned up her face to him, he saw through the film of proud tears the flash of enduring fires.

LI

The door was flung open. Inside marched a squad of British soldiers, their crossed belts white in the candlelight, their ornaments sparkling upon their scarlet coats.

The barkeeper straightened up, wiped his hands upon his apron. "What would you gentlemen wish?" He wiped the bar with the cloth tucked into the belt of his apron.

"We don't wish anything. I suggest you'd better get your hat and coat and get out if you wish to keep your whole skin."

The fellow's mouth fell open. "But—but—"

"Orders to burn down this rebel's nest. All right, boys—"

"But you can't do that, Captain. Old Mr. Jack's upstairs sick in the bed."

"The hell we can't. It's Colonel Tarleton's orders. Look out the door and you'll see that rebel lawyer's office burning now."

"But you wouldn't burn old Mr. Jack. He's an old fellow—a fine old man, old Mr. Jack is—"

"A fine old rebel against His Majesty. We ought to burn him down with this rat-hole. That would be another damn rebel less—"

Through the door strode a young cavalry officer, a heavy scowl smearing his face. "What the hell, Lieutenant. Nothing done yet? That damned Avery's shack is damn near in ashes already."

The commander of the squad paled. "We'll be but a minute, Colonel Tarleton. This fat fellow here says there's an old man sick abed upstairs."

"Who is he?" Tarleton whirled upon the barkeeper. "Speak up, fellow!"

"Old Mr. Pat Jack, yes, sir!"

"He's the old Irish rascal that owns this place? Got several sons in the rebel army?"

"Yes, sir, that's him."

"We ought to burn him up with the building. 'Twould be his just deserts. But send up and fetch him down, Lieutenant. Bring him bed and all."

The lieutenant nodded to a corporal and several of the soldiers ran up the stairs that led to the rooms above. In a moment those below heard a tremendous commotion that grew louder until the Redcoats returned with Uncle Pat, kicking and squirming in the depths of the big feather bed they were carrying by the four corners.

They set down their burden in front of the bar. Tarleton walked over to old Jack. "Scrappy, aren't you, Grandpa?"

The old fellow sat up on the feather bed in the middle of the floor, shook his fist at the flashily uniformed Britisher.

"If'n I weren't sick, you young divil, I'd give ye a trouncin', I would. Sendin' for to take an old sick man out'n his bed." He pointed a skinny forefinger at Tarleton. "Now ye git these young upstart divils out'n here and be damnacious quick about it!"

"You've got courage, Grandpa, too, damned if you haven't, to be a damned Irishman."

Uncle Pat's face grew livid with anger. "Git out, you—you damned Englisher. Git out afore I have ye th'owed out."

"I wonder if you know whom you are addressing, old man?" Tarleton's face was clouding.

"I don't know and I don't give a damn. All Britishers is the same—all of 'em's a bunch o' lily-livered cowardly damnacious knaves."

"You're talking to Colonel Banastre Tarleton, old man. They call me Bloody Tarleton and they've a right to. I've killed more damned rebels and raped more damned rebel women than any other man in the whole British army." A cold humorless smile played around the corners of his mouth. "You'd better mind your words, old fellow."

"You needn't 'old feller' me, damn you, Tarleton. I've heared tell o' you, and nothin' good. You're a damnacious butcher, and a damnacious cowardly scoundrel to boot, sir, and I aint a-scairt o' ye—" Uncle Pat was rocking back and forth upon his feather bed, shaking his fist, his face purple with wrath. Tarleton moved toward him, drew back his heavily booted foot.

But he didn't kick him. "I ought to kill you, you damned old Irish hellion. But you're too damned old." He turned to the lieutenant. "Have your men carry him into the street, and get to work on this rebel-hole. And no plundering, mind you, Lieutenant. Smash all these damned bottles. The liquor's no good anyway. Break hell out of everything. And then put your torches to it. And don't waste any more time doing it, Lieutenant."

He turned, strode out.

A half hour later Uncle Pat Jack, sitting upon his feather bed across Trade Street, lifted a gnarled fist to high heaven and called down upon King George and the British the wrath of heaven and all Ireland.

But few there were who heard him because of the crackle of high leaping flames and the crash of falling heavy timbers.

LII

"GEORGE, HAVE you ever heard tell of what became of those two Tory lawyer fellows you all got up at Salisbury five years ago and took to Camden?"

"I don't know exactly," George Graham replied. "The last I heard tell of them they were locked up down Charles Town way. I guess they still are. It suits me if they keep 'em down there."

" 'Twouldn't be any more than they deserve. We don't need any more Tories up this way. Duncan Ochiltree and old man Cafferty's enough."

"Wait'll we chase the Redcoats out o' Mecklenburg, George," spoke up Francis Bradley. "We'll have time enough then to look after those two bastards. I'd like to get a crack at both of 'em with this popgun."

"Aint that Major John Davidson's gun, Francis?"

"Yeh, 'tis. And it's a sweet shooting stick, Ed," he answered Ed Shipley. "Made at the rifle works at Charlottetown. It'll throw hot lead through a squirrel's skull in the tallest oak, if you can get a bead on him."

"How'd you happen to have it?"

"Major John has to tote a sword. He's a staff officer. He let me have it. I hope he never wants it back. I could—Shut up, boys. I believe I hear the Redcoats."

"It's them, all right." Jim Thompson had his hand cupped to his ear. "It's a big bunch of them, I'm bound. We better hit it to the woods."

ALEXANDRIANA

Fifty yards behind Mitchell's mill the woods ran up in a thick heavy green mass that in a moment effectively screened the group of Hopewell young men peering out upon the Britishers advancing up Beatty's Ford Road three miles above Charlottetown.

Dragoons rode in front. There were perhaps two dozen of the horsemen. Behind them, their guns held easily across their shoulders, came the infantry. "It's a sight of 'em, all right," said Jim Thompson. "Somebody count 'em."

Behind the infantry creaked the wagons. There were so many of them that the Hopewell young fellows, peeping out from the bushes back of Mitchell's mill, could not see the end of the train even after the first of the wagons had passed around the curve above the mill. "They've got enough wagons to haul back all the stuff in Hopewell," George Graham whispered. "And all those soldiers. We must have 'em pretty well scared up."

After a while the last wagon came into sight and behind it other infantrymen marched in the red dust now swirling above the twisting narrow road. And then came other dragoons. "That's the rear guard," said Jim Thompson. "How many'd you make them out to be?"

"It was about sixty cavalry," said Francis Bradley, "the way I figured 'em, and about four hundred and fifty on foot, and about forty wagons."

"That's a lot for us to tackle, boys," said Jim Thompson. "But maybe we'll get a better chance at 'em. Let's slip through the woods alongside 'em. I've a notion they'll be stopping somewhere pretty soon."

Four miles up Beatty's Ford Road the British foraging party halted. The wagons began pulling off to the side of the road, a large detachment of the infantry and a group of the dragoons moved over into the field opposite a two-story log house that squatted above the little branch paralleling the road.

"They're fixing to clean out McIntyre, Jim." Francis Bradley from behind a poplar could see the Redcoats. "Maybe we can get a shot at 'em when they get busy loading up." Strung along the edge of the thick woods, Thompson and his companions watched

ALEXANDRIANA

the foragers. The officers were shouting commands, the drivers yelling to their horses, and orderlies were trotting up and down the road as the entire party began assembling.

In a few minutes a group of the horsemen took their places in the road and began slowly moving off toward the north. Infantrymen fell in behind them, and creaking wagons joined the procession. "They're dividing," said Jim Thompson. "Some of 'em are going up the road and the rest are going to stay here and clean out McIntyre's stuff. That's all the better for us, boys." He motioned to the others. When they got together around him, he pointed toward a heavy thicket down nearer the McIntyre house. "Let's slip down there behind that thicket, boys. That'll put us a couple hundred yards from the house. From there we can slip up behind that rocky ridge that runs up from the spring to the road, and then we'll be right on 'em and they can't see us for those bushes."

Stealthily they moved down the spring branch to the thicket and across to the new position behind the little rocky ridge. From the cover of this ridge they watched silently as the British began plundering the McIntyre place.

The Englishmen appeared to be having a good time. They had scattered over the fields near the house, the barnyard, the stables, the granary, and some had even ventured to push through the low doorway into the house itself. The Hopewell men listened as the Redcoats pulled the corn in the fields and threw it with dull thuds into the cavernous wagons; they fingered the locks and peered carefully at the priming of their guns as Redcoats with merry shoutings chased squealing pigs and squawking ducks and chickens and guineas.

In the barn doorway a squatty round-faced Englishman with an immense cocked hat and a protruberant paunch was watching the soldiers chasing the pigs and the fowls. Along the garden fence a row of beehives rested upon low oak butt-cuts. When the soldiers; and two or three barking dogs who had joined in the chase, in attempting to hem up a pig in the fence corner knocked over several of the beehives and the insects came streaming out after the flying Redcoats, the florid officer roared and slapped his fat stomach.

ALEXANDRIANA

Thompson and his crowd were so busy watching the Britishers that they had failed to hear a man approaching from their rear until he was almost upon them. When a stick cracked, they whirled about.

It was McIntyre. "Where'd you come from, Mr. McIntyre?" one of them asked him, when he slipped up to them.

"Back there in the woods," he whispered. "I just couldn't stand to go off and leave things to those thieving Englishmen. I reckon maybe I ought to but I just couldn't."

"How'd you get away from the house? How'd you know they were coming?"

"A boy down the road toward Charlottetown was plowing when he saw 'em coming and he unhooked his mule and came on the run to tell the folks up this way. We had just got away when they got here. My folks are farther back in the woods. But I just couldn't go off." He pulled aside a thick plum branch, peered through the little opening. "Boys, they're destroyin' everything I got. Carryin' off all my corn and wheat, killing my pigs and cows—" The squeal of a stuck pig gave emphasis to his complaint. "Boys," he raised his musket, "I just can't put up with this any longer."

"Hold on, Mr. McIntyre, just a minute." Jim Thompson held up his hand. "We've got to scatter out, boys. Get about ten feet apart along the ridge. Everybody pick a man. I'll take that captain in the barn door. As soon as we shoot, everybody run down that way and we'll shoot from over there," he motioned toward the left. "They'll likely be shooting back in this direction. We've got to keep 'em fooled, make 'em think there's a lot more of us."

In the barnyard they were loading slaughtered pigs and cows on the wagons. From the fields other wagons were rumbling out toward the road. Over at the granary perspiring Redcoats were heaving sacks of wheat into still other wagons. A handful of hardy Britishers were trying to rob the beehives. One fellow was slapping at the bees with his high cocked hat. When an insect popped him on the cheek, he dabbed his free hand at the burning cheek and yelled. In the doorway the pudgy officer saw it, guffawed, took off his hat, was raising it to fan himself . . .

ALEXANDRIANA

Muskets roared. The calm quiet above this secluded still farmhouse was exploding over the startled heads of these Britishers out upon a holiday marauding. In the barn doorway the florid captain's hat swooped downward, his loud laughing, as if with the sudden down swishing of some unseen knife, was cut off; he swayed, reached a palsied arm toward the door jamb, missed it, pitched headlong forward into the dust of the barnyard.

Nor was he the only Britisher to meet the fast uprushing earth. A tall lanky soldier in the opening of the loft above him spun crazily and dived out to hit the ground flat with a heavy thud; another Redcoat, reaching for the lines to drive his wagon toward the road, fell forward upon the double-trees, and one of the horses screamed and sank down as the other kicked to free itself of the pulling weight of the dying beast.

Over the barnyard and by the granary scarlet coats sprawled upon the ground, white crossed belts reddening with blood and dirt, horses kicking and screaming and trying to rise upon forelegs or lying still and quiet demonstrated the marksmanship of the unsuspected enemy.

And now officers were shouting commands and quickly British discipline succeeded that first mad confusion, and in but a moment a squad of infantrymen, running in formation, body to body, across the intervening rough ground, were charging upon the thicket that crested the ridge above which the smoke of gunpowder was slowly curling. Bayonets gleamed as the Redcoats charged the plum thicket, fingers caressed triggers . . .

There was no enemy in the thicket. The Redcoats searched, but all they found was the evidence that someone had left on the run. They marched back to the main group, now assembled or coming in on creaking wagons loaded with corn and fodder. And as they came up, another roar from down along the spring branch, and other Redcoats slumped to the ground and other horses screamed and kicked . . .

Nor could the unseen enemy be found this time. Nor was his position indicated until his muskets spoke again . . .

The detachment that had moved on up the Beatty's Ford Road,

ALEXANDRIANA

hearing the firing, had turned and come racing back to McIntyre's. And when the dragoons turned in at the farm, they were greeted with another volley from the thick woods.

The Britishers returned the fire. But they could see no enemy riflemen, and their firing was but a waste of powder and balls. Men were falling, horses were being shot down. The soldiers were fast losing their morale. They would soon be bolting into the woods to escape this stinging unseen death.

The officers shouted commands. The bugler blew the assembly call. Drivers urged their horses with curses and blows, and the loaded wagons lurched out upon the road, turned southward toward Charlottetown. The soldiers formed ranks, marched off smartly. The dragoons fell in behind.

Now a musket cracked and one of the lead horses was down. The driver behind pulled his horses off the road, moved around the cursing driver whose horse lay kicking in the tangled harness. The wagons behind followed him. One drove too near the ditch beside the road, the bank gave way and the wagon slipped over. The axle stuck as the wheel swung free. The driver sprang down, called to an infantryman to help him. He bent forward, grabbed the hub; his arms flew wide, he toppled forward, his head caught in the spokes. Another rifle from above the spring had spouted fire . . .

Soon the retreat had turned into a rout. Drivers cut their horses loose from the wagons, jumped upon their backs, galloped toward Charlottetown. But for the infantrymen, pushing along the narrow red dusty road, there were no horses. And from behind the screen of thick woods, from little hills that looked down upon the straggling column, muskets poured hot and stinging death . . .

When the surviving Redcoats after hours of running this gantlet reached Charlottetown and the comparative safety of their camp and unloaded the dead and dying and wounded at their improvised hospital in Liberty Hall Academy, new work confronted the already overworked British doctors. And soon new red mounds were being smoothed out beside those others in the school yard upon which the loosely patted soil had not yet settled . . .

LIII

THE CHICKEN squawked and threshed its wings about in a futile effort to get away. The queer looking little crippled man shuffling along beside the Redcoat grabbed it by its long neck and the squawking abruptly ceased. "Shet up, damn you; I got a notion to wring yore neck." He turned a grinning, grizzled face to his escort. "These damned Domineckers is the squawkin'est chickens you ever seen but they're powerful sweet meat. I 'lowed the Major hadn't ate much chicken lately."

"Here's Major Ferguson." They stopped in front of a clean-shaven, thin-faced young Scotchman seated on a low stump eating from a round pewter plate. He looked up, and a quick smile spread over his face as he saw the man and the struggling chicken. The Redcoat saluted. "This man has just come into camp, sir; he insisted on being brought to you."

Patrick Ferguson returned the salute. "Well, my good fellow?"

The crippled little man said nothing; for a long moment he stared at the British commander, his mouth half open, his hand throttling the chicken's squawking.

Pat Ferguson set down his plate, shifted his high cocked hat to the back of his head. "Well, what do you think of me?"

"I was looking for Major Ferguson, Mister. Be you his boy?"

"I'm Major Ferguson. What can I do for you?"

"You aint the Major? A young feller like you aint got the charge o' all these soldiers?"

Ferguson laughed. "Yes, I'm guilty. What can I do for you?"

"Well, sir. Now wouldn't that beat you? I'd never 'a' thought

ALEXANDRIANA

a young man like you would be the man what us fokes in these parts is depending on to protect us 'gainst these oncivilized rebels. I been hearin' tell o' you a long time but I figured you would be a man o' some age—"

"Well, I'm thirty-six. I suppose that's old enough." Ferguson evidenced his amusement. "You're not so damned old yourself. How did you get that game leg? Fighting for the King?"

"Me, I was borned that way, Major. It's that leg a-floppin' back and forth which has been a-keepin' me from a-fightin' fer King George. I can't do no good gettin' around. But I do all I can and I keep a sharp eye out fer these damned rebels in these parts, and do 'em all the devilment I can. But what I come fer, Major, when I heared you was in this country, was to fetch you a chicken. I said to myself, 'Joe,' I says, 'you can't do much fer yore King when it comes to fightin' but you're a hell of a good chicken-raiser and you might tote Major Ferguson one o' yore Domineckers—and so I fetched it. It's good and fat, Major, and it'll make a toothsome pot o' dumplings. If'n you'll have some o' yore cooks fix it fer yore supper—" He started to hand the chicken to the Major.

"Wait a minute. I'll let that chicken get away." Ferguson laughed, held up his hand. Momentarily an orderly appeared from somewhere. "Take this chicken and give it to my cook; hold him, he's pretty lively." The crippled man handed the chicken to the soldier. "I reckon, Major," he twisted around to face the British commander, "you'll be eatin' that there chicken fer supper a sight nigher the Catawba than you're eatin' yore dinner here at Peter Quinn's—"

"I see you live somewhere hereabouts. I suppose you know the country. These people are friendly to the King in this part of the country, aren't they?"

"Oh, yes, sir, Major. There aint many o' these blasted rebels in this country. There's a right smart over in Mecklenburg across the Catawba River. But I've a notion General Cornwallis is givin' them rebels over there hell and a-plenty, and rightly he should, Major. I guess you'll find that out soon as you join up with him tomorrow or next day or when you—"

ALEXANDRIANA

"What do you know about General Cornwallis?"

"I don't know nothin' fer what you'd say sure, Major. I jest hears tell things from friends o' the King now and then. I heared tell General Cornwallis was at Charlottetown and a-givin' them rebels over in that country a right smart rough time."

"It's a strange thing I can't hear anything from Lord Cornwallis. I send out expresses and I hear nothing more of them. I've sent this Peter Quinn and another fellow to Charlottetown but they're not back. How do you account for that?"

"It's a lot o' them damn rebels over beyont Tryon County. Maybe some o' them has headed off yore men. But you'll soon be there and—"

"I don't know. I'd like to hear from Lord Cornwallis." He looked the cripple squarely in the face. "Look here, my good man. Have you had any reports about the Mountain Men trying to get me in a battle?"

The fellow slapped his hip, guffawed. "Them Mountain Men? You mean them country fellers with that feller Shelby and old Nolachucky Jack Sevier and them others? I shore reckon they got more sense than to try to put up a fight with yore crowd." All at once he was serious. "But, Major, I tell you what I'll do. If'n you got any idea where I could find them fellers I'll ride back and sort o' scout em' out fer you and if'n I can find out anything I'll come back here tomorrow and tell you. That might be a little service to the King from a crippled feller."

Ferguson considered, smiled. "Well, you might try it if you like. They're back somewhere towards Gilbert Town or maybe closer here. If you can't get any news of the rebels, you might pick me up another chicken."

"Yes, sir, Major, I'll see what I can find out." He started shuffling off. Then he turned. "I'll be back here tomorrow if'n I don't get catched—back here at Peter Quinn's."

"Not here," said Ferguson. "We're leaving here right away. I'll be on top of King's Mountain tonight."

"King's Mountain! W'y, Major, all the damned rebels in Americky couldn't run you off'n King's Mountain."

ALEXANDRIANA

In a minute he had disappeared. Fifteen minutes later he untied his horse in a thicket of plum bushes, swung easily into the saddle, headed westward into the warm October sun. At nightfall he swung into the camp of the Mountain Men at the Cowpens.

He went at once to Colonel James Williams, his commander. "Well, Colonel, I saw Ferguson and talked with him; in fact, he sent me off to scout our bunch. I'm supposed to report to him tomorrow on top of King's Mountain."

"King's Mountain, Joe? Is that where you found him?"

"No, sir. I found the Britishers at Peter Quinn's, some six or seven miles this side of King's Mountain. They had stopped to eat. They were going on to King's Mountain during the afternoon. They're there now, I reckon."

"How many men does Ferguson have?"

"Not more'n fifteen hundred. Maybe not quite that many."

Colonel Williams was silent. "Well, I'll report the news you bring to Colonel Campbell—they've made him the commander." He frowned. "He may want to call a council of the officers. It's his damned business; he's running things. Anyway, much obliged, Joe." He started to walk away, turned. "By the way, Joe, you're from Mecklenburg, aren't you?"

"Yes, sir."

"Report to Colonel Cleveland's command. They've captured a couple of fellows this afternoon who claim they're from Mecklenburg and are scouts for Colonel Davie's cavalry. They aren't sure about the two; think maybe they're Tories spying on us. Go over and see if you know 'em."

"Yes, sir. I'll likely know 'em if they're from Mecklenburg."

After a while he found Colonel Cleveland. The colonel was seated near the low-burning fire over which great slabs of meat, hung across a green limb supported in the forks of sticks driven into the ground, were sizzling. He was biting corn from a long ear that had been roasted in the shucks and grease from meat he had eaten ran down from the corners of his mouth.

"Colonel Ben, looks like you're gettin' a good bait tonight, judgin' from that pile o' corncobs there."

Cleveland looked up. "Hello, Joe. Where'd you get in from? Been out spying, I guess."

"Yes, sir, been over to pay a visit to Major Ferguson. But Colonel Williams said you had a couple o' fellers over here claiming to be from Mecklenburg and scoutin' for Major Davie."

"That's right, I have. They're right over there. I'd like for you to look 'em over. If they're really on our side I want to turn 'em loose; if they're spies I'm going to break their necks and damn soon." He threw down the cob, rose ponderously to his feet. "Come on, Joe; we'll go over there."

They circled the fire, walked across the intervening space to another fire, were circling it, when a man on the other side of the fire shouted out. "Hey, Joe, come over here boy! Joe Kerr!"

The cripple stopped, peered through the smoke. "Damnation! If it aint—" He shuffled around the blaze, his withered leg flapping backward, swinging forward. "Jethro! Who'd'a' thought—Hell's bells, and here's David Barksdale. Who'd'a' thought you fellers was the ones the Colonel was talkin' about?" Colonel Cleveland had reached them now. "Colonel—"

Cleveland, smiling through his greasy whiskers, to which grains of corn were hanging here and there, interrupted. "I see they're our boys, Joe." He reached a big hand into the pocket of his coat, pulled forth a handkerchief, wiped his mouth and chin. "Boys, I'm sorry. But I had to be sure, you know. And I'm damned glad to find out I won't have to stretch your necks, though stretching Tory necks, I'll admit, don't give me any particular pain. Cut 'em loose, Joe."

David shook his hands, struck them smartly together, rubbed his wrists. "They were tied pretty tight, Colonel." He grinned. "It's all right about tying us up. I'd a done the same thing had I been in your place. It's a lot of Tories hereabouts, I'm bound. 'Tis lucky we didn't fall into their hands, or Ferguson's."

"'Tis, at that. You boys had any supper?"

"Nothin' to brag about, Colonel," replied Jethro.

"Well, step back over here with me. You come along too, Joe. I want to hear what you found out at Ferguson's camp. And we got

ALEXANDRIANA

some good meat over there and plenty of roasted corn. We gave old Tory Saunders' stuff hell tonight and we ought o' break his damned neck besides. Captain, I just aint got no love for Tories."

"I haven't my ownself, Colonel."

"Boys, there's plenty of meat. Step over and help yourselves. And corn, too. We killed a bunch of old Saunders' fat cows and we pulled fifty acres of his corn. We ought o' pulled his neck, too. But look here, Joe, how'd you get to talk to Ferguson? And did he ever suspect you at all?" Colonel Cleveland settled his huge bulk on a log pulled up before the fire.

"I don't think he did. At any rate, I got away before he did, Colonel."

"But how'd you get up to him?"

"Well, sir, I fetched him a fat Dominecker chicken so he could have some dumplin's. I told him I wasn't able to fight for the King but I was a good chicken-raiser and I could provide some good eatin' for his Majesty's great soldier."

Colonel Cleveland held back his head and laughed, a great ponderous, full throated laugh. "The hell you did! Joe, you're a good one. But look here, I didn't know you raised any chickens."

The crippled fellow laughed. "Yes, sir, Colonel, I raised that one, all right. I raised it off'n Peter Quinn's chicken roost, the damned Tory."

Cleveland slapped big hand on his knee. "There aint another one like you in the whole damned Whig army, Joe."

By eight o'clock the Mountain Men were on the march toward the Cherokee Ford of the Broad. Nine hundred of the toughest horsemen had been selected to push on ahead in the hope of overtaking Ferguson. Another day's march by the doughty major of the Seventy-first Regiment would put him so close to Lord Cornwallis at Charlottetown that it would be dangerous to risk a battle with him. And despite Joe Kerr's information, the officers of the Mountain Men were not sure that Ferguson had actually decided to take up a position on King's Mountain.

"I've a notion Ferguson will try to get to Charlottetown," Colonel Cleveland confided to David, as they rode along through the

ALEXANDRIANA

darkness. "Yet he may be willing to risk a fight with us. If he's on King's Mountain, he's in a strong position. But it could be a dangerous position for him, too. It would be hard for us to attack him up there, but if we could surround him he'd have a hard time getting away. If we can get organized and stay organized, we'll have a good chance at him."

"There'll be no trouble on that score, will there, Colonel?"

"Well, I don't think so. But there's a little jealousy among the officers. Williams wants the command, but he wouldn't do. Colonel Charles McDowell's in the likely place for it, because this is his militia district, and he's experienced, too; but he's a little slow. Shelby's got around it by proposing Colonel Campbell, since he's a Virginian and the rest of us are Carolinians. He's to serve until a general officer is sent to us by General Gates, likely Daniel Morgan or William Lee Davidson. And Colonel McDowell's gone to Hillsboro to ask Gates to send us a commander."

"But he won't be back in time, will he?"

"No, I have a notion he hasn't got there yet."

They rode a long time in silence and the darkness pressed down heavily upon the long column weaving stealthily through the deep woods. The smell of the woods was sweet in the nostrils of David Barksdale, the smell of autumn compounded of a myriad individual odors, of dusty goldenrod beside the narrow road unseen now in the early morning blackness, of hickory and oak and ash, of pine and cedar and pine needles fallen and browning, of rabbit-tobacco and drying grass and crumpled stiffening leaves.

Sometimes they would come forth from the woods and out upon the sweet odor of the fields, of hay mown and stacked, of red earth upturned to await winter's freezing, of corn ripened and ready for the harvesting, of fodder burning upon the stalks. And always there was the strong acidulous odor of the horses, the musty odor of harness and old leather dried and caked with the sweat of many days' heat, of saddles and saddlebags, and the pungent and not unpleasant smell of the steam rising upon the cool clean October air from the fresh manure of the horses pushing relentlessly along the thread of the narrow road . . .

ALEXANDRIANA

Toward morning it began to drizzle, and men wrapped handkerchiefs and what blankets they had about their muskets' locks; and when the drizzle developed into a heavy rain they took off their shirts and wrapped them about their weapons. Near daylight they came within a mile or so of Cherokee Ford, and they sent Enoch Gilmer forward to reconnoitre.

"Gilmer's a first-class scout," Major Chronicle explained to Colonel Cleveland. "He could fool his own grandmother. He can laugh and cry at the same time; he can act the part of a lunatic so well his own friends would think he had lost his mind, for a fact; and he's sharp as a pin and afraid of nothing."

They crossed the river, moved eastward, and on ahead they saw upthrust into the leaden sky the straggling rough ridge of King's Mountain fifteen miles away toward Charlottetown.

Now the rain began pouring, and the Mountain Men, their hunting shirts wrapped about the locks of their muskets, bent over their weapons to shelter them from the deluge, and the water ran down their bronzed backs and dripped from their feet. But when big Ben Cleveland and Nolachucky Jack Sevier and Virginia's Colonel Campbell spurred their horses forward and proposed to Colonel Shelby that the column be halted to rest, Shelby scowled fiercely.

"Damn it, what'n hell's come over you fellows? We're out to catch that damned Ferguson. This aint a hay-ride. You all can stop if you want to, but I'm going to follow Ferguson until I catch him if I have to follow him into Cornwallis' camp at Charlottetown!"

They rode back to their columns. The Mountain Men continued to move eastward through the pouring rain.

A mile farther on a group of Sevier's scouts came to Solomon Beason's house. "Ferguson's about eight mile up ahead," Beason told them. Five miles eastward they stopped at the home of a Tory. The men there were evasive. If they knew anything of Ferguson's movements, they kept the information concealed. But a girl followed the men from the house.

"How many men you got in your bunch?" she asked, when they were preparing to mount their horses.

ALEXANDRIANA

"Enough to lick Ferguson."

She pointed toward the ragged range of hills ahead. "You'll find him up there on top of that mountain."

It had stopped raining. Now it was clearing off, and a fine cool breeze began to fan the tired, drenched horsemen. Colonel Campbell and several of the other officers were now in the lead of the column and David followed just behind the towering bulk of Benjamin Cleveland. They splashed through puddles that sprayed them with muddy water, pushed across little streams now swollen with the burden of the morning's raining. And after a few miles of riding, they came upon a horse tied at the gate of a notorious Tory's house.

"That's Enoch Gilmer's horse," said Major Chronicle.

"We'll go in the house and have some fun out of him while we're getting the information we're wanting," said Colonel Campbell.

They stamped inside.

"Aha! You damned Tory," said Colonel Campbell, when he spied Gilmer at the table, eating. "We've got you now."

Gilmer did not stop eating. "Well," he said, after a moment, his mouth full of food, "you've got a damned good King's man, all right, whoever you be, and you wouldn't be much, I'm bound."

Campbell scowled, gripped Gilmer's shoulder. "Well, fellow, you needn't bother eating any more. You won't need it now in a few minutes. Major Chronicle, where's that halter we tote for just such cattle as this?" Somebody handed him a rope with a noose in the end. He dropped the loop over Gilmer's head. "Get up and get marching; I'm going to hang you to that cross-piece over the gate. You'll make a nice decoration for a Tory hole like this."

Chronicle stepped forward. "Colonel Campbell," he said, "these people here are Tories, 'tis true. They're for the King. But they're good people, Colonel. I know them; I'm from this section, you know. They've been led astray by Ferguson's promises and frightened by his threats. Colonel, I'd hate to see you hang this reprobate to their gate-post. His ghost will haunt these ladies, who you see"—he pointed to the women in the room—"show by their tears that they are not without some of the finer feelings. I beg of you, Colonel, that you take him on down the road a way before you hang him."

Campbell was silent a moment, as if weighing carefully the request of his subordinate officer. "Well, Major, I'll do that. I'll carry him down the road until I come to a nice, convenient oak limb. But I've a notion 'twould do these ladies justice to have to put up for a while with the ghost of this sorry knave."

They led Gilmer from the house, the rope still around his neck, handed the end of the rope to a horseman. The officers swung into their saddles.

"Aint you goin' to let me ride?" Gilmer inquired loudly of Colonel Campbell, so that the women watching from the porch could hear.

"Let you ride? Like hell. You'll be riding soon enough, you damned King-lover." He picked up the reins. "Let's get going, boys. I want to get this fellow swung up before he has a chance to get away." They moved off down the road, with Gilmer, the rope around his neck, his hands pinioned in front of him, stepping along at a right lively gait.

A half mile away they stopped, slipped the noose from his neck. He mounted his horse, which one of the Mountain Men had been leading. The officers grouped about him. "Ferguson's on top of King's Mountain, Colonel. I learned that from one of those women back at that house. She was over at his camp this morning and had just got back a little while before I got to her house; said she took Ferguson some chickens. They're strong Tories and I put on mightily about how I was standing by the King. Fact, we got along so well together that both those women give me a good kiss apiece." He grinned.

"Did they say on what part of that spur you'd find Ferguson?" Colonel Campbell asked.

"Yes, sir, I asked them about that. I made out that I wanted to go join up with him. They told me I'd find him on a ridge between two branches at a place where some deer hunters camped last year."

"I know where that is, Colonel." Major Chronicle pushed into

ALEXANDRIANA

the center of the circle. "Captain Mattocks and I had that camp there. We're the hunters she was talking about. I know exactly where it is."

"Good! Now we know what we're doing. We'll stop here and agree upon a plan for going after Ferguson, and then we'll explain it to the men." Colonel Campbell was almost jovial. "All you officers, let's ride over there and figure it out."

They started forward. Colonel Cleveland nodded to David. "Come along, Captain. We want you in on this, too."

"Just a minute, Colonel!" Enoch Gilmer rode up to Colonel Campbell. "I was about to forget to give you this." He pulled from the pocket of his hunting shirt a folded paper. "Those women at the Tory house showed it to me and I slipped it. It's some of Ferguson's stuff. They talked like he sent out several papers like this about the country." He handed it to the Colonel.

When the officers had assembled Colonel Campbell opened the paper. "It's addressed 'To the inhabitants of North Carolina,'" he said. "I'll read it."

"'Denard's Ford, Broad River, Tryon County, October 1, 1780.'" He paused. "Denard's Ford is about eight miles from Gilbert Town, isn't it?"

"Dat's right, Colonel," volunteered Lieutenant Colonel Hambright, in his thick German guttural. "I know all dat country."

"October 1. Let's see. This is Saturday the seventh. Ferguson wrote this last Sunday. Is that right?"

Several of the officers nodded their confirmation. "Well, I'll go on. 'Gentlemen:—Unless you wish to be eat up by an inundation of barbarians, who have begun by murdering an unarmed son before the aged father, and afterwards lopped off his arms—'" Colonel Campbell stopped reading. "That makes me mad as hell, boys," said he. "That's a damnable lie. But excuse me. I'll go on. '—and afterwards lopped off his arms, and who by their shocking cruelties and irregularities, give the best proof of their cowardice and want of discipline; I say, if you wish to be pinioned, robbed, and murdered, and see your wives and daughters, in four days, abused by the dregs of mankind—' Damn the lying bastard. '—in short, if you wish or deserve to live, and bear the name of men, grasp your arms in a moment and run to camp.' "

"Ferguson iss scairt," observed Colonel Hambright. "Dat iss it."

" 'The Back Water men have crossed the mountains,' " Colonel Campbell resumed the reading. " 'McDowell, Hampton, Shelby and Cleveland are at their head, so that you know what you have to depend upon. If you choose to be degraded forever and ever by a set of mongrels, say so at once, and let your women turn their backs upon you, and look out for real men to protect them.' It's signed 'Pat. Ferguson, Major 71st Regiment.' "

Colonel Campbell folded the paper, put it in a pocket of his coat. "Yes, Hambright, you're right; Ferguson's scared. And he has a right to be."

The officers decided to move forward stealthily and surround the hill upon which Ferguson had encamped. They disclosed to the men the plan of strategy, and soon the Mountain Men were again upon the march. David moved back along the column to find Jethro, and together they rode toward King's Mountain. The sun was shining brightly now, and the steam rose from the fields. The men spread their wet hunting shirts upon their horses' rumps to dry and guarded carefully their muskets' locks as they rode beneath overhanging branches along the winding narrow road through the deep wet woods.

Close to the foot of King's Mountain a young boy came galloping across a field. Quickly they caught him, brought him to Colonel Campbell. "Vell, vell," exclaimed Colonel Hambright, riding along near the commander. "If it issn't John Ponder his ownself. V'ere you goin', John, in such a hurry? You vouldn't by any chance be comin' from dat Ferguson's camp, v'ot?"

The boy grinned shamefacedly. " 'Taint no need to lie about it, Mr. Hambright. Yes, sir, that's where I've been."

"I figured you had, John, knowing you had brothers mit dot damned Ferguson. V'ere iss he now?"

The boy hesitated. "He's—" He paused.

"V'ere? You just as vell tell, John. Ve'll find him."

"He's on top that ridge over there." The boy pointed. "A little piece down the road you can likely see his tents and wagons. And now can I go on home, Mr. Hambright?"

"Not till ve see vot you got on you, John. I've a notion you might be headed over Charlottetown way to see Cornwallis mit a letter from dot Ferguson." Quickly they searched him. "See? I t'ought so," said Hambright, when they pulled a letter from his pocket.

Colonel Campbell took the letter, broke the seals, unfolded it. "We're getting a lot of reading matter from Ferguson today," he said, as he glanced down the sheet. "Uh-huh—He's scared, all right. He's wanting help from Cornwallis. Wants Tarleton sent with his dragoons. Here, Chronicle—" He handed the dispatch to the subordinate officer. "Read it to 'em."

"Now what'll we do with this boy, Colonel?" one of the officers asked, when Major Chronicle had finished reading Ferguson's dispatch.

"We ought to hang the damned little Tory," spoke up Colonel Cleveland. "But I guess he's a little too young. How old are you, boy? And don't you tell me a lie, neither."

"Fourteen."

"Dot's right, Ben," said Colonel Hambright. "I remember v'en dot boy vas born. Dey're goot people but dey're on der vrong side."

"Son—" Colonel Campbell looked the boy straight in the face. "You're lucky you're so young, or else you'd been hung or shot one—"

"He is at that," Ben Cleveland interrupted. "If he'd got over about the Catawba River or across into Mecklenburg some o' Davie's boys would have already got him."

"Son, you turn that horse towards home," Colonel Campbell went on, sternly, "and don't you stop until you ride up to your stable. And don't you leave the house again this day. Do you understand?"

"Yes, sir."

"Well, get moving now and—"

"Vait a minute, Colonel." Hambright turned to the boy. "John, vot kind of clothes has dot Ferguson got on?"

ALEXANDRIANA

"He's got on a fine uniform, Mr. Hambright. But you can't see it very well on account he's got on a big checkered shirt over it to keep it clean."

"Goot. Now I know who I'll be vantin' to see."

"Is that all, Colonel Hambright?" the commander asked.

"Dat's all."

"All right, Son. Get moving. And don't forget what I told you."

"No, sir." In a moment the boy disappeared around a bend in the road.

The officers returned to their commands to give final instructions for the approach upon the enemy. Colonel Hambright informed his men of the checkered duster Ferguson was wearing. "Vell, poys," he said, "don't forget, v'en you see dot man mit a pig funny shirt over his clothes, you will know who dot iss, and you can mark off dose checks mit your muskets, see?"

Now the men formed into two lines, Colonel Campbell at the head of the line on the right, Colonel Cleveland leading the other. Silently, as silently as doom itself, they moved off through the quiet wet woods. Silently they passed along beside a little branch, through a ravine, between rocky knobs; and after a time they emerged to see ahead of them the little mountain and the enemy's camp upon the top of it.

Behind a screen of trees and bushes on the east side of King's Creek a little way above the point where the Quarry Road crossed it, the Mountain Men halted.

"Dismount and tie your horses." The command came down the line, from man to man. "All that have on greatcoats take them off and tie them and your blankets to your saddles." The command passed along the line.

The horses were given in charge of a few of the men despite their protests, for these men, too, wanted to push up those rugged slopes.

Now Colonel Campbell was moving from company to company. "If any body in this crowd, officer or man, is afraid and wants to go home, now's the time." The commander's words passed back and forth. But not a man stepped aside.

ALEXANDRIANA

"Up yonder, boys," Colonel Campbell pointed toward the crest, "is the man we've been following all this time. He's got with him some of the worst scoundrels in all Carolina—murderers, thieves, rascals of the first water. Now let's go get 'em. All right, fresh prime your guns, and every man go up that hill to lick 'em or fight till he dies."

LIV

MAJOR PATRICK FERGUSON of His Majesty's Seventy-First Regiment lay relaxed the length of his bunk in his headquarters tent at the edge of the little flat of land atop the northeastern end of King's Mountain.

The mountain itself lay like an immense green gourd the handle of which was pushed high and narrow toward the Cowpens. Here at the gourd end where it widened into a little plateau smooth and bare of the trees that jutted thickly up all its sides, his Provincials had pitched their tents in the center of their wagons placed to form a makeshift defense.

But Major Patrick Ferguson seemed not to be giving thought to shapes or contours or elevations or defenses outside the four walls of his tent or even beyond the narrow confines of his bunk. He seemed instead to be regarding through half closed eyes only the toes of his shining boots hoisted upon the low foot-piece. Up past the top of his polished boots ran the smooth rounded curve of his legs showing neatly beneath the smart breeches of his uniform. But at the hip they disappeared into his checkered duster that muffled him to his shoulders and clashed sharply with the skirt that flowed smoothly around the curvesome hips of the girl upon whose lap his head was resting.

She was stroking his hair, pulling her white fingers gently and rhythmically back and forth through the thick curling mass.

"I had a most fearsome dream last night," she said, after a while.

He smiled, but his eyes remained half-closed. "'Twas your deserts," he said. "You were late coming to me. Where did you go? To Captain DePeyster? Lieutenant Allaire? Some of the men, perhaps?"

"You're joking, Pat Ferguson, but 'tis unkind anyway. You know since we left Charles Town I've never gone to bed with another man. You well know it, 'deed you do."

"I believe you, Sally. I could never have asked for a more faithful cook."

The girl laughed.

He looked back over his head without moving it from her lap. "But you are on the rolls as my cook, you know."

"Yes, and so is Virginia Paul. And I don't like that."

"But a man on the move like I am needs two cooks."

"Yes, two cooks. But not two—" She paused. "I should think I should be enough. It's Virginia Paul that's been visiting in other tents. But that's all right. Let her go."

"I wouldn't want to start a quarrel between two ladies, my dear. You mustn't be jealous. Am I not good to you, Sally? Aren't you well paid?"

"Yes, but 'tis not shillings and pounds and pretty clothes sent up from Charles Town by the post at Ninety-Six that I want, Pat Ferguson. 'Tis you your ownself."

"You have me, Sally. But you mustn't think too much of me, of an adventuring man like Pat Ferguson, a man who never knows where he'll be next year or next month or even tomorrow."

She stopped stroking his hair, bent down to look in his eyes. "Is that why you got into this war, because you're an adventuring man?"

"Yes, I suppose so. That's why I got into the army, and after having got into the army I was sent to America. A good place for a second son."

"A second son?"

"Yes. My father's a lord, Lord Pitfour, in Aberdeenshire. My mother's father was a lord too. There are enough lords back of me. But I was a second son, and second sons, being of no use at home, join the army. I joined up when I was fifteen. And I've served in it ever since—over Germany, Flanders, the Caribbee Islands, Nova

Scotia, up and down America. So you see—" He twisted his legs around, sat up. "I've been around. But look here, Sally, it's about time for tea."

She got up. "I'll fetch you some."

"Don't make any eyes at those men, Sally," he warned. "Aside from my hundred Provincials—and I wouldn't trust them far with a redheaded woman like you—I've got eight hundred of the damnedest knaves in Christendom."

After a few minutes she returned, poured him tea. "You never did ask me what I dreamed," she scolded.

"What was it? Did the Mountain Men come upon us with their long knives?"

" 'Twas just that," she said. "They came climbing up this hill from every side like—like so many monkeys."

"Well, they'll be monkeys if they ever try it. Even the damned rebels in these parts have too much sense to attempt that. This place is perfect, Sally, perfect. It's a natural fortress. There's but one entrance, that narrow flat bottleneck down at the other end, and we've got sentries out in front of it and a detachment of soldiers up there." He slapped his hand upon his knee. "As for the rest of it, there's no way of getting to us, except coming up these steep, rocky sides. All we have to do is stand up here and shoot them down as they come up. And even if a few should get to the top, we can poke them in the face with our bayonets."

Major Ferguson stood up. His silver whistle fell to the floor; he stooped down, recovered it, stuck it into his waistcoat pocket. He stretched, stood on tiptoe, flexed the fingers of his uninjured left hand, moved gingerly his right arm. "I guess I'm needing exercise. Haven't been in a fight for days. Maybe your dream's coming true is what I'm needing."

"I don't think so."

"Well, don't worry, Sally. There's no chance of its materializing. I could whip those rebels in the flat country, but I'm being unusually cautious. I've sent dispatches to His Lordship in Charlottetown asking him to send Tarleton and his dragoons to reinforce me until I can join him over there. Until Tarleton gets here—and he should be here any time now, for I've sent several expresses to His Lordship—all we need to do is just sit here on this mountain and wait—"

"How do you know the expresses got through to him? He's likely been sending messages to you, but you haven't been getting them."

"Listen, Sally, that dream's got you upset. You'll be getting me nervous, too, the first thing you know." He turned to face her, to scowl at the woman sitting calmly on his bunk. "I tell you we're safe here. Damn it, Sally. All the damned rebels in hell can't drive us from this mountain!"

He sat down again, twisted his legs around to rest them again on the foot-piece, placed his head in her lap. She began stroking his hair; he closed his eyes. "I'm glad the sun's out again. This blasted rain gets on a fellow's nerves, even a fellow from Scotland. It's so—"

"What's that?" Off toward the northeast a musket had fired.

"One of my foragers, perhaps, has bagged a turkey—or maybe some farmer's pig."

"Or maybe a Mountain Man has bagged one of your foragers."

"There you go again."

"I can't help but think such—"

She stopped. A woman stood in the tent's opening. "Oh, excuse me."

Major Ferguson twisted his head around. "Come in, Paul, old girl. Come right in."

She was scowling. "I see you're busy. Sal there seems to be entertaining you all right. Scratching a man's head's a way I'd never thought about. I guess it's the best she can do for you."

"No, Paul, not the best." He was talking without moving his head from the red-headed woman's lap. "But it's a right soothing entertainment when a man's tired and has an arm that's a long ways from healed and maybe's touched with a little malaria from that damned Low Country. Come on in, Paul, and sit down. I'd like to have an account of your conduct of recent evenings, and how you find the company of Captain DePeyster—"

ALEXANDRIANA

"Damn DePeyster and you too, Pat Ferguson." She stamped her foot, turned to leave, whirled about. "And damn you, too, Virginia Sal, you red-headed hair-scratching whore!" She stamped off.

Sal tugged at Pat Ferguson's head. "Let me up; I won't take that from her!"

"Be still, Sally. Don't get excited. The lady's just a bit overwrought. Perhaps a touch, just a touch, of jealousy—"

"Her calling me a whore. I'll—"

"Of course. 'Tis a most vulgar epithet. Indeed, 'tis a most disgraceful word. And how should one ever imagine it's being applied to you, my dear, such a disgraceful bawdy word—"

He stopped short. From the valley below, at the end of the mountain, toward the Cowpens, came the sudden staccato rattle of musketry.

Pat Ferguson bounded to his feet. And in the same instant an orderly dashed through the tent's opening. "The Mountain Men, sir! They—they seem to be all around the mountain!"

He grabbed his sword hung upon the tent pole, raced past the orderly. Outside he blew a long shrill stirring blast on his silver whistle.

LV

F LAMES SPOUTED from the muzzles of a thousand roaring muskets; the flames patterned themselves into a film of sheet lightning that flickered upon the green sides of King's Mountain; the individual metallic sharp explosions flowed together in a crashing symphony of ungoverned sound.

From deep within its rocky bowels King's Mountain, tormented now after millions of years of undisturbed supine slumber, seemed to quiver and groan beneath the smoke that curled along its slopes and fanned across its narrow summit.

Under this weaving, shifting gray blanket the Mountain Men had come upon their day in history; on this warm October afternoon, upon this jagged rough mound, laid out like a scar's welt upon the red flat land of this border country, they would put an end to British hopes in this quarter or give themselves as a gory sacrifice to freedom sought and lost.

But of such things Jethro O'Flannagan, pouring powder into the muzzle of his musket, was just now not thinking. Many weary miles Jethro and David had ridden in search of the Mountain Men, and having found them, other weary miles they had ridden with the Mountain Men in search of Pat Ferguson and the marauding Tories who had come flocking to him.

Nor was he thinking of David, from whom he had become separated in moving around the base of the mountain. David was somewhere back there with old big Ben Cleveland, and he smiled to himself at the thought of Cleveland's three hundred pounds of sweating flesh pushing its way up these steep slopes.

ALEXANDRIANA

Just now Jethro had in mind a man up there somewhere on top of that hill, a man in a checkered night-shirt over his uniform. He had seen a flash of that night-shirt—it looked like one, at any rate—as he had neared the top a few minutes ago, but before he could get his musket loaded again Redcoats had come charging down upon Colonel Campbell's boys with those shining bayonets. He pulled from his mouth the wadding he had been chewing, crammed it into the barrel, rammed it down. Maybe there'd be another chance at the checkered night-shirt . . .

But Colonel Campbell was shouting. He had thrown off his coat, too. The colonel was going back up that hill. And his place was the steepest part. "Come on, boys," the colonel was yelling. "Holler like hell, and fight like devils!"

They were surging up through rocks and trees and bushes. They had forgot those shining bayonets, those Mountain Men left up there at the first charge, that big mountaineer across there with his head split with the sword of a British officer who swooped down upon him on his horse and killed him with one blow. They were thinking instead of those Redcoats who had screamed and pitched headlong into the rocks or had crumpled silently with bullets through their skulls.

"Holler, boys, holler like hell! They don't like to hear you holler!" Colonel Campbell, pausing to call his men, was clambering over rocks, around trees, pushing steadily toward the summit. "Wait till you get a bead on 'em before you fire, boys. Make every shot count for a Tory bastard!"

Ferguson's men were falling back, pushed relentlessly to the top of the slope, pushed back from its edge, toward those Redcoats crowding up from the deadly fire of Shelby's men on the other side.

But now up along the narrow backbone of the ridge's top came a thundering white horse and a shrill high whistle blew and Jethro saw the flash of a checkered long shirt . . . But smoke swallowed the man on the horse and down from the flat place along the top came a charging horde of Redcoats, and the sun still high above King's Mountain flashed and flickered and danced upon a line of polished bayonets . . .

ALEXANDRIANA

Jethro's musket crackled. He saw a gap blasted in that gleaming line of steel. But the gap closed quickly. And Jethro turned and ran down the slope behind the fleeing Virginians.

Toward the foot of the steepest part he turned. Isaac Shelby's men were racing across the flat narrow neck and piling down the slope behind the Redcoats, firing into the backs of the Britishers charging Campbell's men. And now the Britishers faced about, clambered back to regain their position, and Shelby's men gave way, slowly, from tree to tree, behind rock and bush and jutting crag.

Back up the slope charged the Virginians now to catch the Redcoats in the cross firing. And the men in scarlet coats were dropping. Before the sure unerring aim of the mountaineers they were being pushed back, back upon themselves to the center of the ridge's thin neck. And after a while they were crowding down upon the wagons and the tents at the wide point of the crest as Campbell's Virginians and Shelby's Carolinians surged across to close the trap at that end.

But up the other slopes of the mountain men were charging too, men from Surry and Tryon, from South Carolina and the border section, from Mecklenburg and Rowan, the Watauga Settlements, the foothills of the Blue Ridge, and beyond it. Up the rocky, jutting sheer sides at the northeastern rounded end of the mountain they were fighting their way. Firing from behind trees into the massed Britishers above them, dodging out from sheltering rocks to pour their volleys of death upon flashing scarlet coats, they moved upward . . .

The ring of spouting flame was drawing in upon the Tory soldiers of King George. Below Shelby, at the point where the mountain began to widen to make way for the encampment, Colonel James Williams was leading his men upward like Indians from tree to tree and rock to rock to pour flaming volleys into ranks of the invaders, and around the rocky sides of the flat upon which the camp sat the men of Lacey and Cleveland and Hambright, of Winston and McDowell and Jack Sevier had joined with Campbell's fighting Virginians to close the ring.

As the surrounded Tories and Provincials began to push down-

ALEXANDRIANA

ward from the high narrow ridge to the wider rounded area on which the camp had been pitched, Jethro moved slowly around the fringe of the summit's southeastern side. Perhaps he might come upon David down there somewhere with Ben Cleveland's men; perhaps he might get another chance at that checkered shirt flashing along on that proud white horse . . .

At the northeast end of the mountain he came upon Major Chronicle's detachment. The major was talking to his men down below the hill near the branch. "Boys, they're right up there at the edge of the bluff. They can't get down the other side. We're going after them from this side. Keep behind the trees and rocks on the way up. Don't shoot till you're close enough to pick you a man and bring him down. All right, let's go." The men scattered along the base of the steep slope, began the sharp climb.

But they had hardly started when bullets whizzed above their heads from the height above. Chronicle turned, waved his cocked hat. "At 'em, boys." He faced about toward the enemy, stepped forward, crumpled, rolled backward two paces, caught against the slender stalk of an oak. Six feet from him another man threw out his arm, dropped his musket, pitched forward on his face.

Jethro, panting after the exertion of rounding the base of the hill, pushed up the steep rise behind Chronicle's men. Above him they were nearing the crest. Their muskets roared out. Through the screen of bushes and trees and small sharp rocks he could see Redcoats venturing near the edge of the flat ground crumple . . . But now Ferguson's men were firing, and down the slope they came, their bayonets shining as they crossed little spaces where the sunshine pushed through.

They came on down the hill. Over there ten paces away behind a log a boy was feverishly reloading his gun. He jerked out his ramrod, threw the musket to his shoulder, was cocking it . . . But the Redcoat was upon him. Jethro heard the sharp rasp of metal upon metal, saw the bayonet glance along the crouching boy's musket barrel, plunge through his hand and into his thigh. A roar drowned the boy's screaming and smoke shrouded him and his assailant.

He whirled about. Just above him flashed sunlight upon a gleam-

ALEXANDRIANA

ing long slender blade, upon crossed white belts . . . Jethro fired. It was the coordination of eye and trigger finger; he had had no time to aim. As his musket roared and flame shot out he dodged behind the little tree by which he had been pulling up . . . In the curling smoke he saw the Redcoat leap forward; his gun flew from his hands, he landed upon his head and twisted about in a gruesome, crumpled mass that quivered a moment and was still.

Jethro ran across to the boy who had been transfixed by the bayonet. A man was tugging at the Redcoat's gun. The Redcoat had disappeared but blood spattered the leaves where he had been. The man pulled and the bayonet slipped from the boy's thigh. Blood spurted and a muddy red smear circled outward from the cut in his breeches leg. But the bayonet was still sticking through his hand.

The man jerked. The boy screamed. "Don't, Bill. I can't stand—" The man had his foot on the boy's hand. He jerked harder. The boy screamed again. But the bayonet wrenched free.

"Hated to, Bob; but I had to get it out." He was helping the groaning young fellow to his feet. Jethro caught him under his shoulders, held him up. Blood was streaming from the hole in his hand.

"Son, you got nerve, damn if'n you aint. That must 'a' hurt powerful bad."

"You're dang right, friend," said the other man. "This boy's nervy. This here's Robert Henry, Mister, and my name's William Caldwell. What might be yore'n?"

"Jethro O'Flannagan, from Mecklenburg."

"You aint in Major Chronicle's crowd, are you?"

"No, I was a-scoutin' fer Major Davie and I runned into this here scuffle."

Caldwell grinned. "It was a hell of a fight just to run into, all right. Now, if you'll help me get Bob down the hill before some more o' those danged Redcoats come bustin' down on us, we'll be right much obliged, Mister."

They helped the boy down the steep hill to the spring branch, laid him gently down. "I'll be back in a little while, Bob," said

ALEXANDRIANA

Caldwell. "It aint goin' to take much longer to kill off these danged Tory fellers. Then I'll fix you up."

And now King's Mountain had become a volcano of fire and thunder. Along the crest Major Ferguson, heedless of the stinging hot lead thrown up from the slopes all around his sorely pressed Redcoats, dashed upon his white horse, rallying his men, shouting commands, imploring them to fight back every charge of the Americans.

But slowly the Redcoats, herded on the little treeless area on which they had camped, were giving way. Their morale was being shattered. These Mountain Men would flee down the slope when they charged them with their bayonets, but they would turn and come rushing back. And they could shoot. Their bullets brought death, quick, stinging, hot death; but the bullets showered down upon them seemed to hit only rocks and trees or go singing off above their heads . . .

Through the smoke Jethro caught a glimpse of Colonel Hambright on his horse fifty paces to the right. The colonel was shouting to his men. "Come on, mine prave poys, ve have about finished 'em off." He pushed along, stumbling on loosened little rocks, ducking behind trees, until he was nearer. Perhaps David would be near Hambright.

"Come on, mine poys." The colonel was pointing up the slope. He turned to face forward; Jethro saw him slap his hand upon his thigh. "Damnation!" Jethro said to himself. "He's shot." He ran along the side of the hill toward Hambright.

"I'd better help you down, Colonel," a man was saying to the wounded officer. "I expect we ought to see about it."

Hambright was waving him off. "No, it iss not bad, I t'ink. I feel all right, Sam. If I get down the men dey vill see it. I am all right, Sam." He jerked the horse's reins. "Come on, mine poys, ve'll soon have 'em." His men swarmed up the rocky slope, pausing behind trees and protecting rocks to fire whenever Redcoats revealed themselves.

Jethro slipped along behind Hambright's men until he had reached a point where he could look out upon the level place of the encampment. He could see wagons twisted about, tents down, men lying flat upon the ground, motionless and dead, or stirring feebly. Above the rattle of the muskets he could hear groans, calls for help, sudden shrill screamings, curses . . .

He ducked behind a big pine tree, fired from its cover at a Redcoat coming cautiously toward him, his gun at his shoulder. The fellow dropped with a scream, crawled back on hands and knees toward a camp wagon. Jethro, his back to the tree, waited for the smoke to clear. Off to his left someone was shouting . . . "Jethro! Jethro!"

He peered through the rising smoke. "Davy!" David was down the hill a way, off to Jethro's left. "How're you, boy? Aint we givin' 'em hell?"

"I'm all right, fellow. How're you doing your ownself?" He was shouting. "Any Redcoat— Hey, Jethro, look!" He was pointing toward the crest. "Ferguson! That checkered shirt!"

Jethro faced about, peered from behind the big tree. Up toward the center of the flat ground a man on a white horse, his sword in his left hand, was violently shaking his head as another horseman, evidently a British officer, was gesticulating. Jethro braced his back to the tree, quickly began reloading his musket. When he faced about the white horse and his rider had disappeared. Jethro pulled out the wadding he had been chewing, rammed it in behind the powder and balls.

A man near him was yelling. "There goes Ferguson, Robert; shoot him, boy! My damned gun's snapped. Shoot him!"

The fellow behind a rock six feet away jerked his musket to his shoulder. "I'll try and see what Sweet-Lips can do."

Jethro whirled around. The man in the checkered shirt over his uniform was charging across the open space, making for the gentler drop of the hill over toward McDowell's men. The white horse was nearing the edge; several other Redcoats were plunging behind him. Ferguson was waving his sword. In the flash of an eye Jethro saw that the sword was broken in half . . . He raised his musket, drew a quick bead upon the checkered shirt. "I'll see what Flossie Belle can do, too." He squeezed the trigger. His musket roared;

muskets roared all about him. Before the smoke thickened he saw the man in the checkered shirt fall forward upon his horse's neck, slide slowly down its white mane, slip from the saddle . . .

A low brush prevented him from seeing the man on the ground. He stepped out from behind the tree. Ferguson's foot was still hanging—A sudden immense blinding light blasted his eyes, the earth ripped open with a deafening great roar, King's Mountain rose into the air, turned slowly along its green jutting length, and fell darkly across his face . . .

LVI

Upward from down deep in the core of the earth, upward through the rock-hard black center of King's Mountain toward the crust of the ridge miles above, Jethro burrowed his way like an eyeless blind mole, burrowed upward with his right arm, for the mountain lay upon his left arm and he could not raise the mountain . . .

Upward through long ages from the bottom of this great bottomless immense black pool Jethro swam toward the surface fathoms high above, swam with long free powerful strokes of his right arm, for his left arm was small and withered and cold and stiffened and the heavy black cold water sucked at his left arm and he could not force it through the water . . .

Ages he climbed upward, now gaining great distances, now falling to far depths; but always and ever he fought upward toward the point of light that sometimes he could see pushing a warm finger through his closed sightless eyelids. Always he fought upward to warmth and sound and the light of the sun . . .

And now he was nearing the rocky crust of the mountain's backbone, now he was swimming free and fast toward the brightness of the surface of this pool without bottom. Now the crust gave way, the waters fell back, his sightless eyes gained sight, he swam free into the sun—

"Steady, old boy. Steady." Up above were patches of darkening blue sky, of black green leaves. Between them and his eyes a blur, a rounded brown blur that darted and floated and came still. And the blur took shape and settled, and was David's smiling sad face.

ALEXANDRIANA

"Steady, old man. You're all right. Just keep quiet. Just lie still."

"But the Redcoats, Ferguson's—" Jethro stopped. He heard his own voice and it was strained and weak and low, like an old woman's or a small boy's.

"Ferguson and his Redcoats will never trouble anybody again, Jethro. Just lie still, old boy; just keep quiet."

"But, but—"

"Ferguson's dead, Jethro. And all his men are dead or caught. The Mountain Men cleaned him up. Pat Ferguson's dead; he's lying right over there."

"Over there—" Jethro turned upon his left side to look, turned but a little way—and screamed, a shrill high weak scream.

David was over him, turning him back toward his right, propping a blanket under his left shoulder. "I'm sorry, old man. You didn't know. Your left arm's gone, Jethro. That's why you're like you are, old man. Be quiet and rest, and I'll tell you about it in —in a little bit."

He lay still. His stomach churned. He closed his eyes, and circles, yellow and pink and pale green, swam before him, expanded, contracted, moved in and out of themselves. He felt David's hand under his head. He opened his eyes. "Take a drink of this rum, Jethro; it's good stuff, from a cask captured from the Redcoats. It'll give you strength." He swallowed the rum, and it burned his throat and burned its way to his stomach, and the churning in his stomach ceased. The circles fixed themselves, and faded. And the green leaves darkened above him and the sky was black and he rested.

When Jethro awoke it was dark, and he was stronger, but the pain below his left shoulder burned and stabbed and he fancied the fingers of his left arm were cramping . . .

David sat beside him, and when he saw Jethro had awakened, he propped him up and gave him more rum. Over beyond him, over nearer the spring where the steep slope here on the southeast side of the mountain flattened out, he saw a mound of fresh red dirt, and over beyond the mountain a naked white body, white except for blotches of blood now dried. David saw him looking.

ALEXANDRIANA

"That's Pat Ferguson," he said. "They stripped him to count the bullet holes, they claimed, but I reckon some of them wanted his clothes."

"They shouldn't ought 'a' done that," said Jethro.

"One got his pistol, and another his big watch, and another his silver whistle."

"Was he hit many times?"

"A right smart many. Some said six bullets, some eight. Some bullets could have made two holes. His hurt right arm was broken by a ball and another hit him in the thigh. There were some in his chest, too, and one struck him fair in the brain. He didn't suffer after that, likely."

Men were standing around the body of the dead Britisher. Jethro looked again, closed his eyes as if to clear them for a better view, opened them. "Davy, aint that a woman over there? Looks like long red hair and a dress—".

"Yes, Jethro, they say she was one of his women—or maybe just one of his cooks. The poor fellow's dead now; I wouldn't say."

They were picking up Ferguson's body now. Jethro could see, for David had propped up his head a little. They carried it a few paces, deposited it gently.

"What's that they're puttin' him in, Davy?"

"It's the hide of a beef freshly skinned this morning."

"That's a hell of a thing to bury even Pat Ferguson in, I'm bound."

" 'Tis, Jethro, for a fact. But there's not much choosing for these Tory fellows tonight."

The men walked with their burden toward the freshly dug hole. Others held torches. They let the body down into the hole, bending low to let it down gently. One of the men, when they had straightened up again, pointed toward the dead woman. "We aint got no other grave dug. How about putting her in with him? They say she was—"

"It'd be all right," another man assured him. "Fetch her, boys." He held a torch high for the men to see.

They laid the woman in the grave. They were ready to begin

filling the grave when a woman, on her way back toward the summit from the spring, stopped to peer into the shallow pit. "Hold your torch over that way, Mister," she commanded. The man moved the torch, she looked down upon the two bodies a moment, turned and trudged up the hill. Jethro motioned toward her.

"That was his other woman, they say," David answered. "But you mustn't talk, Jethro. You're weak; you lost a lot of blood before I found you, and that Tory doctor was a long time getting to you."

"Tory doctor?"

"Yes, Dr. Johnson. He saved your life, Jethro."

Jethro frowned. "A damned Tory doctor. Hell, Davy, you ought 'a' let me died." A grin spread over his pale face. "But damn if'n I aint glad you didn't."

Through a night of fitful dreaming and waking, a night in which his own groans and feverishness, his delirium and vague senseless talk joined with the groans and screams and piteous low pleadings over the whole face of this black mountain's steep slopes, David watched over him. From time to time he forced rum between his teeth and at times he bathed the raw bloody stump with the rum . . .

"The Mountain Men'll be getting away up the country today with the prisoners," someone ventured as he paused to talk with David a moment on his way to the spring the next morning. "They're 'fraid Tarleton'll be comin' from Charlottetown to catch 'em and turn the prisoners loose."

"There's about as many prisoners as there are our crowd, I've a notion," David observed.

"That's right. It's a powerful lot of 'em. But they'll pretty soon start thinnin' 'em out soon's they can git up the country where Tarleton can't bother 'em and where they'll find plenty o' good limbs to stretch their damned necks on. Mister, Ferguson's crowd was plum' full o' the damnedest lowdowndest scoundrels in this whole western country. Hangin's too good for 'em, I'll vouch."

But David didn't wait to see the Mountain Men start their march down from the mountain. Early in the forenoon he found his

ALEXANDRIANA

horse and Jethro's tethered down near King's Creek. He rode his horse and led Jethro's down along the branch of Clark's Fork that skirted the base of the mountain until he reached the spring.

And after Jethro had slept a while and had awakened refreshed, he helped him astride his horse, swung into his own saddle, and they moved slowly eastward along the road that led out from the high rounded northern end of the mountain.

Two miles away they paused to rest. David pointed back toward the ragged blue range of hills. "I've a notion there never was another such battle, Jethro. I've a notion yesterday was a great day for America, a fair great day. A day as won't be soon forgot."

Jethro grinned. "I'm damned shore I won't fergit it fer many a day."

They reached the Tuckaseegee Ford that night, and stayed with a friend on the Tryon side. The next morning they crossed the ford, and rode slowly toward Alexandriana.

Toward noon they rounded the bend in the Great Road below the house. "Hell's bells, Davy. Whatever—"

"The damned British! Damn Cornwallis's lousy hide!"

Thin twisting columns of smoke were curling slowly up from the ashes and charred ends of timbers now sunk down upon the site where had sat McKnitt Alexander's barn and granary and bulging storehouse.

"Why didn't the scoundrels burn the house, too?" David asked, after Jeanie had ordered Jethro laid in the company bed and had sent Cato galloping for Jethro's wife.

"Cornwallis doesn't believe in burning down people's houses; you'll have to give him credit for that," McKnitt replied. "Nor did he burn down the other buildings. Cato beat him to it. And, David, they didn't get an ear of corn or a sheaf of wheat."

LVII

"Governor, I do not wish to appear blunt, but I think what you are doing is a waste of time and effort. These rebels in this province will pay no attention to your appeals, I am convinced, sir."

Josiah Martin laid down his pen. "But Your Lordship, I am still their rightful Governor, and you represent the power of British arms. I should think that they would be glad of an opportunity to join our cause now that our success is assured. With you here and Major Ferguson over west enlisting men loyal—"

"But is he, Governor? That's just it. I don't know. I have not been able to get any information concerning Ferguson's plans or even his whereabouts. This morning I sent Colonel Tarleton out in search of information."

"Your Lordship, certainly you are not apprehensive about Major Ferguson?"

"Indeed, sir, I am. I've been two weeks without hearing from him. That is a most alarming circumstance. I fear for Ferguson. I urged against his undertaking this mission with militia. I did not believe they could be trusted, Governor. Colonel Tarleton agreed with Ferguson, however, and I gave my permission reluctantly."

"But Colonel Tarleton will shortly join with him and—"

"That I cannot say. This is rebellious country, Governor. Your assurances that once we had crossed into North Carolina the people would flock to us have failed to materialize, failed entirely, sir, I might add. We have marched into a thoroughly hostile country. This Charlottetown, Governor, is a veritable hornets' nest. I send out foragers and there's a damned rebel behind every bush. These Mecklenburgers shoot down my men and then fly back into the woods. Our presence, instead of causing them to enlist with us, is serving to make them even more hostile to the King, I'm convinced. I'm really apprehensive—" There was a knock at the door. "Come in!"

The orderly saluted. "Two friends of the King have just come into Charlottetown, sir, with news from Major Ferguson. 'E's—" The orderly, his face white, hesitated, swallowed.

"Go on! What's happened to Ferguson?"

"Bad news, sir. Major Ferguson's entire command was defeated last Saturday in a battle with the Mountain Men—"

"His entire command? What happened to Major Ferguson. Go on! Speak up!"

" 'E's dead, sir."

"Dead? Pat Ferguson dead?" Cornwallis's round red face was paling toward the color of his iron gray hair. "Killed. Pat Ferguson." He stroked his hair slowly, lowered his eyes to stare unseeing at the polished top of Thomas Polk's table. Suddenly he looked up, spoke to the orderly. "This could be no rebels' ruse?"

"I don't think so, sir."

"Very well. Thank you. You may go."

The orderly slipped unobtrusively from the room. His Lordship glared at Josiah Martin. "And you said I had no cause for apprehension, Governor! You promised me your North Carolinians would flock to me. And now Pat Ferguson's gone—killed. My whole left wing's wiped out. And this damned Davidson's hanging on my flanks, and so's Davie, damn him." He stood up. "Governor, you can stop that damned writing. It's no good, sir." He went to the door, opened it. "Orderly!"

The soldier stepped into the room. "Notify all the officers to prepare to evacuate. Tell Webster to send after Tarleton and have him recalled. We're leaving this damned hell-hole. All right, that's all." The orderly saluted, disappeared.

"Damn it, Governor Martin, I should never have allowed Ferguson to be detached without support and put such a river as the

ALEXANDRIANA

Catawba between us. I should never have listened to Ferguson or Tarleton, or you, sir. And now my entire left wing's gone, the damned rebels are pricking us on all sides, my whole damned command is sick, Hanger's got the fever and not over his wound besides, Tarleton's still sick, and I feel like hell myself. But I'm damned if we'll stay here and die in this nest of rebels. There's enough of my men out there in the damned school yard already. I'm leaving if I have to haul all my officers out in wagons. Damn your North Carolina, Governor." He strode on his short heavy legs from the room, and the door slammed behind him.

LVIII

JEANIE TWISTED over upon her side. That hammering . . . It kept ringing in her ears. Building the granary . . . Raising a new barn to take the place of the one burned by the Redcoats . . . Driving in pegs . . .

She turned again, this time on her back. That hammering . . . Why did one build barns and storehouses in the nighttime? Slowly she opened her eyes as the knocking grew more insistent.

She jumped from the bed, slid her feet into her slippers, threw on her wrapper at the foot of the bed. Downstairs she lighted a candle, went toward the front door.

"Who is it?"

"Mistress Alexander, this is Duncan Ochiltree talkin' to you. Is Mr. Alexander at home, ma'am?"

Jeanie, her hand upon the bolt of the door, drew back.

"Why do you want to know, Mr. Ochiltree?"

"Mistress Alexander, won't you let me in, please ma'am? I'm in trouble, great trouble. I knew Mr. Alexander to be a kind man, a kind, forgiving Christian man, and I have rode out to ask his help. I wonder if you won't call him down and let me see him."

"McKnitt's not home, Mr. Ochiltree."

"Not at home? Where's he at, Mistress Alexander?"

"That I won't tell you. Do you think I'll have you setting your knavish, murdering Redcoats on him?"

"I don't mean no harm, Mistress Alexander. I wouldn't harm a hair on his head, nor yours nor anybody's here at Alexandriana. You've been good customers o' mine and I wouldn't do you no

ALEXANDRIANA

harm. I'm just here askin' for help from one as can help me and will for old times' sake, I'm bound. If Mr. Alexander is not here, won't you tell me where he's at so's I can go beg him to help me out, please ma'am?"

"Mr. Ochiltree, you'd best be going somewhere else for help. You might go to your friend Cornwallis. I'm not going to tell you where to find McKnitt Alexander. And that's a settled fact."

"But, Mistress Alexander, I can't go to Cornwallis. He's left Charlottetown, ma'am. That's why I've got to get help. If some of the good folks don't help me out they'll destroy all I got and likely kill me besides—"

"Which they maybe ought to do, Mr. Ochiltree."

"But you all are good people, good forgiving, Christian people, Mistress Alexander. You'll help a poor fellow out to save his life, I'm bound. If you won't tell me how to find Mr. Alexander, won't you send somebody to fetch him—"

"I don't see how I could do that. There's only my ownself and the Negroes and the children. And I won't leave the children."

The merchant was insistent. He pleaded, he would not be put off. After a while he reached his sword through the window to Jeanie. "I'll pledge my honor, Mistress Alexander—"

"Your honor? And you trading with the Redcoats against your own country and folks?"

"But you'll please send for Mr. Alexander?"

Jeanie relented. She awakened Venus and Peggy. "Peggy," she said, "I want you to ride with Venus to get your pa. He's at the militia camp in Sugaw Creek down at your Aunt Jemima's place. Tell him Duncan Ochiltree's here and begging right smart to see him. You won't be afraid, will you, Peggy?"

"No'm; I'm thirteen. I'm not afraid of the British—"

"Ochiltree says they've left Charlottetown anyway. That's why he's so powerful frightened; his protection's gone and left him. I hate for you to go, but with Venus along 'twont be anything to fear, Peggy. If Davy were just here; but then maybe he'd kill Duncan Ochiltree. If you see Davy before you see your pa, Peggy, don't tell him about it."

ALEXANDRIANA

Hours later the little girl and the Negro woman returned with McKnitt.

"Ochiltree," he said, after the storekeeper had pleaded for mercy, "If I had met you any other place I would have killed you like a dog. Here at my house your life is safe. But I am not going to help you. You have been a traitor. You have been the quartermaster for Cornwallis. You set his Redcoats on the farms and storehouses of the people all over this country. Likely you sent them up here to Alexandriana. Likely you—"

"No, no, Mr. Alexander. I didn't do that. I had nothin'—"

"Hold your peace, Ochiltree!" McKnitt Alexander's tone was sharp. The fat little round man stopped abruptly, swallowed. "You have been a traitor to your country, Ochiltree. You signed our declaration of independence and then you turned a traitor for a little filthy money. But your name's no longer on that paper, Ochiltree. I struck it off, sir! It'll not be there alongside the names o' such patriots as those others. No, sir. It'll not dishonor that proud paper."

He sat silent a moment. "As I said," he resumed his speaking, "if I'd met you anywhere else I'd shot you down, Ochiltree. But you're safe here for the present. I'll advise you, though, to get out of this country in a hurry, Ochiltree. You'd better start ridin' and ridin' fast, and I've a notion you better put the Yadkin between you and Mecklenburg 'gainst daylight—or as much ground as you can. And now, Ochiltree, you'd better start ridin' before I change my mind!"

LIX

SOUTHWARD ALONG the Nation's Ford Road toward the crossing of the Catawba rumbled the wagons of Lord Cornwallis. In front of the wagons and behind them walked the Redcoats; farther in front and back behind the last plodding infantryman rode Tarleton's dragoons.

The scowl that clouded the dark face of Banastre Tarleton plainly revealed the dark thoughts of the young cavalry leader as he rode beside his commander, his thick, heavy legs clamped against the flanks of his horse, his small dark eyes looking straight ahead into the sun dropping now low over the plantations of Steele Creek.

Cornwallis, slumped forward in his saddle, rode along, too, without speaking. His round pink face was flaming in the light of the dying sun, his lips were dry and the skin was taut across them.

After a while Lord Cornwallis turned wearily to the man on the other side of him from Tarleton. "I'm very tired, Mr. McCafferty, and well nigh sick. I believe we should camp for the night shortly. My men are in poor shape. Hanger and five other officers are back there lying on straw in wagons. They're very ill of the yellow fever—"

"This road up here a little ways leads to the ford by a nigher way, Your Lordship. We'll turn down it and there'll be a good camping site."

"Very well. But we'd best be stopping soon."

McCafferty jogged up his horse toward the head of the column, and shortly the Redcoats turned off to the right. He rode back to rejoin Cornwallis, and the column plodded onward along the narrow red road, sticky after much raining and more difficult now that the sun had dropped below the woods and the long October night had fallen.

They moved forward another mile, and then Cornwallis spoke. "Mr. McCafferty, we must stop. How far ahead is the place you suggest?"

"General, I'm sorry; I'm greatly sorry, sir, but I believe we're on the wrong road." Cornwallis was frowning. McCafferty could see even in the dimming light the deep displeasure evidenced on the face of the Redcoats' commander. "But we haven't lost any time, sir. I know where I am now. I hadn't been in this section in some time and for a moment I lost my way. The road we should have traveled is just a little piece over here to the left, sir. We can get to it in no time, and then we'll be almost at the place to stop for the night. If you'll stop your men and just wait here a minute until I can ride over that way a short piece and locate that road—" He clucked to his horse, moved off across a field.

Nor did he stop riding until he had regained the Nation's Ford Road, and after hard galloping until past midnight he rode into the camp of Major Davie to report that Cornwallis had evacuated Charlottetown.

Meanwhile, fearing that McCafferty had been captured by Whig horsemen or had betrayed them, the Redcoats attempted to move to the left, and in the black darkness of this moonless night they became separated into parties. By midnight they were scattered through the woods and fields, and it was noon the next day before they were reassembled. And behind them, fallen into little ravines or wedged between trees, some forty abandoned wagons held the baggage of Tarleton's dragoons and much of His Lordship's badly needed stores.

When the British finally reached the ford, they found the Catawba's waters too high to attempt the crossing. Lord Cornwallis, too, could ride no farther, and the physician ordered him to bed. It would be two days, said the physician, before His Lordship could even endure the jostling motion of a straw-filled wagon.

ALEXANDRIANA

While they waited for the flood waters to subside the Britishers fanned out over the countryside in search of provisions. When a detachment rode late in the afternoon into the yard of Captain John McDowell and began chasing the chickens, the irate Jane Parks McDowell sought the officer in charge.

" 'Tis a right cowardly act to come robbing an unprotected woman with three small children and her husband not at home," she declared, with much feeling.

"Madame, where is your husband?"

"He's in the camp beyond Charlottetown doing all the damage he can to your knavish Redcoat friends over there."

"But we aren't there any more, Madame. We have left. We are going back to South Carolina, down to Winnsboro. And we lost our supplies and that's why we're having to take your chickens. I'm right sorry, but soldiers must eat, Madame."

"Yes, and so must little children. I wonder how you would feel did some knavish scoundrels come robbing your own wife and your little ones."

The Redcoat officer smiled. "Well, I don't suppose, Madame, I'd like that. But war is war, you know, and—"

"What might be your name, sir?"

"McDowell, Madame, McDowell from Scotland."

"McDowell? 'Tis a great pity a McDowell would come robbing another McDowell. My husband's a McDowell, sir, John McDowell, and he's from Scotland. You all must be cousins, sir."

"Well, now that is strange, Madame. I suppose we must be." He hesitated, then he shouted to one of the non-commissioned officers.

"Tell the boys to turn Mistress McDowell's chickens loose, Sergeant." He faced the young woman. "War, Madame, is a mighty bad thing, a mighty bad thing."

When the Redcoats rode away, she lifted her two-year-old son John from his cradle, wrapped him well, and ran with him to the stable. Having saddled her horse, she mounted him and galloped up the Yorkville road toward Charlottetown. Nor did she pause until she reached the camp of the Whigs out at Sugaw Creek.

"The British have left Charlottetown," she said. "They're down in our country destroying things, and they're aiming to cross the river as soon as the water's low enough."

News of the flight of the British came quickly also to General William Lee Davidson, hovering northward from Charlottetown at Camp McKnitt Alexander a few miles above Alexandriana. And soon from north and east the patriots were converging upon the discouraged Redcoats, and to hunger and fever and swollen rushing waters were added the stinging pricks of the hornets, the hot biting death from the canebrakes and the thickets and the suddenly shattered calm of the deep dark woods . . .

LX

THROUGH the gates of Alexandriana into the still silvery haze of a late October morning David Barksdale rode eastward along the Tuckaseegee Road. This morning he rode alone, for Jethro had not recovered strength enough for long days in the saddle. There would be time enough for thoughts . . .

At the rise of the slope he turned in his saddle to look back upon Alexandriana. Quiet and serene and comfortable, it sat unpretentiously upon the crest of the little hill above the spring, where flamed the sugar maples and the gums and the poplars thrusting up past the somber green mass of the cedars. A moment he looked upon the house and the trees and the gray blackened patch across the Great Road where had sat the barn and the storehouses. And then he turned and rode into the sun pushing round and red above the hills toward Poplar Tent.

Over the long miles ahead there would be time for much thinking. He had had little time for thoughts these last months, he reflected. He had been too much in the saddle, scouting the Redcoats, bearing information to young Davie and William Lee Davidson and General Rutherford until that disastrous fight down Camden way, too much chasing the British or being chased by them. But now General Rutherford was free again, exchanged for a captured Redcoat officer, and he was going over into the Scotch country for General Rutherford.

There had been even little time for dreaming, and what dreams there were had been of fighting and being pursued and pur-

ALEXANDRIANA

suing . . . Now he was going eastward toward Cross Creek, toward Pleasant Grove, toward Tories and lurking danger. General Rutherford was organizing a new force to move against those Tories, and he needed information. Alone, David was riding forth to get it. And he smiled as thoughts began to take shape . . .

At Phifer's Mill he rode down along Rocky River and swung eastward toward Mask's Ferry on the Yadkin, where he put up for the night at a little tavern. Crossing the river the next morning, he continued eastward until he struck the main road to Cross Creek. But he turned off to the right before he reached Cross Creek and moved southward along the Camp Fear. The Redcoats had been driven from Mecklenburg and Cornwallis for the time, at least, had abandoned his plans to conquer North Carolina, but in the Scotch country it was still necessary that one exercise caution. Still there were Tories in the Scotch country.

And so after days of hard riding and scouting and quiet listening David came late in an afternoon to lift the big brass knocker upon the paneled front door at Pleasant Grove.

A stooped, white-haired old Negro man opened the door.

"Is Mistress MacDougald at home, Uncle?"

"Yes, suh. I'll call her, suh. Jest come have a seat in the parlor, whilst I go fetch her, suh." He slipped noiselessly along the carpeted hallway.

David heard her coming. He turned to face her as she stepped through the doorway into the parlor. She stopped, raised a white hand to her breast. "David Barksdale! Wherever in the world did you come from, David?" Quickly she walked forward to meet him, her hands extended. He took them in his own, bent over to brush his lips against them. Then he looked up, and there was a broad grin upon his face.

"A far piece, Belinda. And I'm right powerful glad to see you again."

"Well, David—" She was smiling up at him.

"Aren't you going to tell me I've growed a lot?" He laughed. "You always told me that before."

"The same David, for a fact. Yes, and you have growed a lot, as we used to say. But there's the same look in your eyes."

"You haven't broken any your ownself. And your eyes have the same teasing sparkle. After all, it hasn't been so long since—"

"No, David, not so long. It's just that so much has happened."

"So much, and yet so little." There was a half-smile on his lips, and little crinkles webbed from under his eyes. She saw them.

"You haven't changed a bit, David."

"And you're—"

"Yes, I'm glad." For an instant she looked out upon him from underneath her long lashes. But only for an instant. "Please excuse me, David. Do sit down. And you're staying for supper."

"But—"

"No excuses, David. It'll be no trouble at all. I'm here all by myself, and supper's almost ready. I'll just have another plate put down, that's all."

They sat down together on the sofa. The old Negro man appeared, carrying a candle. " 'Scuse me, Mist'ess," he said, as he placed it on the stand.

"Thank you, Uncle Jerry. We'll have supper when it's ready. Tell Chris to put down two plates."

"Yes, ma'am." The old man bowed, slipped out.

"Well, David, tell me about yourself. And Alexandriana. And Charlottetown. A lot must have happened in all this time. And they say Cornwallis is in Charlottetown. I don't suppose that sits so well with you Mecklenburgers. I don't—"

"He's not there now. We ran him back into South Carolina, down Winnsboro way. We made it too hot for him. But he did some damage. He burned the barn and storehouse and granary at Alexandriana, and he burned Waightstill Avery's law office in Charlottetown, and—" He paused.

"And what?"

"And he burned Pat Jack's Tavern, Belinda."

"Pat Jack's Tavern. I—yes, I remember Jack's Tavern."

"I'll never forget it, Belinda." Her hand was upon her knee beside him. Lightly he put his hand upon it. "Those Redcoats burned it down, but they couldn't burn away my memories."

"That was five years ago this summer past."

"The last day of May. I remember because of the second meeting of the convention at the courthouse."

"That's why you remember?" Her eyes were challenging.

"That's why I remember the date. How's your father, Belinda."

She laughed. "Yes, David, you remember that night, I'll vouch. Father's all right, I suppose. He was last week when I saw him. But he's very upset about how the fight at King's Mountain turned out, and poor Pat Ferguson. He's down at Wilmington now—something about rallying the Royalists."

"He's still for the King."

"Yes."

"And you?"

"I still abhor politics." He thought he saw a frown that quickly disappeared. "And I still don't see how your crowd is capable of running a government that will keep things in order. But, David, for heaven's sake let's don't talk about it. "Let's talk—"

"Supper's ready, Mist'ess." The old Negro's grizzled head bobbed through the doorway.

"Thank you, Uncle Jerry." She smiled at David. "Let's eat." She took his hand; they walked into the dining room.

"And now let's go back into the parlor; it's more comfortable," Belinda said, when they had finished.

"I reckon I'd better be going on over to Cross Creek before it gets too late." He arose from the table.

"Oh, no, David, you're going to spend the night here at Pleasant Grove. I've plenty room; all this big house to myself. The Negro woman sleeps in her cabin down at the quarters, and Uncle Jerry has a little room on the first floor at the back. It's no trouble; the guest room stays ready and—and it's been so long since I've seen you."

They sat down on the sofa in the parlor. "I'd like nothing better than to stay, but I really should be getting on back toward Mecklenburg. I've got to make my report to General Rutherford. I have some right important matters to report and—"

"But you'd gain little time by going to Cross Creek. And Lovelace would be asleep before you could get there anyway. You can get up early in the morning and see her tomorrow." She smiled, and there was a coquettish twist to her head as she looked up through her long lashes. "You must stay at Pleasant Grove tonight, David."

"Well, perhaps it would be sensible. It's dark these nights and I'd be late getting to Cross Creek, that's a fact."

"And there might be Tories riding."

"I'm not afraid of them. I've not been caught yet down this way. And if they knew what I was bearing back to General Rutherford they might want to detain me—"

"I'm glad you're staying, David." She picked up a small pillow, laid it across her knee, pulled at its fringes. "There's so much to talk about, and I'm always so lonesome."

"You're not called on to be lonesome, Belinda, not with all the suitors you're bound to have. One would have thought you'd have been married again before now. How'd you manage to escape?"

"Well, David, I have had some suitors and I've been asked to marry." Her tone was matter of fact. "But somehow I haven't been greatly interested—or, I don't think so, at any rate."

"I reckon your suitors have been dashing young Tory officers, or else Redcoat colonels or generals?"

"Well, there have been supporters of the King here. And I might add, rebels, too."

"But you were more interested in the King's crowd?"

"Perhaps. I wouldn't say. Not because of their politics though. You notice I don't hold your politics against you."

He turned to face her. "Belinda, your husband was a King's man. Your father's one. Naturally, I suppose, you'd be a supporter of the King. But just how do you stand?"

"If you want to know, David Barksdale, I take little stock in what you call political principles. I think most of it is a lot of talk and twaddle. I don't believe in this radical doctrine your Mr. Jefferson so glibly preaches. I think there is a small class of the best people who should run things and I think they should have a care for the good of those other folks, too. But I think little of this preaching that everyone has the same rights, and all that, this democracy business. I believe in a stable, orderly government, and I think that the King is more likely to provide it than your Mr. Jefferson or your George Washington or even your Mecklenburg leaders who seem to be so bent upon destroying the King's authority in this province." She stopped, smiled brightly upon him. "But my views do not alter my—my feelings for you."

"And, in the same way, I suppose they don't change my feelings for you." said David, but his thoughts were his own.

They talked on in the glow of the candle on the stand and those in the hall whose flickering light made the shadows of the furniture move upon the wall. After a while Uncle Jerry slipped quietly into the room, and she dismissed him for the night. They heard his door close off somewhere in the rear.

But David did not move to put his arm about her shoulder pressed against his in the soft yielding comfort of the sofa's back. There was no occasion for hurry, he reflected. Many nights he had dreamed of this night; in his dreams he had charted his course in every delectable detail. In his dreamings, in his daylight quiet imaginings he had invariably been drawn into a frenzy of eagerness, of wild, ungoverned hurrying . . .

He was surprised now to realize his utter calmness, his absolute control, his mastery of his every emotion. He cupped his palm over her little hand lying relaxed upon the pillow on her lap. He gave it a gentle little squeeze, and then he drew his unhurriedly away to demonstrate to himself his ability to discipline himself. Out in the hall he was conscious of the grandfather clock's ticking. No need of hurry . . . no need of hurry . . . no need of hurry. Even the old clock was calm, unhurried. A late October night was a long one . . .

After a while he placed his arm about her, quietly, calmly, and her head fell snugly into the little depression between his shoulder and his chest. And sitting this way, comfortable and relaxed and looking into the small fire, lighted against a slight fall chill, they talked of many people and many things, or fell silent and sat unmoving.

ALEXANDRIANA

It was after one of these long quiet moments she leaned forward, turned to face him. "David, you said a while ago that you were carrying an important message back to Mecklenburg about the plans of the Tories in these parts. What if you should be caught?"

He tapped his forehead. "I carry 'em right here. I don't carry letters. It's safer to carry information in your head. I've got all the plans of your Tory friends filed right up here in my head. I've got all the information on what Colonel McLean's—"

"Colonel McLean? Is it—" She stopped abruptly, and David knew that she regretted having shown interest.

"Is he one of your friends, one of your suitors, perhaps?"

"I do know him. I hope you're not planning to injure him." She shrugged her shoulders. "But that's war, I suppose." She leaned back, her head against his shoulder. In a moment she sat up again. "That candle. It's shining right in my eyes." She stood up, walked over to the candle.

"Blow it out if you wish," said David. "There'll be light enough from those in the hall."

"No, I'll just move it over here." She carried the candlestand across the room. He noticed that she set it in front of one of the windows opening upon the Wilmington road down at the end of the lane.

"David," she said, after they had talked longer, "I suppose we should be going to bed if you are to leave early. What do you think?"

No need to hurry. An October night is a long night. "I reckon we'd better," he said, though. "But it's mighty comfortable like this." After all, even October nights come to an end. "You're going to show me where to sleep?"

"Yes, you'll stay in the guest bedroom just across the hall from mine. I'll take the candle in here; you can get one of those in the hall. I'll show you to the door." She walked over to pick up the candle.

"When you were a guest of old Pat Jack in Mecklenburg I did more than show you to your door."

ALEXANDRIANA

She wheeled about, laughing. "You certainly did, young man, I'm bound. Had it not been for Father— But your windows are already opened and there's no occasion for my going any farther than the door." He had picked up a candle to follow her. "But, listen, David—" Her foot was upon the first step of the stairway. "How about your horse?"

"Damn! I'd forgot him entirely, Belinda. He's out there at the hitching-post—if he hasn't broken loose long before now." He set down his candle. "I'll go put him up right now."

"Do you know how to find the stables? Should I wake Uncle Jerry?"

"No, indeed, I know where they are. I'll be back in a jiffy. Do you want me to throw the door bolt when I come in?"

"Yes, please. And I'll go on up. I'll call good-night to you when you get back. Don't forget your candle. And blow out the others."

He went out the front door. It was very dark. He was feeling his way along when a square of light bobbed out ahead on the lawn. He looked back toward the house. Belinda had gone into her bedroom. He saw her place the candle on the mantle. She stood there an instant. Then she walked out of his line of vision and reappeared in a moment with a floor candlestand. She placed the candlestand directly in front of the window, went to the mantlepiece and picked up the candle, brought it back toward the window, placed it upon the stand there.

"I wonder—Hmmm. I wonder could she—" He walked out to the hitching-post, untied his horse. But he did not lead it to the stables. Instead he led it into the woods down beyond the stables and tied the rein to a small sapling. He walked slowly back to the house, circled it, came in the front way. The candle still burned brightly in the window above.

He threw the bolt of the front door, picked up the candle, blew out the others. "Your room's right over there," Belinda called out, as he reached the top of the stairway. "Good-night, and happy dreams, David."

Her room door was ajar. He walked boldly in. She was in bed. Quickly she pulled the sheet up past her shoulders. "I'll blow out your candle for you, Belinda, and besides, that's no way to tell your company good-night." He set his candle on the mantlepiece.

"No-o, you needn't, David. And you must go to bed. You shouldn't have come in here. It does beat all how you come pushing right on into ladies' bedrooms—"

"It's always to give them help, Belinda. You know your ownself you'd never have managed those stays that night at Jack's—"

"Well, I've managed them tonight, and I'll thank you, sir, to go to bed and—"

He sat down on the side of her bed. The light from the two candles flickered across the bed, making queer changing patterns of the dancing pieces in the patchwork quilt. Her bare white arm lay lightly across the quilt and the dancing pieces gave more color to her cheeks. She had unbraided her hair and now it fanned out across the whiteness of the pillow. "You're a pretty little devil, Belinda, a fair tantalizing morsel o' womanflesh."

"You must go to bed, David. You'll be wanting to rise early—" She paused, and David realized there had been a nervous tense ring in her words. "You shouldn't have come in here. You must go now. You must go."

"I just stopped in to blow out your candle." He was smiling. "I only wanted to be of service, my dear. I'll do it now and—"

"Oh, no, don't, David. Just leave it burning. I'll attend to it later. Just run on and undress and—"

But already he had lain back upon the pillow, his head near hers, his nostrils inhaling deeply the fragrance of her hair, of her warm white flesh but lightly imprisoned beneath the starched crisp sheet . . . "It's so quiet and peaceful here," he said, and his tone was casual . . . Still no need to hurry, no need to hurry. He could hear the quickened pumpings of her lungs. He closed his eyes, opened wider his nostrils to the fragrance, his ears to the increasing tempo of her breathing . . .

Her heart was pounding. He could hear it, hear the steady thump—thump—thump, hear it growing louder. He clamped his eyelids to shut out everything except that beating, pounding.

But it wasn't her heart. Hoofbeats. The pounding of horses' feet

ALEXANDRIANA

down at the end of the lane. And they were coming up the lane to the house. He opened his eyes. That candle in the window. Her signal. The whole thing flashed across his brain. Yes, she was signaling her Tory friends to come and catch him, to trap him in her house, his horse unbridled and unsaddled in her stable. Well, she had failed on that score. The horse, he thanked his stars, was safely hidden out down there in the woods. She was lying there quietly now, her eyes closed, waiting for him to be trapped. The spider in the parlor, luring the fool fly. Luring with her beautiful body, her warm enticing flesh, her red warm moist lips half-parted in the flickering yellow glow of the two candles. No wonder she had wanted him to undress, go to bed, his horse stabled. Then he would have had less chance of escaping. But he hadn't stabled his horse, and he hadn't undressed.

She lay there beside him, her eyes closed, her long black lashes spread in a dark curve along the white glowing flesh above the pink of her cheeks. She lay there waiting for the bound-boy to be bound again, bound and delivered safely into the care of her Tory friends. Years ago in Charlottetown she had arched those beautiful brows, lifted those long lashes when that damned Tryon had mocked him. Now that he was a captain in the American army it made no difference; he was still a backwoodsman, an enemy of the King, a follower of Tom Jefferson; she would turn him over to those horsemen coming up the lane, and she would laugh . . .

Yes, she had wanted him. He knew it. He felt it. He had known it. She wanted him that night in old Pat Jack's Tavern. She wanted him this night. He knew that too. But she had wanted more to deliver him over to her friends, and laugh.

She lay there, quiet but for the swelling and falling of her bosom under the sheet, under the soft clinging silk of her night dress. She lay unmoved as these black thoughts raced in the small part of a moment across his mind. She lay there beautiful and beckoning. Dark thoughts swelled up within him. One swift grasp of the sheet, of the clinging soft silk, one flaming ungoverned wild beastial beautiful moment as those horsemen came galloping up the lane, and he would be off, off to the woods, off to his horse and the freedom of the dark night, to the memory of a vengeance well performed. One quick jerk—

"David!" Belinda sprang up from the pillow, and the sheet fell to her waist. "Horses! I hear them coming up the lane. You must get out in a hurry. But wait! Don't get up until I blow out those candles. They may see you. Oh, David, oh—" It was almost a moan, as she threw back the sheet with one swift fling of her arm, and her slim white legs threshed out from beneath it. She bounded toward the mantlepiece, extinguished the candle flickering upon it, walked quickly to the stand at the window. One calm instant she stood there, her figure sharply outlined in the candle's light. Then she blew it out.

"You must go down the back stairs, David. Hurry. They're coming. Oh, and you've got to bridle and saddle your horse. Hurry, David, they'll run to the stables to head you off."

David sprang from the bed. Now his mind was befuddled. He had been wrong about Belinda. Yet that candle in the window— But there was no time for thinking.

She caught him at the door, clung to him, pushed against him. "Oh, David! Oh—" She found his lips, hung to them. "Oh, David, do come back. They'll be gone soon. I'll send them away. And if they leave and the coast's clear, I'll put a candle in the window here at the side next the stables. Oh, oh, you must go—" She kissed him again. "Please come back. You didn't that night in Charlottetown at the tavern—" She pushed him away. "Down the hall, David, down the back stairs. And do hurry."

He ran along the dark hall, slipped down the back stairway, ran like a cat around toward the front, crouched behind a big boxwood. Two or three men were approaching the house. Several were waiting down at the gate at the head of the lane. He could hear the horses of other riders moving toward the stable.

One of the men was pounding upon the door. In a moment a candle was lighted in Belinda's bedroom. A minute later another flickered in the front hall. He could hear Belinda's voice challenging inside; he couldn't understand what she was saying. Quickly the man at the door answered.

ALEXANDRIANA

"Friends, Mistress MacDougald. From Colonel McLean's command."

He heard the bolt slide, and the door opened. He could see Belinda's head, and then she stepped through the doorway. She had thrown on a dressing robe belted about her waist.

"We're right powerful sorry to be disturbing you, Mistress MacDougald," David could hear the man saying, as he peered cautiously through a little open place in the big boxwood clump. "But we are searching for a right dangerous spy who has been down in this country and we're afraid has got some mighty valuable information about Colonel McLean's plans. We're trying awful hard to catch him. We saw your candle in the front window—"

"What sort of looking man was he?" Belinda interrupted.

"He was a young fellow, some twenty-five years old, I'd say, a big, broad-shouldered fellow and tolerable handsome. They do say, Mistress MacDougald, you know a lot o' handsome men."

David could see her face in the flickering light of the candle she was holding. He could see her coquettish smile, the half-shy twist of her head. "I do know a right many, including your colonel."

"Yes, ma'am. We wondered whether such a fellow might have stopped here. And coming along and seeing the light and knowing we had a good crowd and could handle any small size bunch of rebels, we rode up the lane."

"There was a man here early tonight who might have been the man you were looking for. He was from over in the western settlements and he did say something about Colonel McLean. There were a few men along with him and that's why I put the candle in the window. You see—" she smiled again—"Colonel McLean rides here some nights and I didn't want him to come riding up into danger unawares should he come along tonight. And when they left I forgot to take down the candle."

"So they're gone?"

"Yes. They left pretty early."

The man continued to stand, his hat in his hand. "The tracks down at the gate seemed pretty fresh," he said. "And we made out it wasn't but one horse. O' course, we could 'a' been mistaken.

ALEXANDRIANA

It's mighty dark and we didn't have much light. Which way did he go, Mistress MacDougald?"

"He—they went off toward Wilmington; at least, that's where they said they were going."

"We didn't meet anybody. But they could have ducked in the bushes till we got by. You don't suppose he's likely to come back by this way tonight, Mistress MacDougald?"

"Oh, why, no, of course not. No, indeed!" There was emphasis in her tone.

"I meant no offense, ma'am. It's just that we're powerful anxious to catch that fellow." He turned toward the steps. "We're sorry to have bothered you, ma'am. We'll be going soon. We'll hang around a while down at the end of the lane just in case he might be coming back up toward Cross Creek. Thank you, Mistress Mac-Dougald. Good-night, ma'am."

"Good-night." She closed the door. He saw through a window the mellow light of her candle as she moved along the hallway toward the stairs.

"His horse wasn't at the stables," one of the riders reported, as the group came around the other side of the house.

"Well, maybe he's gone like she said, but I wouldn't be too sure. We'll wait around a while. I've a notion that fellow aint so far away and may try to slip back. I couldn't blame him. I might try it my ownself did I have to run off like he might 'a' done." David heard him chuckle as he walked down toward the gate, and his right hand, as he doubled his fist, itched along the knuckles. He slipped noiselessly away, though, through the blackness beside the house, moved off toward the woods, where he hoped mightily he would find his horse.

When he had found the animal and untied the rein, he swung into the saddle, rode quietly along a farm road that ran away from the house. After a while he turned through a field from which the corn had been harvested, and pushed toward the main road. Gaining it, he turned in his saddle. Through a second floor window at Pleasant Grove he could see the faint flicker of a candle . . .

ALEXANDRIANA

A moment he looked, and smiling, he reined his horse toward Cross Creek. No hurry, no need to hurry. Now there would be time for thoughts.

All at once it came to him that there would be no thinking to do. It was strange. No need to hurry. Yes, that was all over now, finished. He didn't know why, exactly. He only knew that he did know. He was glad she hadn't been planning to betray him. He would have a tender feeling for her, he supposed, when in later years he would infrequently think of her. Years ago she had scorned him, and though through the years since she had continued to want him, to be fascinated by him, he had the feeling that she had still felt a slight contempt for the bound-boy. Perhaps he had been wrong in thinking it. But he had felt it, and he had determined to make her come asking for his favors. He had instinctively followed Jeanie's suggestion made that day out in the kitchen at Alexandriana. He had set out to make Belinda take a strong liking to him. Tonight in her dark bedroom at Pleasant Grove she had dropped all pretense, all indifference; she had confessed her desire for him, she had begged him to return to her, she had confessed his mastery.

Yes, it was all over now. His mission had been completed. His two missions had been completed. He had obtained valuable military information for General Rutherford. And he had obtained even more valuable information for himself . . . Perhaps some day he might stop in again at Pleasant Grove, for man's flesh is weak. But now he knew his mind. He dug a heel into his horse's ribs. At Cross Creek he would find a safe shelter for the remaining hours of the night. In the morning he would ride for Mr. McNeill's.

King's Mountain won, the British are gone, Cornwallis has fled Mecklenburg, North Carolina's saved, soon General Washington will be coming south—

David, galloping toward Cross Creek to the music of the nightbirds and with the smell of the swamps heavy in his nostrils, broke into a rollicking verse of *Barney Linn*. Suddenly he stopped singing. He had forgot he was still in the Scotch country, where Tories abounded. But no Tory could still the singing in his heart . . .

LXI

HARD UPON the dragging weary heels of the retreating Britishers winter pushed its invasion of the Carolinas. Another Christmas was approaching. Flames roared high in the big fireplace at Alexandriana, and long into the night before the fire Jeanie sat knitting; and out at Rural Retreat, snug under the hill from the cold winds blowing down the Catawba, Violet Davidson's flying fingers guided her swift needles . . .

Snow poulticed the wounds of great logs freshly peeled of their bark and shaped at the ends against the day when the neighbors would gather and help McKnitt raise his barn and storehouse and granary. Snow lay lightly upon a red mound in Hopewell graveyard where not a month ago they had laid big, bold, gay Francis Bradley, ambushed by Tories sent from over the river to kill him. Southward in Charlottetown snow mantled the scars of many red mounds in the yard of deserted Liberty Hall. And westward along the border upon an upthrust long stony welt it hid the bones of dead men upon whom wolves these many weeks had been fattening and lay white and smooth above a rocky grave near a little spring from which the water trickled cold and slowly.

To Thomas Polk and McKnitt Alexander, riding night and day to wring supplies from the chastened land, the snow was a burden; but it pressed but lightly upon laughing, straight-shooting Francis Bradley, safe now from all lurking Tories; it was not heavy above uncounted, unknown dead Britishers at ease in the red soil of Charlottetown or sprawled for their long rest upon the rocky slopes of King's Mountain; nor was it cold upon the back of courageous,

ALEXANDRIANA

debonair Pat Ferguson, billeted and warm in eternal dark embrace . . .

Charlottetown had become the headquarters of the American Army in the South. General Washington had sent doughty Nat Greene to succeed vain, unstable Horatio Gates; quickly the brusque, efficient veteran of Valley Forge and the campaigns in the North had reorganized the shrinking militia and the discouraged continentals. Having been Washington's quartermaster-general, Nathanael Greene understood well that an army cannot travel upon empty stomachs.

"He's got plenty of business about him," McKnitt reported on his return home one cold night from Charlottetown. "He knows what he's doing. When he took charge last week, Jeanie, there wasn't more'n three days' supply of rations. Now he's got stuff coming in fast. You knew he'd put young Davie in as quartermaster-general instead of Tam Polk?"

"No, I hadn't heard tell."

"Yes, Tam begged off. He is getting a little old for such hard work. And he's done his share, I'm bound. He's about given away all his own property to get food for the army. And he's seen hard service in the army his ownself, and so's Will. And that boy Davie'll make him a good man."

"Yes, Will Davie's a fine young man and a smart one, too. But what sort of a man is old General Greene his ownself?"

"He's not an old man, Jeanie. I was surprised. He's not forty yet. But he doesn't have overly much to say and though he's polite enough he's pretty plain-spoken. He means business, and he's a hard worker. He told me he hadn't had a furlough since he joined the army. I've a notion he's the man we need in these parts."

"Do you suppose he can stop the men from leaving and going home?"

"He'll stop it if he has to hang the last man. When he got to Charlottetown Gates turned over to him only some two thousand and they were running away pretty fast; I've a notion by Christmas though Greene will have a sight more than Gates left him. And he's got some good men, too; I took a right smart liking to General

ALEXANDRIANA

Dan'el Morgan, that old wagoner from up in the Valley of Virginia. I've a notion those fellows will start after Cornwallis as soon as the weather begins to break a little."

At Charlottetown General Greene found awaiting him a message from Lord Cornwallis protesting vehemently the hanging of the Tories after the battle of King's Mountain, and threatening retaliation. But bluff Nat Greene was not to be frightened.

"I am too much a stranger to the transactions at Gilbert Town to reply fully to that subject," he sat himself down in his headquarters and wrote his Lordship. "They must have been committed before my arrival in the department, and by persons under the character of volunteers, who were independent of the army. However, if there was anything done in the affair contrary to the principles of humanity and the law of nations, and for which they had not the conduct of your army as a precedent, I shall be ever ready to testify my disapprobation of it.

"The first example of it was furnished on your part," General Greene continued, "as appears by the list of unhappy sufferers enclosed; and it might have been expected that the friends of the unfortunate should follow it. Punishing capitally for a breach of military parole is a severity that the principles of modern war will not authorize, unless the inhabitants are to be treated as conquered people and subject to all the rigor of military government. The feelings of humanity will forever decide when the rights of humanity are invaded. I leave them to judge of the tendency of your Lordship's order to Lieutenant-Colonel Balfour after the action near Camden, of Lord Rawdon's proclamation and of Tarleton's laying waste the country, and distressing the inhabitants, who were taught to expect protection and security if they observed but a neutrality. Sending the inhabitants of Charles Town to St. Augustine, contrary to the articles of capitulation, is a violation which I have also to represent, and which I hope your Lordship will think yourself bound to redress."

With this message General Greene sent a list of some three dozen Americans wantonly hanged.

"No one, except a deserter, has ever died by my order," he said,

ALEXANDRIANA

as he handed the dispatch to the courier. "I will permit no officer in my department to imitate the cruelties practiced by the British."

Quickly the new commander of the army in the South demonstrated the accuracy of the report that had come ahead of him to Mecklenburg that he was a man of action. Candles burned late in his headquarters; officers came and went throughout the night.

The men had been leaving the camp at their own pleasure to make visits to their homes, to overstay their furloughs when they had taken the trouble to obtain furloughs, to remain at home if they chose. Nat Greene issued orders that this was to stop. The first man caught violating the order was stood up before the troops and shot.

Discipline was being restored; Charlottetown, like Valley Forge after the coming of Baron von Steuben, was becoming the fountain head of a new hope, a new daring, a new promise of victory when the spring should break.

But the country roundabout Charlottetown had been stripped bare of food upon which to feed two thousand hungry men. In the fall the Redcoats had pillaged and the patriots had burned; and after the Redcoats there were the men of Davidson and Davie to feed and their horses to keep. The farms of Mecklenburg and Rowan and Tryon, like the fields at Alexandriana, had been ravaged.

Already Greene's force was small, but he determined after a quick survey of the situation to divide his forces. Daniel Morgan he confirmed in his independent command and sent him southwestward across the Catawba and the Broad to make camp on Christmas Day on the north bank of the Pacolet. Kosciuszko, who had been busy making observations on the roads in the country and the fords and capacity for transportation of the rivers, he sent ahead eastward from Charlottetown to Haley's Ferry and down a few miles into South Carolina to select a site for an encampment. And here, at the head of transportation on the Peedee, Nat Greene established himself.

"This is a fertile and unexhausted country," he explained. "Here I will have an opportunity to look around a bit."

ALEXANDRIANA

At Charlottetown he left General Davidson in command of the militia. It would be his central force and it could move quickly in support of Morgan, or it could come eastward to his own aid.

Seventy miles westward from Nat Greene Cornwallis lay at Winnsboro and sought to recuperate from the vicious stings of the hornets he had left in Mecklenburg. And slowly toward Cornwallis a new army was preparing to move.

Four days after Christmas David rode with William Lee Davidson into the camp of Dan Morgan. "I've brought you a hundred and twenty men, General," General Davidson reported. "And I'll bring you more as soon as I can collect them."

"I may need them, General. We've been giving these Tories hell. I've a notion Cornwallis will soon get wind of it and send Butcher Tarleton after me. And then I'll either have to do some powerful fightin' or run like hell."

David was home at Alexandriana and General Davidson had stopped for the night at his cousin John Davidson's at Rural Retreat when the year ran out on cold winds that gnawed at the thin breeches and worn hunting shirts of the militia hovering about Charlottetown.

"It's been a great year," said McKnitt Alexander at the breakfast table, after he had thanked God for deliverance during the year now ended and had prayed for divine protection during the year just beginning, "a year of great trial but a year, too, of great promise. We should be thankful."

"But this year, Uncle Mac, will be our big year. This year we will run Cornwallis out of the South and out of America, too, I'm bound."

"That's powerful much to expect, Davy, boy, what with only a handful of our men under arms and Cornwallis pressing again from the south, and little provisions for the troops and no money from Congress and a lot of discouraging talk."

"It was right much to expect that Ferguson and his crowd would be wiped out, too, wasn't it?"

"That it was. And King's Mountain may well have been the battle that won our freedom, if indeed, 'tis won in the end."

ALEXANDRIANA

"It'll be won, Uncle Mac. Even Jethro can shoot again. I saw him rest his musket on his nub the other day and knock a squirrel out of the top of a high hickory. That's a good omen."

In the early days of January David lived in the saddle. Wearied almost to exhaustion, he would ride into General Davidson's camp, deliver his message, and throw himself down for a few hours of heavy sleeping. And then he would be off again with Davidson's reply to the camp of Daniel Morgan on the Pacolet or Nat Greene on Hick's Creek. For Cornwallis, readying himself for a sudden sallying forth upon the Americans, was between Morgan and Greene. And it was necessary that communications be maintained. Cornwallis and Ferguson had lost contact . . .

So McKnitt Alexander was not surprised when an hour before daylight on a morning past the middle of January he was awakened from sound slumber by David's shouting beneath his window. He went downstairs quickly, threw back the bolt. "Come in, Son, you must be half-frozen." They went into the sitting room, McKnitt raked back the ashes from the coals, threw on fat pine and firewood, blew lustily upon the coals.

David rubbed his hands together, turned his back to the flames now beginning to blaze up. After a moment he slumped down into a chair. "I'm tired, Uncle McKnitt. Been riding all night. And it's been right smart cold. I've got to find General Davidson. That's why I came by here. Thought you'd likely know where he'd be. And then I've got to head off to General Greene."

"But what's up, David? Why such a hurry, Son?"

"I've come from the Cowpens. There's been a great battle down there, Uncle Mac. General Morgan—"

"Dan'el Morgan's not killed, David?" A shadow, a shadow as of a sharp sudden pain, as of a wound deep down and beyond relieving, darkened the ruddy face of McKnitt Alexander mobile now in the play of the mounting flames.

"General Morgan's not dead, Uncle Mac. Instead of that, he's licked the fair daylights out o' Butcher Tarleton and—"

"Thank God!" McKnitt sank down into his big armchair. "Thank God, thank the kind Heavenly Father. For a moment

ALEXANDRIANA

I was fearful that you bore bad news, Son." He stood up again, turned his back to the fire, faced the young man seated before him. "And now, David, tell me more about it."

"Well, Uncle Mac, 'tis not so much to tell, I reckon. Yesterday morning early Butcher Tarleton caught up with General Morgan. He had been following him as fast as he could and the Old Wagoner had been backing up after he found out that Tarleton had a lot more men. General Morgan stopped, though, on this side of Thicketty Mountain and waited for Tarleton. Tarleton rode all night and started the fight early yesterday morning without letting his men rest. He was afraid, I reckon, that the Old Wagoner would beat him across the Broad River, so he sailed into him and—well, we gave them a first-rate licking." David stood up, turned his back to the fire.

"But the Old Wagoner's in bad danger, Uncle Mac, and that's why he's sent me on the hunt of General Davidson. You see, he killed or captured about all of Tarleton's infantry, took most all their guns, two or three dozen wagons, about a hundred horses of his dragoons, and he's got a turn of stuff that will slow him up coming this way, especially the prisoners. There's five hundred of them, I'll vouch."

"What became of Tarleton, Son?"

"He got away, with most of his dragoons, and headed back to Cornwallis. Colonel Will Washington came nigh getting him, too, Uncle Mac, whacked at him with his sword and cut him on the hand, but he wheeled around and shot Colonel Washington in the knee. But I don't think the colonel was badly hurt."

"What did he want you to tell William Lee, David? What I have in mind is to let you stay here and get some sleep and some breakfast whilst I go give William Lee your message. I think he's over at John Davidson's house."

"He wants him to get his militia lined up and ready over here on the Catawba to help him get across and help hold back the British till he can join up with General Greene this side the river. And he wants me to go on and tell General Greene what's happened and ask him if he won't come across and meet him with

ALEXANDRIANA

his soldiers. You see, Uncle Mac, Butcher Tarleton's crowd, those that were left, joined up with Cornwallis, who had been coming along behind Tarleton and has got as far as Turkey Creek, which isn't more'n twenty-five miles, I'd say, below the Cowpens. So the Old Wagoner hasn't got much of a start and it looks like it's going to be a hot race. Morgan's figuring on going on up into Virginia to get rid of his prisoners if he can keep ahead of Cornwallis. And he doesn't dare risk a fight, not with all those prisoners."

"And so you've got to notify General Greene, too?"

"Yes, sir, General Morgan sent some other couriers straight across towards Greene but he wants me to go, too, just in case something should happen to those others."

"Well, David, I'll find William Lee. You get a little nap and a good breakfast and then you can start for Greene's camp. And tell Jeanie to fix you up some rations to carry along. It'll be a long hard ride, Son."

"Yes, sir, and I've got to be starting pretty soon. You see, Morgan and Greene and Cornwallis are all about the same distance from Virginia and Greene can't afford to be late getting started, I'm bound."

LXII

"It's BOUND to be the work of Providence, William Lee. In the Bible days the waters were rolled back to let the Children of Israel across in safety ahead of their enemies; it's right smart like that now, with the Catawba fordable until Morgan got over and up when Cornwallis got to it, so that while he's waiting for it to drop Morgan's crowd can be getting a long jump on the Redcoats."

"Yes, it does look that way John. Another day and Morgan would have been headed off and we couldn't even have got across to help him. But the water's dropping now, and that means that we'll likely have business tomorrow." General Davidson arose from the table at Rural Retreat. "Excuse me, John, for eating and running, but I've got to be getting along the river to see if everything is in readiness to receive his Lordship in proper style."

"Have you got all the fords covered, William Lee?"

"All the likely ones. I've got men at Toole's and Tuckaseegee, and up at Cowan's and Beatty's and on up as far as Sherrill's. He's bound to try to cross at one of these places. If we can delay him a little, Morgan's troops should get a good start. This is turning into a pretty race, John. If Greene can manage it, it will go down as the most successful retreat in the whole war, I've a notion. But it's going to take some good work to keep Cornwallis back until Morgan can get safely into Virginia."

Major John Davidson fumbled in the pockets of his waistcoat for his pipe. "I reckon old Jacob Forney's sorry it rained." He found the pipe, poured tobacco into it from the pouch he had also

ALEXANDRIANA

pulled from a pocket, packed it in the bowl with his thumb.

"The Redcoats are certainly destroying all Forney's stuff. Cornwallis is putting up at his house, I hear. When they march away from Forney's, they won't leave him a bushel of wheat or one skinny cow, I'll vouch."

"By the way, William Lee, what's the latest word you've had from General Greene?"

"He's sending his troops north from Hick's Creek to join with Morgan's up about the Yadkin at Trading Ford. That's the word young Barksdale brought me this morning. General Greene's coming across to Sherrill's Ford to meet Morgan who sent his men on ahead under the command of Howard, and when we get together we'll figure on some way of holding Cornwallis back until Greene and Morgan can get safely out of his reach."

General Davidson rode down to Tuckaseegee Ford, inspected the detachment there, and then proceeded up the river to Toole's Ford and beyond to Cowan's. By nightfall of this cold, gloomy last day of January he was at Beatty's Ford up the river southwest of Centre Church.

It was past midnight when General Dan Morgan and Colonel William Washington rode down from Sherrill's Ford. The colonel's knee was bandaged beneath his military breeches from the shot fired by Tarleton, but it appeared not to be giving him much pain.

Ten minutes after their arrival, General Greene and his aide, Major Pierce, rode into camp. General Davidson greeted them cordially and the officers walked into the edge of the woods and sat down upon a log. A half hour later they had made their plans, and the visitors rode off into the night toward Salisbury.

On the other side of the river the Americans could see Redcoats moving along the water's edge. When a company of horsemen galloped rapidly along the western bank, pausing here and there to study the campfires of Davidson's men across the swift flowing cold waters, the defenders took the leader to be Lord Cornwallis himself. They gripped their guns. Soon now there would be work to do . . .

ALEXANDRIANA

Long before dawn Cornwallis had begun to move his men out from Jacob Forney's plantation five miles back from the river. But instead of marching eastward to cross the river at Beatty's Ford, he swung sharply southward and moved toward the stream at the less traveled Cowan's crossing. The detachment under Colonel Webster, however, he ordered to move eastward and cross at Beatty's Ford.

Cowan's Ford was a difficult crossing to persons not familiar with the rocky bed of the Catawba at that point. From the Tryon County side it moved straight out into the river along a little rise of smooth stones to near the center of the stream. At this place one route led straight across. It was called the Wagon ford. The other turned southeastward, went obliquely to come out upon the bank a few hundred yards downstream. This was the Horse ford. Between the two was a mass of haws and persimmon trees and dense, matted briars.

It was a cold, raw morning. Mists hung low upon the murky waters. The campfires of General Davidson's men blazed high upon the eastern bank. Near the place where the Horse ford emerged upon the Mecklenburg bank lay Lieutenant Tom Davidson with some twenty-five men, their muskets primed and ready. Close by, Joe Graham, now sufficiently recovered to be back in the saddle, awaited nervously with his newly organized cavalry volunteers the coming of the Redcoats. A large body of infantry, their muskets also held in itching palms, stood silently in the gloom of the early morning haze.

But Cornwallis could wait no longer. Daylight would soon be breaking, and Cornwallis was racing with time, for Dan Morgan was making fast muddy tracks toward the Yadkin and time was upon the side of the Old Wagoner and Nat Greene.

The light infantry of the Redcoat guards, their bayonets fixed, their empty muskets carried on their left shoulders at the slope, their cartridge boxes fastened upon their left shoulders, and each man equipped with a long light sapling with which to brace himself against the push of the current, stepped off into the cold dark water, splashed outward toward the Mecklenburg bank.

ALEXANDRIANA

Behind them came the grenadiers and behind the grenadiers came battalions pushing in platoon formation along the little ridge of rock that formed the ford.

Half way across the Redcoats heard the angry challenge from Tom Davidson's sentry. But the British pushed stolidly on through the cold black water ... A shot skimmed the surface and after the shot came the crack of the musket upon the bank.

The easier route would have been along the Horse ford. But the Redcoats, reaching the dividing point, kept straight eastward toward the bank, splashing, slipping on upthrust slimy stones, holding to each other for balance. General Davidson, some distance from the ford when he heard the firing, with young Will Polk and Pastor McCaules of Centre Church, came racing to the river.

Bullets now were whistling above the Catawba's dark surface. Joe Graham was shouting commands; his cavalrymen swung into their saddles, moved up the rise from the river to protect the rear against a possible British attempt at surrounding the Americans. Tom Davidson pushed along the bank from the Horse ford with his men. They dropped to their knees to aim long barrels at the British now nearing the bank.

His musket resting on a fallen tree trunk near the water's edge, Jethro O'Flannagan, with the nub of his left arm steadying the weapon, drew a bead upon a solitary horseman near the head of the floundering Redcoat infantrymen. The man was moving steadily forward, Jethro's trigger finger was drawing in—

The Redcoat fell out of the circle of the bead Jethro had drawn upon him, plunged into the water, his horse rolled over him, he disappeared. But now he was on the surface again, and Redcoats were clutching for him. And ten yards away smoke was curling from the muzzle of Tom Barnett's musket.

"Damn if'n you didn't beat me to him, Tom," yelled Jethro. "He must 'a' been a officer, too. Pity 'twasn't old Cornwallis his self." He patted the lock of his own gun. "Well, Flossie Belle, you can git his Lordship." He lowered his musket, shook his right arm a moment, leveled the weapon again, drew a quick sight, squeezed the trigger.

ALEXANDRIANA

"By George, you got that one, Jethro!" The man at the right was peering out through the cane thicket towards the bank up which the Redcoats were clambering now. "Looks like you can still shoot first-rate, in spite o' gettin' yore left arm shot off at King's Mountain."

"Yeh, I can still shoot pretty good, Ab. But my fingers bothers me bad. If'n I could jest scratch 'em. They're always itchin' like and always got a cramped feelin'. They buried them fingers twisted up crooked, I'd bet a half-Joe."

The British were clambering up the bank, fanning out. Jethro turned his back to the log to reload his musket. As he clamped it between his knees to pour in the powder, he saw out of the corner of his eye a man on a horse, a broad-shouldered, stocky Britisher, round-faced and ruddy. The horse was pawing to gain a hold upon the bank. That man had a familiar look—

"Hey, Ab; Over there! That big blocky fellow. That's Cornwallis! Shoot 'im!" He pushed his wadding in behind the powder and ball. "It would be just my luck," he mumbled, "not to have Flossie Belle ready when Cornwallis come a-ridin' up."

The man beside him raised his musket, fired. From along the bank the men in hunting shirts and coonskin caps, in linsy-woolsy and three-cornered hats, were blasting away at the advance company of the Redcoats, now forming along the flat corn ground to load their muskets. Jethro, watching the ruddy-faced broad man on the horse, saw the animal stumble, sink down, begin feebly to thresh out his hind legs. Cornwallis sprang from the saddle, ran along the shelf of the bank, caught at some low bushes for support, pulled himself up.

Now the Redcoats were throwing a steady hail of hot lead into the defenders. General Davidson galloped toward the river bank. "He's coming to get us organized better, Ab," said Jethro, pointing. But as he looked, he saw the general reel backward, as if struck a mighty blow in the face with some unseen hammer, and slowly roll from the saddle to pitch heavily to the ground. The riderless horse turned, and with one long shrill whinny, bounded up the slope from the river.

ALEXANDRIANA

Rapidly now the British were emerging, wet and shivering, from the cold Catawba, and under the protecting fire of their comrades already formed in fronts just below the landing point of the Wagon ford, were loading their muskets to pour another volley into the disorganized Americans. There were too many Redcoats. The militia gave way, scampered back along the bank, ducked into the cover of the woods above the Horse ford.

Jethro was climbing into his saddle at the top of the rise up from the river. A horseman reined his animal toward him. "We're ridin' on up the Beatty's Ford Road to get in front of them again," he announced. "They'll have to stop here a while to bury that bunch we killed. That'll give us time to get set for 'em. It's Cap'n Graham's orders."

"Where're we goin' to meet at?"

"Torrence's Tavern." The fellow galloped off.

Nearing Torrence's Tavern, the assembling militiamen found the roads choked with fleeing refugees from the river lands. "What you all doing, Mister, takin' all yore stuff off like this?" Jethro asked an old man leading a mule hitched to a cart piled high with feather ticks and other household goods.

"We heared the shooting. It rolled down the river like thunder. It was shooting up at Beatty's Ford and down the river, too, 'bout Cowan's or Toole's, I 'lowed. That's why we're leaving. Them Redcoats'll burn down our houses on our heads if'n we don't git out."

Militia from other parts of the countryside had already reached the tavern when Jethro got there. The yard and the building itself were overrun with laughing, cursing, loud-talking soldiers and country people. They were carrying out whiskey in kegs. Half the soldiers were staggering already.

In the midst of the confusion a horseman came charging up the lane. "Tarleton's dragoons are coming!" he shouted. "They aint but a little piece down the road! Cornwallis sent him on ahead. He's nigh here right now!"

Drunken soldiers straightened up, examining with squinting eyes the locks of their muskets; some ran to their horses at the hitching-rack. But when in a moment Butcher Tarleton's dragoons came racing up the lane, there was no organized defense. They poured one stinging volley upon the Redcoats, saw several of them pitch from their horses, saw horses stumble and sink upon their haunches—and then they turned and ran for the woods.

Jethro circled a field that opened out upon the tavern, keeping within the protection of the screening thickets, and watched the Redcoats as they smashed the furniture and ripped open the bedding of the terrified country people . . . Then he turned southward and after a while came out again upon the main road. The candles had been lighted when he reached Samuel Wilson's four miles northwest from Hopewell Church and east two miles from Cowan's Ford.

Mrs. Wilson, her eyes red and streaming, and still wearing heavy mourning clothes for her father, old Pat Jack, gone now with his tavern in Charlottetown, answered his rap upon the door.

"The men are in there," she said, when she had welcomed him. " 'Tis a sad gathering you have come to."

He walked into the dimly lighted room. Richard Barry sat just inside the door, and young David Wilson, Samuel Wilson's son and Violet Davidson's brother, and several of the neighbors were there, and over on the bed, straight and stiff upon his back, a sheet pulled lightly up to his shoulders, a man lay.

The men nodded stolidly to Jethro, who walked slowly across to the bed, looked down upon the closed eyes of the dead man. Jethro felt himself going sick in the pit of his stomach. The man on the bed was General Davidson.

"His horse came back to Rural Retreat," said Richard Barry, after Jethro had walked slowly away from the bed. "Violet Davidson knew something bad had happened. She gave the alarm and David here went with me to Cowan's Ford. We found him lying on the ground pretty nigh naked. There was one shot went in about the left nipple, Jethro—" He fumbled in his pocket, pulled out a small dark round object. "This fell out of his undershirt. It went through him. I'd like for you to look at it and say what you think."

Jethro took it, walked over to a candle. " 'Tis plain to see what it is. It's a ball from a rifle. You can plainly see the markin's." He examined the ball closely, turned it over, weighed it in his palm. Slowly a scowl crossed his face. "And I know who's gun fired that ball, too. It was that damned Fred Hager's."

"That's what we said, Jethro," said Richard Barry.

"The damned bastard of a Tory!" Jethro handed the ball back to Richard Barry. "Damn his lousy soul!"

"We'll get him," said young David Wilson. "He hasn't got many more days in these river bottoms."

"We've sent young Templeton up to their home at Centre Church to get Mary Davidson, Jethro," Richard Barry announced. "I want you to go on over to McKnitt Alexander's and put out the word. There was a gathering of the militia there after the battle at the ford. Tell any of their friends you see that we're going to bury him tonight at Hopewell Church."

By the light of torches held high they lowered William Lee Davidson into the grave a few paces from the mound above Francis Bradley. "Ashes to ashes, dust to dust," intoned the minister, as the stiff red clods fell with a dull thud upon the box.

For a moment they looked upon the smooth red mound. Mary Davidson, her head hidden beneath her heavy veil, stood quietly between John Davidson and Violet. John Davidson put his big arm about the young woman's slender shoulders. "He has left us for a little while, Mary. He has given his life for his country. He has brought honor upon the name of Davidson as long as our land shall endure. He was my cousin; I loved him, too, Mary. I—" But he said no more. His arm drew tightly about her shoulders. And beneath his arm he felt her slim body wrenched in the grip of a shudder that pushed upward from depths far down within her.

But not a sound came from Mary Davidson's lips.

LXIII

MRS. ELIZABETH STEELE from an upstairs room of her tavern in Salisbury looked down upon the man coming slowly to her front door. She could see, despite the lateness of the afternoon and the slight drizzle that added to the gloom of this first day of February, that the man's shoulders sagged, that he was tired almost to exhaustion, that weariness and discouragement had ridden with him on a long day's riding.

And now Dr. Read was advancing to greet him. "How do you do, General Greene?" Mrs. Steele stepped back from the window. So the stranger was General Greene. General Nathanael Greene, Washington's commander of the southern army, coming here to her tavern.

More cautiously now she peered down upon the two uniformed men. The general was stretching forth his arm to shake hands with Dr. Read. "I'm right glad to see you, Dr. Read," she heard him say.

"Welcome, sir, to Salisbury. And how do you do, sir?"

She saw the general shrug his shoulders. "I'm tired as a dog, hungry, alone, and penniless, Doctor. I'm about as low as a man can get and keep his wits. And how goes it, sir, with you?"

"Well, sir, General, I've been right busy with some of General Morgan's prisoners. Our men were right rough on them at the Cowpens, and the fast retreat hasn't helped them. And we have some pretty bad cases our ownselves. As for myself, I'm quite well, sir, I thank you."

"And is General Morgan confident he can get safely over the Yadkin before Cornwallis—"Mrs. Steele couldn't hear any more,

ALEXANDRIANA

for the men had entered the front door. She walked over to her dresser, busied herself a moment before the mirror. Then she went into her closet, withdrew with two small bags, which she placed in a pocket beneath her apron.

When after a while she came downstairs the two men were seated at the table eating, a roaring fire in the fireplace at their backs. They arose. "Mistress Steele," said Dr. Read, "I have the honor to present General Greene of the Continental Army."

Mrs. Steele dropped a curtsy, extended her hand, which General Greene bent low to kiss. "I am most honored and happy to make your acquaintance, sir," she said. "You are most welcome. And now, you gentlemen do sit down and finish your supper." She ran her eyes over the table hurriedly. "Is there anything I could see to having them bring you?"

"No, Mistress Steele," said General Greene, seating himself again. " 'Tis a most excellent meal, and especially to one so tired and hungry as I am at this moment."

"I am right glad you are enjoying your supper, sir." She hesitated, set straight a piece of china in the corner cupboard near which she had been standing. Then she advanced nearer General Greene. "I must beg your pardon, General Greene," she said hesitantly. "But I overheard your conversation with Dr. Read when you said you were tired and hungry and friendless and penniless. That cannot quite be, sir. You are, no doubt, tired and hungry, but you cannot be without friends, for all this wide land is praying for you, General, and is depending upon your great wisdom as our leader next under our great Washington to deliver us from the enemy." She raised her apron, drew forth from the pockets of her skirt the two small bags. "And here, sir, is a bit of money. 'Tis what I have saved these years from running this tavern. 'Tis not so much, but it may help you a little, and I can get along without it. Take it, sir, and use it for our cause, and may the good Father bless you."

General Nat Greene arose. There were tears in his eyes as he took the bags from her hands. "Mistress Steele, I don't know how much money there is in these bags. By the weight of them I suspect there's much, but much or little, Mistress Steele, it has already been of inestimable value to me, ma'am. I came into your house wet and tired and greatly troubled; I shall go from it a new man." He dabbed at a tear that broke from his eye and ran down a cheek. "Yes, ma'am, we'll get across the Yadkin, we'll outrun Cornwallis, we'll win this race yet. God bless you, ma'am, and all the fine women of America."

He sat down. Mrs. Steele had already slipped from the room. General Greene pointed to the bags on the table before him. "Read, you have just seen the thing that's going to win this war for us. A million Redcoats can't beat that sort of spirit." He slammed a heavy fist upon the table, and the dishes rattled. "Damn it, Read, I came in here a damned whipped coward; that little woman's made a man out of me. We'll get over that damned Yadkin ahead of Cornwallis, we'll let him run us till he's worn himself down, and then up about the Dan we'll turn on him, run his tongue out, and then beat holy hell out of him!" He gulped down a last swallow of coffee. "And now to find my damned orderly and get on over towards Trading Ford. We've got work to do, Read, and work to do tonight. It looks like this drizzle might turn into a big rain and it would be hell if we got caught on this side the river with the damned Redcoats coming like all fury from the Catawba." He stood up, smiled. "And on the other hand, it would certainly be something to write General Washington about if after we got over it started raining like hell and kept Cornwallis back two or three days."

LXIV

AND SO once again the red soil of Mecklenburg was free of the foot of the invader, and old Dan Morgan was safely across the Yadkin ahead of Cornwallis, and Morgan and Greene raced northeastward from Guilford Courthouse toward the Dan.

And when the great retreat had ended and Cornwallis, weary and worn with chasing, turned southward in Virginia and moved down to Hillsboro, the Americans turned, too, and followed almost upon the swift tracks they had made going north.

Word came occasionally to Alexandriana of the marchings and the skirmishings of the Redcoats and the patriots, and one day past the middle of March David Barksdale, riding home upon his spent and lathered horse, told how General Greene had finally turned and on a flat stretch of rolling fields and woods near little Guilford Courthouse had battled Cornwallis. The Redcoats, David told McKnitt Alexander, had claimed the victory; but Cornwallis had moved southward and turned out east with the remnants of his sorely tried army, and behind him he had left a land dotted with mounds patted smooth above dead and bloody Redcoats.

"They do say Cornwallis is headed down Wilmington way," said David, "and General Greene's already started south and 'tis thought he'll strike for South Carolina."

So there was time for raising the outbuildings at Alexandriana and for plowing the red fields and planting a new crop against the fall days and empty granary and storehouses. And the buildings covered the scars from the visit of the Redcoats the fall before,

ALEXANDRIANA

and soon the fields turned green again, and new grass grew upon the graves of Francis Bradley and William Lee Davidson and eastward in the center of Poplar Tent graveyard old grass sprouted anew above the closed still lips of Hezekiah Balch . . .

Nor was McKnitt Alexander greatly surprised when one day at the courthouse in Charlottetown a trader heading into the western settlements from Wilmington gave out the word that Cornwallis had left Wilmington and set his columns northward toward Virginia.

The soft sweet winds of spring were blowing up from the trees ringing the spring at the foot of the slope behind Alexandriana when one afternoon a horseman rounded the bend of the Great Road and came slowly toward the gate. McKnitt, smoking his pipe in the cool of the shade trees, heard the plodding of the horse's hoofs. He looked up from the month-old *Cape Fear Mercury* he had been scanning.

"The man on that horse is sick or else he's powerful tired out," he said to Jeanie, seated near him, her fingers flying above the fancy work in her lap. "He has a powerful familiar look about him, too. Jeanie, do you reckon—?" He got up from his chair, walked out toward the uppin'-block. "Jeanie," he called back, "I do believe—. It is, for a fact!" He ran toward the man on the horse, now almost opposite the gate.

"Ephraim! Boy, is it you? Is it you, Ephraim, for a fact!" Jeanie now was running toward the gate. "Jeanie, 'tis Ephraim back! The Lord be praised. 'Light, boy, and rest your saddle. And you look all tuckered out your ownself."

Ephraim Brevard climbed wearily from the saddle. Standing beside it a moment, one hand still upon the horse's mane, he swayed. But he caught himself, stood erectly, held out his hand to McKnitt. "McKnitt. Jeanie. 'Tis fine to see you again. 'Tis fine indeed to be back at Alexandriana."

"But you must come sit down, Ephraim. You're tired. Sit down and rest whilst I go fetch you a drink."

"Thank you, Jeanie. I believe it would brace me up a bit. I'm a right smart tired after the ride from Charlottetown. I borrowed

ALEXANDRIANA

this horse and I'm heading up to Centre Church to see the folks. But I wanted to stop here, of course, and see you all."

McKnitt took his arm and they walked toward the house. "When did you get to Charlottetown, Ephraim?" McKnitt asked, when they had sat down in the sitting room.

"Just this morning, McKnitt."

"From Charles Town?"

"Yes, they finally paroled us. But they well nigh ruined me, McKnitt. I'll never get over the treatment on those prison ships."

"You do look pretty thin, Ephraim. But a spell o' hot sun and good Mecklenburg rations will get you back on your feet first-rate."

Ephraim Brevard smiled wanly. "No, I'll never get over it, McKnitt, I reckon. It just took too much out of me. Had it not been for those good women—by the way, McKnitt, what became of Mrs. Jackson after she got back to Mecklenburg? She was a powerful fine woman to us down there. I've often wondered—"

"She never did get back, Ephraim. She died of the fever on the way home. They buried her somewhere along the road, but nobody knows just where. Her boy Andy was in Charlottetown the other day and he told me about his mother. He got a nasty sword cut his ownself down below the Waxhaws last year when a Redcoat officer threw his boots at him and ordered him to clean 'em, and Andy gave him some right pert back-talk."

They put Ephraim Brevard to bed at Alexandriana that night. Nor did McKnitt and Jeanie have the courage to tell him that after the skirmish that February day at Torrence's Tavern Butcher Tarleton's dragoons had burned his mother's home to the ground and had even threatened the old lady herself because, the Redcoats told her with many an oath, she had sent eight sons to the rebel army. Nor were they sorry they had not told him. For days later, tired and worn and racked with a burning fever, Dr. Brevard died, the thin hand that had penned a declaration of independence clasped in the big strong hand of McKnitt Alexander.

"A great man has gone, Jeanie," said McKnitt, when he had closed the tired weary eyes of Ephraim Brevard, "a great man and a good man, a man Mecklenburg will long look up to."

ALEXANDRIANA

"Yes," answered Jeanie, and tears were welling in her eyes, "he was a good boy, Ephraim was, and a great man, and he was a man after the fashion of young Preacher Balch, a fair fine clean man, was Ephraim."

LXV

THE BRITISH had gone from North Carolina, the dust had settled from the last weary horseman plodding along in the rear guard of Cornwallis' column crossing into Virginia. Southward General Nat Greene pressed relentlessly toward Ninety-Six. Far to the north General Washington was turning hopeful eyes toward the south. But at Alexandriana peace had settled with the soft summer haze upon the wide rolling acres.

Down in the Scotch country, down in Bladen between Cross Creek and Wilmington, the Tories, however, were still marauding. Upon the heels of the retreating Britishers they were burning and robbing and killing. When early in September the startling word came to Mecklenburg that the Tories had surprised Hillsboro and taken Governor Burke prisoner, old Grif Rutherford instructed Joe Graham to raise a troop of cavalry to move down into the Tory country.

David Barksdale joined the dragoons. "He can't settle down; he's got to be doing something," Jeanie told McKnitt, when David had gone away.

"Yes, that's partly the reason; but had you ever thought about the country they're going to, Jeanie? It's another good excuse for getting back down Cross Creek way, I'm bound. Nor do I blame the boy. I only hope he'll soon be fetching her back with him."

Stories shortly began coming back to Mecklenburg of the fighting. "Our boys gave those Tories a big licking in a swamp down nigh to Wilmington.," McKnitt reported late one afternoon upon his return from Charlottetown. "The word's just got back. That

ALEXANDRIANA

boy Joe Graham is a born leader, Jeanie. And after the way the British cut him up and shot him over at Sugaw Creek that day last fall it's a wonder he's alive."

"Was there any word of David?"

"Not a word. I reckon that means he's all right."

Traders coming up from Wilmington fetched other stories. There had been fighting at Alfred Moore's plantation close to Wilmington and down at the Waccamaw Lake, and the Tories were running from swamp to swamp, from thicket to thicket . . . There had been stories, too, brought by travelers from Williamsburg and Richmond that General Washington and the French were closing in upon Cornwallis.

And one late October night McKnitt came riding back to Alexandriana and the light of a thousand fires danced in his eyes. The children were in their beds. A crackling fire lighted the sitting room. He walked over to the fire, stood before it to warm his back. He turned to face the warming flames, turned again to face his wife. And the fires blazed in his eyes.

"I'll fetch your supper in here, McKnitt," said Jeanie. "We can sit and talk whilst you eat. You can tell me the news from Charlottetown. You can— McKnitt, whatever in the world is possessin' you? You can't keep still. There's something you're fair dying to tell. Your eyes are fair on fire."

"Jeanie, I can't keep anything from you. I meant to eat first and then tell you. I reckon it was sort of saving the dessert to the last. Jeanie—" He moved forward a pace, took his wife's hands in his own. "Jeanie, the word came today. I was at the courthouse when the man got there and gave out the news. I heard it my ownself from his lips. I—"

"For heaven's sake, McKnitt, why don't you—?"

"Jeanie—" The fire was leaping in his eyes. "Cornwallis has surrendered to General Washington!"

"McKnitt, it—it can't be!" She buried her head on his chest. "Oh, it can't be!" The tears streamed out upon his waistcoat. And as he held her tightly in his arms and felt her little bosom heaving with a thousand emotions long imprisoned but now given play,

ALEXANDRIANA

tears dropped from his eyes and he buried his face in her hair.

They sat long before the fire and talked.

"Was there a great battle and many killed before the surrender, did the man say, McKnitt?"

"No, there was no use of a battle, Cornwallis saw. General Washington and young Lafayette had him surrounded, and there was the French fleet behind him. There was nothing else to do."

"Where was it?"

"I hadn't told you that? 'Twas at a place they call Yorktown, Jeanie, a place down on the water nigh to Williamsburg. It was Williamsburg the man came from."

Jeanie was staring into the flames. "And now there'll be peace and an end o' killing. God be praised, I'm so glad." She faced her husband, and the flames from the fireplace and from the fire deep within her blazed in her eyes. "And now, McKnitt, we're free. We'll be a free country, an independent nation our ownselves?"

"Yes, my dear, God willing, now we've but to form our own government and—"

"And George Washington will be our king?"

"Not likely our king, Jeanie." McKnitt smiled and little crinkles ran out from his eyes. "The title of king isn't so popular in America, you know. George Washington will be our ruler, I'll vouch, after our government's fully set up, but he won't be a king, you can bet your life, Jeanie. He wouldn't want to be, anyway, not General Washington."

"And now we are finished with the British forever."

"Not forever, Jeanie. England's our mother. We'll never be finished with England."

"But England fought us, tried to make us slaves, McKnitt. England killed William Lee and Ephraim and that fine young Hezekiah Balch and heaven only knows how many other fine young Americans, McKnitt, and destroyed our houses and barns and crops and—"

"It wasn't exactly England, Jeanie. 'Twas those stiff-necked, unprincipled Tories and that bull-headed German King George. Many of the finest people of England—most of them, I'll vouch—

were on our side, really hoping we'd win our independence. We must always remember that, Jeanie."

"And we'll be friends, after all, with England?"

"I hope so, Jeanie. I think in the coming years it will be up to us—to England and America—to stick right smart together. After all, Jeanie, we got most of our finest things—our laws and our language and most of our customs, and our great love of freedom, too—from our mother country. We see most things pretty much out of the same eyes. And now that we're free and will have our own government, I've a notion we should start right away being friends with the Britishers."

Jeanie sat silent. After a while she looked up, turned her face flushed by the flames toward him. "McKnitt Alexander, you are a strange man, the most powerful strange man I ever heard tell about. Imagine you saying we ought to be friends with the British!"

McKnitt laughed. "But now that we've licked 'em, Jeanie, why shouldn't we be friends? General Washington would say the same thing, I'm bound."

"General Washington's a powerful strange man, too."

"And a powerful fine one, too, God bless him! He's still got a lot ahead of him, I'll vouch."

"Yes, McKnitt, but General Washington'll know what road take."

"He always has so far, Jeanie, and that's a fact."

LXVI

CATO WAS holding David's horse at the uppin'-block when Jethro rode up. McKnitt came out along the walk between the boxwoods.

" 'Light, Jethro, and rest your saddle. David'll be out in a little bit. I reckon Jeanie's giving him some last-minute instructions on how to get married." He noticed the pack behind his saddle. "Looks like you're taking a lot of stuff with you, man—like you might be getting married your ownself."

"I got them clothes in there that I'm goin' to wear when I stand up with Davy, Mr. Mac. I know I'll look like a plum' fool in that there rig. But Molly made me go down to Charlottetown and buy it. I'd a-ruther wore a clean huntin' shirt, but Molly said that'd never do fer no weddin'." He spit a stream of tobacco juice toward the Great Road, grinned. "And I got to do all my chewin' this side o' Cross Creek, too. Molly gived me orders 'bout that. Wimmen's funny critturs, Mr. Mac, but damned if'n you can do wit'out 'em."

McKnitt laughed. "I reckon that's David's idea, or 'twill soon be."

"That's right. But you can't tell a young feller nothin'. They couldn't tell me, and they couldn't tell you, and now we can't tell Davy." He rolled his tobacco in his cheek, spit again. "But I reckon a feller could do worse'n git married. But look a-here, Mr. Mac, where's the horse for the bride?"

"She'll have her own horse, Jethro. That'll be part of the dowry, I reckon. Mr. McNeill, in spite of the war, can still afford to provide a pretty nice dowry, I'll vouch."

ALEXANDRIANA

"Yes, sir, I reckon he could. Where's they goin' to live at when they git back?"

"They'll stay here at Alexandriana this winter, Jethro. This spring we'll raise 'em a house over east toward Poplar Tent. I'm going to give David a tract over that way. Then, too, David's still got some property from his father's estate up in Pennsylvania, but he turned most of it over to Will Davie to help raise pay for the men, and I'll say I advised him to do it, too."

"David'll git along, Mr. Mac. That boy's got plenty o' sense. And with that purty little gal to help him he'll do first-rate, I'm bound. Mebbe some day he'll be the Guv'ner. Mebbe—There he comes now."

Jeanie was walking with him. He threw up his hand. "Hi, Jethro, old fellow. Ready for the hanging?"

"All set to pull you over the limb, Davy."

David shook hands with McKnitt, kissed Jeanie, gave her a big hug. Quickly he swung into the saddle. "Let's go, Jethro," He pulled on the rein.

At the gate, he turned in the saddle, waved. McKnitt and Jeanie, beaming, were standing beside the uppin'-block. "Good-bye!" he yelled.

"Good-bye, Son!" McKnitt called. "Give the bride a kiss for me."

"I'll do that fer you, Mr. Mac," Jethro shouted back.

Jeanie threw him a kiss. "There'll be a big infare waiting for you all when you get back, Davy."

They rode eastward into the early morning. At the top of the ridge, David halted, looked back. Jethro stopped his horse. "Many a day we've ridden off from Alexandriana, Jethro, and so far we've always made it back safely."

"But you aint never been on a dangerous trip like this here one before. You aint never faced nothin' before but old Tryon and them danged Redcoats."

"It looks mighty quiet and peaceful like back there, Jethro. You wouldn't a thought the British were there a year ago. You wouldn't—"

ALEXANDRIANA

"Hell, Davy, you wantin' to go back?"

David laughed. "Not me, old man. Not till we finish that little business over Cross Creek way."

He jerked the reins.

"Giddap!" said Jethro.

They jogged eastward along the Tuckaseegee Road toward Poplar Tent. Behind them the sun had found the topmost branches of the oaks at Alexandriana.

(THE END)